SHELTER AND SKY • 1

# Even After This

## DEBORAH CLACK

Haven
a division of Baker Publishing Group
Grand Rapids, Michigan

© 2026 by Deborah Clack

Published by Haven
a division of Baker Publishing Group
Grand Rapids, Michigan
HavenFiction.com

Printed in the United States of America

ISBN 978-0-8007-4694-0 (paper)
ISBN 978-0-8007-4740-4 (casebound)
ISBN 978-1-4934-5141-8 (ebook)

Cover illustration by Nate Eidenberger
Cover design and type by Laura Klynstra
Interior design by William Overbeeke

Baker Publishing Group publications use paper produced from sustainable forestry practices and postconsumer waste whenever possible.

26  27  28  29  30  31  32      7  6  5  4  3  2  1

*For my mother.*

Who did that thing that moms do when they know their kids better than their kids know themselves, and who quietly, nonchalantly, and so unassumingly that I didn't bristle at the idea suggested, "You should be a writer someday." She gave me so much freedom in her simple statement that ten years later when it was time for me to write, I was ready.

Because she was my mom. And she knew.

*I miss you, Mom. You were a gift.*

Please don't tell my thirteen-year-old self, but I wish you were here to correct the grammar in my stories.

# 1

THE ELEVATOR DOORS SLIDE OPEN to the exquisite Penrose Room, and for the first time in four years, I question if I'm some kind of masochist widow. My colossal baby step out of hiding no longer seems like a good idea.

Mustering shaky confidence as a party of one, I press my shoulders back and enter one of the most romantic restaurants in the country. My smile threatens to falter at the sight of couples adorned in sparkling cocktail attire swinging around the parquet dance floor, their faces radiating delight.

I clutch my sequined mulberry-colored purse, wishing my anxiety was snapped tight inside. My matching dress is a simple knee-length A-line with long sleeves and a boat neck, paired with nude, patent leather platform shoes. It's been so long since I dressed up like this, I didn't realize people were wearing the 1970s monstrosities again until I shopped at the mall last week.

"Hello," I say to the maître d'. "My name is Meredith Harper, and my reservation is for seven o'clock."

"Hello, Ms. Harper." The kind smile complements the grandfatherly appeal of the stout older gentleman. He types into his workstation and stares at the screen. For a moment he appears puzzled, then masks his reaction and pulls on the cuff of his tuxedo. He shoots a compassionate glance at me, pauses, and returns his focus to his monitor.

While eating alone in the Colorado Springs AAA Five Diamond restaurant must be rare, I can't imagine I'm the first. Confusion joins my jittery nerves, and I shift from my left foot to my right.

"Let me check on your table," he finally says.

Just as he turns to leave his stand, a woman bursts into the lobby from the kitchen, bringing with her the sound of clanging pots and the piquant aroma of gourmet cuisine. "Will you please check to see if the Wilsons have arrived?" she asks the maître d'. The second her gaze hits mine, she halts midstep.

The navy pantsuit tells me she doesn't work for the Broadmoor Hotel, but her clipboard and sharp hand gestures show she's a woman of authority. Who is she?

The maître d' shifts so his back is to me, blocking my view of the fierce woman. My proximity only allows me to decipher pieces of their discussion.

I hear the words "VIP" and "special circumstance" in his low voice.

"That will not work" is her reply. She darts an icy glance in my direction.

Are they talking about me?

My aching feet match my insecurity in uncomfortableness. I lift my right foot out of its shoe to relieve the pressure on my toes. These new heels are supposed to be part of tonight's leap off the comfort zone of my couch. Now I want to throw on my running shoes and hightail it back to Texas to sink into the safety of my pedestrian life.

A tall, well-built man saunters in from the dining room and steps close to the woman. "Penelope, I found Drew Wilson and got him squared away with tonight's schedule. Everything else okay?"

Decked out in a fitted charcoal suit and an azure dress shirt with two buttons undone and no tie, he oozes masculinity. No skinny pants for this guy. The tousled dark toffee hair and matching rich eyes are entirely too mesmerizing.

Why does he look so familiar?

I comb through the Rolodex in my brain while the three talk in hushed tones. Every so often, one of them peeks over at me.

Despite my irritation that I geared up for tonight's emotional challenge, I should tell them I can reschedule.

My wobbly ankles make walking with mettle in these trendy shoes difficult, but I make an approach. "Excuse me. Is everything all right?"

The group's full attention is intimidating. The maître d' offers a pity-filled smile. Blue Suit Lady squints at me. I don't dare look at Handsome Man.

"My apologies, Ms. Harper." The maître d' bows his head. "The hotel made an unfortunate error. The restaurant is booked for a private event this evening. At the same time, my computer also shows your VIP reservation."

"VIP?" I ask.

Blue Suit Lady taps a fingernail on her clipboard. "A memo—"

"Everyone at the Broadmoor is a VIP." The maître d' raises his voice the appropriate amount to regain command of the conversation. But I want to know what she was going to say.

What is she talking about, a memo? Something's not adding up here. I glance at each person in the group. This crew could be cousins of the Seven Dwarfs. Regretful, Seething, and Charming all wait for my reply.

"I'm sorry. I made the reservation a while ago, but I can come back another time. I'm here for five days." *Bracing for tonight was difficult enough. Please don't make me come back.*

"Thank you for the offer." Blue Suit Lady dismisses me with a sharp nod.

Handsome Man places his hand on her arm. "Penelope, it's fine."

He must possess superpowers because the vein in her forehead disappears and her face transitions to resignation.

Handsome Man shifts to me. "Penelope did an excellent job planning our event for this weekend. The good news is we can spare a table for you tonight." He sweeps his arm toward the room. "Please stay and enjoy dinner."

"Really? Oh, goodness. Thank you." My sigh of relief is louder than I intend. If I stay, I get this social experiment over with now. If I go, I'll have to do all of this over again.

Worse, I'll have to find another outfit.

"Thank you so much. I promise, you won't even notice I'm here."

Penelope returns my peace offering with a blank face.

Once the maître d' settles me into my high-backed booth, I gaze over the Penrose Room. My view of the live band and dance floor is unhindered. The open semicircle seats allow guests to sit next to their dining partners instead of across from them. But my solitary status places me at the center of the plush leather cushion. I recall previous trips to this historic hotel and the familiar burgundy, royal blue, and golden hues that cover the room in luxury.

As if it remembers I'm returning to the restaurant, this time without my husband, the opulent booth welcomes me back into the safety of its cove.

But sitting alone isn't for sissies. I can almost feel curious stares aimed in my direction.

When I lean forward to unravel my swan napkin, I catch someone approaching the table in my peripheral vision.

"I owe you an apology." Handsome Man, wearing a sheepish smile, moves to stand in front of my table.

"You didn't need to accommodate me. My schedule is flexible

this week. I could have come back." I try to hold his stare, but it feels like I could drown in those beautiful deep brown eyes, and I'm not sure I want to go swimming yet.

"Our group is a little high-maintenance." Handsome Man shrugs, but instead of making him appear boyish, the gesture exudes calm confidence. "I didn't want to ask the hotel to make one more exception for us."

"Yeah, but double-booking is their mistake."

"Agreed. However, I'm confident you can behave yourself."

I ignore the gleam in his eye and nod to where Penelope stands, her clipboard hugged to her chest as she surveys the room. "Your friend might not agree with you."

Handsome Man glances over his shoulder. "Penelope? Her heart's in the right place. She's my assistant, and the details for tonight kind of fell in her lap. I told her a bad joke and made her laugh, so that should help."

"A bad joke?" My tone feigns offense, but I add with a smile, "Is that how you always deal with women?"

What am I doing? My attempt at flirting was not only rusty but a complete surprise to me. I want to disappear.

The man's eyes flash, and he breaks out a roguish grin. "No. Sometimes I ask them to dance."

Wait. What?

Does he mean me?

"I'm sorry." I tilt my head. "I didn't catch your name?"

He studies me for a beat, and his grin shifts into a blinding smile. "I'm Harlan Holcombe."

Oh no. I cover my face with my hands and start rocking back and forth, shaking my head. Invisibility seems impossible at this point. Can I will myself into spontaneous combustion? "No, no, no."

"You're going to be fine." His playful tone belies the seriousness of the situation.

I rub my temples. "You're Hercules."

"No, I'm not." His words break through a chuckle.

"Yes, you are." I snap my head up. "I saw it." Hyperventilating is a real threat at this moment. Of *course* he looked familiar.

Harlan Holcombe, the Hercules of Hollywood's silver screen. Which is bad enough.

But he's also Harlan Holcombe, the Hercules of hometown heroes.

Two weeks ago, he saved a teenage girl from drowning in a river. A bystander posted the event on YouTube, and it went viral within two hours. His celebrity status took on a superpower of its own and skyrocketed through Social Media Bizarro World and straight to Planet Infamy.

My teenybopper niece wore her "Vote for Hercules" shirt the last time we were together. I've done my best to avoid Harlan's rescue video, but it's impossible to go to the grocery store without seeing this man's face plastered across the magazine aisle.

I place my elbows on the table and rest my forehead on my fingertips. My brow is sweating.

Is thirty-six too young to get the vapors?

He puts his weight on his hands and leans into the table. "Are you okay?"

Cringing, I look to him and whisper, "I'm not allowed to talk to famous people."

The confession earns me a deep, barking laugh. "I'm not that famous."

"Really?" I rub my sweaty palms on my dress. "Various social media outlets continue to spread a nationwide petition for you to be *People* magazine's Sexiest Man Alive."

"Magazines get recycled to line the bottom of cat litter boxes." He flashes the same grin I saw splashed across the airport bookstore stands earlier today. "And why aren't you allowed to talk to famous people?"

My shoulders slump as scenes of my most embarrassing moment flash through my mind. "It's a long story involving a book-signing event."

He shakes his head and chuckles. "Meredith? Is that right?"

"Yes." I exhale.

"I tell you what, Meredith. I'm going to order you a drink. All right?"

Dabbing my forehead with my napkin, I peek up at him. "Can you make it a double, but nonalcoholic? Sugar is my preferred coping mechanism."

"Yes, ma'am." He raps his knuckles on the table twice. "Then get ready for that dance."

I blink. "What?"

But Harlan Holcombe is already walking toward the bar.

The server approaches and sets a crystal goblet of water on the table. I don't even try to disguise my bewilderment. Heat drains from my face, and I imagine my color turning from teenager crimson red to hotel-sheet white because in about twenty minutes, I need to remember how to waltz. With a bona fide celebrity.

"Ma'am?" The server points to my clutch. "I think your phone is ringing."

The tone breaks through the calm dinner atmosphere. It feels almost as embarrassing as if my phone was going off in a movie theater.

"Oh, sorry." I scoot out of the booth. No way am I answering a call in a fancy restaurant. Digging through my purse, I reach past my small, worn accordion folder for my cell. As I pull it out, my big sister's name flashes on the screen.

Of course.

I scurry down the hall to the bathroom to take her fifth call of the day in privacy.

With floor-to-ceiling dark wood doors, lush padded fabric walls, and a full stock of velvety toilet paper, the decor insists I forget I'm in a room with a commode. The ceilings are high enough that, with a few changes, they could add lavender-scented rock climbing to the restroom amenities.

"Hello?" I tromp to the last stall.

"How's your trip?" The voice at the other end is too chirpy for this annoying call.

"Molly. This is my night at the Penrose Room."

"That's why I'm checking on you. How's it going?"

"Something's not right." Using my free hand, I scrunch my hair on top of my head. "The restaurant was booked for a private event, but the maître d' made an exception for me to dine here tonight. Someone mentioned a memo and I—"

Details of the day shutter through my head like I'm watching an old movie reel. An eerie understanding clicks into place. This isn't the only abnormal exception the Broadmoor made for me today.

"Molly, I don't understand what's going on, and you're the only one who knows I'm at the Penrose Room tonight." I drop my hair and press my palm flat against the door. "What did you do?"

Silence causes me to pull the cell down and confirm the timer is ticking off the live call.

When I put the phone back to my ear, my sister's demanding voice says, "Promise me you'll be open-minded about this."

"Spill it."

"I called the Broadmoor last week and talked to a manager. Since you wouldn't let me go on this trip to be your buffer, I asked them to take care of you and to be your advocate."

In the dictionary, under the word "vigilant," it says "See Molly."

Frustration surges through me for not anticipating this move. Trying to keep my voice level, I ask, "What did you tell them?"

"When you check in with their dining rooms, the spa, or your realtor, anyone who assists you views a memo requesting sensitivity to your situation." Her words spew out in rapid succession.

The conversation comes to a standstill while tears prick the back of my eyes. "I just want to be normal, Molly." My voice sounds garbled, and I lean my weight into my forehead, now pressed to the fabric wall. I'm hoping my waterproof mascara serves me well.

To others I will always be That Woman. The Widow. The One Who Lost Everything. I can't blame them. Horrible things happened. And I am That Person.

However, four years later I'm starting to breathe again. And for the first time since the accident, I wonder if I could become another person.

"I think this will help." Molly forges forward. "Didn't you once say telling new people is always difficult because you end up emotionally managing their reaction? Now they'll already know, and you can skip the hard part and talk about the weather."

Tears stream down my cheeks.

Molly's loud sigh breaks the silence. "Are you there, Meredith?"

"Yes." I grab some of the impossibly soft toilet paper to use as a tissue.

"I could still come to Colorado. A flight from Dallas will only take a few hours. I don't think you should be by yourself."

"Please don't. I need to do this." I close the lid of the toilet to create a place to sit. One hand holds the cell to my ear while the other presses the wrinkled toilet tissue to my cheek. "If I fall apart, I'll come home in a week, and you can say you told me so. But I need to try to do something different with my life." A stray tear falls to the marble tile. "There has to be more for me in this life than being alone, doing volunteer work, and living out a sad story."

"Okay." The voice coming through the phone is thick. "But call me every day."

"I love you. I'll call you when I can."

Stepping out of my stall, I glance at the mirror and recognize a familiar reflection. Not tonight, I vow as I pull my makeup bag from my purse. I won't wear the face of grief. Tonight is about the comfort of an old place that might kindle a new beginning.

Tears are allowed, but they don't get to rule the evening.

While I blend concealer under my eyes, two beautiful women walk into the room. No, beautiful isn't accurate. Exquisite? Glamorous? Otherworldly? Or, just wow.

I've missed some movies over the last four years, but not enough not to recognize these women as actors. One is the leading lady of a rom-com, the other a longtime lead for a television drama, now turned movie star.

Oh man. I'm at a real live Hollywood party, and the hotel handed my life tragedy on a silver platter to one of the most famous men in the country.

As I wrap up my eye makeup repair, I know what I must do.

Shoulders squared and chin up, making great effort not to hobble in these silly shoes, I enter the dining area and place my purse at my booth. Turning on my heel in platforms proves to be more difficult than I anticipated, and I twist and fall into the arms of a wall. A hard, well-defined wall of muscle. Strong hands grip my biceps to steady me. I draw my eyes up, and up, and find a second chiseled Greek god staring down at me. Only this one is young. Jailbait young.

"Are you okay, ma'am?" The dimples. His dimples are speaking louder to me than his question.

"Nice catch, Charlie." Harlan Holcombe's words pull me out of my drooling stupor as he claps the man-child on the shoulder.

Charlie releases my arms, and his crystal-blue eyes dance from Harlan to me.

"Meredith, this is Charlie Boyd. He's an up-and-coming prodigy. If he stays focused, you'll be seeing his work headlined on the big screen one day."

Charlie slips his hands in his pants pockets and shrugs in an endearing aw-shucks manner. "He mentors a couple of us newbies. We're all glad he's back and hope he rubs off on us somehow."

"Charlie, this is Meredith." Harlan nods to me, his dark eyes gripping my attention with their intensity. "She's about to make me grateful my mother forced me to attend cotillion."

These two are like a testosterone commercial, and I pray my deodorant is holding up to its advertised standards.

"What kind of event is this?" I ask, looking around the room and spotting a few more familiar beautiful faces. "Is this a fundraiser? Or did they move the Golden Globes to Colorado Springs?" I gasp. "Is there a secret famous people convention at the hotel? I won't be able to handle that."

Charlie grins. "We're all on a movie set together close by."

"It's been a brutal schedule," Harlan adds. "And something went wrong behind the scenes that delayed filming. The studio gave us the weekend for some R and R while they work out the details."

"Harlan set it up for all of us to come here. And he paid!"

Harlan glares at Charlie. "That's enough. I'll take it from here."

"You paid for all of this for them?" I ask, not knowing how to filter that information but not being able to ignore how moved I am at his generosity.

Instead of explaining, he wraps my arm around his elbow.

We walk the plank toward the dance floor.

Everything about him is overwhelming. His solid presence, his masculine scent, his confidence. If I'm unable to form coherent thoughts, how do I pull out of this?

As we reach the edge of the inlaid hardwood, I tug on him to stop our forward movement. I bow my head and study my toes.

Harlan's body angles toward mine, appearing almost protective. "Meredith?"

I lick my lips, tasting overpriced lip gloss and a hint of insecurity. Staring at the safety of my shoes, I ask my question. "Be honest with me. Did you let me stay and dine with your group because you found out about the memo?"

"No. Yes." His laugh fractures, and he gentles his voice. "Maybe."

I nod at the floor.

"But I asked you to dance with me in *spite* of the memo."

Any other answer would have driven me straight back to my table. However, this one robs me of the frequent-flier excuses I use to insulate my widowed, risk-averse life.

Harlan leans in. "What do you say? Dance with me?"

The low timbre of his voice coaxes me to respond. I lift my head and stare at him. Can he see the stars swirling in my eyes? He doesn't need *People* magazine to affirm his looks. This man would make anyone forget how to speak.

Four years. No doubt I've been in the presence of attractive single men over the course of the last four years, but this feels like the first time I've noticed one. I just can't believe the one my body chose to notice. How can anyone converse with someone so beautiful?

"I could be a complete nightmare, you know," I say.

His broad shoulders, still shielding me from the room, shake with his light laughter. "You aren't. In my entire life, I've only misjudged one person." His eyes seem to dim a touch, though it's almost indiscernible. "I won't make that mistake again."

"Famous last words. But if you're willing to risk it, so am I."

He doesn't waste a moment ushering me to the dance floor, allowing me no time to ask the obvious.

I place my right hand in his left, then set my other one on his shoulder. When his palm hits my waist, I shudder. The surprise of his touch clashes with the memory of the last time I danced with a man in this room.

"You okay?"

After gulping down my uncertainty, I offer him one curt nod. I can do this.

The piano, saxophone, and upright bass play the opening notes, and as the first words of "The Way You Look Tonight" roll out, I start to understand that we have actually made a mistake of epic proportions.

Clunky doesn't begin to describe our movement.

Unsurprisingly, Harlan leads well. Yet he is about a quarter of a beat off every fourth step.

Our feet are dancing on different planets.

I lower my head and stare at our disastrous strides, unable to figure out how to fix this. We knock each other's toes, our arms sway off-kilter, and if our proximity narrows, one or both of us will be in danger of a concussion.

*Bam.*

"Whoa. Sorry there, bud." Harlan offers a chin lift to fellow A-list dancers caught in our path.

*Pow.*

"Nope. Not that way." Harlan pulls me into him and scoots us around a tall couple, offering a dashing, apologetic smile as we pass.

*Schmack.*

I now fear we look like Batman and Robin participating in hand-to-hand combat.

"Harlan." I lean toward him in laughter. "We're terrible at this."

Harlan bites his lower lip in concentration, looking over my shoulder. "Nah."

Glancing around, I note we are now being given a wide berth. I catch the eye of a blond with hair big enough to rival the women of Texas. She smiles at me with a cross between sympathy and amusement. Her dance partner winks.

Wow, these people know he's terrible. And it appears they choose to love him through it anyway.

The second I think we're safe from another disastrous collision, my ankle falters.

In Harlan's only smooth move of the night, he steadies me against his chest. "Gotcha." He locks his eyes with mine. "Your hair smells amazing."

"The lady at the salon said I needed a dash of vanilla in my milk-chocolate hair." I close my eyes, lamenting my brilliant response. When I look back to him, he's still staring so I keep saying words. "She used a lot of food items to describe my coloring and makeup. Strawberry-shortcake cheeks. Red-apple lips. This only made me hungry." *Oh my gosh. Someone make me stop talking.* "When she mentioned my eyes being the color of Twinkies, I asked for a snack break."

Yes. Yes, I did just say that.

The left side of Harlan's mouth twitches. "Your eyes seem more of a golden hazel to me than Twinkie yellow."

The last few bars of Frank Sinatra's song decrescendo, and, God help us, Harlan moves to dip me.

Jumping out of an airplane can't be as terrifying.

After surviving the plunge, I pat my hair back down from the stratosphere and attempt an escape to my table. However, he doesn't loosen his grip. His grin sends me a silent invitation for a second whirl around the floor. At least his abysmal dancing skills help me relax, causing me to almost forget his celebrity status.

But will I survive another go-around?

During the first few measures of "Come Away with Me," I'm relieved at the musical choice of a straightforward waltz. However, as each set of three beats pass, it's clear Harlan prefers to count to four.

The slower pace is in the best interest of crowd safety, but this new category of awkwardness makes me yearn for the earlier slam dancing.

"What brought you to Colorado Springs?" he asks.

Interesting that he thinks he can handle talking and dancing at the same time.

"I'm looking at properties in the area. A realtor from the Broadmoor sent me some options. I'm supposed to meet with her tomorrow."

His dark eyes light up in what appears to be recognition. "Prissy? Prissy Prestidge?"

I smile my affirmation. Can there be another person in the world named Prissy Prestidge?

We continue to sway to the music in Harlan's head. That is to say, I'm clueless when each movement will happen. But we're dancing without violence, which I count as a victory.

"How do you know Prissy?" I ask.

His shoes scuff the edges of mine. "I grew up outside of Colorado Springs. Prissy's one of my mom's best friends. You're in good hands. She's a legend in the real estate world."

Harlan continues to drop breadcrumb details of his life. But I don't know if they lead to a safe home or to a mean lady who wants to eat me alive.

He uses gentle pressure on my waist to guide me sideways in a motion resembling quintessential awkward junior high dance moves. "Why are you looking for property here?"

What I want to say is I fell in love with this place the first time my husband and I visited. But what's the protocol for talking about your dead spouse to someone you're dancing with? "I guess I thought it would be a good place to start."

Harlan stills our movement, pulls back, and stares down at me. "A good place to start what?"

"I don't know, exactly. Start over." Shifting my gaze to his shoulder, I swallow. In the safe corner of a small dance floor in the heart of Colorado, I ask a complete stranger, "Do you ever wonder if there might be more to your life? A purpose? Something you're missing, but it might be obtainable if you search hard enough?"

The squeeze he gives my waist feels like a reflex. "Most days."

His gravelly words draw my eyes to his, and I search the face of the man in front of me. "Charlie mentioned he's glad you're back," I say. "What did he mean?"

"I guess I got a little off course."

His words don't make sense to me. "You saved someone's life. You couldn't be that far off course."

In spite of our close proximity, the shadow in his eyes makes him look far away. He clenches his jaw. "I guess being a hometown hero isn't all it's cracked up to be. We can get a little off course too."

21

I tip my head. "Is that what you're doing now? Getting your life back on track?"

He takes a sidelong glance across the room. "Yeah," he says quietly. "I guess it is."

His confession moves something inside me, but I don't have time to reply because he schools his face into a charming smile. "But for now, I need an outlet to show off my mad dancing skills." With dramatic flair, he swoops us back to the center of the dance floor to finish the waiting waltz.

We dive back into the anti-Fred-and-Ginger show, concentration imperative so as not to send anyone around us to the emergency room.

Once the song ends, Harlan takes my hand and leads me to my table.

I might be wrong, but I think I detect a collective sigh of relief from the other dancers when we exit the dance floor.

As I scoot into my booth, the adrenaline rush from the precarious waltz drains from my body, and I'm stumped as to what to say to this man who stands before me, larger than life.

"Thank you for the dance, Meredith." Harlan bows his head, his glittering eyes never leaving my gaze. "Maybe I'll see you around the hotel this weekend. But if not, enjoy your time in Colorado. I hope you find what you're looking for."

He turns to leave before I can respond with anything resembling the English language.

Trying to process the wide pendulum swing of the last thirty minutes, I bring the edge of my glass to my lips. A shocking thought occurs to me, and I almost spill the drink.

The most surprising detail of the evening isn't the botched dinner reservation, my sister's scheme, or the handsome man with two left feet and a broken metronome in his head. No, the most surprising part of the evening is, by far, my desire to know what it is Harlan Holcombe is looking for.

Or maybe *who* it is Harlan Holcombe is looking for.

It's unexpected and uncomfortable to be drawn to someone for the first time in four years.

But not altogether unwelcome.

---

A one-hour time change from Dallas, a five-course meal, and two life-threatening dances have zapped me of all energy. I enter my room hoping to drop into bed as soon as possible, but my phone buzzes with a text.

**MOLLY**

Did you survive your night?

I roll my eyes. The woman has a husband, a ten-year-old, and a fourteen-year-old. Surely she had something better to do tonight than to wait for my call.

Yes.

As I sit down to soothe my ankles, I come to the disturbing realization these shoes might be easier to walk in than remove.

I worried about you all night when I didn't hear from you again.

If she only knew. Risking injury on the dance floor worried me too.

Even though she can't hear me chuckle, my lack of answer must have stressed her out because my phone vibrates with another text.

Are you drunk? You should remember that your typical half glass of wine is more potent in the altitude of the mountains.

"No, I'm not drunk." I grunt as I pry off the right high heel. The left shoe removal requires the same unfeminine sounds. I roll my ankles in the air, and once circulation returns to my feet, I text my answer.

> Not drunk. Impeccable service, amazing food, and I danced with Harlan Holcombe.

That should get a good reaction.

Dress still on my body, I crawl into bed, pull up the covers, and enjoy my smug moment.

> Harlan Holcombe?

> You are drunk.

> Sleep it off. Proud of you.

My life hasn't afforded me many secrets over the last four years. I revel in keeping my death-defying dance with Hercules the Hometown Hero just for me.

Eyes drooping, breathing slowed, I glance at the new message.

> Can you imagine? The thought of you meeting him is disastrous. You're on Famous People Probation.

Snuggling into my pillow, hands nestled under my chin, I close my eyes and grin like an idiot. I am. I am one hundred percent on Famous People Probation.

Which is perfect because I won't see him again.

# 2

FALLING ASLEEP while wearing Spanx was not one of my better decisions.

As I sit in the hotel spa waiting room this morning, I'm thankful for my upcoming eighty-minute hot stone massage. With a considerable amount of pampering, my body should forgive me for dozing off in the spandex vise.

I'm hoping my masseuse can also work out the giddy memories of last night dancing through my head.

The purpose of my trip to Colorado Springs is to find a charming investment property, not fall for a charming actor with a killer smile and dangerous dancing skills.

But my reality taps me on the shoulder, and I release a weighty breath.

Not even Hercules can carry the baggage I travel with, despite his disarming smile.

Clamorous laughter across the room disrupts my sobering thoughts.

The plump woman on the chaise lounge next to me rests her elbow on the arm of her chair and leans in my direction. "Who thinks cackling in the quiet room is okay?" She nods toward the loud talkers.

I offer a smile of solidarity and shrug.

When I go to the dentist and the assistant tells me to go to my happy place, my mind takes me to the Broadmoor Spa. Panic attack in a packed elevator? Broadmoor Spa. Talking to my sister about her latest bra-purchasing adventures? Broadmoor Spa.

The irony is not lost on me that I'm having to make great effort to be happy in my happy place because of some insensitive clients *in* my happy place.

My partner-in-annoyance glances around the room. "I hope my appointment's soon."

I want to say "Me too," but I'm holding the line on the whole quiet room thing.

The woman next to me doesn't take the hint. "I'm getting a body wrap, and afterwards going downstairs for a pedicure. Do you know, when I checked in, this nice girl told me about a cancellation and asked if I also wanted a Tuscan fig sugar scrub? Can you imagine the self-control required not to eat the treatment?" She shudders. "No one needs that kind of stress while trying to relax."

Covering my mouth, I stifle a giggle.

"Are you getting your hair done?" She nods her head in the direction of my makeshift bun.

The messy pile of hair gives the appearance that I fought a fierce battle with a beehive. Remnants of last night's makeup only confirm my loss in the war.

"No." My hand reaches in vain to smooth down some of the destruction. "I went to the salon yesterday."

"Okay, honey." She pats my hand twice and turns back to her book. "Whatever you say."

As the slight patronizing tone in her response lingers, I'm overwhelmed with the urge to tell her I don't believe people should dress up to visit the spa. But a staff member arrives and whisks her away before I can dive into my diatribe on proper relaxation practices.

I snuggle deep into my chair and curl my arms around my body. The Broadmoor Spa is well known for its impeccable services, but for me, the decor buries me into a relaxing state. The varying striped chairs, pillows, and fresh flower arrangements all coordinate different hues of blue, yellow, and brown throughout the Mountain View Room. Even the provided cornflower-blue robes add an element of harmony.

When I'm here, I can only think of peace. The room won't allow for anything else.

Except when the group of women behind me lets out another roar of laughter. Then my peace flies right out the grand windows.

Who do these people think they are? Don't they understand the rules? I'm all for fun on vacation, but pick a room without a polite sign directing everyone to honor the quiet atmosphere.

The remnants of my water-with-cucumber drink need to be thrown away, and on the way to the trash can, I notice a few of the ladies are looking at me and whispering. I'm having a paranoid moment, I'm sure. I flash them what I hope looks like a genuine smile.

I've tried in vain to block out the chatter. Should I say something?

Deciding I don't want to be that person, I exit the room and head down the carpeted hall to find my second-string happy place.

An unfortunate pop sounds with each step of my resort-administered flip-flops. Never one to criticize the serene ambiance, I worry I'm betraying Spencer and Julie Penrose, creators of this oasis, as I question the choice of these shoes.

But then a woman approaches, and I'm dumbfounded to find her identical spa shoes don't make any noise. It must be me. I offer a silent apology to the Penroses and continue down the hall, this time making great efforts to mute my flip-flops.

My mind wanders to last night's dinner at the Penrose Room, and a feeling of unease hits me. I stop.

Oh no. I recognize two of the women in the quiet room. I think they *were* talking about me. They watched me dance with Harlan Holcombe. I should go back and tell them dancing with movie stars never happens to a person like me. Moreover, I'm not even sure it occurred. Altitude sickness does weird things to people. The chances are quite high I dreamed about Hollywood last night.

But why does it feel like giddy butterflies have landed in my stomach? This must be another symptom of altitude sickness. I make a mental note to ask the concierge for pamphlets on the topic.

As I plod forward and take a left into the women's-only section, I locate the entrance to the Fireplace Room and come to a complete halt. The reality of meeting Harlan Holcombe is in full view. But instead of it being a dream, it has become a nightmare.

Sitting in a chair next to the glowing fireplace, stiff, upright, and looking like she needs a massage more than the rest of us, is Penelope. Last night's gatekeeper to the Penrose Room, also known as Harlan Holcombe's assistant.

Every cell in my body wants to stride right back out the door. But the space is so small, leaving is impossible to do without looking impolite.

I decide to put on my big-girl panties and stay in the room with the tiger.

In a ridiculous turn of events, this makes me want to go to my happy place.

Penelope glances up. At the sight of me, her blank expression remains unchanged, but her hands clutch the newspaper she's reading, causing a soft crinkling sound.

My guess is her facial expression hasn't changed since 1998. Or her makeup. A closer look reveals her jet-black hair is pulled back in a tight bun, and her face sports a fresh coat of battle paint, brightening her already piercing green eyes.

I fight the urge to ask if she came here to unwind or to hold a board meeting.

"Would you like to sit here?" She nods to the chair across from her in the room's only other seating option.

My hesitation is part shock and part fear that she will throw me into the blaze of the fireplace. Unable to help myself, I peer at her for a beat. She holds my gaze, but we're not in a stare-down.

Almost as if she wants me to see her vulnerability, I remember what I know to be true.

Everyone has a story.

I exhale some of my tension before I risk sitting three feet from her and scoot into the offered seat. I'll try to get her to share her story before she rakes me over the coals. "Thank you."

As I sit down, I pick up a blanket from a basket on the hearth to drape over my legs. The tan piece of fabulousness is fluffy and divine.

Penelope interrupts my thoughts of developing a new wardrobe line with the blankets and shocks me for the second time today. "I'm sorry about last night. I'm not proficient at being flexible."

I pick up my robe's belt and wrap it around my left palm. "No need to apologize. The hotel made the mistake."

"I know."

My guess is Penelope uses the words "I know" on a regular basis. My next guess is that it's hard to be Penelope.

She drops the paper to her lap and smooths the creases flat with her palms. "It wasn't going to bother anyone for you to enjoy your meal. I should have let it go."

"Do people tell you to let it go often?"

Her eyes flash, but she doesn't answer.

"Harlan Holcombe sang your praises last night." I unravel the belt off my mummified hand, creating a long spiral. "But I also get the impression you consider it your duty to protect those around you."

"My job is critical. If someone from the outside compromises his reputation because they want their fifteen minutes of fame, it falls on me. The work is unremitting."

29

My head jerks back in response. What a life she must live, guarding Harlan Holcombe's private matters in the middle of the boundaryless realm of social media.

Penelope chooses to take responsibility for both the overexuberant fans and mindless haters in Harlan's world. For someone as competent and capable as her, the burden would be consuming.

No wonder she looks rigid while sitting in a spa. She's like Superman, ready to pull her hair down, tear off the spa robe, and reveal a full suit so she can go save the day.

"You're excellent at your job," I say. "I hope you let yourself off the hook sometimes."

She releases a sigh. "Well, I think last night I could have handled the situation better."

I quiet my voice. "Are you saying that because the maître d' told you my story?"

"Maybe," she tells the fire. "Or maybe you're a reminder that not everyone wants to take something from me."

Interesting. I cock my head to the side. "Harlan Holcombe is special, isn't he?"

Her eye twitches. "Yes. But not in the way you might think." She reaches to the small mahogany table next to her chair and picks up her hot tea. "He hired me when no one else would. He saved me."

I nod. "And now you protect him."

After returning her cup to the table, she leans in, clasps her hands, and pierces me with her eyes. "My concern is, Meredith, will you?"

The question is so shocking, my entire body pulls back, and I gape.

*It was just a dance* is what I want to say to her. But her intensity steals the words before they can escape my mouth.

A masseuse appears and interrupts our moment. "Penelope?"

"Yes."

"I'm Patty. If you're ready, I'll take you to your room."

Penelope picks up her treatment folder and cup of tea and rises from the chair. Before she passes me, she pauses. "I hope you find what you need while you're here, Meredith."

*I need an investment property, not a bad dancing partner who just happens to have a kind heart, killer-watt smile, and plays a Greek demigod on the big screen,* I want to assure her.

And myself.

Instead, I offer a smile. "Thank you. Enjoy your well-earned massage."

With their departure, I'm left alone in the room, and I'm conflicted. Since she didn't throw me into the fire, talking to the tiger a little while longer might have been enjoyable.

While replaying the conversation in my head, it occurs to me I've lost my own treatment folder. Paperwork representing health inventories, therapy needs, and personal schedules are tucked away in brown padded folders for each patron to hand to the staff member in charge of their care. I need to track mine down.

I exit the women's-only section, trace my oafish steps back to the Mountain View Room, and, upon arrival, am relieved the exuberant women are now gone. Scanning the lounges, I spot the lost item. As I approach, my shoes announce my presence with their intrusive flip-flopping.

Without looking up, I address the person in the chair as I lean down to snatch my abandoned folder off the neighboring table. "Sorry, I'm just going to grab this."

"Shh. Do you mind?" The voice of the chair's occupant sounds familiar, and I glimpse down. And stop breathing.

A grinning Harlan Holcombe continues. "This is the quiet room, and those shoes could start a stampede."

Oh my word. My face burns as my hand travels to lightly touch the disastrous hair-don't on my head. Trying to save my pride, I stand tall. "You know what could start a stampede? Your dancing."

An unrepentant, slow smile crosses his face. "I must have made a real impression on you for you to remember the dances we shared."

I blink. No words. Just blinking. In what world is Harlan Holcombe flirting with me twice inside of twenty-four hours?

My flirting is like my first flip phone now housed at the back of my kitchen drawer. Wow, even if it wasn't cool, it *felt* cool back in the day. But it needs a total reboot, and I'm not sure any amount of updates could make that old technology work in today's world. Certainly not on the Harlan Holcombe megawatt-smile data plan.

Which is why, after the brilliance of my blinking, I finally say, "We danced. Last night. Yes."

I thought he would make fun of me. *I* would have made fun of me. But instead his eyes soften, a really good look on him, and he motions to the chaise lounge next to him. "Do you want to sit down?"

"Oh." I straighten the tie on my robe, as if speaking to a celebrity dressed in a robe while I'm also wearing a robe is a normal, everyday thing for me. There's no excuse for me to leave. Nowhere I need to be. If I say no, what does that look like? "Oh, um. Okay."

I sit in the chaise, staring out at the golf course, my back ramrod straight, my knees locked as if an Olympic judge is going to give me a score for my form.

In the silence, Harlan is so loud.

A chuckle sounds from him. "Meredith?"

"Yes," I tell the fourth hole on the green.

"I don't feel like you're relaxed."

"Of course I'm relaxed. This room is my happy place."

"Have you already shopped properties with Prissy this morning?"

"No. We'll go this afternoon," I say, proud of my brain for coming up with a complete response this time.

"She's trustworthy." His tone fills with sincerity. "She doesn't want you to buy something you don't want. So if you have thoughts about the process, it will work well for you if you're completely up-front with her on what you need and want."

His sincerity touches me. He's still an interplanetary movie star who saves children in his spare time, but his sincerity touches me all the same.

"And what are you treating yourself to here at the spa this morning?" he asks.

"A massage."

"Going to try to relax before Prissy runs you around?"

And then a flicker of courage hits me. I don't know where it came from. It's like my flirting flip phone got charged for a few minutes and is ready to talk. I kick my lips up in a half smile and look at him. "I'm getting the massage to recover from your smooth moves on the dance floor last night."

Something sparks in his eyes, and his shoulders shake with silent laughter. "Is that so?"

"I called downstairs to ask for their recommendation, and when I described my sore muscles, they suggested the extra-long appointment with the hot rocks."

He cocks his head and says in all seriousness, but with a glint in his eye, "I think maybe that means we need to practice more."

"I—I—um . . ." *Mayday. Mayday. The flip phone has failed. Step away from the conversation. I repeat: Step away from the conversation. The flip phone has cosmically failed.* "I can't dance in a robe."

My skin is on fire.

"Meredith." He does that thing again where his eyes soften, but this time they're filled with amusement and . . . affection? "Are you okay?"

My flirting flip phone shorts out completely, and my flustered self blurts, "I need to go find my happy place." I suck in a breath, stand, and turn on my heel to leave.

Only to have the most beautiful, deep laughter follow me out of the room.

—

"I don't think I want a golf course in my backyard." Looking out the bay window of a Broadmoor West Residence condo, my arms crossed, I stare at color that would make the fields of Ireland jealous.

My first property viewing is a mirror to my life.

It's fine. It just doesn't feel quite right.

"Colorado's Front Range is behind the golf course." The ultimate businesswoman, my realtor makes this obvious statement without an insulting tone.

"I know," I say. "But it feels a little manufactured."

"People pay significant amounts for this view."

"Yes." Turning to her, I nod. "But I bet they actually *play* golf."

At this point, I consider joking that I am the problem client, but I'm afraid the statement might hold some truth.

Besides, Prissy Prestidge is too professional to appreciate that kind of comment. She epitomizes efficiency. My guess is her assessing gaze means the cogwheels in her brain are calculating how to find my dream property.

She offers a curt nod. "Of course. This isn't right for you. Let's drive to the next option."

Prissy's deceiving name is her first line of defense. Her reputation as a bulldog real estate negotiator is legendary. But at this moment in time, I covet her ability to wear a suit. How can someone look so fabulous in what I consider the dress code for the FBI?

I need to rethink my entire wardrobe. In spite of the pashmina I added to spruce up my outfit, the pink cashmere sweater and black NYDJ ankle-length pants don't hold a candle to Prissy. I'm underdressed to be a passenger in her car.

After we meander through Colorado Springs for viewings at three other Broadmoor estates, the final one we hit is perfect.

In theory.

Leaning against the marble countertop in the state-of-the-art kitchen, I imagine cooking in front of the island's six-burner stove and gazing across the open floor plan to my extended family seated in a giant, comfy sectional framed around the tall stone fireplace.

Prissy's high heels click on the textured, wide-plank hardwood floors. She reaches the custom windows and pulls the curtains to capacity, exposing the full glory of the mountains. "What do you like about this house?"

I cross the room to the hearth. "This wall of ledgestone is inviting. You can come home, throw your jacket on the back of the couch, and take a load off. Whereas the fabric-covered walls in the last house wouldn't allow you to relax." Twisting my torso, I glimpse back at her.

Her eyes narrow. "What do you dislike about this home?"

"I'm torn. I loved the brownstone because of the location and access to hotel amenities." I clear my throat. "However, farther out from the city, the properties have more character."

*Click, clack, click, clack.* Prissy stands by my side, looking at the mantel. "What else?"

"Why do you think I have a 'what else'?"

"In my experience, a lot of clients bury the lede. Our initial appointment is helpful, but new information reveals itself after the third or fourth showing."

She's good.

But I don't know how to answer her question. I don't know how to define it. This is a wonderful home, but it isn't the one.

"I came here because I wanted a getaway home for my friends and family." I pause, trying to decide if I want to say what's really on my heart. I swallow. "But sometimes I wonder if there's more out here for me."

In a surprisingly affectionate move, she grasps my hand. "What do you mean?" Her words gentle. "Is there more here for you?"

"Listen, I know what I'm about to say next are not a realtor's favorite words, but I don't know what I want. A vacation home has its appeals. A permanent move for me is a more loaded decision. I just . . ." I shrug. "Don't know."

"No, Meredith." She shakes my hand and slows her words. "What did you mean when you said that you wonder if there is more out here for *you*?"

The memo.

During last night's restaurant fiasco, Molly admitted the memo had been delivered to my realtor. Prissy knows my history.

But it's more. Her sixth sense for selling properties seems to be fueled by her spot-on intuition.

My gaze remains on the stone as my voice hitches when I whisper my answer. "He left me an obscene amount of money, Prissy. We took out huge, cheap life insurance policies in our early twenties. His original policy provided enough for me to fall apart in the event of his death, but still be financially secure and able to care for any children we might have. My losing everyone never occurred to us. And after the funeral, our lawyer told me about additional insurance Steve bought, unbeknownst to me." I swipe tears away with my free hand. "It's so much money for one person. I think I'm supposed to do something with it."

Her thumb sweeps over the back of my hand in comfort.

"Or maybe the money is supposed to do something with me," I whisper.

I lack courage to ask Prissy the question that started burning in my heart a few weeks ago. *Is it possible there's still something left for me in this life?*

We turn our heads toward each other, and our eyes lock. She nods, purses her lips, releases her hold on me, and walks away to close up the house.

I gather my purse, take out some Kleenex, and pull myself together.

She may be supportive, but that doesn't mean I want to cry all over her gorgeous suit.

Prissy's sleek black Mercedes SUV defines first-world comfort. I'm so enthralled with the individual seat controls, I'm giddy. Sleek buttons marked with colorful symbols cause my fingers to twitch. I glance to the heated steering wheel. Would Prissy slap my hand away if I leaned over to touch the warm leather?

"Meredith? Would you be comfortable in a property farther away from town?" Prissy asks.

"I think so." I punch an arrow indicating it will increase my seat temperature. "I like the amenity packages some of the Broadmoor estates offered, but the advantages may not outweigh a different kind of property."

"Priscilla." A soothing male voice from the car speakers interrupts our conversation, and every muscle in me freezes. The voice continues, "You are driving over the speed limit."

"Stop nagging at me, Derrick," Prissy snaps, then gnashes her teeth.

Two questions. Is that her car's name? And can it hear her?

"My husband bought this car for me because it can monitor my speed." She presses a button, muting the disembodied voice. "But instead of decreasing my traffic tickets, I now suffer from road rage."

I'm so surprised that I can't mask my response. I throw my head back and laugh. If I'm not mistaken, a smile tugs at Prissy's cheek.

She leaves both thumbs on the wheel while stretching her fingers out, revealing an impeccable manicure. "Meredith, did something unpleasant occur at the hotel?"

"Yes. Harlan Holcombe danced with me in the Penrose Room." The answer blurts out before the words register in my brain.

Her heavily made-up eyes slide in my direction, pause for a second, and return to the road. "Some would consider meeting a celebrity a perk of sorts."

"Well, those who don't make a habit of hyperventilating around famous people probably *would* call it a perk."

She laughs, and her silver, football-shaped hair shifts back and forth in one unified movement. "Did you also have a moment at the spa with said celebrity?"

"What? No. There was no moment in the spa. Why would you ask if there was a moment in the spa?" Heat crawls up my neck, and I paw around my seat, looking for the temperature controls.

"No reason." She looks over at the oncoming cars. "Only that Harlan texted me from the spa informing me to take good care of you today during our viewings."

This time, instead of the heat crawling up my neck, it seeps into my chest. Or maybe it's just warmth. That was kind of him to text on my behalf. Maybe even sweet. "What did you say?"

"I told him he knows better than to discuss privileged client information and that he needs to mind his own business and go have lunch with his mama."

We approach the stately circular drive at the hotel, and she delivers a stiff wave to the gate guard. At the doors to the hotel, she shifts the car into park. While we wait for the valet, she turns to me. "I need to do some research about another property. Is your schedule open tomorrow?"

"Does your plan involve any famous people?"

She pauses. "Not at the moment."

I flash a smile. "Then I'm game."

# 3

**I WALK OUT** of Prissy's office with a head full of floor plans, and my phone rings. After rummaging through my purse, I'm able to see that my friend Stanley is calling. I hit the screen to send him to voicemail, but it's like the buttons don't work and it takes a few tries. Focused on silencing my phone, I almost miss the little boy running at me at Mach 5.

"Toby!" A flustered woman balances a tearful baby on her hip while whispering to her other child at the loudest publicly appropriate volume. I fear little Toby's life could be shortened today if he doesn't obey her. She apologizes to me as she tries to take his hand.

"It's okay. He's adorable." I crouch down, disregarding my knees' protest. "How old are you, buddy?"

Three chubby fingers thrust into my face.

"Wow. Three. That's awesome. Toby, my name is Meredith. It's nice to meet you." I ignore the memory flash of another three-year-old boy I once knew and stand to face his mom. "Can I help you with anything?"

The woman shifts the child squirming in her arms and glances at me. Moisture gathers in her eyes. "I'm so sorry. I don't know what's wrong with me."

Meltdowns are always better with privacy, and if the tear that just slid down her face is any indication, she's about to have one. I decide to guide us in the direction of a bench around the corner. Once seated, I hand Toby a brochure for Jeep tours in Colorado Springs, hoping this occupies him for more than ninety seconds.

"Jeep!" He grabs the glossy pages.

"I'm trying to get to the movie room, and Toby keeps running away, and Layla's diaper just blew out, and now I need to change clothes but I'm late, and I can tell we're disturbing the peace, and I keep trying to smile at everyone to make it okay, but we're getting some rude stares, and I know that all sounds small, but I'm just so overwhelmed." The woman's lips quiver, and tears spill onto her cheeks.

In response to her stress, I lock into some kind of automatic-pilot mommy mode. One I haven't experienced in four years. "I'm Meredith. How can I help?" I point to the diaper bag on her shoulder.

She drops to her knees, and I follow suit and start searching to find what we need. I pull a changing pad out and lay it down for her to place the baby on.

"I'm Sally. This is Toby and Layla." Even through her blubbering, this woman is stunning. Long brown hair tied back in a loose ponytail, displaying a pert nose and wide, long-lashed, indigo eyes.

"How old is Layla?"

"She's almost one."

The painful flashback to a different sweet baby shoots right through my gut, and I pause to take in a breath. I push past, though, because this mama needs help.

"Arms up, sweetie." As she tugs the soiled dress over Layla's head, I force a smile.

"Well, they're beautiful children," I say.

After Sally finagles Layla onto the changing pad and removes her diaper, I'm relieved to see it's only a wet blowout. Sally draws her head up and catches my eyes. "Aren't you going to add, 'and a handful'? People seem to make that comment when my kids act up."

"I wasn't thinking about your children." I offer a small smile. "I was thinking about how hard it is to be a mom of little ones."

"I'm a mess." She murmurs the confession on a sigh. Her tears slow, and she takes the diaper I hold out for her, slips it under Layla, and secures the tabs.

"Did you feed your kids today?" I ask.

Sally blinks.

I hold up a clean, ruffled replacement romper I found in the diaper bag. "They're obviously clothed in appropriate attire. So you dress them too."

She opens her mouth, but nothing comes out.

"That's all that's required of you," I say, rolling up the wet diaper into a ball. "Feed them, clothe them, keep them safe. Some days, accomplishing those three things is all you can do. And, Sally, that just has to be okay. You're doing an excellent job."

Slumping over, she shakes her head in her hands. "We met two minutes ago. You don't know that."

"Now, Miss Layla, I think you're all set to go." While she holds my hands, her chunky feet find the floor in an effort to stand. Layla gives me the sweetest two-tooth smile, wobbles, and falls on her baby bottom with glee.

Toby continues to rip the Jeep brochure apart as if his life depends on it, his little-boy brow furrowed in concentration.

"Toby and Layla can't tell you this right now," I say, "but they're so glad you're their mommy."

"Being a mom is an impossible job. It feels like any mistake will send my kids straight to therapy." Using the back of her hand, Sally brushes a lock of hair out of her eyes. "Do you have kids of your own?"

It's an innocent question. A natural one, really, from what's just unfolded. But I can't. It will change everything. "Oh, let's focus on yours. I'm on vacation."

Sally shifts her attention to the wet area covering a fourth of her belted, pale-green sweater dress, then looks to me, a little panic-stricken. "We were going to the hotel movie theater. My husband, Spencer, is here on business and the company organized several family activities, but now I'm covered in tinkle."

"Here." I remove and offer my pashmina. "Use this to cover the spot. Then head to the bathroom just outside the theater. The stalls are stocked with body spray. No one will have a clue."

She looks at me, awe filling her eyes. "Are you a superhero?"

I blink. Superhero? A lump forms in my throat as something dawns on me.

I've been useful to someone.

The realization feels more than sweet. It's thick with meaning. *Yessssss.*

I thought my purpose, my worth in this life, had been swept away with my cataclysmic loss. Who am I if I'm not a wife or a mother? But helping Sally chisels away at the falsehood.

After draping the pashmina over her shoulders, Sally scoops up Layla and grabs Toby's hand.

I take her in from head to toe. My black scarf coordinates with her dark knee-high leather boots as if the entire ensemble came from her closet. "You look perfect."

She flashes a smile at me as I pass her the diaper bag. "We'll be done around five. Can I treat you to dinner for helping me? We can meet in the mezzanine."

Sharing a meal with a new friend. Who has young children. The thought doesn't hurt nearly as much as it usually does.

In fact, the thought feels warm, like it could be safe for the first time in a long while.

*Shut up. Shut up. Shut. Up.*

The torturous, beeping alarm badgers me out of a deep sleep. My hand blindly slaps the side table until I annihilate my target. Lifting up my sleep mask, I lean over the bed and peer down at the injured clock on the floor.

"Ugh." I roll to my back and stare at the ceiling. Details from the day trickle through my memory. House shopping with Prissy. An unfortunate mention of Harlan Holcombe. Sally, Toby, Layla, and the blowout. A monster nap.

I blink. Sally. I'm supposed to meet Sally and her kids for dinner.

Disoriented, I fumble around until I sit on the side of the bed, hotel phone in hand, and stab the operator button.

The voice greeting me is too loud for my not-quite-awake ears. "Good afternoon, Ms. Harper, how can I assist you today?"

Still in a post-nap fog, I hear unplanned words tumble from my mouth. "I need to report a homicide."

The voice clears its throat. "Excuse me?"

"I murdered my clock while trying to turn off the alarm." A yawn interrupts my confession. "I'm so sorry—please charge it to my room."

Stifled laughter comes through the phone. "That won't be necessary, Ms. Harper. However, I will contact housekeeping and have a replacement sent to you right away."

I wind the cord around my forefinger. "Don't enable my poor behavior choices, otherwise I'll never learn."

"My pleasure, Ms. Harper. Can I help you with anything else?"

Once the blood in my finger is cut off, I unwind the cord the opposite direction. "No, but I can't guarantee the safety of the other small appliances in the room."

"We'll take it one incident at a time, Ms. Harper. Thank you for making me smile."

He thinks I'm kidding.

I rejoin the phone to its cradle and hang my head in my hands.

The crankiest of moods accompanies me as I rouse from my dead-to-the-world nap. What is wrong with me?

*This isn't hard, Meredith. You're triggered.*

Long, deliberate breaths start to ground me.

Grief is stealthy.

I don't choose when it rears its ugly head. My only options are in my response.

When I left Sally and the kids, I floated back to my room on a cloud of anticipation and hope. Allowing myself to dust off the cobwebs of my mommy skills somehow liberated me. I felt grateful for the opportunity to jump outside of myself and encourage someone else. I'd really leaned into the situation. A sense of pride had washed over me, and my grief didn't immediately steal it away.

But the reminder of my personal catastrophe settled over me like a wet blanket while I slept. Instead of a suffocating ache, I woke up to a seething spirit. The fatigue, moodiness, and hungover feelings are all familiar foes. They know they aren't welcome. And they know I'll take time to wait them out.

Deep, long, deliberate breaths.

The question is, will I risk being around Sally and her children again, knowing there could be consequences like this episode of emotion?

Over the last four years, I've lived life as if I'm playing a game of dodgeball. My reality is so painful, I take care to hide in the corner, avoiding the different spheres of loss.

At first everyone else protected me. Birthday parties, weddings, and baby showers passed without invitations in my mailbox. At some point they resumed, but it became more comfortable for me to ignore them, and I disappeared right off the social grid.

That's just it. The corner is safe.

I benched myself from my own life.

And for the first time in four years, I'm curious. I want to come out and play. I do. Even if it hurts.

The question I was too scared to ask Prissy runs through my head like a news ticker across the bottom of a television screen. *Is it possible there's still something left for me in this life?*

Stretching my arms, I stand on my tiptoes as I inhale once more. I fold my body over, my hands touch my feet, and I exhale. Back curled, I turn my head and talk to the deceased clock on the floor. "Let's suit up."

---

When I arrive on the mezzanine level, it's a bustling hub of connection. Three helpful staff members pack the concierge desk. Those waiting for their parties lounge on various plush couches, chairs, and ottomans. The hotel bar welcomes guests for late-afternoon libations.

Sally isn't difficult to find. Toby and Layla, noses and hands pressed against the floor-to-ceiling windows, gaze in awe at the swans floating in Cheyenne Lake.

At the sight of the children, my heart pangs. But my optimism bats away the feeling. My past is what it is. Today the present is tempting me to settle and stay a while.

Toby attempts to follow another family out the door, and Sally twists toward me to shout her greeting while grabbing Toby's hand. "Meredith."

I bend down to reach for Layla, who is crawling to a great escape. She giggles through the swoop into my arms.

With Toby's steps redirected, Sally calls to someone a few feet behind me. "Spence, come meet Meredith."

Layla leans over my arms and tries to catapult herself to the man who is strolling in our direction. "Da!"

The man snags the little girl before she drops to her demise and plops her on his hip. "Hi there. I'm Spencer, Sally's husband."

Someone hits the pause button, and I gawk at this demigod.

Spence is Spencer. Spence is Spencer Dean. SPENCE IS SPENCER DEAN.

Spencer Dean, famous for his leading role as a crooked lawyer in a John Grisham blockbuster, is standing in front of me.

"Hello?" The only word I can remember breathes out as my eyes dart between Sally and Spencer Dean.

Spencer smiles, hand held out. "Is that a question? Hello?" He winks.

Spencer Dean winked. At me.

My brain lopes behind the scene like a hound with floppy ears. I am one giant delayed reaction. *Get a grip, Meredith.*

His eyebrows arch. "I'm sorry, I didn't catch your name."

Spencer Dean appears amused.

Meredith Harper is mortified.

"Spence, this is Meredith," Sally says. "She's the one I told you about."

Precious Sally doesn't understand I'm frozen somewhere back in the giddy land of junior high school.

Spence's expression changes to one of recognition. "Yes. Meredith. You're my wife's superhero." He closes the gap between us, bends in to grasp my hand, and shakes.

This is getting worse. I have a rule. When I meet famous people, I am not allowed to talk during the first five minutes of the interaction. Anything that comes out of my mouth before the five-minute mark will only be stuttered, jumbled, giggling, nervous, and full of bad jokes. Molly made me swear to this after I met Rachael Ray and pitched the idea of an adult version of the Easy-Bake Oven to her. My sister then sentenced me to Famous People Probation because for me, the initial exhilaration of talking to a celebrity is not worth the aftermath price of humiliation.

But there is no time to wait the required five minutes because I am now BFF status with Sally, the wife of Spencer Dean. Acting cool is imperative. I am just meeting my friend's husband. Say it again. *I am just*—breathe—*meeting*—breathe—*my friend's husband.*

"Meredith, are you okay?" Sally purses her lips and her cheeks twitch. Apparently I'm not fooling her.

"Yes, Meredith, are you okay?" booms a voice behind me.

As if I needed another reason to fall into hysteria, Harlan Holcombe saunters into our exchange.

"Hey, man." Spencer Dean is now talking to Harlan Holcombe. Which might be less alarming if I were watching a movie instead of being in person, with my participation in the discussion required.

"Hi, Meredith." Harlan observes me, mischievous eyes sparkling.

My lips try to move but fail, and my eyes are wide, frozen in shock. For once, I'm not trying to adhere to the five-minute rule. I am simply immobile.

Harlan joins my worst nightmare as the group studies me. His body remains facing mine, and slowly he stiffens, as if to mirror my stress. "What did you do to her?" he says out of the corner of his mouth.

My face contorts, and it's regrettable when I use my out-loud voice. "I'm on Famous People Probation."

Sally snickers in the background, but I can only see Harlan's head, now cocked to the side. "What?"

"Okay." A huff of breath escapes and I wring my hands. "I don't understand what happened, but by a complete fluke, I walked into someone else's life. Now I must leave." I start to turn. What else is there to say? Tears are forming. Why tears? I don't know. Rather than blush like an ordinary person, I am dying.

Their collective laughter follows me as I turn to escape. I will be an entertaining story at their next Hollywood stars support group.

"Hey, hang on." A chuckling Harlan uses his long, jean-clad legs to slide in front of me and cut off my getaway. "What's wrong? You survived meeting me the other night. And you survived our moment in the spa."

"You guys had a moment in the spa?" This from Spence. Super-Famous Man number two looks to Harlan, who is nodding.

I squinch my eyes. "We did not have a moment in the spa. We had a short conversation."

"It was definitely a moment. But you have a point. I can't prove that one."

I have a point? There are no points. There are no coherent thoughts in my brain right now. How can there be points?

Oblivious, Harlan keeps talking. "But you did dance with me. There were witnesses. And you survived."

"Barely. No thanks to your dancing." Filtering doesn't occur to me or my flailing hands. "Let me start from the beginning. I met Sally today and we had a wonderful conversation. I thought she was just a normal person." My torso twists, and I whisper at her through clenched teeth, "*I thought you were normal.*"

Sally slaps a hand over her mouth, and her shoulders shake in muffled amusement.

My body spins back to Harlan. "Apparently she isn't normal, because a few minutes ago, I found out she is married to Spencer Dean and they are friends with Harlan Holcombe. All are delightful people but also frequent the cover of *People* magazine's Most Beautiful list."

Harlan clutches his navy Henley shirt over his heart, feigning hurt. "Only once."

"Twice for me," Spencer says in a cocky voice.

Harlan half turns to punch him in the shoulder. "Jerk."

Spencer returns his focus to me. "Why is this a problem?"

Exasperated that they can't understand, I open my arms wide. "Because you aren't real people. Besides"—I squeeze my eyes shut—"it's painful to talk to you."

Harlan nudges me with his elbow, and my eyes pop open. Good Lord, he just touched me. He leans in and says in a low voice, "But isn't it also just a little bit fun?"

Spencer studies me. "We went to high school together. Why is this a problem?"

I point between both of them, my finger wagging in the space between us. "Don't try to make this okay."

Spencer grins. "High school puts everyone on the same playing field. We're normal. He and I played football together. Doubled to homecoming. Spent countless hours playing Nintendo." He kisses little Layla's hand. "Listen, we're going to grab something to eat. The studio switched up our schedule, which means the next few hours are free. Why don't you come with us? I'll tell you all about this guy's ninth grade mullet."

Hmm. Hearing about Harlan Holcombe's unfortunate hair days *would* knock him down a few notches.

Sally chimes in with a chagrined smile. "Spence called right before I left the room. What do you think?" She leans closer to confess and conspire. "I'm a real person. Ignore them."

With cautious movements, I shift to inspect each person. Surreptitious Sally. Spellbinding Spence. Hero-worshiped Harlan.

Nope. Not ready yet. I lift my hand and make a shield to block my view of Harlan's face. "Why don't you let me babysit so the two of you can enjoy a romantic date alone?"

Harlan's suave voice breaks through my hand barricade. "Can I stay and help you with the kids?"

My arm dips, and when he comes into view, I glare at him. "Absolutely not." I shoot the barrier back up.

Two women eyeing our discussion scoot past Sally, and she takes a step toward me. "No, no. Thank you so much for the offer. But the kids are super excited about hanging out with their daddy. Plus, they love climbing all over Uncle Harlan."

On cue, Toby swings on Harlan's arm.

In one of my more courageous moves of the afternoon, I glance at Harlan.

His laser eyes are directed at me, and I'm stuck in his tractor beam. "You made plans with Sally," he says. "No pressure, but refusing is not an option because we know you're available."

I release a long, dramatic sigh. "Are any other ridiculously famous people joining us for dinner?"

Grinning, he shakes his head once. "Nope."

Sally must sense my resignation because she reaches up, squeezes my hand, and pulls me forward. Harlan's fingers graze the middle of my back to guide me to the exit. I ignore the confusing shiver down my spine.

Toby hangs off Harlan's left arm with every stride. Spencer kisses Layla on the cheek over and over, causing baby babbles while he ambles toward the door.

As the six of us leave the Broadmoor together, I shake my head and start talking to myself. "I am going to dinner with Spencer Dean, his wife and kids, and their good friend Harlan Holcombe."

"Meredith," Harlan calls behind me. "Referring to me by just my first name might help."

"Of course, Harlan Holcombe. I will try that."

Is it too late to go back to the corner in my dodgeball game?

**"THIS PLACE LOOKS** like Chuck E. Cheese created a love child with Janis Joplin," I say.

Somehow I've made it through the drive, getting seated, and ordering dinner without making a complete fool of myself. I can't say the same about the server who delivered our food. Total teenage fangirl. However, now I take time to observe the ambiance of the restaurant.

"Right?" I ask the table. "This place has multiple personalities."

Harlan's deep laughter causes squishy sensations in my belly. I shift in my seat to shove the warmth away, simultaneously conjuring up things I can say to make him laugh again. The interior design isn't the only thing in the room that can't decide what it wants.

Our red faux-leather booth holds six people. When I scooted in first, I thought Toby would sit next to me and be the kid buffer to help my celebrity personality problem. Though untested, I am confident I can function like a normal human being around famous people's children. However, Harlan zipped in first, which placed his body two inches from mine, with little Toby betraying me and sitting on the other side of him.

This could be a long night.

Sally leans over to attach a bib around Layla's neck while Layla squirms in protest on her high chair. "The reviews claim food the parents will love, with a germ-infested arcade the kids won't want to leave."

"Everything on the menu is organic, free range, food of the hippies, topped off with captivating psychedelic decor." Harlan shovels a bite of bread covered with bruschetta into his mouth. "Quintessential Colorado."

The tie-dye napkins are an amusing touch. I couldn't care less if the cheese came from a free-range cow that only eats dandelions at dusk. The food choice is genius in calming my frayed nerves because pizza is the great equalizer. All levels of income, class, and celebrity love the coma-inducing Italian pie.

"I want Wocky." Toby spits bread onto the table while he points and talks.

Following the direction of his pudgy finger, I see a person wearing a disturbing animal costume. "What. Is. That?" I ask.

Layla lifts her little arms and tries to echo her big brother. "Was!"

The menus sit between the condiments and the wall, and Harlan stretches across me to grab one. This causes me to lean way back, squeeze my eyes closed, and say a prayer he doesn't touch me. Does. Doesn't.

Doesn't.

Setting the laminated page in front of me, he points. A picture of a proud Rocky Mountain bighorn sheep greets me alongside a written explanation.

"Okay. I recognize Rocky is the Colorado state animal, he's endangered, and he's a magnificent creature. But that thing"—I hitch my thumb toward the disastrous mascot—"is like the Stay-Puft Marshmallow Man went through a car wash, drip-dried, and got some horns stuck on him." Glancing down at the real picture, I note the atrocious costume at least got the massive curling horns correct.

A small roar comes from across the room, and we shift again to gawk.

Rocky has a wife.

Dressed like a sheep in Little Bo-Peep's clothing, she sports the same giant horns tacked to her head.

With my mouth gaping, I can't tear my eyes away from the scene. "This could be something out of a horror movie. Don't they scare the kids?"

Sally smiles and shrugs as she shifts her attention to Layla, who is trying to launch herself at the dynamic sheep duo. "Layla and Toby, Rocky and Rockina will come over to our table when they make it to our side of the room. Let's eat some dinner, please, while we wait." She offers a carrot to a distracted Toby.

I turn back to Harlan. "Maybe your costume department could help these poor souls. Or maybe I should excuse myself when they get here so I don't have nightmares."

A low, rumbling chuckle escapes Harlan, and he steals a glance at me while he returns the menu to its spot against the wall. This time, I lean back and ignore how good he smells.

"How did your day go with Prissy?" he asks me while Spencer and Sally deal with the kids.

"She gave me something to think about."

"She does that."

"Meredith," Spencer asks, "what do you think of our boy here's latest celebrity stunt?"

Harlan rolls his eyes, shaking his head. "Spence, let it rest."

"What? Last I heard, you're supposed to be the next Bachelor," Spencer says.

My stomach clenches, and I chance a glance at Harlan. But instead of irrationally worrying about twenty-five women vying for his attention, I'm intrigued by the flash of pain that crosses his face.

What is that about?

He picks up a piece of toasted crostini and points it at Spencer. "You need to stay off social media, man."

Sally mashes a banana with her fork. "Harlan, what you did was a big deal. Seriously, we're all very proud of our Hercules."

"It's not that big of a deal." Some of the shoveled bruschetta overflows from his toast and falls back to the plate. "And if we stop talking about it, it will disappear into the graveyard of runaway social media spotlight stories."

Spencer grabs a fork and a knife. "Meredith, have you seen the video?"

"Oh." Cheese from the piece of pizza I grab off the pan stretches long, and I wrestle it from the neighboring slice. "Uh, no, I haven't watched it. I don't watch that kind of . . . thing. I'm a little bit sensitive. Sorry." I throw a half-hearted smile to Harlan.

He turns to me, studying my face. "You haven't seen it?"

I shake my head.

"That's the best news I've heard all day," he says softly.

"Well, um, full disclosure. I've seen pictures." I forget I'm holding a slice, and my hand gestures flop the pizza around until I set it on the plate. "My niece and I are close, and she might be your biggest fan. Hannah's personally responsible for at least a thousand of your millions of YouTube likes. She would have a coronary if she knew I was sitting here with you."

"It probably wouldn't have been that big of a deal"—Spencer leans over to cut Toby's pizza—"if you didn't take off your shirt at the end of the video."

Staring at Harlan, I concentrate on his shoulder so I don't picture the shirtless photograph showcased on several tabloid magazines this week. Stupid airport bookstore.

"I didn't know the kid was filming. I was just trying to—" Harlan grabs his napkin, swipes his mouth, and balls a fist around it. He sighs, closing his eyes. "Never mind."

My hand twitches, wanting to offer him some touch of encouragement. "I don't know, Harlan. Maybe this kind of attention will open doors for you. You could be the next Rocky the Bighorn Sheep." I smile. "You could have a real future in mascot wear."

While the others laugh, his gaze meets mine, and something passes between us. Something electric that causes my belly to flip.

Exhaling, I shift my focus to the Deans. "Do you all get to the Springs often?"

"Every now and then," Sally says. "I'm from Nebraska. Spence is the one who grew up here, but his family has scattered over the years."

"What about you, Harlan?" I ask, proud of myself that my voice only shakes a little when I pose my question to Super Famous Man.

"I make it back more than Spence." Shaking his head, Harlan grabs another piece of pizza, sets it on Toby's plate, and says in an unmistakably bitter tone, "The hills of Hollywood have nothing on Colorado mountains."

The table freezes.

Harlan glances around, wipes his hand on a napkin. "Sorry." He offers a grin that doesn't quite reach his eyes. "Maybe I should look into that mascot thing after all, Meredith."

"Your future looks bright in mascot wear." I let out a puff of laughter, knowing full well I'm about to make a terrible joke. "You do look a little *sheepish* right now."

After a beat, Harlan throws his head back and laughs.

My face flushes as my shoulders shake, and I peek up at him from under my lashes.

He aims a dazzling smile my way. "Did you just make the world's worst joke?"

I grin proudly, then glimpse over to Sally.

Her head is cocked, her gaze equal parts amused and observant. What does she think she sees?

Spencer reaches across the booth, picking off rejected pepperonis from Toby's plate. "Meredith, I didn't ask you where you met Harlan. Have you guys known each other long?"

"Oh yeah," Sally says. "You didn't mention it this morning."

"Why would I have mentioned it this morning?" I ask.

"I assumed you saw the movie crew and knew I was with them." She takes a baby spoon and scoops up a bite for Layla.

"No, if I had known you were connected to anything Hollywood, I would have panicked, run away, and never spoken to you again."

Sally tilts her head. "So if you didn't know, how did the two of you meet?"

I take a sip of my water and, without thinking, answer her question. "Well, I ate dinner at the Penrose Room last night."

"I thought the room was cast and crew only," Spencer says out of the side of his mouth while chewing. "Wait, a woman showed who lost her—" He clears his throat.

Awareness burns through me like fire catching a newspaper.

Molly's memo is going to be the death of me.

The banana-filled spoon in Sally's hand stops midway to Layla's mouth. Her pained eyes find mine. "That was you? But you said . . . you said—"

Her whispered words of shock cause a fracture straight from the top of my heart to the bottom.

She squeezes her eyes shut and shakes her head. "Doesn't matter. That was you?"

Layla's little hands bounce in protest of the paused dinner.

Sally's emotion spills from her eyes, and she touches a hand to her cheek. She breathes her declaration, "That was you."

Holding my breath, all I can do is nod.

"I just—I just need a moment. Excuse me." She sets the spoon down and pushes on Spencer's shoulder, prompting him to move out of her way.

"Sally . . ." I'm frozen as I watch her scurry from the table.

Harlan grabs Toby and moves out of the booth. "Meredith." He calls me out of my stupor and nods in Sally's direction. "We've got the kids. Do you wanna go . . . ?"

"Yes." Scooting out from behind our table, I lower my head, hoping my hair covers my flushed face. "Thank you."

When I reach the bathroom, I crouch down to check under the stall doors. Her black boots contrast with the checkered red and white tile, confirming she's the source of the sniffling. "Sally? Sally, I am so sorry."

"Meredith, don't apologize." Her thick, soft voice floats over the room. "Please. Can you give me a minute?"

"No." I take a few steps in, pressing my hand on the black metal door. "I'm afraid if I leave, it will only give you more time to decide why we shouldn't be friends. And I would hate that, Sally."

"That was you." She lets out a sob. "Spencer told me the rumor about the woman who joined us in the Penrose Room who had lost her husband and two small children in an accident." A hiccup. "I was sick, Meredith. Sick with grief for a woman I didn't know. And it turns out to be you."

"Oh, Sally." My hand strokes the door as if it could comfort her.

"I'm so stupid," she says with tears in her voice. "This morning I was a wreck over what? A diaper blowout? I can't believe I acted upset about such a small thing when you're dealing with a loss of astronomical proportions."

Seconds plod by.

When she finally steps out, I shift back and rest my hips against the black Formica countertop. Red rims her eyes, and her fist clutches a wad of toilet paper.

Approaching with caution, I catch her open hand in mine. "Do you think I could explain a few things to you?"

She purses her lips, nods, and turns to exit the bathroom.

We find a semi-private table in the sparsely filled restaurant away from the games. On the way, I glance over to our booth and see the gang receiving their much-awaited visit from the infamous sheep.

After we take our seats, she begins ripping the toilet paper into small pieces, replicating her son's actions this morning.

"I'm sorry, Sally. Discussing Steve and the kids is complicated. When people find out, they struggle. I thought withholding information would protect you. But it only protected me." Moisture hits the back of my eyes. "Most won't talk to me about their children because they can't handle what happened or they're afraid of hurting me." My palms spread flat on either side of her shredded toilet paper mountain. "I was a mom for three years, Sally, and it's almost as if I'm not allowed to acknowledge it. To own it." A lump of frustration builds in my throat. "You can't know how refreshing it was to be a normal person with you. A normal mom." I keep talking, more to myself than to Sally. "I'm still a mother. And I have something to give other moms. Even if my children aren't with me anymore."

She stops tearing the paper and stares at me with what seems like a mix of confusion and awe. "Meredith," she whispers.

"When we met, I figured we were vacation friends, so I kept it simple." A biting laugh escapes my mouth. "Except my worlds collided when I ran into you with Spencer and Harlan."

The edges of her lips tip upward.

If people treat me with kid gloves, how can I experience life and determine if there's more for me? Before this moment, I'm not sure I understood how much I needed Sally. If I had anticipated this friendship, I would have feared it. But I think life is gracious to have brought her to me. Even if only for a short time.

She clutches my hands, takes a breath, and almost chokes on her question. "How old were they?"

Holding back excruciating sorrow causes my head to pound. My eyes bore into hers, willing her to find the answer that I don't want to have to say out loud.

A terrible understanding crosses Sally's face. "Toby and Layla." Her eyes close, causing brimming tears to overflow.

When she returns her teary gaze to me, I offer a small nod.

Yes. My children were three and one when I lost them, very close in age to her precious Toby and Layla.

She releases her grip and wipes her hands over her face. "My support system is sparse. Spence's work calls for a lot of travel, and the women I meet in the industry aren't the greatest source of authenticity. I'm a mess, and I never feel like I fit anywhere. But this morning? We connected and I drank in your words." Her index finger stabs the table with resolve. "I want to be your friend. After you leave Colorado, I'd love to stay in touch. But, Meredith, is this really okay? I just . . . I don't want to hurt you."

"For a few moments in the lobby, Sally, I had a purpose." A few tears stream down my cheeks. "I wasn't the Woman Who Lost Her Family. I got to be a friend with something to give. While it sounds like a contradiction because you see my tears, there is significant joy in being able to come alongside you and encourage you as a mother." I grit my teeth. "*That* is living. I'm not saying this will be easy. Our conversations are sure to trigger grief. But *that* is also living. So, if you can sit in the uncomfortable grief with me sometimes, I would love to be real-life friends with you. Because you are a gift to me."

She reaches over to the napkin dispenser, grabs a few, and offers them to me. "What do you need from me? How can I know I'm not hurting you?"

"I need you to trust me." I dab under my eyes, knowing I'm wiping off any remaining concealer. "Another time I can fill you in, but just know that I've done the work. There are professionals and unprofessionals alike keeping tabs on how I handle life. It took a committee meeting for this trip to be approved."

She opens her mouth to respond, but looks confused and says nothing.

"No, not really." I chuckle. "But enough well-intentioned people already tiptoe around me. I need you to be you. I need your precious kids to be the amazing little people they are." I shrug and lean in, offering a small smile. "And I need you to promise me you don't have any more quasi-famous friends."

Sally grins but clenches her fists. "Okay. I won't treat you any differently than I did today. But I need you to promise to tell me how you're doing."

Relief settles over me, and I nod. "Deal."

After a long hug, with our arms linked, Sally and I rejoin our crew. Harlan glances up at me as he slides Toby out of the booth to allow me entrance. I curl my hair behind my ears as I scooch back to my spot.

The kids are preoccupied with the coloring books and crayons Rocky the Wonder Sheep bestowed them on his visit. As I place my napkin in my lap, I catch Spencer's attention across the table.

"I'm sorry," he says. "I should have been more forthright." He switches his tone to playful. "Listen, the real story last night was the babe who danced with Harlan."

His backpedaling is almost audible, but I appreciate the effort to help move the conversation to an easier place.

My giggle breaks the solemn mood. "Spencer, I mean this in the nicest way possible. You are the worst liar on the entire earth."

Yup. I just told a Golden Globe nominee that he was essentially not good at acting.

"I know." Sally beams with pride. Patting her husband on the arm, she leans over and grabs a leftover scrap of garlic bread. "I married him because he can't lie. He isn't wired for it." She angles back and plants a kiss on his cheek.

"Thank you? I think?" Spencer sports a smirk aimed at his wife. He shifts his gaze to me and lowers his voice. "I'm sorry, Meredith."

"Why? I *am* the widow who crashed the private Hollywood dinner at the Penrose Room. I'm so proud of it, I may add it to my résumé." I flash a smile. "So, Spencer, to answer your original question from half an hour ago, that's how I met your friend."

Harlan cranes his neck so he can speak into my ear. "I did dance with a babe that night."

Unfortunately, he chooses to do this at the exact moment I take a sip of my water, thus causing me to choke.

While pounding me on the back, he twists to everyone else at the table. "Listen, I think this whole thing is a diversion. You're all avoiding the inevitable."

My cough calms down enough for me to clear my throat of the last of it just as Harlan's hand on my back slows to gentle circles.

After a pause to the group, he says proudly, "The Skee-Ball tournament."

"We aren't in town often," Spencer explains to me, "but when we are, this is tradition."

"I don't want to play." Sally displays her French manicure. "Going back to get my nails fixed is not worth the effort."

"I think it's because you don't want to lose to me." Harlan winks at Sally, only receiving an eye-roll response in return. "Layla forfeited due to the height requirement. But Spencer and Toby are in. So that leaves you, Meredith."

"That leaves me what?"

Without removing his hand from my back, he angles his body toward mine. The warmth of his touch seeps through my skin just like the warmth in his smile.

But then his smile turns into a smirk, almost challenging. "Would you like the opportunity to lose, thus crowning me Skee-Ball Champion the sixth time in a row?"

Oh no he did *not* just challenge me.

My head turns to look at him dead-on, and I ignore how close we are. Because my competitive streak just swiped away all warmth coming from him and stomped right over my nerves. I cock my head just a touch. "It's going to be so embarrassing for you when I take you down in front of all these people. You're about to be a YouTube sensation for a completely different reason."

# 5

I GLANCE AT THE SPEEDOMETER on Prissy's dashboard, and my blood pressure rises. "How come your car hasn't rebuked you yet?"

This morning, we're driving thirty minutes outside of town to look at a property. She asked me to wear jeans and keep an open mind.

I'm not sure this bodes well for me.

Prissy slides a triumphant glimpse in my direction. "I disabled the monitoring system. You can find how to do anything on YouTube."

In spite of my giggle, I'm a little nervous. I glance at my white knuckles clutching the door handle. "How long before Derrick notices?"

"I feel sure when I immobilized it, the Bat-Signal alerted not just my husband but my insurance agent and the police departments in three surrounding counties." Her black leather–gloved hand swirls in the air for dramatic effect.

My love-hatred of Prissy grows. No suit today. She sports a pair of age-defying jeans that imply gravity hasn't taken a toll on her backside. She paired the dark wash with a thin red cashmere sweater. But the black-and-white woven wool poncho is what gives her the sass.

"Forty-two speeding tickets in twenty-five years of marriage," she declares.

I laugh at the window as we pass open fields. "Prissy, no."

"After yelling at each other about the first ten violations, we came to a truce. He installs every gadget on the market to help me stop breaking the law, but doesn't react when I come home with a citation. In return, I choose to view his monitoring me as an act of love instead of a violation of my privacy." She shrugs. "It works for us."

I can remember a thousand incidents for which I want to apologize to my late husband. My biggest guilt comes from the energy I wasted criticizing Steve for the mundane. None of my grumbling complaints matter now.

Who cares if he wanted to wear his grandfather's old, worn, plaid shirts?

Who cares if he didn't cut the apples for Clayton's lunches the "right" way?

Who cares if he missed the turn to the highway for the seventy-fifth time and we added three whole minutes to our drive time?

None of it matters today.

It shouldn't have mattered then.

Our marriage wasn't perfect. It was perfectly normal. Two flawed people deciding to do life together. Ten years that weren't always easy but held a lot of wonderful times.

Steve died, and there are no regrets about where our relationship ended. We said everything there was to say. Our goodbye is our legacy of respect for one another, the love we showed by serving each other, and the efforts we made in our purposeful parenting. That knowledge has to be enough because I wasn't afforded a chance to say the word "goodbye" to him.

Something that only took me a few years of therapy to believe and accept.

Elbow pressed to the window, chin resting in my palm, I watch the clouds race our car to the mountains. *Steve, I know. I know it was all so stupid. I know how amazing you were. I get it.*

I get it now.

I hate that I get it now.

Prissy's talk about her speeding tickets truce is a reminder. *It just doesn't matter.*

I sense Prissy's scrutiny as she slows to turn right on a county road. "What's going on in that pretty head of yours?"

Reaching for my purse, I weigh my words. "My brain is jumbled."

She maneuvers the car to a stop and shifts into park. Her hair doesn't move when she pulls off her sunglasses to reveal understanding eyes that seem to be waiting for my reply.

I angle my body toward her and plop my purse on my lap. "Steve is at the forefront of my mind today, and I can't figure out why."

She cocks an eyebrow. "Is it necessary to figure out why?"

"For me, yes." I toss my hair over my shoulder and let out a frustrated sigh. "I'm not sad today, which catapults me into guilt over not feeling sad today, which catapults me into anxiety."

She remains silent, and I shake my head. "No, that's not it. I'm always sad he isn't here. But today I don't miss him."

I sit in those uncomfortable words for a beat.

"Yes," I murmur to myself. "That's it. I'm sad he's not here, but I don't miss him, which catapults me into guilt, which catapults me into anxiety."

Prissy clears her throat in a way that sounds almost judgmental. "Could this have something to do with a certain Hercules?"

I'm too young to know what a hot flash feels like, but I'm guessing what I'm feeling now must be similar because my face is on fire. "You're ridiculous."

*Tap, tap, tap.* Her pristine index fingernail sounds like a gavel calling our meeting to order. "Did you or did you not go to dinner with him and his friends last night?"

Wait a minute. "What? Why would you know that?"

"The Broadmoor is like a small town. The doormen gossip like girls. News travels fast."

I blow out an unladylike breath. "Okay, fine. Yes. We ate a very benign dinner. Pizza, for goodness' sake. There is no way some guy from Hollywood is interested in me."

She pauses and stares, long enough for discomfort to crawl through my nerve endings. "Do you have an open mind?"

With theatrical flair, I lean forward and put my head on the dash in protest. "Prissy, I do not want to talk about Harlan Holcombe."

"Meredith."

Out of the corner of my eye, I see her arm pointing. I sit up straight and follow her lead until I find the target.

"Do you have an open mind?" she asks again.

Past the spot where we pulled over, a dirt road leads to a wide metal-framed entrance. High above sits a sign.

Twelve Bluebells Ranch.

I almost snicker out loud. It's a full working ranch. What is she thinking? I am City Girl with a capital *C*.

She maneuvers the car to a narrow strip of gravel, heading to the open gate. "This property has unofficially been on the market a while."

"What does that mean?" As I squint down the lane, a darting animal catches my eye. Was that a cat?

"Around here, the locals try to keep the land within the community family. But the current owners, the Carsons, are shaking things up a bit."

"That's nice." I place my purse on the floorboard and lean toward the windshield.

The home in front of me demands my attention. The main building, so grand and inviting, is a gorgeous combination of logs and stone. Off to the side is a more utilitarian addition made only of logs.

"It's nice until they become stingy about buyers. This ranch is a bargaining chip between a few neighboring families. The price goes up or down depending on who is interested." She clucks her tongue twice. "But now Twelve Bluebells is represented by a professional, and they don't have the freedom for under-the-table talks. Because you're an outsider, selling becomes a little more interesting. You're either viewed as safe because you have no stake in the ongoing feuds, or you're a threat because you're an unknown."

Pulling my gaze from rockers on the front porch, I turn to face Prissy. "Why would I want to be in the middle of all that tension?"

She answers me with a knowing smile. What she knows, I have no idea. But she's the expert.

As I step out of the car, my phone alerts me to a new voicemail. I peek at the screen and find I missed two calls from Stanley. Wonder what that's about.

Glancing up to the house, I freeze. "Prissy?" I speak out of the side of my mouth. "A cow is approaching the vehicle." I wonder if my poorly chosen tennis shoes can outrun this heifer.

Not even glancing at the beast, she glides toward the house, dirt crunching under her designer boots. "Just ignore Isabel. She won't hurt you."

I believe her. Prissy would take down a massive bovine with her bare hands if it threatened a possible real estate deal.

The cow must know this.

As we tour the primary residence, there's something intangible I'm drawn to. This doesn't make sense. Why would I move all the way out to the countryside? What would I do with all this space?

Exposed logs and stone fill the walls of the house. Old hardwood covers the floors throughout, and the countertops switch between butcher blocks and stained concrete. The deep colors and materials give a rustic vibe, but everything is updated in modest decor.

Staring at the giant deer head mounted above the fireplace, I debate the buck's exact level of creepiness. He continues to stare at me. "Prissy, what am I going to do with a working ranch? The last time I rode a horse was two decades ago at summer camp."

The clack of her high-heel boots announces her approach behind me. "It's not up to me to discern what you could do with the property."

I twist my torso, scrunching up my nose in disapproval.

"There are several options to consider," she says. "You could retain the hired ranch hands to run the place. They've worked the land for years. If that doesn't pan out well, you can always keep the house and a few acres but sell the surrounding estate. Your neighbors would want first crack at the land, and it would be a quick sell. Little hassle."

I suck in my lip and catch it between my teeth. "I guess you've given me something to think about."

A proud smile crosses Prissy's face but is quickly masked. However, her eyes still sparkle a bit.

Annoying. Annoying woman with her fabulous clothes and bizarre wisdom.

"Let's go see the boardinghouse. Twelve rooms, four giant bathrooms, and a full functioning kitchen."

I want to ask her what I need a lodge for, but I fear she'll give me a frustratingly Zen answer. However, I think there's value to this stranger's perspective. Her view of me isn't distorted by my complicated backstory, and in an odd turn of events, I trust her as more than just a fierce real estate negotiator.

---

As we exit the boardinghouse, a primitive wooden sign above the door grabs my attention.

I nod at the word carved across it. "Alba?"

Prissy pushes the door open and steps on the porch. "The

history of the ranch." She approaches the corner of the house and crouches down.

I follow suit and wait.

"The original settlers who claimed this area were from Spain. They were hunting for silver. Story is the husband wanted to keep moving north, but the wife insisted on putting their stakes here."

"Why?" A fly thinks we're friends, and I swat it away to tell it otherwise.

Prissy stands. "I think they were right here in this spot." Her eyes search beyond, then fall on me. "Colorado is known for its Rocky Mountain bluebells. They're a beautiful hue of blue. Almost purple. But the wife found twelve flowers that didn't match the others. White Spanish bluebells. She believed it was an omen signaling where they should settle."

"Twelve Bluebells Ranch." The wind carries my whispered words away.

"Hyacinthoides hispanica. 'Alba.'"

"What does 'alba' mean?"

Prissy's baby-blue eyes laser into mine. "Dawn."

Her response almost takes my breath away.

Dawn. Beginning.

Breaking our gaze, I stand and consider the area where the flowers once grew. Slowly I spin, taking in each piece of the ranch. The vast fields, the sturdy boardinghouse, the brown wood fence delineating the property line to the neighboring ranch. In spite of my fleece jacket, chills race down my arms.

Could this be where I belong?

Prissy walks past me, heading in the direction of her car, her platform boots covering the gravel with unexplained grace. "Legend goes, the Spanish bluebells haven't appeared here since. The following spring the field was covered only in Rocky Mountain bluebells."

An odd sensation washes over me, and I find myself hoping I'll be visiting next spring to witness the blue blanket of beauty.

Maybe even catch a glimpse of an inspiring white bloom.

# 6

**MY HEAD SPINS** like a cheap plastic top. Round and round, until it twists right off the table into oblivion.

What does Twelve Bluebells Ranch mean for me? A simple catalyst to consider new options? Or is the land somehow my alba? My dawn. My beginning.

What the heck would I do with a full functioning ranch? "Native Texan" doesn't mean we're all born with cowboy hats and spurs attached to our bodies.

Without my prompting, Prissy cancels the last two property showings to give my brain a rest.

We agree to touch base later, though I make no promises about my ability to express coherent thoughts. When I say goodbye, I picture her snapping her fingers to transform from her magic jeans back to her power realtor uniform.

While cruising through the lobby, I decide I need to figure out when the hotel shuttle leaves next. I want to make a visit to the Cheyenne Zoo. A stroll in the fresh air will get my blood pumping and help sort things out in my head. Plus, they revamped the elephants' section since my last trip, and I want to check out the new digs.

On my way to find a hotel shuttle, through the hustle of the arriving crowd, I clock Harlan in a corner talking on his phone. Heat flushes my face, my pulse picks up, and I stop in my tracks.

Dressed in business casual khaki pants, he looks quite dapper today. The white oxford shirttail hanging casually underneath his navy sweater presents a boyish air. However, he's all man.

What is the appropriate behavior? Do I smile at him as I pass? Or am I supposed to stay and talk to him? What's the protocol for someone famous who is starting to become familiar on vacation but you probably won't ever see again?

I don't have that manual.

I approach him, gritting my teeth as I prepare to act normal.

Look at me, I'm really growing.

Running his hands through his hair, face contorted in frustration, Harlan pulls his phone down and stares at it.

Two teenage boys shove a piece of paper and pen in his face. Harlan gives them a smile that doesn't reach his eyes while he signs his name and says something that makes them all chuckle.

His acquiescence is generous, but I find myself wondering what it costs him to interact with passing fans. Then I think about me standing there waiting to . . . what? Talk to him?

Nope. I'm not growing anymore. I start to turn on my heel to retreat before I also look like a fan.

Harlan jerks his head up and spots me. "Hey there." A tight smile accompanies his greeting.

Oh-kay. Apparently we're doing this. I'm going to speak with Harlan like a regular human being.

My hand offers a small wave, and I take another stride forward. "Hi. Um, hi."

He says nothing, and I realize my epic mistake. I was just going to say hi. And now I've accomplished my goal. I was so focused on the one word I wanted to say to him, I had not created an exit plan, and the longer we stand together, the more awkward I feel.

"Um," I say brilliantly while I stall to find something else to say, "are you . . . still recovering from your loss last night?"

I did, in fact, beat him at Skee-Ball, thus proving no skill is required to play the game.

Without responding, Harlan surveys the lobby. Stress seems to come off him in waves, like heat rising from a sidewalk during a Texas summer.

One small step closer and I lower my voice. "Is everything all right?"

"Not exactly." He glances at his watch and releases an exasperated breath.

That's when I catch sight of her.

Giant brown eyes, set in the precious face of a little girl dressed in pink skinny jeans and a waffle shirt, peer at me from around Harlan's pant leg.

"Well, hello there." I crouch down and grin. "I love the monkey on your shirt."

She shies away from me, hiding behind Harlan.

"My name is Meredith. What's your name?"

Three dainty fingers shove into her mouth and impede her answer. "Owlex."

"How old are you, Alex?"

Those same fingers, now covered in saliva, outstretch in front of her. "Thwee."

I gasp in dramatic awe. "Three. You're such a big girl."

Glancing up, I do a double take. Another pair of beautiful brown eyes stare at me. But this set makes me nervous.

I use my knees as leverage to stand. "Is she the president of the PHHFC?"

Harlan's brow furrows.

"Preschool Harlan Holcombe Fan Club."

He rubs his chin. "She's my daughter."

71

My expression freezes as the statement tries to penetrate. An instant later, something in my heart squeezes.

"Oh, wow. What a cutie patootie." Of course she's his daughter. The eyes and hair color are an exact match. Does Alex's smile mirror her daddy's gorgeous one?

Harlan returns his focus to his phone.

"Harlan?"

His eyes dart to mine.

"I don't think you answered my earlier question. Is everything all right?"

We both glance down at Alex, who rummages through a small pink backpack.

Harlan shifts toward me. "She's been having sleepovers with my mom, who brought her by to have breakfast with me this morning." He nods to Alex. "Little Bit's mom was supposed to come pick her up, but I just got off the phone with her, and she can't be bothered with it right now. She's not the most dependable person."

My brain is conflicted between compassion for Harlan and the mayday signals his proximity is causing me.

His gaze flits around the room, never settling on a person for long. "I've got an important production meeting this morning, and my assistant, Penelope, is off-site, so she can't bail me out. I called Sally, but the group is on a field trip riding the train to Pike's Peak. The hotel staff is trying to find someone, but they're swamped with two new shuttles of arrivals, and no telling if or when help would be available." His jaw tics. "This is so like Olivia. I cannot believe . . ."

I imagine a deep thicket of history behind the words he doesn't say.

Ignoring the tension in Harlan's body language, a woman walks by and snaps a photo without asking permission. Harlan takes a protective side step to conceal Alex's presence and gazes down at the floor.

I glare at the clueless tourist, wondering again what fame costs Harlan. "How long is your appointment?"

"I'm not sure. We're meeting with a college buddy of mine, Landry McKay. He's an FBI agent and serves in a consulting capacity for the movie. It depends on his availability, but if I had to guess, we should finish up midafternoon." He shakes his head. "I'll just skip it."

With a deep breath, I find some confidence and make my proposal. "Okay, listen. I know you don't know me well, but I can take Alex. I don't carry a résumé with me, but if you need a professional reference, call Sally."

He cringes. "Meredith—"

"Harlan, I'm serious." I lean forward and rest my hand on his arm. "I can take her."

Harlan's eyes travel from his phone, to Alex, to my hand, and back to my face.

Before I hyperventilate or he files a restraining order, I let go of him. "I was about to leave for the z-o-o." I have no clue if Alex can spell. But if Harlan says no and she wants to go to the zoo, he'll have anarchy on his hands. "I'd love to take her with me."

He squints, and I'm just sure that red splotches are climbing up my neck. I either need to move forward or bail.

Mommy mode takes over. "Bottom-line these details for me. Any food issues or allergies?"

"No."

"Does she take a daily nap?"

"Rest time at 2:00."

"Has she eaten breakfast?"

"Yes."

"Is she potty trained?"

"Yes."

Thank God. "Is her backpack stocked for the day?"

"A change of clothes, extra shoes, light jacket, her blankie, lunch, some emergency snacks, and a sippy cup."

"Impressive."

Harlan rolls his eyes. "Yeah, well, I can't predict what Olivia will or won't have. Sometimes I'm parenting them both. But I can't take credit. Penelope packed the bag."

I scrunch up my nose. Olivia sounds like no walk in the park I want to take.

Harlan crouches down and explains the new plan to Alex.

She glances up at me, and I wink and flash an overenthusiastic smile.

When he finishes, he stands and slides a room key out of his back pocket and hands it to me. My heart stops beating. This feels like a complete lack of judgment on his part. It also feels like the opening to a stalker movie starring myself.

"If you guys come back here, use my suite," he says. "Rest time will be easier with all her stuff in her own room." He taps at his phone. "What's your phone number?"

Numbly, I give it to him. The stalker movie feels more real.

"I just sent you a text with my room number," he says as if that's normal.

I turn my attention to the beautiful three-year-old at hand. If I focus on her, I can ignore that Hercules just sent me his number.

A strand of sadness from my past mars the overarching excitement about spending the day with a child. But I push through. I want to see what this day holds.

Harlan leans in and lowers his voice. "I need to tell you one more thing."

I want to lean into the rumble of his voice. In an effort to focus, I blink.

He smells amazing.

In a second effort to focus, I blink again.

Seriously. I can never date again.

"Her mother is super unpredictable. Olivia was supposed to pick Alex up for the rest of the weekend. She might show up in an hour, she might not show up at all. I'm hoping you don't have to interact with her, but I need to communicate to her where you'll be in case she decides to be a parent today. I want to warn you"—he shifts as if he's uncomfortable—"she's not entirely pleasant."

I give him a slight nod, hoping I'm masking my internal deer-in-the-headlights reaction.

Harlan takes one last unsure glance around and clutches the back of his neck with his hand. "You know what? Never mind. This is too much to ask you to do this. I can't put you in this position."

"Harlan, it's fine." I bend down to pick up Alex's backpack and sling it over my shoulder. "Alex and I are about to have a blast. I promise not to let her play with the lions or bring home a pet elephant. We will wash our hands, walk on the sidewalk, and eat healthy foods. And if I run into Olivia, I'm a big girl. I can hold my own."

Smoldering eyes lock with mine, and he nods once. "I bet you can."

I order whatever animal jumped in my stomach to cool it. "We'll head back to your room afterwards for rest time. If Olivia changes her mind or your schedule changes, text me. We're good. Promise." I shoo him away with my hand. "Go be a big, famous movie star."

Harlan levels his eyes at me as if he doesn't like me calling him that. Then a small smile crosses his lips, and he shakes his head before he bends down to Alex. "Okay, beautiful. Have so much fun at the zoo today. Make sure you obey Miss Meredith."

Alex captures her daddy's cheeks, both of her little girl hands splayed across them, and in her earnest child tone adds her goodbye. "I wuv you, Daddy."

"I love you too, Little Bit."

My heart squeezes again, this time just a bit more.

Alex grasps my hand. "Let's go, Miss Merweradith. I want to see the giwaffes!"

Smiling down at her, I feel something new. Different. I am at peace holding a child's hand. I am at peace holding *her* hand. "How would you like to *feed* the giraffes?"

"Yes!" She jumps several big little-girl jumps.

"Meredith." Harlan grabs my hand and squeezes. "Thank you. This is crazy. So just . . . thank you."

Before I can respond, Harlan turns, scoops Alex up, and gives her one last giant hug.

I'm tempted to ask if I get one too.

Goodness. The animal that was jumping in my stomach just swooned.

We need to leave. Now.

# 7

**"MR. PENROSE NEEDED** to build a zoo because he received a pet bear as a gift." I hold out the brochure to Alex, displaying the sepia-toned picture of a handsome man sporting a handlebar mustache and baggy riding pants. He resembles the villain from *Penelope Pitstop*.

"I want to take a hippo home," Alex says.

"Nope. Sorry, kiddo. Promised your dad we would leave the animals here." I pick her up and shift us to face the rest of the wildlife park. "But how cool is this? Penrose put his bear and all the other creatures he collected right here and carved a home for them on the side of this mountain. It's like they're still in the wilderness."

Her face scrunches up in a serious manner. "Does Wocky live here?"

I bite my lip to censor myself before I can tell her that Rocky the Wonder Sheep would scare away not just the children but the entire zoo population. "No, sweetie." I cough to disguise my laughter. "Rocky lives in his home with Rockina." And some very unfortunate-looking costumes.

"Can I wide the animawls?"

*Can I wide the animawls?* Wide . . . ride. Can I ride the animals.

Alex is patient with me, and her demonstrative little arms clarify as she points to the historic Allan Herschell carousel.

"Hmm." How do I ask a small child if she struggles with vomit issues? Better question—how do I explain to a small child what a vomit phobia is? It's not one of my more attractive qualities.

My imagination hijacks my rational thinking, and I visualize my full-on panic attack when Alex pukes on the merry-go-round as paparazzi report, "Harlan Holcombe's Child Abandoned by Fainting Caretaker."

So, no. We're not going to *wide the animawls.*

"Alex, let's wait a little bit because lunchtime is soon." I slide her body down the side of mine, and when her feet hit the ground, I grasp her hand. "We also need a potty break."

Navigating the small, personable zoo is easy. We pass a woman pushing a sturdy stroller with a pink bundle inside, bringing the zoo patron total to seven. Signs lead us up a hill to the food court, and I feel a tug on my arm.

"I need my foose fried."

"What, sweetie?" Foose fried. Foose fried. What in the world?

"I need my foose fried." Her face contorts and she stomps her foot.

Sometimes I wish children Alex's age came with a professional translator. My grown-up intellect cannot come up with anything useful. Up until this point she hasn't been frustrated with me, but now she's thrusting her foot to the ground in earnest.

Foose fried. Foose fried. I crouch down so my face can be at her level. "Alex, you're doing a great job using your words. Do you think you can show me what you need?"

"She needs her shoes tied, you idiot." The sharp voice pelts me from a few feet behind us.

Tingles of complete shock skitter over my body.

As the savage comment registers, Alex peers around me. Her

face turns from caution to excited recognition. "Mommy!" She abandons me and runs.

This must be Olivia.

I exhale and close my eyes. Wanting to move to friendlier territory, I stand and turn toward the mother-daughter reunion.

Her toned arms open in a dramatic manner. "Hi, baby."

Alex takes a flying leap to her mother.

Harlan's ex-wife is striking. Long, gorgeous dark hair frames the face of a porcelain doll look-alike. Her eyes are an intoxicating green, and I'm not even focusing on her rock-hard body. Yup. She could date a movie star.

Olivia carries her child two steps and pauses in front of me. "Who are you?" She barks her words. "The flavor of the month?"

In spite of Harlan's warning, I'm caught off guard by her disdain. My face flushes with embarrassment at the public scene, but I'm more upset she's chastising me with Alex as the audience. I plaster a smile on my face. "Hi. You must be Olivia. My name is Meredith."

Alex claps her hands. "Merweradith."

"Whatever." Olivia's eyes roll in disgust. "Do you have Alex's bag?"

Is she threatened by me? I'm nobody. I'm the babysitter for the day.

These are new waters, ones I'm unsure how to navigate. I stay on the shore and pray for safety. "Her backpack's right here. We were about to go use the potty and sit down for lunch. Alex has had the best time—"

"Listen, I don't know who you are, *Meredith*"—her emphasis on my name drips with condescension—"but I don't want a rundown on what my daughter needs from someone who clearly should go get children of her own."

I hear the sound of my gasp, but my world stops.

My bottom lip starts to quiver. No doubt those around us can pick up the sound of my heart cracking, but if it isn't audible, blood should be spilling out of me any minute now.

In one long moment, I take in a labored breath and ask my emotions to do something for me. I ask them to wait. Beg them to wait. As I gulp down the knot in my throat, my damp eyes meet Olivia's.

Unable to mask the tremor in my voice, I strain for a gracious tone. "I'm so sorry. There's been a misunderstanding. I'm just a friend who wanted to help out. Alex and I have had a wonderful time today. You're raising an amazing little girl."

Olivia's glare doesn't soften, and she exhales through her nose like a bull about to charge in the rodeo ring.

We stand in loaded silence, and I'm not sure what else to do or say. My emotional dam is about to break, and the impending tears don't care where they flood.

I fix my attention on Harlan's daughter. "Alex, I had a blast with you today. Thank you for hanging out with me. Have so much fun with your mommy."

She flings herself at me, causing Olivia to step forward and allow the awkward embrace.

Her tight, earnest hug slays me.

I need to escape to an isolated location, because my impending meltdown isn't going to be pretty.

Olivia grabs the backpack from my hand and huffs as she walks away.

Heading to the nearest exhibit, I swipe away teardrops and search for a secluded spot. When I discover no one in the vicinity of the moose habitat, I give myself permission to let go.

Olivia spewed unfair judgment, yes. But this explosion of feelings has been building the last few days. I shoved down too much, and everything is coming to the surface with a vengeance. Grief found me. It even waited on me. And it will wait no longer.

My emotional pain manifests into physical. Clutching the railing with one hand, I grab my writhing stomach with the other.

Why did I come here? Why did I think this trip would be valuable? Why was I stupid enough to believe there was something for me here?

I'm spiraling down to the Bad Place at an alarming speed.

*Think, Meredith.* I suck in a choppy breath. Hot tears stream through my closed eyes and down my cheeks.

Molly. Tell Molly.

My touchstone.

I reach inside my purse, grasp the accordion folder, run my thumb across the folds, then release it. After fumbling for my phone, I drop my purse on the ground. My vision starts to blur as I scramble to text my flare for help. A flower emoji. Our symbol that tells Molly I'm not okay.

Her response is immediate.

> Loving you.

A few seconds later, my cell buzzes again.

> You can do this.

I pitch the phone on top of my belongings and grip the bar again. At the exact moment I think I will double over, I see a shadow.

Someone is here.

Shoot. Someone is here.

"Hey there." A palm puts gentle pressure on the center of my back. "Meredith, it's Harlan." He covers my hand on the rail with his.

No. Not him. Not now.

"I . . . I . . . I . . ." My quivering voice sounds like that of a child.

The hand on my back steadies me. "It's okay." He stands perpendicular to me, his face a few inches from mine. "Don't talk."

I try to control my twitching body as my eyes dart around the area.

"No one's coming back here," his deep voice soothes. "You're okay. Just breathe."

In spite of my best efforts, I cry out. Grief's agony sears through me with relentless force, and I release a curse through my sobs.

Harlan says nothing, his hand stroking my back. His presence gives me a temporary reprieve, and my breathing, though still choppy, isn't as strained.

"Meredith, do you think you can walk a couple of steps and rest on the bench back here?"

Without making eye contact, I nod once. Maybe if I sit down, he'll leave.

He grabs my purse, his hand on my back guides me, and I lean my weight into his side. When we take a seat, he faces me, places a protective arm around the back of the bench, and rubs his thumb on my shoulder.

My broken inhales struggle to grant passage to the calming oxygen. I'm so mortified. "I'm sorry. I'm so sorry."

"You aren't the one who should apologize. Take a *deep breath* for me. I'm here. I'm not going anywhere. I just want to sit with you, if that's okay."

On my next inhale, I whimper.

Waves. Unrelenting waves of mourning.

I think I'm okay, then I can almost make out Clayton's laughter. I think I'm okay, then I picture Chloe's silly walk. I think I'm okay, then I remember Steve's last words to me.

Unforgiving waves of agony threaten to drown me.

After several more minutes, Harlan squeezes my shoulder. "Meredith, what can I do for you?"

"There's"—I clear my throat—"water in my purse." My limp hand casts a half-hearted gesture to my bag.

Harlan releases his secure grip on me, and I regret asking him to move. My body shakes in his absence.

He bends to retrieve my purse, returns to me, and rummages through the contents. When he finds the water, he twists open the cap and hands me the bottle.

My unsteady hands grasp the container.

I gather some courage to glance up at him. What I find surprises me.

I thought he would appear uncomfortable at the very least and fearful at the very worst. But the man returning my gaze can only be described as concerned. His compassionate eyes match his calm demeanor.

It's surprising. Maybe comforting. But also confusing.

Why is he still here?

When I think I can form words again, I pull in a breath and exhale. "I'm sorry. The bad grief isn't as frequent now. At home, I'm usually alone and no one else has to deal with it. I'm just"—I pick at the edge of the bottle label with my fingernail—"sorry."

"You don't have to justify yourself to me." He strokes my hair with a gentle touch. "I'm glad I'm here with you."

I don't understand why, but in the middle of this profound moment of sadness, he is able to provide a foundation of peace, to endure and wait while the anguish passes.

As we sit a while longer, my breathing slows and my other senses return. The bright sunlight streaks through the clouds and draws lines across the moose that relaxes twenty feet from us. When did he show up? An elephant calls from over the hill.

Instead of being consumed with torment, my brain is functioning again. Words and energy evade me, but I'm grateful to be on the other side of the beastly grief attack.

Harlan clenches his jaw, then glimpses around and back to me. "Let's get you back to the hotel. I think you'll be more comfortable there."

My eyes are filled with moisture yet scratchy at the same time. Vitality has drained from me. But I stare at him with a boldness I don't often allow. "Okay."

On our way out, it occurs to me that I enjoyed being friends with Harlan, if only for a brief while. But I won't hear from him after today.

The only people who stick with me through similar episodes

are either in my support group or my immediate family. No doubt my massive emotional attack has scared him away.

Meeting Harlan Holcombe will soon fade to an amusing story to tell at parties.

But secretly I will know.

I will know that one beautiful autumn afternoon, Harlan Holcombe bore my sorrow like a champion friend.

And secretly I will know that on that same beautiful autumn afternoon, I fell a little bit in love with him because he did.

# 8

"I TAKE IT BY YOUR CLOTHING CHOICE we're staying in for room service?"

I blink. Am I still asleep?

Harlan Holcombe. At my hotel room door.

I blink again.

"Don't get me wrong." Harlan leans a shoulder against my doorjamb and crosses his arms. "I dig the pink camouflage sweatpants, but the shower cap might draw some unwanted attention."

Shower cap?

*Shower cap!*

"I smelled like a giraffe, so I took a bath." Unable to decide which half of my statement is more embarrassing, I move on to figure out what's happening. "Um." My hand reaches nonchalantly to drag the cap down the back of my head. "Why are you here?"

He pushes off the frame and stands alert. "When I dropped you off at your room, I told you I'd check on you for dinner. Do you remember?"

Grief makes my life hazy. Not in an I-just-need-to-take-a-mental-break way, but in more of a did-I-forget-to-put-on-deodorant kind of way. I tap my fingers on my lips as the montage of the day runs through my mental movie reel.

Yes. He mentioned dinner, but I didn't believe him. I don't trust most of what I remember because it resembles a bizarre dream. One where Harlan Holcombe held my hand all the way back to the hotel, walked me to my room, removed my shoes, and tucked me under a blanket to sleep off the rest of my tears.

He nods in the direction of the table right inside the door. "May I?"

The hand with the shower cap points. "Use my phone?" When I spot the outstretched cap, I whip my arm behind my back.

The side of his mouth quirks. "Yeah. I need to touch base with room service."

"Sure, but be nice to that phone. Things didn't end well for its cohort."

Harlan pauses, receiver in midair.

I turn and call back over my shoulder, "Long story."

While Harlan rings downstairs, I stride to the bathroom, push the door closed, then dare to peek in the mirror. The grief hangover doesn't look as rough as I thought it might. My head feels swollen like a tight balloon, but only my eyes are puffy. My typical post-sobbing headache is minimal, helping me save my supply of ibuprofen.

I start to powder my nose while I eye my lip gloss. If I apply a thin coat, will it look like I'm trying too hard?

"They're going to bring us a hamburger and a chicken salad something-or-other for dinner," Harlan calls to me. "You can pick what you want, and I'll eat the rest."

It sounds like furniture is being moved, and Harlan keeps talking as if what separates us isn't a bathroom door. "I thought about bringing a pizza, but we ate pizza last night. Man can't live by pepperoni alone."

Forgoing the lip gloss, I opt to run a brush through my mangled hair. "You've single-handedly crushed the teenage population with that statement. Your fans will stone you for blasphemy."

"Good." He chuckles. "Then maybe they'll leave me alone."

His response intrigues me, but I can't focus on that direction.

The elephant in the room reminds me that I went against Harlan's wishes and brought an animal home from the zoo. Only this elephant is Harlan's history with a five-foot, nine-inch beauty who happens to be his daughter's mother.

Opening the double doors to the bathroom, I note the makeshift dining area Harlan set up in the corner. While this is a kind gesture, he needs to leave.

"Harlan, I'm sure you had other plans tonight. You're not obligated to check up on me. I'm fine." I wring my hands, knowing I buried the lede, then take a breath. "And I'm embarrassed. I'm sorry you had to deal with all of . . . that."

"Okay, good." Not looking at me, he moves the Broadmoor Hotel literature from the table to the coffee bar. "Let's tackle this head-on." He shifts to step toward me and holds my eyes in his. "First of all, I don't want to be anywhere else tonight."

Oh.

*Oh.* What just happened?

"Second. Meredith, you have nothing to be embarrassed about." He runs a hand through his hair but stops when it reaches the back of his head. "I'm trying to find a way to apologize to you."

I spiral the drawstring at the bottom of my hoodie around my forefinger. "Why would today be your responsibility?"

"I shouldn't have asked you to babysit Alex." I want to protest, but he puts a hand up. "She had a wonderful time. But I was so focused on my stupid meeting, I didn't think through the entire situation. I know your history, and Olivia's fangs are no secret. I never should have put you in that position."

A pang shoots through my gut. The reality hits me that he knows some version of what happened today with Olivia.

But it doesn't matter. I need him to know this wasn't his fault.

"Harlan, please understand. I don't need a reason for an episode like today. My husband and two children died in a terrible accident. That's enough to make me go to the Bad Place at any given moment. I'm just embarrassed you had a front-row seat."

He stares back at me but says nothing.

"And," I say, "you can't take on the behavior choices of the mother of your child. My presence triggered her, and she operated out of fear and insecurity. I get that."

"But, Meredith," he says, his voice apologetic, almost in agony, "what she said to you."

The memory of her words tries to take another stab at me, and I cringe.

His arm sweeps to the window, and he points outside. "I ran up the mountain to find you the second she told me."

He ran up the mountain. To find me. And now he's in my room. To check on me.

I'm frozen in confusion, but the knock on the door causes me to jump out of my thoughts.

Harlan squeezes my arm as he walks past me toward the door. "Room service."

"They're sure fast," I mumble to the spot he touched.

He opens the door, signs the bill, and pulls in a cart. "I had the food on standby because I didn't know how tonight would play out." He picks up a covered dish. "Do you want the burger or the salad?"

"The hamburger?"

Grinning, he removes the silver cover from one of the plates, finds my meal, and sets it in front of the chair closest to me. "I'm glad you have an appetite. Besides, I have to mind my girlish figure."

"You've never been labeled girlish a day in your life," I murmur.

He chuckles. "What was that?"

"Nothing." I flash him a smile.

Awkward feelings swirl in my stomach. It's bad enough we're

having a meal in an oversized bedroom. Add to the scenery one famous, tall, dark, and handsome man, and I'm out of my element. I'm not even in the stratosphere of my element. Instead, I'm frozen in the corner of the room like a wallflower at a junior high dance.

He places rolled-up silverware on the table and turns to me. "Bon appétit." But instead of eating, he takes me in from head to toe, his gaze moving to the food and back to me. "I apologize. I just realized that after today you may not want company. I'll take mine and let you have dinner in peace." Harlan starts to pull his plate.

"No, wait." Letting out a breath, I shake my head. He's sweet, but he has it all wrong. "Sorry. I'm fine."

I move toward my chair and sit. I can do this. I can eat a meal by myself with Harlan Holcombe.

As I unroll my utensils and place the napkin in my lap, Harlan sits across from me. It's then I realize my grave culinary mistake. My stomach spoke louder than my brain. Hamburger consumption is not always graceful.

Great. I'll start with the safety of a French fry.

Struggling with the miniature ketchup bottle, I break the silence. "Can I ask you a question?"

"Sure." He leans over and snags the jar from me, twists the top off, and hands it back.

"Friends who've known me my whole life aren't able to handle my grief. But you were really good with me today. How is that?"

Harlan takes a drink of his water, sets the glass down on the table, and rubs his thumb over the condensation. His eyes find mine, and he holds my stare for a second. "Five years ago, my dad died of a heart attack. Unexpected." His voice is thick. "We were close."

"I'm so sorry, Harlan."

He nods. "He was a man of great character everyone wanted to either be around or be like someday. When we lost him, I didn't know how to deal with it."

I divide the ketchup between the hamburger bun and a spot on my plate as I listen.

"In spite of how I was raised, I made some pretty big mistakes trying to avoid the pain." He grimaces. "I chased things that would help me forget. Enter Olivia." He shakes his head as he pours dressing on his salad. "I had no capacity to recognize it at the time, but she was running from her life too. She didn't share with me that her solution to all her problems was pregnancy."

I try to stifle my gasp. Precious Alex.

Harlan's expression hardens, and his hand clenches on the table. "A lot of ugly things came out. Turns out she got pregnant to make her ex-boyfriend, the father of her firstborn, jealous. What better way to do that than with a movie star?"

I gape. "Oh, Harlan."

"Justified anger is powerful. I ran from her and denied the entire thing for a while. My brother handed me some ugly truth about taking responsibility for my actions." His jaw tightens as he shifts his gaze to the window. "My behavior after Dad died disgraced his legacy."

I tentatively touch my hand to his. "We're all vulnerable under the stress of grief. Sometimes we make unwise choices. It's how we find our way."

His eyes return to mine, and he releases a breath before he makes his next statement. "I want to hear your story."

"I'll tell you sometime." I offer a small smile. "But I'm here to listen to the rest of yours if you want to share."

His stare is scrutinizing, but then he nods. "My career choice puts a lot of stress on relationships. So I quit." He shrugs. "We tried to make it work. Got married. Moved to Colorado Springs to start fresh and be with my family."

I lean in close as his words lure me to the painful train wreck I suspect is coming.

"Not long after the ceremony, I knew we couldn't put the pieces together. Olivia has bipolar disorder." He seems to think about this for a second. "She really flourishes when she follows her doctor's care, you know? She's capable of so many good things. But when she's off her meds, her emotions are a roller coaster. Which I found to be the majority of the time during our marriage. It was intense. I feel guilty saying this, but I was relieved when she told me she still loved her ex." He stops to take a bite of his neglected salad.

I reach for my water glass, stalling to process his words before I speak. "Your efforts to right the situation were honorable."

"Doesn't matter. I was wrong about everything." After focusing on the table for a moment, his brown eyes, full of shame, find me again. "I fell apart. For the first time since my dad's death, I was alone with my grief. On top of it, the reality of my complete failure with Olivia and my new daughter almost did me in." He draws the butter knife up and turns it end over end. "If I'm honest, I lost my purpose long before any of that happened."

Lost his purpose. My heart constricts in pained empathy. Our stories have different names, but they are kindred spirits.

"Somehow my brother sat with me during my toughest moments. He understood better than anyone why I didn't want to get out of bed, and he patiently waited until I was ready to pick myself up and move forward. At any rate, to answer your original question from ten minutes ago, I don't know." His smile is genuine and heartbreaking all at the same time. "Your emotions don't scare me, Meredith. Neither does your story. I hate it for you, and I wished today at the zoo that I could take away some of your pain. But since I couldn't, I just decided to sit in it with you."

Why would Harlan Holcombe . . .

I blink. I blink as if my eyelids are windshield wipers and can swipe the old view away and bring up a fresh, different one. He's no longer Harlan Holcombe to me anymore, is he?

He's just Harlan.

And he didn't have to know me for a lifetime to understand what I needed today.

Before I can think about what I'm doing, I rise, move toward him, and hold out my hands.

He pauses, not taking his eyes from mine, then stands and places his hands in mine.

I push up on my toes, his grip tightens in mine, and I press my lips to his cheek in a soft kiss. "Thank you." My voice, thick with emotion, is barely audible.

He draws me to him and wraps his strong arms around me, one hand sliding to my waist, the other gently sifting through my hair before he presses my head to his shoulder. And then he pulls me in tight, his warmth engulfing me.

After what seems like an eternity and a quick second all at the same time, he says, "Meredith?"

"Yeah?"

"I'm glad you don't smell like a giraffe anymore."

# 9

"**WHAT IS HE DOING?**" Last night I thought I traded my famous-people panic disorder for a friendship with Harlan Holcombe. However, as I half hide behind a giant green plant in the lobby of the Broadmoor Hotel, I realize my current behavior belies my newfound role.

Prissy slides her eyes in my direction. "He's meeting with the guys. It's his thing."

"His thing?" I shift forward, and the word "thing" is pushed out along with a branch caught in my mouth.

"Everywhere he goes, he's a mentor. Peer helper in junior high, football captain who headed up service projects for the team in high school, creator of a Big Brother program in college." She adjusts the bangles on her wrist until they form a pristine row. "This isn't the first group he's brought to the Broadmoor. I've seen this play out numerous times. Without fail, Harlan gets up each morning, plants himself down here in this corner of the lobby for a couple of hours, and meets with whoever wants to show up."

A warmth fills my chest, and I am once again surprised at

Harlan. This new information spurs twenty-seven questions, but I don't voice them because the group stands.

Five hulky men of varying degrees of beauty, including Charlie Boyd, say their farewells through man-grips, hugs, and slaps on the back. I worry someone will need medical attention by the time they finish.

While shaking a hand, Harlan catches my eye. His face lights up, and he flashes a smile my way.

Prissy raises her slim eyebrows. "Nothing going on, huh?"

My face flushes. "I mean, we're just—I kind of—you know, yesterday we—it's not a definite, you know." My hands try to help my non-explanation but instead resemble flailing fish.

Prissy's eyes glitter with amusement but shift with mine to observe Harlan sauntering in our direction.

"The queen of England called, Mrs. Prestidge. She wants her clothes back." In one smooth move, Harlan takes her hand and kisses the top.

"Don't be silly. The queen could never pull off this look. Stop with the vain flattery, Harlan Christopher Holcombe." Her eyes narrow. "I changed your diapers, caught the show when Carissa Jo turned you down at the homecoming dance, and your mama would support me if I found cause to put you in your place."

Prissy's bad-to-the-bone display is entertaining. By the time she's halfway through, Harlan has moved two feet over and side-hugged me. We're now standing with his arm draped around my shoulders. I'm surprised my sharp, rigid posture doesn't hurt him.

It's not that Harlan Holcombe is touching me. It's that *Harlan* is touching me. Somehow this is so much worse.

Harlan's head turns, his mouth aimed at my ear. "Breathe." He lets go of me but remains close. Prince Charming starts back in on Prissy. "Why are you cranky this morning, Mrs. Prestidge?"

I gape at him. No one messes with Prissy. I'm afraid of the consequences Harlan will face for poking the immaculately dressed bear. "Don't give her a hard time, Harlan. She's not pleased with me after this morning's meeting."

Harlan tilts his head, and his eyes dart between us.

Prissy shrugs and clasps her hands. "I've been in this industry a long time, Meredith, and seen every scenario. Clients who make hurried decisions. Ones who don't recognize what they want. Others who purchase property for the wrong reasons. My business is leading them to their choices."

Gnawing the side of my lip, I consider her words. "And me?"

Her astute gaze remains locked on mine. "Some clients are too paralyzed to make decisions."

I play with the hem of my shirt. "Prissy, I—"

She steps forward and gives my hand a squeeze. "Feeling anxious is normal. Just don't allow fear to be the guest who won't leave. Doubt should never take up residence." Her focus transfers to Harlan. "And you, young man. What are your intentions with my client?"

Ohmyword.

Where is the eject button for this conversation? I spot a fire alarm across the room and want to spring over and pull it with all my might.

Harlan crosses his arms over his chest and cocks an eyebrow. "My intentions are to take her to the Garden of the Gods today."

"I'm depending on you to do an upstanding job representing Colorado Springs."

"Yes, ma'am."

Prissy gives a sharp yank to straighten her crisp jacket. "Many wishes for a lovely day, you two."

Harlan and I watch as she marches through the lobby, the crowd parting like she really *is* the queen of England. While my focus doesn't leave her grand exit, I nudge Harlan in the side. "I cannot believe you talk to Prissy as if she's a normal human being instead of the bulldog businesswoman in couture that she is."

"Are you kidding? She's a teddy bear. Plus, she's hilarious." He turns me to the exit and offers a gentle nudge to prompt forward movement. "Did you catch what she said? Prissy's a realtor, and she told you she didn't want doubt to take up residence. Brilliant."

---

"I wanted to introduce you to my friends earlier, but I hesitated." Harlan brings his black Jeep Wrangler to a halt in a parking lot closest to the Perkins Central Garden Trail.

Thank God we're taking the easiest path in the park. I strain forward to tie my shoestring. "Why's that?"

"Well, those guys aren't famous yet, but they will be. So, do you also hyperventilate around future famous people or only current celebrities?" He sports a playful smile and reaches over to squeeze the back of my neck.

With a huff full of feigned attitude, I open my door and try not to fall out of the SUV. However, I can't stretch out my fake dramatic reaction too long because in front of me is pure, unadulterated beauty.

Pure, unadulterated beauty being interrupted by a vibrating phone in my back pocket. I yank it out and am beyond annoyed when I catch Stanley's name at the top of the screen. We're friends, but we aren't call-each-other-on-vacation friends. After powering down my phone and stashing it back in my jeans, I refocus on the scenery before me.

About twenty minutes from the Broadmoor, the Garden of the Gods holds a series of breathtaking sandstone rock formations with a backdrop of Pike's Peak. In 1893, Katharine Lee Bates penned a poem describing this view, which later became the patriotic song "America the Beautiful." Frustration fills me because I can't think of any competing intelligent words to describe what my overwhelmed eyes see.

It is, simply, beautiful.

Harlan rounds the hood to join me. He shrugs on his backpack and grips each shoulder strap. His intense gaze skitters across the natural structures in front of us. "It's like muscular, salmon-hued hands of the earth grasping at the blue heavens to declare their love."

Ugh. Really? "Show-off." I stomp in the direction of the trail, calling back to him, "Why can't you just call the scenery beautiful like the rest of us normal people?"

Harlan's chuckle gets louder as he catches up to me. "Okay, Meredith. You mentioned you're not a hiker, so we'll take the concrete path to find our bearings. No elevation climbs. The view from the base is still spectacular. If you're lightheaded or need to rest, we'll stop." His thumb hitches behind him. "My pack is well stocked with water and snacks."

Last night, the only thing Harlan told me about our plans was to wear jeans and running shoes. I understand some women love being super girly and dressing up in fancy heels and shiny lipstick, but telling me the attire is sweatshirt-required is like some kind of foreplay.

Not that I'm thinking about foreplay. Ever. With Harlan Holcombe. Or anyone. What's wrong with me? Must be the beginnings of altitude sickness.

We settle into a comfortable pace, and Harlan glances at me. "Can I ask you a vain question?"

"Sure."

He clutches the back of his neck with his hand. "How much do you know about me?"

"About what?" I kick a rock to the side before taking my next step.

"About my life. Who I am. With this ridiculous media thing going on around me, I don't know what to expect from people I just met."

With a half cringe, half smile, I answer, "Next to nothing. I know your acting career is extensive, but I think I've only seen one of your movies. I only knew about the YouTube video because of my niece. But I haven't seen the actual footage. I'm, um, not so good with videos or stories about accidents."

His eyes flash, but he stays silent.

Something else occurs to me, and I hold up a finger. "Oh, and I have no idea why they call you the real-life Hercules after the save you made, but I can make a guess."

"I like that." His hand drops from his neck, and he repeats, "I like that. A lot. Maybe you can get to know the true me instead of the tabloid version of me."

Get to know him. Now? In the future? He cannot possibly think that after my trip we would ever see each other in real life. And yet, I can't help myself from asking the next question. "So, what's not in the *E! True Hollywood Story* version of you, Harlan?"

As we stroll, he describes growing up on a ranch not far from here, the life of an all-state quarterback, and his childhood starring role as Joseph in a church play. "I thought it would be funny to stand up and yell 'Let my people go,' Charlton Heston style. My brother took great pleasure in crushing me with the humiliating information that Heston played Moses, not Joseph. Right there on stage for everyone to hear."

Chuckling, I dig in my pocket for a ponytail holder and start to pull my hair back. "Sounds like typical brothers. Does he live in Colorado Springs?"

"Yeah. He runs the family ranch. Has a wife and two boys."

I wind the rubber band around my hair a few times and pull it tight. "Doesn't seem like messing up your lines ruined your acting career, though."

"Let's stop here for some water." Harlan slips the backpack off his shoulders, fumbles with the zippers, and digs through the contents. "I just kind of fell into my career. Some agent found me on stage in college and threw me into a shampoo commercial with Spencer. Before I could blink, we were cast as brothers in an obscure Western, and life began to snowball." Handing me a water, he shakes his head. "It wasn't supposed to be like this."

My stupid dry hands chafe against the ridged bottle cap as I twist it off, causing me to wince. After a gulp of water, I study his face. "What was it supposed to be like?"

His sigh is heavy as he stares off into the rocks. "I'm the first-born. I was supposed to take over the Holcombe business and live out the legacy. But when I went to college, I figured out I like working with people more than I like working with cows. I thought I'd enjoy being a drama minor but get a job in finance in the long term. My family couldn't understand why I'd turn my back on the legacy. The land has been with us for generations, and the men in our family worked it like they couldn't breathe without it. I had found something different for myself in college. But . . ."

He continues to look off in the distance, and I get the feeling he's seeing some combination of his past, present, and maybe even future in the complicated colors of the rocks.

"But?"

"But then I got that commercial. And my newfound career spun so quickly, I didn't think about it. I didn't think about how much I liked studying finance or what my life would look like with fame added into the mix." He pauses so long, I don't think he's going to continue. Then he shakes his head with an expression that seems almost like disbelief. "A thousand guys would give their right arm to do what I do. It's a once-in-a-lifetime chance. Some actors love the craft like they can't breathe without it."

Gently I ask, "How's your breathing, Harlan?"

A breeze passes between us and almost carries away his soft words. "I need more oxygen." His piercing eyes find mine. "But when my dad died and everything happened with Olivia, I moved us back here as quickly as I could. I live every day regretting the time I didn't work side by side with him on his land."

"Even if it's not what you wanted to do with your life?"

"It would have given me time with him."

I take another swig of water, draining the bottle and thinking about the pain I hear in his words. "I get that. I do, Harlan. But you might have been miserable living a dream that wasn't yours."

He opens his bottle and guzzles the water down in less than twenty seconds. "So here I am, living in my hometown, helping my brother with the ranch when I can, full custody of my daughter, and dealing with an unpredictable ex-wife on occasion."

"And now you're back to acting?"

"Not really. I mean, yes, I'm on set now for a minor role I was already contracted for. But I'm trying to stay off the radar as much as possible. Olivia is clickbait waiting to happen. I want to give Alex a normal life here in the Springs and figure out what else I can do with my life. I was toying with the idea of mentoring and consulting with actors. Keeps me low-key and allows me to help them get their feet on the ground for the long term." He places our empty bottles in his pack and turns his dark look to me. "But then a stupid video rattles across America claiming I'm a hero, when my real life has imploded and the only time I'm a hero is when I'm pretending on the big screen."

"Maybe heroic acts aren't for heroic people. Maybe they're just for ordinary people who are in the right place at the right time. Just living their lives."

He doesn't look like he's buying it, so I try for a different angle. Maybe the most important angle, at least to me.

"You're a hero to that teenage girl you saved," I whisper, my voice thick. "To her family."

Anguish crosses his face. "Meredith, I'm sorry. I wasn't thinking about your loss."

I clutch his forearm and shake my head. "This isn't about me. Now, I know you played Hercules on the big screen. Tell me why they call you the real-life Hercules."

He takes a deep breath. "When the girl was safe on the ground, gasping for breath, getting rid of the river water, I realized her shirt was torn pretty badly. No way could she get up and walk to her friends without exposing herself. So I peeled my shirt off to give to her, we got her covered up, and I carried her up the bank to her friends." He rolls his eyes. "I had no idea anyone was filming, but if you watch the video, someone in the background yelled that I was her personal Hercules. It sort of took on a life of its own."

Pursing my lips as hard as I can, I'm still unable to rid myself of the smile breaking across my face, so I lower my head. My shoulders shake. "I'm gonna—" I cough to rid myself of the laughter building in my throat. "I'm gonna have to figure out how to watch that video."

"Oh, really?" Harlan says, part offense and part humor in his voice. "Then maybe I'm gonna have to leave you on one of these rocks."

"Listen," I say as I stand, "you're not the only famous person here. My junior high marching band played the halftime show of a Dallas Cowboys game." I singsong the last few words as I strut down the next section of our path.

Harlan jogs a few steps to place himself in front of me and taunts, "Show me some of your moves. Come on, I know you've still got it."

"I'm sorry, but no. I don't do public performances anymore." My attempt at a coy smile is successful right up until I trip over a pile of small rocks.

He grabs my elbow while chuckling. "Maybe you *don't* still have it."

"Shut up" is the brilliant response I laugh through while I regain my footing.

Before I know what's happening, he slips his hand around my waist and angles me perpendicular to him while he lifts his phone in his other hand to take our picture. "Smile."

Smiling isn't a hard request. I seem to do that a lot around him. But him wanting a picture of the two of us feels meaningful. Significant.

When I turn to him, his hand slides away from my waist, but we're still very close. As in I-could-count-his-eyelashes close.

A fire flashes in his eyes. "I kind of want to kiss you."

"Kind of?" I say on a rushed breath.

"No. Not kind of. I definitely want to kiss you."

"But you said 'kind of.'" Somehow we're even closer. So much so that I place my hand on his arm because now I'm losing my balance for a different reason.

"I didn't want to scare you." His deep, quiet voice settles over me. "We haven't talked about that sort of thing."

"It's, um . . ." I look over his shoulder, trying to make sense of the seventeen thoughts scrambling through my head, then I look back to him. "It's been a while. For me. With the kissing."

He glances at my lips. "It's like dancing. You don't do it for a while and once you get back on the dance floor, you just automatically remember and everything falls into place."

I try to keep a straight face but fail. "Okay, first of all, I think you mean it's like riding a bike," I say through chuckles. "But in your case, I seriously hope you kiss better than you dance."

He winks, and there is nothing cheesy and everything good about it. Then his face turns a little more serious. "I'm wondering how you feel about it. Me kissing you."

Reflexively, I squeeze his arm. Is this hard? This is a no-brainer, right? I swallow and steady my voice, hoping it sounds calm when I say, "I feel fine about it."

Fine?

I just told Harlan Holcombe that I feel *fine* about kissing him. As if he asked me how I feel about having green beans with dinner. Fine. What do I think about getting Grandma a scarf for Christmas? Fine. How do I feel about people who wear corduroy pants in April? Fine.

He smiles at me.

It's a drawn-out, dangerous smile. The kind that starts in the lines at the edges of his eyes right before it adds a spark of mischief to them, then slowly spreads to his curving lips.

"Fine," he says. But somehow his "fine" implies so much more than mine.

Still holding my eyes with his, he slides his hand from my

elbow down my arm and laces his fingers with mine. "Later," he says, his breath feathering against my lips.

While my nerves feel like a pinball pinging across my body, he leads me down the path.

"Later" sounds way too far away and terrifyingly close all at the same time.

After we pass the Tower of Babel formation, I catch the Siamese Twins in the distance. I stride over to the side of the trail and stop to face the orange rock formations with the majestic purple mountain backdrop.

The scenery seeps serenity into the nervous energy that his promise of a kiss had placed there. A breeze brushes my face, and I close my eyes, inhaling a deep breath through my nose.

Harlan's shoulder gently nudges mine. "What are you thinking?"

I open my eyes and turn my head to find him staring at me, his face full of curiosity and maybe a little concern. "Sweet moments in life are precious. I'm intentional about grabbing hold of them."

His Adam's apple bobs as he swallows. He stares at me, studying me, and I let him. It feels significant, this moment.

"What do you want to ask me, Harlan?"

"Meredith." My name releases from his lips in a growl, and he looks unsure.

I offer a small smile of assurance. "It's okay," I whisper. "I won't break."

He faces me. "After everything you've been through, how do you keep going?"

Tears prick my eyes. My nose stings.

"I'm sorry," he says. "Oh, Meredith, I'm so sorry I asked. I should've kept my mouth shut."

I square my body to his. "Harlan, listen to me. Thank you." I reach for his hand and squeeze. "Thank you for having the courage to ask me something so honest. It's an important question." Facing the mountainous rocks again, I clench my teeth and lock down the grief to give a voice to the sentiment forming in my gut. "Because life doesn't come with guarantees."

A tear falls to the ground. Only this time it isn't mine.

"We make up rules for how our lives should run and then make ourselves live as hostages under our own expectations. When life doesn't go the way we planned, the way we expected, we can't forgive our expectations. And it gives us a reason to walk away from living." My voice hitches. "I was driving a few cars behind my family when an eighteen-wheeler crossed the middle of the highway and crushed my husband of ten years, my three-year-old boy, and my one-year-old daughter."

Harlan gasps, and I beat back the pain I see in his face. He laces his fingers through mine, his grip whitening his knuckles, and I have no idea if he is comforting me or if he needs my comfort, but it feels nice to be in this conversation together. Holding the tension of life together.

"I have a choice," I say. "I either hold life to my unrealistic, unfair requirements, or let go and try to live again."

His head jerks back, and he blinks. "How do you do that?"

"It's gritty. Some days I'm angry. Irate. Other days I'm indifferent. But on a few precious days, I have peace. So I hope." I catch a glimpse of Harlan's water-filled eyes and push through. "I choose to hope. Because some days hold sweet moments. Like this one. This particular moment reminds me of life's beauty."

He nods, and we stand in silence and stare at each other while a family walks around us.

"What about you?" I finally ask. "How did you keep going after you lost your dad and Olivia left you?"

He releases my hand and throws his arms up in the air, almost in exasperation. "Our losses aren't the same, Meredith. In our brains, we expect our parents to die when they're old. My dad lived a long, fulfilling life. And the consequence of my personal choices resulted in my situation with Olivia. What happened to me is part of regular life." His forefinger points down. "But what happened to you seems . . . cruel. Unnecessary. I can't believe you get out of bed every day."

A scoff escapes my throat. "You're impressed with my ability to get out of bed every day?" My fists tighten, fingernails biting into my palms. "Harlan, it's been four years since the accident. I spent a nice chunk of that time curled up in a ball, paying people to make sure I ate and slept. It took a group of very committed, loving professionals to help me function again."

The rise and fall of Harlan's chest slows as he gains control. "So how did you do it?"

"Early on, my friend Claire sent me a card. She said she prayed only one thing for me, the words of Rainer Maria Rilke. 'Flare up like flames and make big shadows Meredith can move in.'" I shrug. "That was my lifeline. I could picture taking baby steps within the protection of the fierce blaze."

Harlan drops the backpack on the ground and rifles through until he finds a red and blue plaid blanket. He shifts behind me, wraps the blanket around my shoulders, and folds his arms across my collarbone, pulling my back to his chest.

Slowly, slowly I wrap my fingers around his forearms.

He tucks his head down and brushes his cheek up and down against mine. Three times. Three times I feel his skin against mine. Three times I feel the faint whisper of his breath on my neck. Then he tightens me even closer to him. To his warmth.

Affection. It's been a long time.

"Meredith." My rumbled name vibrates against my ear. "You're a gift."

I don't know how long we stand there. And I don't know exactly when his arms around me shift from something deep and meaningful to something . . . different. What I do know is that as he nuzzles my neck, his lips brush across a sensitive spot.

When he turns me around, he takes my face in his hands and locks his eyes on mine.

"Is it 'later'?" I whisper.

A small smile tugs at his mouth. "It's 'later,'" he says just before he brushes his lips against mine.

My breath catches, and I clutch the fabric at his waist.

When the kiss ends, he pulls back just a touch, waiting. Watching.

I stand on tiptoe and wrap my arms around his neck. In a quiet voice, I ask, "Can it be 'later' again?"

I barely see his grin before he kisses me. For several "laters."

# 10

> I kissed a boy.

**CLAIRE**
> WHAT??? What in the world happened?!
> You're in Colorado!

I smile goofily into the phone. My childhood best friend is definitely the right person to tell.

> I know.

> I need details. Now.

> Don't hate me, but I can't go into it right now.

Partly because I'm about to meet Sally. Partly because the screen on my phone has decided to act like a rebellious teenager and only work when it wants to. Composing a coherent text now takes several tries.

> This is the meanest thing you've ever done to me, and that's saying something since you tied my shoelaces together in the third grade.

> I know. I love you.

> I'm proud of you. I hope you get to kiss him again.

Claire was the first person I told when I kissed Mickey Ranger on the playground during recess in the fifth grade. She was my first phone call after the post-homecoming kiss Eddie Watson gave me our freshman year. Not one heartbreak has passed in my life without Claire to ground me. It just feels right that I'd text her about my first kiss as a widow. Only . . .

> I didn't feel like a widow.

> What did you feel like?

I don't have to think before I type my answer.

> A woman.

A beautiful, desired woman.

> You're torturing me. You can't give me any details?

> No. I love you.

Ten minutes later, Sally sits in the passenger seat of Harlan's Jeep, looking at me with wide, astonished eyes. Even if she wants to comment on my music choice, the reverberating sounds of Rush fill the space to capacity. Harlan had to work today but let me borrow his SUV. I'm hoping I don't blow out the speakers.

A few blocks later, I brake at a stoplight, turn the volume down, and grin at Sally.

"What is wrong with you?" she asks through giggles.

"What?" I pull my sunglasses down the bridge of my nose and wink. "Tell me you don't feel better with this song vibrating through your body."

Her shoulders bounce up and down with her laughter. "Okay. I might feel a little better."

Yanking the glasses off, I grab her hand. "Sally, listen to me. This is my last day here, and if you learn nothing else, promise me this one thing will stick." The left-turn arrow cycles, giving me a few more seconds. "When Toby poops all over his room and Layla is getting her two-year molars and you've absolutely had it with life. When the dog days of motherhood hit and you aren't sure why you chose to do this, or if you can even pull off this gig. When you can't fill anyone else's needy requests one second longer because you are on fumes. That. *That* moment. Are you with me?"

"Yeeeeeessssssssssss." She leans in and clutches my hand tighter.

"Leave the house. Farm your kids out to the closest human being. Get in your car and push play on this song." I thrust my pointer finger at the radio. "And just start driving."

The light turns green. I rev the engine and peel out while Sally shouts a woo-hoo.

"L-o-u-d loud music, Sally. You spend your days watching gentle cartoons and listening to the Playgroundigans."

She leans out the window so everyone within ten feet of our car gets wind of her battle cry. "I hate the Playgroundigans!"

"Motherhood is a thousand series of just a few minutes that have the potential to make or break you. So if you need this four-minute, thirty-seven-second song to deal with life, you take it." Our bodies rock forward as I shift gears.

"You remember how long the song is." With a grin on her face, she shoves my shoulder. "Amazing."

I used to listen to five different songs for this purpose. The washed-out-mommy vibes were always forgotten within the first thirty seconds of the Rush selection.

As I laugh with Sally, my heart seizes at the thought of saying goodbye to my new friends, their celebrity status not so glaring.

But our worlds will never cross. What would I say? Let's carpool to the Academy Awards?

I dipped my toe into the waters of normal life. I met new people. Hung out with children. Found small pieces of usefulness. Shared a few sweet moments with a man. And now, maybe, I'll go home and wade a little further into the pool.

I wish I could bring these lovely people with me.

But maybe this path doesn't have to end here.

Maneuvering us to a parking place, I take an overly dramatic breath. As I pull the brake, I shift my body toward her. "Sally, you are in the battle. You are a mother of two small children, trying to survive each day. And today, we arm you with more weapons."

Sally's eyes follow to where my hand points, and she gapes.

The mecca of motherhood, All Things Baby Mart.

Her face shifts to a smile and she shakes her head. "I haven't come here since I registered for shower gifts."

"Also, you've never been here with me, which I think you'll find is a game changer." I snag my purse and exit the Jeep. "Come on. Let's go make your life easier."

After I grab a cart, I throw my purse in the kid seat. My phone dings to call my attention to a new voicemail. I must not have heard the ringer over our rebel mom music mix. I sift through my purse contents. Once I find my cell, I cringe.

Stanley.

Okay, I'm officially weirded out by how persistent he's being over "just wanting to catch up." Typically, we talk once a month. Maybe twice. I don't know what to make of this week's calls.

Sally and I enter the store, and we're greeted by a mommy-and-me clothing display. The matching Wonder Woman T-shirt and little-girl dress are perfect for Sally and Layla, and I throw them in our cart.

"Has anyone told you that you're a dead ringer for Wonder Woman?" I ask.

"Oh." Her face turns red. "Spence thought I should've auditioned for the role, but I don't act."

Conversations like these, where no one is joking, never cease to blow my mind. "You resemble her even after having two kids. Which I hate you for in the most loving way possible."

While throwing her head back and laughing, Sally takes over the cart and pushes forward. "Shut up."

I crane my neck and glance at the overhead signs to get my bearings. "Hold up there, Lynda Carter."

She pulls the cart to a stop.

"Okay." Grabbing her shoulders, I narrow my eyes. "I'm going to ask you a question, and I want you to say the first thing that comes to mind without censoring."

Sally squares her body to me, fists on her hips. "I'm ready."

"What thing do you secretly hate but don't want to replace because guilt plagues you and you're too tired to think about it? Say it." I tap her forehead to prod her answer. "Say the thing in your mind right now."

"My stupid portable crib." Her mouth forms an *O* and she pauses. "Wow. I had no idea. You're good."

We head to the appropriate aisle.

"Okay, my dear. Pick your very favorite one on the entire earth."

Sally wiggles her fingers in delight and walks straight to one decorated in psychedelic circles of pink. She pauses with her arms reaching out for the item. "Wait. Do we need to research this?"

I shake my head once. "No way. All you need to understand is this sucker is not the one you hate."

Someday I'll write a book about the psychology behind this process. I don't have credentials and my theory will be made up, but it will climb the bestseller list because tired moms across America want permission to hate their already-paid-for, perfectly usable portable crib. Or high chair. Or bottle sterilizer. On any given day, there is one item sucking the life out of a struggling mother, and she needs the freedom to walk away.

Automatic bestseller.

After traveling a few rows over, I stop. The squeaky wheels of our cart announce Sally's arrival, and she comes to a halt near me.

She sidles up next to me, stance broad with arms crossed, mirroring mine. "I hate sippy cups." Her seething voice fills the space.

"Preach it," another woman says from the end of the aisle. "I'm convinced the makers of sippy cups are evil. It's impossible to find one cup to meet all your needs."

"Humph." Sally nods.

Our new friend down the way repeats her affirmation as she strolls closer to join us. "The worst part is when you find the one that fits in your car cupholders, won't break, doesn't spill, is covered with your kid's favorite character, and allows the correct liquid flow. And your child will not drink from it. All after spending the money to try eight different cups. No one tells you sippy cups should be a separate budget line item."

Spreading my arms to take command, I begin the evaluation process. "Okay, ladies. Let's talk." I pull down each brand of cup, and we partake in sippy cup therapy. After twenty-five minutes of debating pros and cons, we put our new choices in our respective carts.

Our new friend wanders off with her cart, muttering words about investing in the sippy cup industry.

"On to the potties." I charge a few rows over and push the cart to a stop. "Sally, this is potty dating, a close cousin of speed dating. Answer the questions. Don't overthink them."

Covering her mouth with one hand, she glances around furtively, then checks out the choices in front of her. "Did you just imply we're on a potty date?"

"Affirmative." I don't take my eyes off the colorful choices. "Do you want a child seat to attach to your existing potty, or a small plastic mobile one you clean out?"

She shrugs and throws a Lightning McQueen portable potty in the cart.

"Do you want to throw Toby in the backyard naked to tee tee, or use bulldozer targets in your house bathroom?"

Sally pulls the targets off the hanger. "I want these, but Spence reserves the right to throw him in the backyard."

"Absolutely." I balance daily, weekly, and monthly calendars across my arms. "Would you prefer a sticker chart or candy as an incentive?"

Her hands sweep over the cover of each chart. "Um, it depends. How long is potty training going to take?"

*Until the next millennium*, I want to say. "Let's review these books and programs. Potty train in twenty-four hours, three days, five days, a week, or over a six-month time period. What's your poison?"

She scrunches up her nose. "I want the one that works."

"Sure." I give her a side hug. "We all do."

She turns her head to me. "So, what's going to work?"

"The one your child responds to." Shoulder squeeze.

"How would I know the answer?"

"You don't until you try." Tighter shoulder squeeze. "But the good news is I tried all seventy-three programs with mine, and I am an expert in the field while also being a total failure."

She scoffs at me. "You're just trying to make me feel better."

I wish. With all my heart, I wish.

We come up with a plan, and out of love, I don't tell her it won't work. All potty training plans fail. Bless her heart when she calls me to come up with another strategy. Been there. Bought the T-shirt.

While we walk a few more aisles, my phone's default ringtone sounds. I glance down, and the name of my caller pops on the screen. Hercules. I purse my lips and try to tone down my grin. My stomach whooshes like I'm on the downside of a roller coaster hill. "It's Harlan."

Sally's eyes bug out, and her gleeful smile almost blinds me.

I turn my body and hug the diaper shelf. "Hello?"

Nothing.

The phone continues to ring, and I stab repeatedly at the screen to accept the call, lamenting the untimely loss of its sensitivity. I'm going to have to get this fixed when I get home.

Finally, my phone acquiesces and answers the call.

"Hey." My breathy answer releases as I knock down a tub of Vaseline.

"What are you doing?" His deep voice resonates in my ear.

I place the fallen product back on the shelf. "Looking at rash creams."

Silence.

Oh, shoot. My hand slaps my forehead. "For bottoms." I nod at the Desitin as if he can see me.

More silence.

Oh, shoot again. Fix it. Fix it fast. "For babies." My high-pitched voice carries through the store.

Harlan's boisterous laughter causes me to pull the phone away from my ear.

I blow out a loud sigh. "Can I have a do-over on this conversation?"

"Sure. Hey, Meredith"—his voice rumbles with amusement—"what are you up to?"

I try to mask my mortification with a neutral tone. "I'm at All Things Baby Mart with Sally."

The ominous sound of a distorted electric guitar, followed by a computerized "I am Iron Man," causes my head to snap up.

Sally bounces on her toes. "It's Spence." She fumbles through her purse for her phone.

Harlan calls my name through my cell.

"Oh, sorry. Spence is calling Sally. His ringtone is the theme song from *Iron Man*."

"He wishes," Harlan says. "He played a small role in the first one. Spence talks schmack to Robert, claiming he would've made a better Iron Man."

Robert. As in Robert Downey Jr.

"You people aren't normal," I say with breathy exasperation. Harlan chuckles.

"Babe." Sally beams at the ground, her phone to her ear. "We're at All Things Baby Mart." Pause. "I agree, but Meredith is a genius. She's revolutionizing our lives with this one trip." She flashes a smile at me, then stares back at the floor. "What, babe?"

I turn my attention back to Harlan. "Did you call for something in particular?"

Sally's hand waves. "Meredith, Spence and I are wondering if we can crash you and Harlan's fancy dinner plans tonight so we can spend one more meal with you. Would you guys mind?"

I hold up my finger. "One sec." As I tuck my chin down and turn, the butterflies in my stomach and I address Harlan. "Um, do I have fancy dinner plans with you tonight?"

"That's why I'm calling," he says. "Would you like to have fancy dinner plans with me tonight?"

My face flushes, and I hover over the baby wipes section. "I would. Thank you." Now I'm grinning like an idiot at the travel-sized packages of disposable wipes for sensitive skin. "Sally said she and Spence want to join."

Harlan growls. Like, a real-life growl. "Tell her I'll share you for part of the night, but after dinner I'm kicking them out. I want you all to myself later, even if it's only a little while."

The butterflies in my stomach go wild. "*Later*," I say, my voice filled with giddy excitement.

"*Later*," Harlan says, his deep voice saying the word so much better than I do.

I am really starting to love the thought of later.

I turn around, give Sally a thumbs-up, cover the speaker of the phone, and hold it away while I whisper like the giddy junior high girl that I am, "He says dinner is fine, but he wants me all to himself after that."

Her eyes light with a twinkle of mischief. "He wants you alone for dessert?"

Horrified, I gasp. "What? No. Just to have some time alone."

The twinkle sparks brighter. "For dessert."

"No!" I lower my voice and lean toward her. "No. Just to . . . just to . . ." Just to what? How am I supposed to fill in that answer?

How do I *want* to fill in that answer?

She turns the cart and heads to the recliners, laughing all the way.

I shake off the butterflies, kind of, and remember what I wanted to say to Harlan. "Can you do me a favor? Can you please go check on Penelope? We left her with the kids, and this outing is taking longer than planned."

"I'll check on her, but I'm sure she whipped them into shape. How's your day going?"

"Well, I think," I say, my voice excited, "I'm useful. I have a purpose. I mean, no way am I going to tell Sally potty training will make her question her sanity, but I'm getting to encourage her and talk her through what she needs, and it feels . . ."

Harlan's low voice fills my ear. "What does it feel like, Meredith?"

"Like living," I whisper, the answer causing tears to prick my eyes. Yesssssss. This feels like living.

"That's wonderful," he says. I can hear the smile in his voice coupled with something that makes me think he gets it. And maybe even that he's proud of me.

"Gotta go, Harlan. We still need to hit three more stores." My eyes follow Sally to the gliders. "By the way, who are Sally's friends who dropped the ball and let her get this far into motherhood without covering the basics?"

"From what little Spence has shared, she doesn't have the best support system. My guess is life in and around Hollywood can't help. You're probably a breath of fresh air to her."

"Oh." I take the cord from a nearby wipes warmer display and wrap it around my forefinger.

"Hey, before I let you go," he says, "when you said potty training will make Sally question her sanity, does that also apply to nighttime training? Alex has mastered daytime control, so now she's working on keeping her panties dry through the night. I just bought this book, and it says I should give her a giant party each morning she succeeds. Apparently she'll be trained within a week. It doesn't seem hard."

"Right." I suck in my lips to stifle my laugh. "We used that method."

Four times.

# 11

**"'INVINCIBLE,'" HARLAN SAYS** as he reclines in the high-back restaurant chair, crossing his arms over his vast chest.

Sally scoffs. "The Pat Benatar song or the Kelly Clarkson song?"

"Yes, Harlan. Which girl-band ballad do you want to be your signature ringtone?" Spencer shifts to kiss Sally on the cheek. "Good point, baby."

"Scratch that." Harlan scoops up his unused spoon and sweeps it through the air. "New idea for the ringtone that truly represents me. 'Unforgettable.' Can't go wrong with Nat King Cole."

I fold my napkin lengthwise and then fold down a corner. "How about 'You're So Vain'?" A half second after the words escape, I slap my hand over my mouth.

Harlan's gaze slices from Spencer to me. "Traitor."

"I know." Sally's hand waves like a schoolgirl wanting the teacher to call on her. "'Let's Hear It for the Boy.'"

As the three of us laugh, Harlan shakes his head. "Let's be clear. I'm no boy." He angles his spoon to point to his heart. "I'm all man."

With the last crease in place, I stare at my napkin creation. "Yes, you *are*."

It dawns on me no one is talking, and I glance from my blossomed flower napkin to the rest of the table.

Everyone is frozen, and a split second later laughter erupts.

Apparently I said that in my out-loud voice.

My face heats up, and I pull my napkin out of the floral shape to curtain my face. "You guys. Just love me through it."

Harlan reaches over and yanks my napkin shield down to the table. "You proved my point." He shifts his attention and points his spoon at Sally. "Why does Spence get the Iron Man ringtone? I'm Hercules, for goodness' sake, which means I deserve a better one."

Sally twists her torso and lifts the strap of her purse off the corner of her chair, transferring it to her shoulder. "I'm no help to you." She flashes a smile at Harlan, then addresses the rest of us. "If you will excuse me, please, I have to go to the ladies' room."

As Sally rises to exit, Spencer and Harlan scoot their chairs out to half stand.

My last dinner in Colorado is divine. Ristorante del Lago is one of the newer dining options at the Broadmoor, and its elegance doesn't disappoint. The terra cotta tile and exposed wood beams complement the authentic Italian menu filled with house-made sausages and pasta.

A server walks away with my empty plate, and I wonder if this is the kind of restaurant that brings their guests after-dinner mints. The spaghetti puttanesca's garlic, anchovies, and black olives took my taste buds to a new level of bliss. But my dinner mates will have to forgive me when they're knocked over by my breath.

Spencer stretches his arm across the table, encircles my wrist, and squeezes. "Meredith, I need to thank you. Sally is a changed woman because of you."

My torso jolts in surprise at his kind comment. "Oh, gosh, no, I—"

"Neither of our families can help us out." He releases me and pulls back. "Having two babies in a row almost did her in, and a lot of times I have no clue how to help." His gaze falls to his fisted hands. "She hates it when I suggest hiring someone."

"It's a loving gesture, Spencer." I wrap my napkin around my hand. "It just might not be for her."

"This week, Meredith . . ." He clears his throat. "This week, she's the woman I fell in love with. Less nervous. More laughter. Confident. It's because of you."

Stunned, I flex my hand, causing the napkin to unravel and fall to the table.

"We'd like to stay in touch." Spencer leans back in his chair, hands resting on his thighs. "Make sure you look us up when you visit Harlan."

I inhale a sharp breath. Back up the wagon, Spencer Dean. Harlan and I may not speak again after tonight.

Without breaking eye contact with me, Spencer gives Harlan's head a playful shove. "Okay, forget Harlan. We'll dump him and adopt you."

Harlan clutches his chest and yanks out an invisible dagger. "Does decades of friendship mean nothing to you?"

Before I'm forced to acknowledge the social grenade Spencer dropped about visiting Harlan, Sally returns from the restroom. She stands with her pink-tipped fingernails clutching the back of her chair. "Oh, Spence, did you break the news to Harlan that we're trading him in for Meredith?"

Harlan throws his hands up in the air. "Unbelievable." His body sags, adding to the dramatics, until his head shoots up and he snaps his fingers. "That's it. That's the ringtone for me. 'Unbelievable.'"

"Do not dishonor the glory of the nineties by picking that song." Spencer pushes out of his chair. "Harlan and Meredith, thank you for sharing your dinner with us this evening. As promised, we're going to let you two enjoy your dessert alone." He turns to his wife. "You ready to go?"

In spite of standing in the middle of a fancy restaurant, the second I rise, Sally throws herself into my arms. "Call me anytime," I say into her ear. "I will always want to hear from you. Tomorrow. Two weeks. Two months." My voice cracks, but I rein in the tears. I pull back and grasp her shoulders. "You are beautiful. And you are strong."

Sally swallows, nodding. Pulling my hand down, she thrusts a purple envelope into my grip. "Read it later."

"My turn." Spencer steps in and engulfs me in a giant bear hug.

After a stunned pause, I return the embrace. For a scarce moment, I forget he is Spencer Dean, and I realize I'm going to miss my new friends.

After Spencer releases me, he shakes Harlan's hand, then watches while Harlan kisses his wife on the cheek.

As the couple strolls away arm in arm, Harlan moves to my side of the table to pull out my chair.

"Thank you." I do the scoot-your-chair-in-while-the-man-helps thing. So awkward. After putting the envelope from Sally in my purse, I fold my jittery hands in my lap and wait for him to sit down.

Our server appears out of nowhere. "Can I interest you in a chocolate-filled cannoli or some house-made gelato this evening? We have a lovely selection of desserts I can show you."

Harlan offers a smile, one that doesn't quite reach his eyes. "We don't need the dessert tray, but would you please give us a few minutes with the menu?"

"Of course, Mr. Holcombe." She sets down two leather-backed lists and leaves to assist an elderly woman nearby.

Harlan's deep brown eyes focus on me. His finger draws a figure eight on the tablecloth, then he knocks twice with his knuckle. "So, when you visit Spence and Sally, do you think you'll look me up?"

Can everyone in the restaurant hear my hammering heart?

Menu clutched in both hands, I stretch my arms out, focusing on the after-dinner drink options. "No. You're Chad Tarkington."

Harlan takes his index finger and pulls the card down halfway so he can see my face. "Who?"

"Chad Tarkington. You"—I nod in his direction—"are Chad Tarkington."

He pushes the menu all the way to the table, causing me to release my hold. "What are you talking about?"

"My summer camp romance boy. You know how it is. For seven glorious days, you're thrust into an intensified relationship with someone who would annoy you in real life. You return to your respective homes and grow apart. Or give each other the slow fade. Whichever." I sweep my palm through the air. "For that one week, it was amazing, but the end is the same."

The muscles in his jaw clench, and he taps three times on my menu. "You said so many things I need to unpack, I don't even know where to begin." He observes as I weave my napkin between my fingers. His eyes warm. "Summer camp romance boy. First of all, we established earlier I'm not a boy. I'm a man."

Yes. Yes, we did.

"Second." He plants his elbow in front of him and rests his chin in his palm. "Were we having some kind of a sordid romantic fling this week? Because I would have made different choices, starting by kissing you a heckuva lot more."

My face flushes with embarrassment. "I didn't say 'sordid romantic fling.'"

"It's implied. It's the adult version of summer camp romance."

This has backfired. Astronomically.

He wants to go there? Fine. I knew this was coming. Let's get it over with.

I bite my bottom lip, pause, and take a breath. "Why do you want to be friends with me?"

"I think it's clear I want to be more than friends." Harlan's face blanks. He sits up straight. "Why are you asking me this?"

"If you define me by my grief, this can't be anything. Or if you want to save me from my grief, this will be a disaster." I swallow the lump in my throat and shake my head. "I've lost friends over this, Harlan. People I valued, who are no longer in my life."

There. I've given him a better picture of reality. My emotional minefield should be sufficient to scare him off.

He draws in a breath, waits a beat, and encloses my hand in both of his. "I don't define you by your grief."

Ignoring his hand-holding, I let out a frustrated sigh. "It has to color how you view me."

"Meredith. I define you by the kindness you showed Sally when she was a total stranger. I define you by the faith in life you hold on to despite all reason against it. I define you by your beautiful smile when we drove the Jeep through the mountains." He tugs my hand, drawing me closer. "You'll always grieve your losses. But it's only a piece of your journey. All I want is for you to consider letting me be part of your whole journey. To show me who else you are." One side of his mouth hitches in a half smile as he shrugs one shoulder. "To see a little of who I am."

I gnash my teeth. "I don't know, Harlan."

I'm standing at the end of the high dive, legs shaking, board wobbling, unable to jump.

"Let me ask you something, Meredith." He strokes my hand with his thumbs. "How can you read everyone else, but you can't read me?"

I pull my body back into the deep chair, breaking our connection.

He runs his hands through his hair. "You see people. It's a gift. You may not know the details, but you grasp the depth of their story in a short amount of time. How they're wired. Where they're broken. What they need."

"Harlan—"

"You understand Sally to the core. You tolerated Olivia in an impossible moment." He holds a finger up with each incriminating detail. "And, in a bizarre and miraculous way, you disarmed Penelope in record time."

A puff of amusement escapes my mouth.

He lays his forearms against the edge of the table and leans in. "But why can't you read *me*?"

My napkin seems to be my security blanket. I pick it up and run the seam through my thumb and forefinger, then drop it to the table. When I can no longer avoid the inevitable, I look at him. "Because I'm scared," I whisper.

"Meredith." His low growl mirrors his intense brown eyes. "All you would see is that I like you. That I want to spend more time with you."

His reply hits me in the chest, and I have to draw in oxygen twice to recover from the declaration. We can't do this. I'm too broken.

I shake my head. "I can't do halfway, Harlan. I don't have it in me. No games. No guessing."

He spreads his palms flat on the table and answers without hesitation. "Not one thing I'm thinking about pursuing is halfway."

My eyes widen in shock, but before I respond, one of the servers approaches our table.

My stress level has been rising parallel to my craving for a calming chocolate concoction. I long for the server to bring the dessert tray to the table in spite of Harlan's earlier request to do otherwise.

He disappoints me beyond forgiveness when he pulls a metal straightedge from his apron to clear the surface of crumbs.

I begin to form my napkin into a fan, folding it back and forth. Back and forth, back and forth.

*Think, Meredith. Think. In your gut, what do you know to be true about Harlan?*

As I finish my masterpiece, Harlan's gentle hand pulls the end of the cloth, unraveling the accordion fold. "You have more tricks with this thing than Houdini."

Speaking of Houdini, the server has disappeared into thin air. I am now left without sugar or my origami napkin to help me cope with the impending destruction of the wall constructed around my carefully controlled life.

I mentally put on my big-girl panties and square my shoulders. Pinning Harlan's gaze with mine, I ask, "So what would be next?"

Harlan's grin finally reaches his eyes, and my insides warm with the understanding that I'm the reason for the beautiful phenomenon.

He claps his hands once and rubs them together. "I've got some vacation time coming my way. What about Thanksgiving? That's six weeks away."

I blink several times. "I spend Thanksgiving every year with my family."

"Perfect. May I join you?" He takes a swig of water, watching me over the top of his goblet.

My eyelids flutter as if I've lost control over them. "You want our first date to be meeting my family on a major holiday?"

"Thanksgiving would not be our first date." He sets his water down, thumb rubbing the condensation on the glass. "And yeah, I want to meet your family. Catch a glimpse of your life."

No, I guess it wouldn't be our first date.

When did I start going out with Harlan Holcombe? Later I'll have to figure out how my life has turned into a possible tabloid story.

Scanning the restaurant, I decide to tackle the next server I spot and demand immediate sugar consumption. Is it in poor taste to grab the leftovers from the table next to us?

I refocus on Harlan. "So, Thanksgiving at my house? Where will you stay? What about Alex?"

"Alex will be with Olivia this year." He shakes his glass, jostling the ice. "Avoiding the paparazzi is easier if you don't mind my staying at your house. I don't want them tracking me to find you. But we can work around it if you're uncomfortable with my sleeping on your couch."

He's speaking the English language, but I cannot comprehend what he's saying.

Seriously, why is there not a double order of chocolate cake in front of me to counteract this anxiety-producing discussion?

As our server passes our table, Harlan holds up his hand to signal her and orders two coffees. After she leaves, he sprawls back in his chair and stretches his long legs. "What are you thinking?" He crosses his arms as he waits.

I clench my fists. "Harlan, if you come to my house, you'll see Steve, Clayton, and Chloe everywhere. I don't just mean in the pictures on the walls. I mean no one in my inner circle is allowed to censor stories or feelings about them. Would you be comfortable with that?"

His gaze lingers on me while the server returns and fills our mugs. Once we're alone again, he puts his weight onto his folded arms on the table. "Whatever our relationship is or becomes, Meredith, it includes Steve, Clayton, and Chloe. They're your family." He stops for a moment. "I want you to share your memories with me so I can know them. So I can know you."

My heart beats rapidly, and moisture brims my eyes.

He reaches over with one hand, cups my face, and wipes a tear with his thumb. "What do you think, sweetheart? Can I spend Thanksgiving with you?"

"That's the first time you've called me sweetheart," I whisper.

"It's not the first time I've thought it," he says, watching his thumb brush softly over my cheek.

The answer washes over me. *Jump in, Meredith. The waters are warm and safe.*

"Okay," I say.

The beautiful smile that breaks over his face feels like a reward for my bravery. "Okay," he repeats.

His palm slides from my face, down my neck, shoulder, and arm, to my hand, ending with a squeeze. He cranes his neck, searching the restaurant. "Now, let's find someone who will bring dessert. I'm willing to bet you need massive amounts of chocolate right about now."

I'm grinning like an idiot for the second time today, but I don't care. "Don't suggest we split something." I wave the neglected menu toward him. "I'm not sharing."

⸻

Desserts in our bellies, my elbow in the crook of Harlan's, we enter the lobby, and something on the television at the hotel bar catches my eye. "Come with me." I grab his hand and lead him.

We enter the room, and his long strides slow. He yanks back. "Oh, please, no."

My eyes feel like they're glittering as I flash a smile his direction. "Humor me." Ignoring his groan, I walk forward, weaving through people, dragging him behind me.

On the screen in front of us, a local news anchor stands in a field with a river behind him, reporting on the Hometown Hercules sensation.

As we sneak through the crowd, it takes great restraint for me to resist yelling, "Hercules is here!"

My eyes are slow to adjust to the dark atmosphere. We lean against the wall, and I survey the surrounding patrons.

Three twentysomething ladies lean forward in their bar chairs with their high-heeled feet propped on the crosspiece below. They whisper, giggle, and point to the screen.

"Hercules is haawwt," the brunette says, and giggles spread through the group of women.

Harlan shakes his head.

But one devastating peek at the TV and my critical mistake is staring at me in high-definition.

Panic begins to spread through my gut.

We arrived just in time to see the full rescue video. A video I've purposely avoided.

My eyes barely have time to take in the overcast day, the

browning field of grass, and the group of young people in the screen of the smartphone video. The audience view wobbles as the camera operator follows a dancing girl to a wooden fence, the flowing river in the backdrop. The girl balances on the top of the fence and claims to remember her fourth grade beam routine.

My breath hitches, and I grasp Harlan's hand. I can feel his gaze turn to me, but I can't pull my eyes off the video unfolding on the screen. I whisper what everyone in the room already knows. "She's going to fall."

Harlan wraps his hand around my waist and pulls me to his side. "She's going to be okay," he says into my ear.

My heart can't hear his words. Because in that moment, all I see is that someone's child is in danger.

The crowd in the video screams as the girl's arms windmill and she topples, disappearing from sight. Someone yells that she fell in the river.

Tears sting my nose.

From the top right corner of the camera appears a running hulk of a man. Harlan.

"Help her." My chest hurts as the strained words release.

Harlan's arm around me tightens.

On-screen Harlan slides down the grassy hill in time to grab the girl's arms just before she washes down the river. By this time, the camera operator is rushing to the scene with everyone else. The picture fills with the sounds and movements of mass chaos, Harlan and the girl unseen.

"I got her." Harlan's soothing statement breaks through to my brain, and understanding dawns.

I look up at him. "You got her."

With eyes full of concern, Harlan scans my face. "I got her," he repeats.

The relief. I didn't expect the relief.

A child was saved.

Not one of mine.

But someone's.

A watery smile fills my face, and I throw my arms around Harlan. "You got her." My shaky voice reverberates in my chest. "You saved someone's child." I shift back and place my hands on his cheeks. "Please. I know you hate this social media mess. And I know you don't want to be called a hero. But you saved someone's child. *Please.* Just take that one part in. You saved someone's child."

He nods slowly.

When I turn back to the television, I see that the news story paused the novice video to interview the rescued girl.

Shaking off the moment, I wipe under my eyes.

Harlan places a hand on the small of my back as we watch the interview in silence, the clinking glasses, flirtatious laughter, and busy servers bustling around us.

The anchor redirects his report. "The social media storm that has hit since the incident is a category five . . ."

"That's my cue." Harlan puts pressure on my back and urges, "Let's go."

"Okay." I glimpse at the screen one more time, and instead of allowing Harlan to guide me out, I freeze. Gaping.

Glaring in my face is a shirtless, built, defined Harlan in all his glory. With a fierce scowl, all muscles flexed, he carries the girl to the top of the hill.

Oh. My.

He truly is Hercules. All I can think of are things I wouldn't share with my mother.

"Let's go," I whisper, mesmerized and unable to move.

"Are you gawking at me?" his rumbly voice says in my ear.

I jump and lock my eyes with his. "No," I say, clearly lying. "No. We have to go. You said that. Let's go."

I take his hand and drag him through the lobby, trying to think of something. Anything that would give me a few minutes to get a handle on things. When I spot the escalator down to the ground level, I say, "Hey, let's go see what's playing in the movie theater."

"Meredith, I don't think—"

"Trust me," I say, taking the first step of the escalator, "they always have some fun movie playing that everyone's already seen, so you can walk in and out. Sometimes it's a kids' movie, but other times it's something great from the eighties."

We hit the ground floor, and I tug him down the long hallway.

"Yeah, but—"

"No, no. Trust me. It'll be fun."

"Mer—"

He silences when I hold my finger to my lips in the international sign for be quiet. I gently open the door to the theater and we find the show already playing. The music sounds familiar, but I can't quite place the movie. Slowly I make my way down the side of the theater a few feet and wait for my eyes to adjust. Once they do, I scan the rows to find open seats.

Next to us, three teenagers rest back in their chairs with their sock-clad feet propped on the seats in front of them while they whisper, giggle, and point to the screen.

"Girls," the adult figure next to them admonishes.

And then a familiar voice says quietly in my ear, "You're beautiful."

I shift to lean my back against the wall and look at Harlan. Bashfully, I curl my hair around my ear and say, "Thank you."

He glances at the screen and back to me, the look in his eyes a cross between amusement and bewilderment. "Um, Meredith . . ." He nods at the screen.

Slowly, because mortal fear courses through my veins over the train wreck that I know is about to happen, I look to the screen.

We walked into *Hercules*, starring the man I had dinner with, just in time for the racy make-out-leading-to-sex scene.

Once again, but this time on a larger screen, is a shirtless Harlan in all his glory. My gaze shifts to the goddess in the Princess Leia bikini who is making out with him. I immediately want to rip her eyes out. Two of her could fit into the dress I'm wearing.

I glance down at my body that gave birth to two children. I look pretty good for my age, but certain contents may have shifted during flight. My body doesn't match any superhero's, and I'm more of the dressed-in-a-white-sheet Princess Leia.

"We should go." My high-pitched tone throws a spotlight on my discomfort.

Harlan turns perpendicular to me, crosses his arms, and leans his shoulder against the wall. "Oh?" The screen flickers shapes across his face, but his amusement shines through the shadows.

I open my mouth but can't remember how to speak. Even if I could, what would I say? Instead, I push out of the room, making a beeline for the empty elevator. I pound the number for my floor as a chuckling Harlan saunters to my side and the doors slide closed.

Staring straight ahead, I talk to the elevator door. "Well, thank God you've gained a few pounds and don't look like that anymore. Otherwise I wouldn't be able to contain myself."

Harlan studies his shoes, rises up on his toes, then rocks back to his heels. His cocky vibe bounces off the walls of the confined space. "My trainer thinks I'm in better shape now than I was six years ago when we filmed."

My hands fly out in exasperation, and I still talk to the door. "Would you throw me a bone here?"

His rumbling chuckle is both annoying and attractive, and I can feel him looking at me. "How long until you can look me in the eye again?"

I address the ceiling. "Won't be looking you in the eye if you take your shirt off again."

He leans toward me. "What was that?"

"Nothing." I squeeze my eyes closed and giggle. "Nothing at all."

This is why I can't be around famous people.

On the way to my room, we're silent. I have no idea what's going through Harlan's head, but my head is spinning and trying to put a baggy Hawaiian shirt on my mental image of him. As if he's a benign Ken doll.

When we arrive at my door, I turn to him. I squeeze my eyes shut.

"What are you doing?" he asks with some concern.

"I think this will be easier if I say this with my eyes closed."

"Say what?" Now he sounds amused.

"I think we need to break things off."

"Because you saw me without my shirt on?" Still amused. He runs his knuckles down my arm. I don't think he's on board with what I'm saying.

"I didn't think this part through."

"Meredith." He chuckles, then brushes his knuckles gently down my cheek. "Open your eyes."

When I look at him, he cups my face in one hand and wraps his other arm around my waist. "If it bothers you that much, I'll ask my agent for a part where I have to gain weight."

"Is that a thing?"

"Sure. She'll find a script that has a man in a midlife crisis. She'll put a clause in my contract insisting I gain thirty pounds for the part and that the makeup crew make me look like I'm balding."

"But I like your hair." So do my hands, which is why they've crept up his neck and slid into his soft waves.

He's definitely not on board with breaking things off. Then again, with his thumb slowly grazing the small of my back, I don't think I'm on board with it either.

"Okay. We'll leave the hair as is and just insist on the weight gain." He pulls me in, and now his face is all I can see, his breath against my lips all I can feel.

"Thirty pounds isn't going to be enough," I whisper. "Make it fifty."

He looks at my lips. "Done."

I pull back and blink. "You'd agree to gain fifty pounds for me? There's not one person on the planet I'd agree to do that for."

"Meredith." His shoulders shake with silent laughter.

"Yes?" I lean into him and place my hands on his chest.

His eyes darken. "It's later," he murmurs against my lips.

"It's later," I say on a smile right before he kisses me good night.

# 12

**THE NEXT MORNING,** all giddy memories of Harlan's good night kiss vanish during a call with my sister. Trying to control my anger, I squeeze my eyes shut. I all but growl into my cell. "Forget I brought it up, Molly."

While my sister drones on about things that aren't her business, I pull the phone away from my ear and glance at the screen. Instead of 5:25 a.m., my phone should just say Crack of Dawn. I let Molly talk to the air for a few more seconds.

"Meredith, what if Stanley is the one for you?"

The multi-offensive comment shoots through my heart. "Enough." I bite out my response while shaking my head.

"Why do you sound upset? You're the one who mentioned him."

The early-morning call to my sister is a disaster of epic proportions.

"Did you catch the part where he has left me six messages this week? That's not normal." I cross my hotel room and peer out the window. "I only said something to you about it because I wanted to make sure he's all right. When someone calls that often, you're either in a relationship or something's wrong."

She huffs. "What I'm saying is, as far as I know, everything's fine. And because everything's fine, I think you need to consider Stanley. His interest in you isn't a secret now."

"You don't find this creepy at all?"

"He was surprised when I told him you were out of town—"

"Wait." I tap my finger on my front teeth. "He called you?"

"Yeah. He sounded worried and asked why you aren't returning his calls."

I rest my forehead on the windowpane. "Molly, that's weird."

"Not with your history." She releases a long sigh. "I don't know, what if he's the person you didn't know to hope for? You lost your husband, but the best man in your wedding could be a safe place for you to land. There's something beautiful about it."

The person I didn't know to hope for? As if he alone can solve my problems? Is that what she thinks?

I drift from the conversation. Stanley isn't unattractive. He's a little taller than I am but with a small frame. His green eyes go nicely with his brown hair. But he does nothing for me in the attraction department. To no avail, I spent years during my marriage trying to find some nice, introverted, supportive, homely woman for Stanley.

My gaze follows a black Suburban as it rounds the circle drive to the hotel. I lose track of it when it drives under the awning. "I don't have those kinds of feelings for Stanley. He's a friend. That's all."

Molly groans. "How would you know if he couldn't be more? You don't let yourself think about other men."

A layer of sadness accompanies the realization that my sister isn't always someone I can safely confide in. I clench my fist and knock on the window three times. "I think of other men, Molly. Just not Stanley."

As a matter of fact, a certain beautiful-souled man is due to arrive in a few minutes.

"Well, I think you should reconsider. He's loved you for years and would be a good option for you."

Good option.

Safe.

The person Molly, if she got her way with my dating life, thinks I should hope for?

What would she do if she knew about Harlan? Definitely not the safe option she wants for me. But I've been living safe for quite some time, and it's not doing anything for me anymore.

I crane my neck and catch a glimpse of the clock across the room. Shoot. "Gotta go, Mol. Will you be at the airport when I land, or should I Uber?"

"Of course I'll be there, Meredith." She pauses. "I'm always there."

I wonder if she knows that's kind of a problem. For both of us.

I turn on my heel and walk to the unmade bed. "Okay. See you later."

As soon as she says goodbye, I toss the phone down, plop on the bed, and hold my head in my hands. What's going on? I'm not even home yet, and the luster of this vacation is dulling. Was this trip a total waste?

Prissy won't admit it, but I think she's disappointed I didn't commit to purchasing a property.

Then there's Harlan.

Harlan, who is coming to get me any minute now even though I'm not ready. I shoot to my feet and survey the room.

All of a sudden I'm a human tornado sifting through the space for lost belongings. Brochures, receipts, and chocolate wrappers go flying while I hunt for anything I might need to take home. In spite of its lack of use, I run to check the safe in the closet. Oh no. What if I left my favorite pair of underwear in the mountain of towels on the bathroom floor?

My thoughts are broken by a robust knock on the door, followed by a gruff-sounding "Room service."

Freezing, I contemplate an absurd escape to the balcony. It works in the movies.

"Mer?" Two more knocks.

Shoot. "Coming."

I open the door, and the man in front of me is so ruggedly handsome, I'm embodied by a flaky teenager.

Harlan is dressed in a long-sleeve, navy-blue Broncos T-shirt and faded jeans that fit oh-so-well in all the right places. His brown hair is disheveled, not in an I'm-trying-to-look-like-this way but in an I-just-rolled-out-of-bed-and-couldn't-care-less-how-great-I-look way. But it's the warm mahogany eyes with crinkles around the edges that pull back the chandelier of my emotions and let it swing.

Bottom line, I'm in trouble.

He leans against the doorjamb.

I'm now in more trouble than I was five seconds ago.

"Tell me again why you're leaving so early?" He holds out a cup of coffee.

I cradle the caffeine offering in my hands. "My plane takes off soon?"

"Humph."

I nod to the bakery sack he holds. "Are you going to hoard those treats, or is one for me?"

"Banana nut or blueberry muffin?"

"Banana nut."

He grins. "You gonna let me in, or are we gonna eat breakfast out in the hall?"

Am I going to let him in?

I swallow. "Yes. Sorry." I turn sideways to allow him entrance, grabbing the bag as he slides past me.

He stops, stance wide, left hand shoved in his front jeans pocket, right hand holding his coffee, and takes in my room. "What happened in here?"

"I kind of got carried away." I attempt a sip of my scalding coffee, but the heat emanating from the hole at the top of the cup warns my tongue of its demise.

"Checking for lost stuff? Yeah, I'm the same way. Want a second pair of eyes to make sure you didn't leave anything?"

"No," I blurt out too fast, thinking of the possible stray underwear. In an effort to distract his helpful ways, I set my cup down and distribute the muffins.

Harlan takes a huge bite, chews, and swallows. "Hey, I wanted to ask you something. Are there any significant dates coming up? Hard days? Anniversaries or birthdays?"

I forget to breathe.

"Meredith?"

Shaking my head, I pull out of my awed stupor. "My calendar is like a minefield. How did you know that?"

He wipes a hand on his jeans. "I'm always a bear to be around on the death anniversary of my dad." He shrugs. "I thought I would ask."

Three birthdays, a wedding anniversary, and the accident anniversary. Add my birthday, Mother's Day, and Father's Day to the list, to say nothing of any of the regular holidays like Thanksgiving and Christmas. If I think about it too much, I want to crawl in a hole and hide for the rest of my life.

I swallow down a lump of heartbreak. "Chloe's birthday is October twenty-fifth."

Harlan nods and steps toward me. "What will help?"

I place my muffin on a side table and walk to the window. The light from the lampposts streak the dark, glistening streets.

"I'm not sure how to answer your question. It only took a few failed attempts to realize I can't avoid pain by planning how to cope. I have to lean in. Feel what's there on a specific day. Figure out what I need in the moment." I wrap my arms around myself. "Sometimes I draw the shades and stay in my sweats. Sometimes I go to her grave. Always, there's an exhausting meltdown involved. My sister checks on me, but I usually don't want to be around people."

Harlan clears his throat.

"Thank you for asking." I turn to face him. "It means a lot to me." Tears threaten to fall, so I amble to the bathroom to finish my search.

"Where's your phone? I want to plug in all my contact info."

"On the bed." I close one of the doors and inspect behind it for stray clothing.

"My cell is the best way to get ahold of me, but I'm also going to add Penelope's information. If you can't find me, she'll know how to track me down."

I gasp. Hiding under the bath mat is my beloved pair of one hundred percent cotton, faded pink granny panties. They're so industrial they should be called underwear, not panties. But they are shockingly comfortable. No one makes 'em like these anymore.

"She's not that bad," he says. "I thought you two buried the hatchet."

I glance at Harlan, and he bites his lip while he punches data into my phone. "Um, no. Penelope's great. I, uh, found something I forgot to pack."

"Oh, good. What was it?" he asks, staring at the screen.

"Nothing." I scurry past him to shove the precious commodity underneath every other item in my luggage.

He stabs at my phone, his brows drawn.

"Is it giving you problems?" I nod toward my cell.

"It's kind of special, isn't it. What's going on with this thing?"

"I did some research. Apparently the screen is losing sensitivity and only works when and how it wants to." I kind of wish it had spontaneously stopped working when I was talking to Molly. "I'll get it fixed when I get home."

He continues to work on the phone, then smirks. "Programming my chosen ringtone took a little longer. But it's worth it."

"What?" I dive to grab my phone, but Harlan's long arm keeps it at a safe distance. "What song did you choose?"

His eyes glitter. "You'll just have to wait until I call you."

139

Something in my belly flips. He's calling. Me.

Harlan grins.

My belly flips again. Swinging on the chandelier isn't so bad.

Once I zip my suitcase closed, Harlan pulls it off the bed. I take one last glance around the room, spread my arms out, and drop them. "I guess it's time."

He wheels my luggage down the hallway as if it doesn't weigh eighty-three pounds. When we arrive at the elevator, he pushes the down arrow.

"Um." I adjust my purse on my shoulder. "I wanted to let you know I've thought about it, and I'm not going to cyberstalk you."

Despite pursing his lips, he can't hide his smile. "Thank you, I think?"

"If this is going to be a normal relationship, I need to treat you like you're a normal person. I know you like to lay low and that you want this whole Hometown Hercules thing to calm down. But if it doesn't, I'm not going to check out TMZ to find out where you are. I won't follow your fans on Twitter. I will ignore *People*, *Us*, and the *National Enquirer*. That way, when we do interact, we get to be whatever we want us to be."

The doors open. I take two steps in and turn around.

Harlan stands frozen, watching me.

I stretch my arm to hit the button that holds the doors open.

He shakes his head. "Sorry. I— Thank you. That's thoughtful." The elevator buzzes its impatience, and he rolls my belongings inside.

Turning to him, I point my finger. "If you break your leg, it's going to start trending immediately. Please find a way to let me know you're okay."

"I will." He runs a hand through his hair. "But if you don't hear from me, it doesn't mean I'm not thinking about you."

"Oh." If I don't hear from him? "Okay."

A pang of insecurity zings through my chest just as we hit the ground floor. Harlan puts an arm out to direct me, and we walk around the corner, pausing a few feet from the concierge.

He turns to face me. "This movie's pretty intense. I only have a minor role, but the next six weeks will be grueling. Long hours, an unpredictable schedule, and several tough-to-shoot emotional scenes aren't a great cocktail for the time and energy required in a new relationship. Hang in there with me. Trust me."

The concierge catches my eye, and I address him. "I'm on the six o'clock shuttle. Meredith Harper."

He glances down at some paperwork on the tall, ornate wood podium in front of him. "Ah, Ms. Harper. Yes. We tried calling your room. Your ride is running about ten minutes late due to traffic from an early-morning wreck. We apologize for the inconvenience."

Harlan peers down at me. "I can give you a ride to the airport, you know."

I put my hand on his forearm. "No, my flight doesn't take off for a while. Plus, we talked about this last night. I don't want you to skip time with your guys. If you don't leave now, they may bail on you, and I know it's your favorite part of the job."

Harlan's head tilts and his eyes soften. He tucks a strand of hair behind my ear.

My heart is unsettled, and I offer him a small smile. "Listen, I just—I'm just grateful, Harlan, to have had this week. If we don't ever speak—"

The forward motion of his body stops the words from coming out of my mouth. He cradles my face with his hands, and I clutch his shirt at his waist. He kisses me on the forehead, pausing for two glorious seconds, then rests his forehead on mine. "We talked about this last night." He shifts and rubs his cheek against mine. Once. Twice. Then moves to kiss me. One long, lavish kiss letting me know he has every intention of speaking to me again. Kissing me again. When he draws back, one hand snakes around my back and the other into the hair at my neck, holding me to his chest. "I will see you. In six weeks."

Engulfed in his scent, warmth, sweetness, and the solid beat of his heart, I wrap my arms around his waist and hold on tight. The gentle swing of the chandelier cradles me.

On a sigh, I exhale everything I was going to say to him about how it was okay if we never spoke again, because I know that while this was a short trip, I didn't buy any property, and there is a possibility I'll lose touch with my new friends, my life has shifted monumentally. And on the small, fluttering wing of hope, I inhale all that is and all that could be of Harlan Holcombe and myself.

"I will see you in six weeks," I whisper against his chest.

When he saunters away, I can't help but watch the show. Those jeans could win awards. But I'm distracted when I hear the faint sound of ABBA's "Take a Chance on Me." I peek around the room. The song is an odd choice for piped-in music in the Broadmoor lobby.

Then I discover the peppy chorus is coming from my purse.

Gasping, I reach in to find my cell announcing "Hercules calling," accompanied by the selfie Harlan took of us at Garden of the Gods. I whip my head up in his departing direction.

His arrogant grin blinds the room as he holds up his phone, and I burst out laughing when he turns to swagger away.

Ten minutes later, I'm still smiling.

With my luggage packed into the back of the shuttle and my body tucked into a window seat, I overhear the driver telling someone he could wait a little longer. I glance at the couple across the row. The wife mouths to me, *What's going on?*

Once off the phone, the driver addresses us. "I'm sorry, you guys. One more person needs to catch this ride to the airport, and he should be here in a few minutes. This isn't procedure, but our shuttle times are a little off because of the accident. We don't want anyone to miss their flight. Is it okay with everyone to wait just a few minutes?"

The husband grunts his approval.

"May I run to the restroom while we wait?" I ask.

When he nods, I'm out of the shuttle before he can finish his warning to mind the time. I briskly walk through the doors of the building and head to the bathroom. After taking care of business in record time, I hurry out of the ladies' room, glancing to my right before I veer to the exit. I stop dead in my tracks and do a double take.

Sickening tingles begin in my gut and spread outward to the tips of my limbs.

This is what I imagine a gunshot to the stomach feels like.

Twenty feet away, Harlan hugs a woman. Their bodies are attached toes to hips, his hand in her hair, holding her head to his chest. She turns for me to see her face, and the reality suffocates me.

Olivia.

Only then do I notice Alex, held against the far side of Harlan's body, included in the family embrace.

I hope no one hears the small cry of pain that accompanies the breath I release.

Tucking my head down, I hustle back to my seat on the shuttle. I angle my body to the window, close my eyes, and try to slow my breathing. I'm powerless to stop the hot tears streaming down my face.

The chandelier swung so hard, I was thrown off as if riding a bucking bull. Face-first into a puddle of mud.

Closing my eyes, I exhale. The release of anger, disbelief, and confusion feels harsh to my lungs. I swipe at my wet cheeks with the back of my hand and look at the hotel doors. It's a special kind of torture to wonder if I want him to walk out or not. If I want him to walk out with his family. If I want him to see that I know what just happened.

I place the tips of my fingers on my lips, almost able to still feel his pressed against mine. I must be terrible at interpreting a kiss. No. Kisses.

I'm so stupid. I'm so very, very stupid.

The shuttle jerks me forward as it pulls away from the hotel. My phone chimes to alert me of an incoming text message. I'm not in touch with my body's automatic response to pick it up and check the screen.

**CLAIRE**

You're coming home today! I want the story on this boy you kissed.

I fight back the next round of tears. I'll tell her someday. But I don't want to go into it now.

It turned out to be nothing.

Love you.

And that was Claire. She knew I'd tell her when I was ready.

I set my phone down, and after a few minutes of swallowing down my emotions, I hear it chime again.

**STANLEY**

Safe travels today. Can't wait to see you.

Great. The beautiful man I kissed was just embracing his exwife and their child, and Mr. Good Option just texted me.

# 13

"MEREDITH? DID YOU HEAR what I said? I've got your schedule lined up for the week." Molly slows her red Ford Explorer to pass through the DFW airport toll booth.

Staring out the passenger window, I nod. "Yeah. Schedule."

"The food pantry is starting to get busy with the upcoming holiday season. The director said they could use you a few more hours a week." She sets her blinker and exits onto 635 East.

Her proposed calendar for my life feels like a needle pricking at my skin.

Molly settles the car in her chosen lane and accelerates. "The animal shelter always needs people to walk the dogs, but adoptions don't kick up until much closer to Christmas."

Prick.

"The only other volunteer thing I have for you right now is with the church. They're working on Octoberfest."

Prick.

My cell, settled deep in my purse, alerts me to an incoming text. If it's Stanley, I want to cringe. If it's Harlan, I want to cry. Ignoring the pang in my heart, I refuse to reach for the phone.

I hold my gaze on the passing cars, hoping my sister doesn't see the semi-permanent sheen of tears in my eyes. "We should combine efforts with these volunteer jobs to multitask," I say. "Let's dress the dogs in tutus and trick-or-treat at the festival booths for canned goods."

My sister doesn't laugh at my lame joke. "I think the church could also use some help updating information after the recent financial campaign."

Another prick.

Seething with frustration, I can't hold back any longer. "Can I ask you a question, Molly?"

"Francine Clyde is the point person." She adjusts the rearview mirror. "Yesterday I left her a message asking when she wants to train you on the database system. I assume you'll be in town now because, thank God, you didn't follow through on your whim to purchase property in Colorado."

Prick. Prick. Prick. The tingles on my skin intensify to pain. I reach over to squeeze her arm. "Molly."

She glances at my hand, then back at the road. "What?"

I angle toward her. "Did I commit a crime of some sort?"

"What are you talking about?" Her incredulous tone mirrors the hair-raising lane change she accomplishes by cutting off an unsuspecting Honda to veer around a slow truck.

"You're listing various volunteer projects as if I'm working off some kind of sentence. Al Capone wouldn't have had this many community service hours."

She runs her hands from the bottom of the wheel and around the sides to grip the top. "We're supposed to keep you busy, Meredith."

"I'm supposed to keep myself busy, Molly."

Dealing with grief materializes like a prison sentence some days. Lately I've been itching to make a jail break.

The text alert sounds again.

I curl the top of my purse over as the only way I can quiet the annoying noise.

Molly huffs. "What's wrong? I always plan this kind of thing for you."

Banging my head against the back of the seat, I swallow my frustration. "Why are these jobs in particular a good fit for me?"

She flips her hand through the air and throws it on the wheel, making a thud. "What's that supposed to mean?"

"Am I operating out of my strengths?" I ask the ceiling.

"It's volunteer work, Meredith. It's not rocket science."

Instead of a prick, the hurled comment is a minor stab wound. I snap my head down and glare at her. "What if there's something more for me in life?"

"I don't even know what that means. We're all just living, Meredith, doing the best we can with what we have on board." She exits the highway and pulls to the far right lane.

Another new text comes through my phone, and my arms spasm around my purse at the sound. I sit up. My right leg bounces in nervous energy.

I'm no longer comfortable in my own skin.

Molly offers me the security of a numb life. But this past week I waded in the ocean of the living. Felt the soft coax of the waves.

I shift in my seat to cross my legs. My life feels like scratchy underwear.

Molly drives in silence through my neighborhood and slows to the curb in front of my North Dallas ranch-style home. "I'll text you when I hear from Francine."

I release my seat belt and climb out of the SUV. "I have a few things going on."

She hops out of the car and moves toward the tailgate. "What does that mean?"

My approach to the back is slower than hers, and I murmur the answer to my shoes. "I need to shop for new underwear."

She raises the back door and leans around the corner of the vehicle to catch a glimpse of me. "What?"

"I just have to take care of a few things."

Things like do I need to let my former mother-in-law know I'm dating again?

Wait.

At the top of the list should be to figure out first *if* I'm dating again. Next would be breaking up with the person I may or may not be dating. Also important, fixing my stupid cell phone screen. And last, letting my therapist sort through everything flying around my head. Things like that.

We lean in and pull the gargantuan bag out together, her at one end, me at the other. Without an ounce of grace, we all but drop it on the ground.

She straightens, hands on hips.

I mirror her stance and don't allow her assessing gaze to intimidate me.

Her face softens. "You okay?"

"Yeah." I grasp her hand.

She nods. "I don't understand what's going on with you, Meredith. First you wouldn't let me go with you when you traipsed off to Colorado. Then you come back and you don't want the usual volunteer jobs. Something about you is off." She points a finger at me. "Don't deny it."

Stupid sister who knows me too well. But self-preservation leads me to a silent response.

She sighs. "You talked to Gwen lately?"

My hand jerks at her intrusive inquiry about my therapy, but wanting to keep the peace, I force myself not to let go of her grasp. "I'm supposed to check in with her soon."

"You know I love you." Her voice cracks, and she squeezes my hand.

I return her gaze and wince at the worry in her eyes.

My sister only understands one way to love, and her smothering increases when she's anxious.

"I know you love me." I step around my luggage to wrap my

arms around her. "I'm okay, Molly. Promise. I'm just thinking through what I should be when I grow up."

She pulls back from the hug but holds my shoulders in a firm grip. Her lips purse and twist to the side in her signature face of disapproval. I thought she mastered the expression when we were teenagers, but it matured into adulthood with the addition of a single eyebrow raise.

As she releases me, a text alert sounds again from my bag. I sort through my purse to find my keys, refusing to check the screen on my down-turned phone.

"Those texts could be from Stanley. You gonna answer them?" she calls back as she rounds her car to open the driver's door.

"Yeah," I lie. "Thanks for the ride, Molly."

I stand at the curb while Molly's SUV careens out of sight.

My skin tingles, but maybe the pricks aren't about pain. Maybe I've been asleep so long, the sensation is the nerves coming back to life.

# 14

**AS I GLANCE DOWN** at the bootcut jeans, running shoes, and University of Texas sweatshirt I threw on this morning, it occurs to me I'm not cool enough to be in the Apple store.

A salesman approaches and interrupts my thoughts of escape. "May I help you?"

Can he help me? The super-trendy teenager standing in front of me sports a signature cobalt-blue T-shirt with an Apple icon adorning the center of his chest, paired with dark-wash skinny pants. His brown hair is swished to the side in a way that defies both gravity and hair product.

I shift my weight from my right foot to my left. "Uh, I know there's a fancy system to sign up for appointments here, but could I speak to your manager, please?"

His hair sways with his nod, causing a different but equally perplexing disheveled look. "Can you give me more information about what you need? I know I resemble a twelve-year-old, but I have a college degree and I'm married with a kid on the way."

I can't mask my shock. "Really?"

"No. But I've worked here for two years." His genuine smile improves his appearance, upping his estimated age to twenty. "My name is Cade. How can I help you, ma'am?"

Cade. I bet having a hipster name is required for employment here.

My gaze travels from one side of the store to the other, looking for someone born in the 1900s. The giant room is packed with hopeful patrons, eyes glazed, ready to sign their latest paycheck over to the computer cult to obtain a pristine white-packaged electronic device of the modern era.

"My screen has lost sensitivity, so when I try to do things, either I have to stab the screen into submission or it won't complete the task at all."

"Unfortunately, that can happen," he says. "Can you tell me specifically what doesn't work?"

"Texting. And some settings."

"What kind of settings?"

"I'm pretty sure the problem is the screen."

"You're probably right, but before we go down that path, I just want to make sure I understand the problem and it's not something I can solve with a simple settings adjustment."

I square my shoulders and lift my chin. "Do you have customer privacy rules?"

Cade's brow furrows. "What do you mean?"

I clutch my purse closer to my side. "If I show you something on my phone, are you bound by some kind of agreement not to tell anyone?"

"Yes." He draws his answer out to four syllables and nods knowingly.

Wait. That must have sounded bad.

I hold up my hand. "I just need to delete a contact and a photo."

His face reddens while his body jolts like he's holding back laughter. I made it worse.

"It's not inappropriate." My voice is so loud, a customer nearby glances over with big, round eyes. She leans down and steers her toddling son away from me.

Cade's face is now contorted with a forced earnest expression. "Yours wouldn't be the first awkward photo problem to walk through our doors."

Taking his elbow in my hand, I guide us to the least populated nook of the room. "Someone programmed it with things I no longer . . . appreciate. It's not inappropriate." I crane my neck to search our close surroundings and catch possible eavesdroppers. When I'm sure we're in the clear, I huddle and expend a lot of energy holding my emotion at bay while steadying my voice. "The contact is a celebrity, and I need to know you'll keep what you see confidential."

His eyes narrow. "I will not tell a soul."

Lord help me, I'm going to trust this boy-man. I dig the phone out of my purse, press the power button, turn it face down, and hold it out to him. "Please don't tell me about any of the waiting messages."

He opens his mouth to say something.

"Please." I jerk my outstretched arm. "I don't want to know what they say."

Ignoring Harlan, Stanley, and Molly is the trifecta of avoidance, but once Cade and his hair help me fix my phone, I'll have to deal with them.

"Okay." He takes the phone and stares at the screen. "What are you trying to do with the settings?"

"Several things. But first, a quick question that might solve all of this. Can I exchange this phone for a pager?"

His face contorts in question. "A what? Do you mean an iPod? I think those were around when I was a baby."

"You're making this worse."

"Well, that's not good. Let's go back. Talk to me about the settings giving you issues." He holds up my phone and waves it back and forth in the air.

"Can we talk about the screen first?"

He looks at me expectantly. He might be young, but he's focused. Apparently, I'm not getting out of this conversation until I talk about the settings.

"Okay. When I go to change a ringtone and picture assigned to a certain contact, I can't get it to work." When the words leave my lips, my chest hurts, and I rub a spot beneath my collarbone.

"Oh, wow. Notifications are popping up like an out-of-control fireworks show." Cade turns the phone to show me.

"No." Thrusting out my right hand, I block my view while throwing my left hand over my eyes. I peek at him through my fingers.

"Sorry. What's the contact name?"

Maybe if I tell him, he'll change out the picture and ringtone for me, fix my screen, and I'll be on my way back to the predictable reality of my life.

"Hercules." I make every effort to state this name like it's normal. As if Bambi, Superman, and Princess Leia are also on my list.

He nods and maneuvers my contacts to find the name. His eyes grow into saucers, and his head shoots up. "Wait a minute. Is that really—"

"Hush," I say entirely too loud.

"Sorry. It's just . . . is that really him? I've seen that awesome video of him saving that girl. I mean, it's a cool pic of the two of you. If it's really him."

*Yes, that's really him,* I want to say. That's really him before he told me he wanted to kiss me. And it's really him a few days before he was embracing his ex-wife. I glare at Cade.

"Right." He returns his gaze to my phone.

A UPS guy sporting a fuzzy blond mustache approaches our area. Carrying a large box, he walks past us the exact moment the aforementioned toddler decides my side of the store is more interesting than his mama's. A look of awe shines from the child's cherubic face.

"Whoa there, little man." The UPS guy shifts his hips and legs backward in a partial hopping action while the forward-moving box is lifted higher to accommodate the runaway.

Cade, clueless to the stray child, continues to stare at my phone.

I turn to smile at the boy but instead find calamity looming. He reaches his little arm up to a counter, stretching as far as he can to grasp a shiny new silvery laptop. One of his chubby hands finds purchase on the charger cord, and he pulls the computer just enough that it teeters on the edge.

The UPS guy lowers his box, momentum pressing him forward.

The runaway's mom uses her stealth speed to slide in front of and past the man to save either the laptop or her son.

The delivery man, unprepared for the Olympic-worthy mommy move, loses his balance.

None of this would have mattered to me, except this incident causes the UPS guy to fall into Cade while Cade is pressing commands on my phone.

"Oh, shoot." Cade regains his balance and his head pops up, eyes filled with terror, cheeks fire-engine red. "I'm sorry. I'm really, really sorry." He shoves the iPhone in my face.

"Hercules" and "Calling Mobile" are splashed across the screen, accompanied by the selfie of Harlan and me at the Garden of the Gods.

No. Nonononono. Nooooooooooooo. I'm aware of the computer crash behind me, but all I hear is my pounding heart.

"Did you just—" I slam my hand on my chest. "Did you just *call* him?"

Cade's nod is so vigorous, his hair layers flop like the wings of an eagle.

"What do I do?" I stare at the screen. WhatdoIdo? WhatdoIdo? WhatdoIdo?

The ringing phone taunts my paralysis.

I bug out my eyes at Cade.

He shakes his head strenuously, his hair now resembling twirling helicopter blades. I half expect him to take flight. "You could hang up the phone."

"But then he knows I called!"

If I hang up and don't leave a message, what will that look like to him? Desperate? Aloof? Interested? Insecure? Presumptuous to not at least leave a message? Why can't we live in a time when phones don't document each and every call we make? My parents talk about what it was like to live pre–caller ID, and while it sounded lame to me growing up, it sounds like a pretty great setup right about now.

"This is Harlan, leave a message."

I almost injure myself from whiplash when I snap my head down at the sound of the deep-toned voice coming from my phone.

I have six point two seconds to decide what to do while the automated voice lady explains how to end the call. If I hang up, he'll still see that I called. I'm about to jump into shark-infested voicemail waters.

My shaky hands bring the iPhone up to my ear while I pray I don't vomit all over Cade. Though it might serve him right. I hunker over the display next to us and place my free hand up to my head to brace for the ominous beep.

"Hey, uh, it's me." I clear my throat. "It's Meredith. From the Broadmoor. I mean, there are probably a lot of Merediths who've been to the Broadmoor. I just mean it's me. Meredith." I cringe my eyes shut. "I didn't mean to call you. I mean, it's good to hear your voice. Or, uh, the six words you left on your outgoing message. Not that I called to hear your voice. I didn't mean to call at all."

Someone please bring me some Imodium for my diarrhea of the mouth.

I glance over at Cade. His lips purse as he sweeps his forefinger across his neck in a swift motion signaling me to cut off the call.

*Think of something. Think, think, think.*

"So, uh, yesterday I drove east on Highway 30."

Cade grunts and jerks his hands out in question. Even his hair looks upset.

I shoo him away and fold back over the shelving for privacy. "There's a billboard that has bothered me for a couple of years. In big, giant letters it says, 'Stop his snoring ladies.' There's no punctuation on the sign. And so when you read it, it sounds like someone is saying something about snoring ladies. 'Stop his snoring ladies.' I had to pass it a few times to figure out that was, in fact, what it says. But then you go by another few times and look at the other information on the sign, and you realize it's an advertisement for a product to help people stop snoring. But they left out the comma." I'm on a roll now, gaining confidence as I ignore the grunting sounds from Cade. "They want the sign to say, 'Stop his snoring, comma, ladies.' They want the ladies to stop his snoring. But without the comma, you think they want someone to stop a group of snoring ladies."

It's true. I keep talking while throwing out an animated hand during my enthusiastic monologue.

"So, anyway, yesterday I drove by the sign, and after two years, someone corrected it. They put a comma in between the words 'snoring' and 'ladies.'" I giggle into the display of phone chargers. "It's hysterical. I have so many questions. Did people complain about the typo? Was there a company meeting where it got addressed? Who paid to correct the sign?" My chuckle calms. I take a breath and lower my voice. "I just wanted to share it with you. Maybe you had a long day and this will make you laugh."

Hitting the screen to end the call with more force than necessary, I freeze. The remaining oxygen whooshes out of my mouth as the brutal cascade of reality flows over me in a tingling sensation from my hair follicles all the way down to the tips of my toes.

What have I done?

My breathing increases, and I turn to Cade with wide eyes. "I'm not allowed to talk to famous people."

He bites his lip. "I think I know why."

"Can I call back and erase the message?" I shove the phone into his hands. "Fix it. Fix it now."

"I'm sorry, ma'am, there's nothing I can do." He grimaces.

I run my hands through my hair and hold it in a ponytail. "Maybe I should get ahold of Penelope." I pace two steps, turn, and walk back. "No, she'd tell him." Releasing my hair, I snap my fingers. "I'll contact Verizon. They'd be reasonable, right? I mean, I can't be the only person in dire need of erasing a message." My voice rises. "Oh my gosh. What if it ends up on some kind of auditory YouTube? My fifteen minutes of fame." Which, upon reflection, is the length of the voicemail I just left.

"It'll be okay." Cade holds out his hands as if he can push back my hysteria.

I shoot daggers from my eyes at him while I snatch my phone back.

"Look at the bright side." He shrugs, hair calmed down and unmoving. "There's an excellent chance he'll change his number after he hears your message."

Why does that make my heart hurt?

"Listen, ma'am—"

"Stop calling me 'ma'am.'" I stomp my foot. "You're making me wish I had gone to the Verizon store. Normal-aged people wearing mom jeans and flats shop and work at those stores."

Cade fights a grin and loses. "Listen. I'm sorry I accidentally called him. But I'm thinking"—his amusement vanishes, and he rubs the nonexistent stubble on his chin—"that maybe that call happened for a reason."

Wonderful. The lead in a boy band just played the fate card. And the worst part is the tears pricking my eyes.

He points to the phone dangling in my hand. "Have you backed up your phone?"

"I did it before I left this morning."

"Do you have current AppleCare coverage?"

"I'm pretty sure I do."

"Good. Let's look at your options for replacing this phone. I think it's probably your screen."

Oh my word.

I give him my information, and while he types into an iPad, he says with a small smile, "I think you're my favorite customer of all time." Before I can protest, he holds up a hand and clarifies. "My favorite customer of all time who I can't tell anyone about."

---

After wandering the mall for who knows how long, I make it back to my car and sit lifeless in the front seat, staring out the window.

I walked into that store wanting to rid myself of my asinine crush on a Hollywood boy. I walked into that store seeking closure to a ridiculous dream.

I walked into that store wanting to shut down the ache in my soul over seeing Harlan with his ex-wife.

I knew. I just knew if I got my phone fixed and could change the picture and the ringtone, it would bury the evidence of my feelings for Harlan. Maybe it would bury the feelings themselves.

While I ponder calling the FBI for disastrous voicemail retrieval aid, my cell's text alert dings. I grab my purse from the passenger seat and scramble for the phone. My heart stops at the words from Harlan staring at me on the screen.

> Greatest message EVER. Thank you for making my day, sweetheart.

"I hate boy bands!" My yelling is heard by no one. I fall forward in defeat, gently banging my head against the top of the steering wheel.

Repeatedly.

# 15

"I'M SO PISSED YOU get to spend Chloe's birthday with her." Standing in front of the most unfathomable site on October twenty-fifth, I whisper the irrational words while tears stream down my face.

Placed in the ground before me are three plaques representing the three loves and losses of my life. I stretch my foot to rub off some dirt collected in the corner of Steve's grave marker. When the soil doesn't clear, I huff frustration and drop to my knees, ignoring the pain from the bruise I know I just caused. My attention focuses on clawing away the muck.

As soon as the plaque is once again clean, I settle on my haunches and rest my hands on my hips. I angle my head and shrug my cheek onto my shoulder, using my shirt to soak up the tears. Maneuvering to sit cross-legged, I lean forward and place two hands on the marker in front of me. "Hi." My eyes cloud over, but I beat back the despair. "I know if you were here, you'd tell me I'm being ridiculous. But seriously, Steve, grief isn't logical. And right now, I'm so mad at you because you three are together celebrating her, and I'm . . . here."

Twenty feet away, a peaceful creek manufactured by the cemetery runs through the back half of the property. The sound of two ducks quacking draws my attention away from my family, and I glance up. Each duck pecks at something in the water with aggression.

"Do you mind?" I admonish Donald and Daffy. "This is supposed to be a peaceful place."

Lord help me, I'm a little more loony today than usual.

I anguished over choosing these plaques for Steve, Clayton, and Chloe. Should I put the kids together so I can talk to them at the same time? Should Steve be first because I pictured him leading them into heaven? Should all three be on one marker, or should they each get their own? It felt so final.

It was. So final.

Surveying my selections, I'm pleased. Steve's bronze gravestone is in the middle, with Clayton's and Chloe's smaller ones flanking it. It's perfect. I can lean down, place my cheek on Steve's grave, and imagine it being his chest while my arms outstretch to grab hold of the children through their markers.

But now I'm sitting in my anger. My ridiculous, displaced anger, protecting me from the deep cavern of profound sadness.

"I wish you were here." Something in my grief-filled brain wants to negotiate. Okay, I lost my husband. Could I just borrow him for a little bit to be the father of our children? "It's like I wish you were here to help me deal with Chloe's birthday, then I'll send you back." I shake my head. "She's our child. It's our loss." My voice shakes. "But I'm the only parent who shoulders the burden. And today I'm beyond mad at you for not being here to share it with me."

The ducks in front of me quack louder. It's a toss-up whether they agree with me or think I'm warped.

I squeeze my eyes shut, wisps of hair tickling my face. Taking a deep breath, I gather the strength to study the small gravestone to my right.

Chloe Abigail Harper.

I lie down on my stomach, my body lined up with her grave, and my hands frame the name on her plaque. "Hi, sweetie." The iceberg of grief bursts through the glassy water surface, and shards of emotions escape. The sobs of sorrow rack my body, and I rest my face in my palms. Each inhale is a gasp, and the metallic scent of the bronze marker fills my senses.

Several minutes pass, but once my breathing normalizes, I prop myself up on my forearms. "Happy birthday, Chloe Girl. I'm so very glad you were born." A few tears drop to her birth date. My smile wobbles as I remember her pronunciation. "I brought you a bwoon, honey."

I have no idea if five-year-old Chloe would have still liked pink balloons. But I honor the toddler I knew.

Pushing my body up, I lean back to grab the small Mylar balloon from my purse. They last longer than the latex ones. Despite my daughter not being here, I feel like a good mother by picking the higher-quality decoration. I shove the plastic stick in the ground above her marker, and the rose-colored ornament stands at attention.

Crawling over to the far end of my trio, I arrive at Clayton's site. I stay on my knees but lean over and put my face right up to the engraved race car. My draping hair creates a cocoon of intimacy. "Hey, Speedy. I love you, buddy." I picture him going in for a quick kiss on my cheek, then running away with giggles of pure joy.

I move back to the middle of the three graves and stretch to snag my purse again. Thankful I remembered Kleenex, I blow my nose and wipe off mascara remnants from my cheeks. Once I gain a little control, I sit with my feet on the ground, arms hugging my shins, chin resting on my knees.

Looking over, I notice the ducks have made peace with each other. They glide back and forth over the water.

"Hey, baby." I sniff. "I need to tell you something."

This time I want to borrow Steve to be my friend. And then, I negotiate again, I will send him back.

I exhale. "Stanley's been calling a lot lately. I think he might have feelings for me." I can almost catch Steve's laughter in the wind. "Stop making fun. You always said he had a crush on me."

My words and the smile on my face must make me appear odd. I'm glad the ducks are my only companions today.

I drop one of my hands, pick at some grass, and start a pile of blades. "The thing is, Steve, I might have . . . met someone." I shake my head. "I don't think anything will happen with him. But I . . . I guess I needed to say it out loud to you." Tears prick my eyes, and my chin wobbles. "I know you would want me to be happy."

I hate grief. It toys with your logic and has its way with the playground of your sanity. It feels like I'm breaking the family up to find someone new. I know it's not logical. I know it's not true. But my feelings vacillate between reality and distortion. I want off the seesaw.

I repeat the earlier truth to myself. He would want me to be happy.

"You'd love this part. He's a celebrity." My unseeing gaze aims at the birds swimming toward me. All I can picture is what Steve's reply would have been. "You don't need to remind me about Rachael Ray's book-signing debacle. I agree. I can't do famous people."

One of the ducks rises from the water and ruffles his wings in a grand gesture I can only assume is agreement. If only they knew.

After the Apple store, I gave up ignoring Harlan's messages. Not that there have been many. I don't know why I'm dragging out the inevitable, but when Harlan texts me, I text back simple replies.

He's left me two voicemails. One last week, filled with exhaustion and talk of something unexpected that came up. The other a few days ago, garbled and left while he was sitting on an airport runway. "Hey, you might be good at Skee-Ball, but you are terrible at phone tag. That was a lame joke. So, we're about to take off and my phone is dying. I accidentally packed my charger in my checked luggage . . . Man, I really want to talk to you . . . This isn't how I wanted to do this. Okay. Take care of yourself."

*This isn't how I wanted to do this.*

That felt confusingly final. Which leads me to say to my husband's grave, "None of this matters. He's not interested in me." My fingers dig into the bald spot I created on the ground. "But someday someone will be. And I want to thank you for loving me well." The words are almost indistinguishable through my tears. "I won't settle for anything less."

My gaze hits his name, and I sigh.

The wind blows my grass pile away.

On my stomach again, I press my face to Steve's chest, grab hold of Clayton's and Chloe's hands, and breathe in as I embrace my family. "I love you guys."

---

Arriving at my house, I feel like I've been run over by a bus. As I insert the key into my door, I spot dirt shoved into the beds of my fingernails. I glance down to confirm the additional green and brown marks of earth covering my sweatshirt and jeans. A wave of satisfaction washes over me.

Somehow the stains on my body and clothes legitimize today's grief. I stared it in the face, honored it, got dirty with my efforts, and came out on the other side. When I leave the cemetery with a physical manifestation of the emotional turmoil I'm in, my pain is validated.

I realize my shoes are muddy—another affirmation—and toe them off to dry on the porch. As I scoot them aside with my foot, something stops them.

A package.

Wow. I'm so out of it, I almost missed the delivery altogether.

I pick up the brown box, open the door, and enter my house. After I throw my purse on the red bench, I make a beeline for my bedroom. I grab my favorite pair of worn-out UT sweatpants off the top of my hamper and change into them. There's a slim hole next to the monogrammed *U* and *T*. Upon noticing this one day, Molly burst out laughing and deemed these my UTI pants.

Molly.

I heave a sigh. She's called a few times today. My phone's now in my purse. I'll text her later.

The closest shirt, also on my hamper, is a long-sleeve gray Henley. My arms protest with exhaustion as I drag my soiled top off and pull on the cleaner-but-not-clean replacement.

I climb up on the bed with the grace of an elephant and sit cross-legged with my back against the headboard. Turning my head to study the postal box on the table, I wonder if I have enough life left in me to open it.

With my last morsel of energy, I pull scissors out of my bedside table drawer and run the sharp edge down the sides of the package. When I unfold the top, I find a white card with handwritten red block letters resting on tissue paper.

*Meredith—I'm not going to send you flowers, as if those could make you feel better. Instead I hope you can wrap yourself in this blanket and take some comfort. I hate that you have to go through today. I am thinking of you, sweetheart. Harlan.*

As I read the words, a solitary tear, the last piece of emotion I can expend today, escapes down my cheek.

Drawing the delicate pink tissue paper open, I uncover a treasure. I skim the palm of my hand over the exposed layer of velvety fabric, the deep color of the predawn ocean.

Scooting down in my bed, I curl my body into the fetal position while pulling the blanket out of the box to cover myself in the sea of solace.

I have no energy to analyze Harlan and his confusing embrace with Olivia. No interest in dissecting our sporadic texts or his voicemails.

Instead, as I fall asleep, my only thoughts are of the sweet embrace he sent to me.

# 16

SOCIAL PRESSURE TO READ intellectual literature increases with age. If you dare to admit to choosing fiction, dear Lord, make sure it's at least literary fiction. It's as if you need to justify your reading choices by how complex the story is and how well it honors the craft of writing.

But I just can't get me enough of Tris and Katniss.

Because I'm a closet young adult book fan, I can't discuss with anyone the most irritating issue with those stories. There seems to be a common love triangle theme between the damsel in distress—who is not really a damsel in distress because she's so strong but she does need some help—and the two boys whose combined body fat is three percent. I don't want to disappoint the young women . . . or thirty-six-year-old women . . . of America, but I'm not sure this scenario is realistic. On a couple of levels.

Still, *Divergent* and *The Hunger Games* sit in my DVR, waiting for the days I need to escape to a teenage dystopian world.

Before I married Steve, my dating life represented the who's who of misfit toys. I was the queen of attracting the good-guy nerds who lack the chemistry they profess to know so much about. No hot vampires and werewolves fighting to the death for me.

Instead, my world is full of Stanleys.

Maybe Molly's right. Maybe Stanley is a good option for me. Maybe women like me, with stories like mine, need to look for the good options in life.

Claire would hate that I'm thinking this way. Even though we all grew up together, or maybe *because* we all grew up together, it's her life goal to get Molly out of my head. She was kind enough to drop the topic of my first kiss as a widow, but not without telling me over lunch that she was proud of me for taking a risk, something Molly would hate.

Still, can't there be value in good options?

Good options that don't include decreasing, erratic phone calls. Good options who aren't distant, exhausted, and vague when they do call. Good options that don't mention maybe re-neging on their promise to come for Thanksgiving in a couple weeks. What was it he said on my voicemail yesterday?

"I don't know how to tell you this. I really wish we could talk. I am one hundred percent planning to be there on Thanksgiving. One hundred percent. But something has come up that I don't have any control over, and if it plays out a certain way, I might need to miss. I hate this, Meredith. Please know that I hate this. And please call me . . . I know. I know that I'm not around when you call, but that doesn't mean . . . Just call me. Take care of yourself."

What happened to the Harlan Holcombe I met in Colorado?

This morning, Stanley's coming over to drop something off. Instead of looking forward to talking to my good option, I find myself checking for all the possible exit routes from my own home.

After I open my tall oak door, Stanley raises the Styrofoam cup he's holding in greeting. "Hey." As he shuffles by me into the house, he leans in for an awkward hug. His other hand grips a travel mug, and a book is tucked under his armpit.

Our touch is fleeting but ignites nausea. Are "good options" supposed to make you ill at the thought of kissing them?

"I brought you some coffee. Just the way you like it." Shoving the cup in my direction, he loses his arm grip on the book and it falls. "Oh, sorry." As he picks it up, a slosh of his drink spills on my hardwood floor. "Shoot." He pulls the edge of his shirt up over his wrist and rubs the splattered liquid into the cuff of his plaid button-down.

Rather than help him, all I can do is stare.

My gut clenches as I realize I can't be that person for him.

"How is your day?" the nicest man I will never date asks.

"Good. Thanks. Do you want to come in?" I gesture toward the living room.

Stanley, having been to this home many times over the years, enters and sits in a leather armchair. As I pass the coffee remnants on my hardwood, I rub my sock-clad toes over the spot.

He brushes his straight brown hair back and smiles. "I thought of you the other day."

*Oh, please, don't have thought of me the other day.*

I sit across from him in the corner of my couch, tucking my foot under the opposite leg.

"I found this." He stretches his arm across the ottoman to hand me the paperback. "A friend of mine said it was helpful to him."

I run my fingertips over the cover. *The Gifts in Grief*, by Person Who Hasn't Lost Their Husband and Two Children.

What I want to say is "Thank you, but have you read *Divergent*? Lots of people die in that book, but it's more entertaining." Instead, I quiet my inner child. "How thoughtful. Thank you, Stanley."

"I was kind of thinking we could . . . read it together?" He mumbles the question to his hands.

"Oh." I shift forward, trying to squash the twinge of guilt that runs through me for not asking Stanley about his life. "We haven't caught up in a while. Are you dealing with a loss?"

He snaps his head up, his brow furrowed. "No."

I blink.

"Meredith." He rubs his hands together. "I-I'd like to spend more time with you. If you would like that."

Over the years, Stanley has checked on me, left me thoughtful gifts, and taken care to know my goings-on. Sometimes I want to joke that being the best man only applied to the wedding, but I think that brand of candor would crush him.

I pull a striped, square decorative pillow into my lap. "Thank you, Stanley. That's kind of you." I hate this. "But if I said yes, I worry I would be leading you on."

"I don't mean we would be dating. I just thought—" He exhales a breath of frustration. "I mean, I know, Meredith. I know we have a connection and maybe it's—maybe we should look at it." He leans forward, his intense gaze shooting my way. "I was there, Meredith. That day. I was there." He points to his chest. "And that has to count for something. I loved you through that . . . and . . . and I think I love you more than friends now."

I squeeze my eyes shut and take a deep breath.

That day.

A couple of months after the accident, I had a meltdown. My world was filled with a silence so loud, it brought me to my knees. Depression was like a sticky fog that rolled into my life and refused to let go.

Underneath the unfathomable and gut-wrenching sadness, a potent anger infiltrated my every fiber with admirable stealth.

Yes, I was angry at the loss, but I was irate with the people around me.

Well-intentioned friends visited my home, and I was a sitting duck for everyone's opinion. Many of them wanted to somehow quantify the tragedy so it would make sense in their human brains. I was accosted by kind words full of messed-up platitudes that felt wounding to me. Out of self-protection, I started hating people and withdrawing from my life.

I wasn't trying to harm myself. I simply didn't want to exist. So I stopped eating, ignored self-care, and wouldn't answer my phone or door.

My loved ones recognized the suicide attempt I didn't understand.

One day, my family showed up to perform an intervention. Accompanied by a nurse and a representative from a recovery facility in Arizona, they made it clear I was leaving for inpatient care after our discussion.

Unfortunately, Stanley arrived at my house unannounced right as my panic over leaving turned to righteous fury.

When I saw him, I thought he was part of the family meeting. I seethed with pain, assaulting everyone around me with malicious words. To his dismay, this included an unprepared and innocent Stanley.

Someone removed me from the house. I remember a lot of arms and straps. An injection of some sort. Screaming. Then relief.

And I remember the broken expression, full of anguish, on Stanley's face.

So what I am hearing from him in this moment about how he loves me in spite of that day causes my heart to fracture. What kind of a beautiful person can still want to be with me after such destruction?

"Stanley, you've been a valuable friend." I tug at the fringe on the pillow. "I'm overwhelmed by your commitment to me. Especially after what I said to you that day." A tear slips down my cheek, and I wipe it away. "I will always be so thankful for your grace."

Seeing the pools that form in his eyes causes an ache in my chest.

"But I am so sorry. I'm not interested in you in a romantic

way." I bite my lip to hold back more tears. "You are a treasure and such a genuinely good person. Thank you for loving me. I'm just so sorry I don't return your feelings."

He scoots to the edge of the chair, his fists clenched. "How do you know, Meredith? Shouldn't we at least try?"

On an inhale, I grasp at my resolve. "Because I met someone who is also a treasure and a genuinely good person." I offer an apologetic half smile. "Only my feelings for him are different."

What am I doing? Am I channeling my inner teenage girl who likes the handsome man who might never speak to her again? Those stupid YA trilogies are messing with my ability to be logical. As I silently curse Peeta and Four, I lock my gaze with Stanley's.

I have just kicked a puppy.

Standing, he turns to the fireplace. "What do you mean? Who?" He shakes his head and faces me. "Your trip to Colorado. Let me get this straight. I wait for years. For you. You finally decide you're ready, and I miss it by a few weeks?" Crimson anger flushes his cheeks.

"Stanley, I—"

He holds up his hand. "Can he take care of you? How will he know how to help you? Or what you need?" His arms open wide as his voice rises. "I've known you for years, Meredith. That has to count for something."

An unexpected wave of reality sweeps over me. Stanley has known me for years, but he doesn't know me at all.

"Your feelings are honorable, but I think they're misplaced." I whisper my words to soften the blow. "I don't need to be rescued anymore."

His head jerks back. "Tell me who." The quiet, controlled order drips with torment.

"I'm not sure it matters who. More than likely, it won't go anywhere." I clutch the pillow tighter to my stomach. "But I think it matters that I can tell a difference. And I am so sorry."

Stanley's cheek twitches, and he nods. He stares at me for

another miserable few seconds. "Well, then." Looking around the room, he pulls his keys from his pocket. "I should let you go."

We walk to the entryway, and I unlock the door and hold it open.

As he steps onto the porch, he turns and glances over his shoulder. "Take care, Meredith."

Claws of guilt grab my chest. "I'm sorry we lost them." My voice cracks. "I'm sorry you lost Steve."

The sound escaping his mouth is a cross between a scoff and guttural pain. He cranes his neck and focuses on the sky. "Now it feels like I've lost yet another friend."

And on that painful note, my grip on the door is the only thing that keeps me upright as I watch him drive away.

---

A few hours later, I'm still reeling.

Everything's wrong. My top three coping mechanisms didn't work. First, I took a walk and gained nothing but an opportunity to think about what just happened. Second, until I choose to acknowledge Harlan to those around me, talking with Molly or Claire isn't an option. And third, this one possibly being the worst, my long-term companion, chocolate, failed me.

I grab the remote and search on my DVR for my last-ditch effort to find comfort.

Help me, Katniss. I just shot an innocent victim with my bow and arrow.

# 17

**WHACK.**

To my surprise, using a butcher knife can be quite cathartic.

It's Thanksgiving Day, and I haven't heard from Harlan since Sunday. His tired, seemingly apologetic voice filled my voicemail with dull, confusing words about not knowing if he could come to Thanksgiving until the last minute.

Why is he dragging out the slow fade of our relationship when he could sever it with a few words?

"Why do boys have to be so stupid, Aunt Meredith?" My niece, Hannah, rests her hip against the counter and turns to me while I butcher a cauliflower. "I'm serious. Why are they so *stupid*?"

"You're stupid." Her ten-year-old brother, Taylor, ambles to the sink, apparently clueless that his comment just endangered his life.

Whack. Whack. I am really starting to like this butcher knife. "What happened, Hannah Banana?" I ask.

"I'm sure Jackson figured out she's boring." My nephew has put his life on the chopping block. Again.

I lean over and elbow him in admonishment.

Hannah rolls her eyes with such exaggeration, I worry they'll stick behind her eyelids. "I went to homecoming with him. We had fun. He said he'd call, but he didn't."

Whack whack whack. Does she play her dance with Jackson on a torturous looping movie reel the way I play mine with Harlan? "Big jerk," I say to the vegetable in front of me, otherwise known as Harlan's cruciferous head.

"Whoa there, Wolverine." Molly's hands cover mine, and she eases the butcher knife out of my grip. "Let's get you a smaller blade."

"Sure." I angle to the block down the counter and pick a substantially smaller chef's knife. This will do just fine.

Chop. Harlan's lanky carrot figure gets a haircut.

"Anyway, I know football season, especially the playoffs, is super busy." Hannah's fingers make dramatic quotation marks around the words *super busy*. "But he's not too busy"—repeated air quotes, this time with bug eyes—"to hang out with Candace Briggs for study group. Where, I might add, he was seen hugging her afterwards." She throws her arms out in an I-rest-my-case sort of way.

Chop. Chop. Chop. Her story's a little too close to mine for my liking.

"Rebecca says I need to ask him what's going on. Like maybe his parents grounded him from his phone or something. She thinks Candace threw herself at him." Hannah leans in closer to my salad. "Whatever."

Chop chop chop chop chop. "Whatever." I grind my teeth with the forced word.

Molly steps between us. "What is wrong with you?" Her question comes out the side of her mouth while she removes the newest knife from my hand.

I wipe my brow. "Nothing." Nothing at all.

"Boys are stupid." Hannah folds her arms over her chest, glaring at her mother.

"Boys are stupid." I imitate my niece and glare at her mother.

"I think these vegetables have endured enough violence for today. Let's see if you have more gentle ways with the ambrosia salad." Molly takes my elbow and turns me toward the topping and canned fruit. "There's no need to use your aggression. The Cool Whip comes already whipped."

That's unfortunate. Because I am seething.

I've been a simmering pot. Waiting, waiting, waiting, tiny combustible bubbles of emotion on the fringe of the water. Until today.

Today someone turned up the heat, and my feelings are roiling.

This morning my family participated in the Turkey Trot. A three-mile race around downtown Dallas in the most charming display of Thanksgiving pride. When I say charming, I mean 22,000 of our closest friends joined us in the walk. And for 15,840 feet, I listened to Hannah's boy woes. She excelled in fueling the fire under my pot. Roil, boil, roil, boil. Stupid Jackson, stupid Harlan. Stupid Jackson, stupid Harlan.

Clank.

"How could he do that to me?" Hannah, expending too much energy on her crisis to help with Thanksgiving preparations, shakes her long-haired head and waits for my answer.

Clank clank clank clank. Molly misjudged this task. The metal spoon striking the Pyrex glass is quite therapeutic.

I put the bowl on the granite island, turn to Hannah, and take hold of her shoulders. "I don't know, Hannah. How could he do that to you? He said he would call." My exclamation is punctuated with a gentle shake, and I draw her into me for an overzealous hug.

Are her raging pheromones contagious?

Molly moves behind her daughter and mouths to me, *What is going on?*

*Solidarity*, I mouth back.

"Girls are dumb." Taylor strolls by and takes a swipe of Cool Whip out of my bowl. "I'm going to watch football."

"Shut up, Taylor." Hannah clutches me tighter. "You don't understand anything. Gah."

"Anything." I stick my tongue out at innocent-bystander Taylor. No one understands anything.

I've gone to the Bad Place.

"I just want to throw my cell phone away." Hannah muffles my fantasy into my shoulder.

Yes. Let's throw all cell phones away. Because if I check mine one more time without having any new messages, I'm going to scream. I'm stuck in Teenager-Waiting-for-a-Call Land, and it is worse than I remembered.

"Come on, Banana. Let's do it." I dig into the back pocket of my jeans and pull out my phone, hating myself when I glance at the screen one last time. Opening the trash can drawer, I drop it on top of the vegetable rejects.

Hannah freezes, her mouth gaping. "Um, Aunt Meredith, I can't throw mine away. I was going to invite him to Thanksgiving if he called." She stares wistfully at her phone. "Maybe you should call my phone and see if it's working."

Maybe I should never tell anyone that this morning I called my phone from her phone to see if mine was working. I look at the ceiling. "Whatever." Gah.

Leaning into the waste bin to retrieve the bane of my existence, I think I hear something. "Was that the doorbell? Mom and Dad can't be back from their ice run so soon."

Molly scoots past me and rinses a long-handled spoon in the sink. "It could be Stanley."

Her words register as I wipe my phone with a dish towel. I whirl my head in her direction. "What?"

"I invited him to join us for Thanksgiving." She opens the dishwasher and places a silicone spoonula in the top rack. "But he was kind of weird about it. I don't know if he's coming or not." Molly shuts the dishwasher and snaps it closed with her hip. "Taylor, grab the door, please."

I drop my head in my hands. This is it. I'm going to kill my sister. And my only defense is fake teenage hormones.

Muffled voices float to the kitchen. Taylor yells something in our direction, but I don't catch the words because I'm in a panic to appear busy. I snag the bowl of Cool Whip and vigorously fold the canned fruit into the creamy substance. Clank, scoop, clank, scoop. This will be the most thoroughly mixed ambrosia salad in the history of Thanksgiving.

"Aunt Meredith." Taylor's voice is closing in on us, and my heart beats faster. "Did you hear what I said? Harlan Holcombe is at our door. Hercules is here."

Clank, clank, thud.

"What did he say?" I have no idea if I whispered the question because alarms are going off in my head. Piercing, clanging, find-an-exit, stop-drop-and-roll, save-yourself, what-is-happening alarms.

"He said he's an idiot." Hannah picks up my spoon, shoves it in her mouth, and turns on her heel to leave the room. "I'll go see who it is."

"Molly." My voice croaks. "I think I need to tell you something."

I'm paralyzed. All my body can do is stand frozen. Waiting. Watching.

The screech Hannah produces has the potential to shatter the crystal goblets I set out for the meal.

Molly takes a step forward. "What's going on?"

A puff of air escapes my lips. "I might have invited a friend to Thanksgiving."

Hannah's burst into the room causes me to jump. She bounces, her face lit up, eyes darting between her mother and me. "This is sooooo much better than Jackson coming over for Thanksgiving," she breathes.

Before I can explain, react, feel, or hide, Harlan Holcombe saunters into the room.

Harlan.

Holcombe.

In my kitchen.

Not just Harlan Holcombe. Harlan Holcombe and his smile are in my kitchen. He might be wearing irresistibly attractive faded jeans with boots and a wrinkled button-down chambray shirt. But man. His smile has superpowers, and my bitter teen-age angst melts like ice cream on a summer Texas sidewalk. That smile can't silence my doubts from the last few weeks, but it sure can quiet them down to a dull roar.

For now.

He raises his eyebrows. "Happy Thanksgiving?"

I shake my head, trying to clear my brain, and can't really help the smile on my face. "Yes." My legs wobble as I move forward. "Yes. Happy Thanksgiving."

Once I'm in range, he pulls me to him, wrapping one arm around my shoulders and one around my waist in everything that a hug is supposed to be.

"Hi." His deep voice rumbles in my ear, and something zings through me. "Hope it's okay that I surprised you."

Was my moan audible? As I release him, I step back to Molly.

"Okay. Okay. Sure. Everyone, this is Harlan." My open palm gestures in his direction, as if they don't know who I'm talking about. *Get a grip, Meredith.* "Harlan, this is my sister, Molly, her two kids, Taylor and Hannah, and somewhere is her husband, Michael. He'll be in soon to pull the turkey from the oven. Mom and Dad ran to the store for ice."

Harlan leans forward to grasp Molly's hand.

She stares at him, eyes squinting, forehead scrunched as if she's trying to work out a complicated math problem in her head.

Hannah giggles through her own handshake with him, but she's holding herself together well for someone who truly is infested with the plague of adolescence.

Taylor gives him a "hey man" type of greeting, and both guys turn to observe the room of giddy girls.

Not taking her eyes off Harlan, Molly grabs my forearm and tugs me to her. "You weren't drunk that night at the Broadmoor. You totally danced with Harlan Holcombe."

"Aunt Meredith was drunk?" Taylor voices his question to his mom, but Hannah blurts out another giggle in response.

Great. More to sort out later. No need for my niece and nephew to think their aunt is a lush.

Still clutching my arm, Molly gawks. "Dear Lord. It's like staring at the sun. He's so pretty, my eyes are burning."

"Mom," Hannah hisses as her entire body lurches in our direction. "Stop talking. I'm begging you."

Harlan's lips twitch, and he glances at me.

Molly gasps, faces me, and clutches my bicep. "Are you dying? Is this some kind of Make-A-Wish thing?"

A small burst of laughter escapes my mouth as my gaze locks with Harlan's, and I shake my head.

"Should I leave the room?" Harlan asks Taylor.

"No. Stay here." Taylor widens his stance and crosses his arms. "This is when it gets good."

Molly peeks at Harlan, then back to me. "What I can't understand is how you were normal enough to meet him."

Yanking my arm from her hold, I glare at my sister. "I did just fine, thank you very much."

Harlan stares down to his boots while his shoulders shake.

"What?" My arms go out in question. "I think my issue has to do with the little amount of time I spend with famous people."

"Oh, please." My sister folds her hands in a praying position. "Please, Meredith—"

"If I had gotten more time with Rachael Ray—"

"Aaaaaaanndd here we go." She sighs.

"—I think she would have understood my Adult Easy-Bake Oven design. We would have bonded and become best friends."

"No, sweetie." Molly pats my hand. "That was never going to happen. No amount of time changes the fact that in a sixty-second book signing, you pitched the idea of the microwave to a beloved chef."

Harlan grimaces. "That's rough."

I grab a dish towel and wrap it around my hand. Traitor. Does no one understand my ingenious concept?

Molly offers Harlan a tight smile. "That's when we came up with the rule."

Harlan's gleaming eyes sear into mine. "So . . ."

"Yeah." Molly nods. "She can't do famous people. Hence the Famous People Probation." She steps toward Harlan and swirls her finger in the air, directing him to turn around. "So we're going to have to ask you to leave."

"Mom!" Hannah's hummingbird presence takes a splat into a window.

Molly shrugs. "Or give up your super successful career, disappear for about five years, and reenter our lives as a carpenter. Then you might have a shot at being her friend."

"I think I'll take my chances." Harlan's amused brown eyes cut to Molly, then return to me. "Besides, *People* magazine passed on me this year. Which means I'm not as famous as I was when I met her. Things should go a lot smoother now."

"You were robbed," Hannah says under her breath.

Harlan hears it and winks at me.

The YouTube sensation about him died down weeks ago, and *People* magazine's Sexiest Man Alive issue came out this week without mention of the hometown hero. Now he's just movie-star Harlan. Except really, now he's just a man standing in my kitchen with dark circles of exhaustion under his eyes, but eyes full of vulnerable hope nonetheless.

*What happened to you over the last six weeks?* I know he was filming. I know he said he would be busy. But was it more?

"Well, Harlan Holcombe," my sister says, "welcome to our family Thanksgiving. I'm hoping we don't scare you away before dessert, but if we do, it was wonderful to meet you." Molly shifts my direction, and in a quick private moment with me, she bugs out her eyes. "You have a lot of explaining to do."

Trying to conceal my giggle, I cover my mouth and cough just as I hear my parents enter the house through the front door and call out their greetings.

I shoot a panicked look between Harlan and Molly.

My mom walks into the kitchen. "Oh, good, you've all met Harlan."

Because the last five minutes weren't bizarre enough, this happens right as my dad scoots into the room and gives Harlan a manly pound on the back. "Come on in here, son. We'll find a football game while they finish the meal preparations."

Harlan jerks his chin up at me, winks, and leaves the room with my dad.

Glancing around, I take note that we all appear related not because of our common genetics but because of the matching gaping mouths.

My mom approaches and wraps her arm around my waist in a side hug. "He's a nice boy, Meredith."

"But how did you . . . ?"

"He was getting out of his car when we left the house. Don't tell your father, but I think I saw that young man without his shirt on once. All the ladies at Wednesday morning Bible study were watching something on YouTube. If I recall, he has a nice chest."

I'm worried Hannah's head is going to explode after hearing her grandmother talk about seeing a man's pecs. "Gramma. Gah."

My head may explode too, but for different reasons.

Molly turns to her kids, snaps her fingers, and holds out her hand. "Hannah and Taylor. Phones. Now."

The memory of Harlan's pecs is snatched from my mind as reality sinks in. "Oh my gosh. Yes. You guys, you cannot tell your friends he's here. No pictures. No posting anything, anywhere."

"Huh." My mom furrows her brow while she fiddles with her

phone. "I should probably take down the selfie of Harlan and me on my Facebook page."

"Mother." I hold my hand out, opening and closing my fingers twice.

"Look at that. Seventy-two likes." She looks at the screen and her smile wanes. "Oh. Kathryn messaged and she wants to meet him."

"Mom. Gah." I make an unsuccessful nab for the phone.

Hannah snickers.

"I'll fix it." My mom shoos me off. "I'll tell her it was my first attempt at Photoshop."

"Okay. Everybody out." My firstborn, drill-sergeant sister swirls her finger in the air, directing everyone to the door. "There's a Thanksgiving meal to prepare, an explanation to be told, and a famous person in the living room. Man your stations."

Molly stashes the confiscated phones on top of the refrigerator while everyone else shuffles out of the kitchen. The only action I'm capable of right now is blinking.

What just happened? *Blink.*

Why is he here? *Blink.*

How am I nauseated but also full of glee? *Blink.*

With a drone-like perspective of the bigger picture, I pull back. And then it hits me.

"I should have told everyone." Small, panicked thoughts pelt me like a hard rain. Staring aimlessly at the living room, I whisper to no one, "I should have asked if this was okay. Taylor and Hannah were so close to Steve and the kids—what if this hurts them? What if Mom thinks it's too soon to bring someone home? What if Dad doesn't approve?"

Molly takes my hand. "Meredith. It's okay." She squeezes.

Tears prick my eyes. "I want everyone to be normal. If they want to talk about Clayton or Chloe, I want them to tell their stories. And if a memory of Steve comes to mind, they should voice it. I know I didn't tell you anything about Harlan, but he would want us to be normal." My gaze turns to Molly and I swallow.

Her smiling face surprises me. "You asked a handsome man to Thanksgiving. Other than your not sharing the girly details with me, it's fine." She grabs my other hand. "It's time. We all knew this was coming someday."

"Yeah?" I release the word on a shaky breath.

"Maybe not the part where you bring home a movie star." She chuckles, our hands shaking with her laughter. "But we all understood this day would come."

Something small and far away aches inside of me. I miss this Molly. Before life imploded, she was my person. But our relationship morphed into a codependent puzzle that's missing pieces, and neither of us can decipher how to put it back together.

Molly lowers her chin and peers into my eyes. "You wouldn't have asked him here if he wasn't safe. You and I will lead the discussion at dinner by example. Everyone will follow. It will be okay, Meredith."

The downpour of my anxiety decreases to a light drizzle.

But even though her words were calming, her current expression is unreadable. "What are you not saying?" I ask.

"Nothing. I'm withholding my opinions until later."

On a giant exhale, I release some of the tension. "Thank you."

She drops my hands, ambles to the silverware drawer, and pulls out another spoon. "But don't think you're getting away with anything. I want details later. All of them."

She offers the utensil to me and nods to the unfinished ambrosia salad.

I wave off the spoon. Surveying the remaining jobs to be done in the kitchen, I figure out what will help my current emotional state. "I need the cleaver. And the turkey."

---

"Another beautiful bird, Meredith." My mom walks into the dining room, nodding at our turkey in the middle of the table.

"It's only still beautiful because I hid the cleaver from her." At Molly's statement, everyone groans in agreement.

Everyone except Harlan. He hasn't been exposed to the abstract art that is my cutting of the turkey.

We create a circle, connecting our hands for the prayer my dad will pray.

Harlan follows suit.

We bow our heads and listen as my father leads our prayer of gratitude. At the end, his voice takes on a gruff tone and he pauses. "Today we are thankful for the old and the new. Amen."

The echoed "Amen" is tentative at best. There's always an elephant in the room. I just didn't realize my dad would invite it to the table.

Darting glances at everyone, I move to my seat. Harlan moves to the one next to me. Steve's spot.

Everyone stills.

My mom stares at him while he sits. "Perfect." She clears her throat. "Let's be seated."

Following her lead, the others take their chairs.

If Harlan is thrown off, he doesn't show it. But I don't think there's any way he can miss the heaviness in the air.

Sounds of clanking silverware fill the room as we unroll our napkins and release the spoons, knives, and forks.

"Meredith"—Harlan points to the turkey—"since this bird is sitting in front of me, would you like me to do the honors?"

Without my consent, tears sting my nose. That was Steve's job. It was always Steve's job. My father filling in the last few years has been a silent reminder of our loss. But Harlan's request to carve the turkey is a screaming announcement of it.

I shrink into my chair and look down at the table. I am an idiot. I've placed Harlan in a field of emotional land mines. It will be a miracle if any of us make it out alive.

Molly, seated next to me, reaches under the table for my leg and offers a squeeze of support. Or maybe it's that she can't bear the stress of waiting for Dad to respond. Either way, I'm thankful for the contact.

"Son, since you're our guest, I'll take a crack at it." My dad rescues all of us, stands, and positions himself closer to the turkey. He claps Harlan on the shoulder. "Thank you for the offer, though."

I catch Harlan's uncomfortable smile at my dad, and my heart sinks.

In taut silence, we pass the side dishes while Dad works on the turkey, handing out slices as he goes.

"Harlan," my mom says while scooping green beans out of a casserole dish, "does your family do anything special for Thanksgiving?"

"Yes, ma'am." Harlan grabs a roll from the basket in front of him. "Once we recover from the big meal, we play a huge game of Monopoly. It goes on for hours. Through the first round of desserts, the leftovers, the evening coffee. Some years we play late into the night." He hands the basket to Taylor. "I was wondering if Taylor and Hannah wanted to play later."

With wide eyes, I stare at Taylor. His grinding teeth are his only response.

Michael shoots a compassionate look to me, then quietly says to Taylor, "Can you pass the salt, son?"

Sweet, well-intentioned, clueless Harlan concentrates on spreading butter on his roll. "I'm usually the race car."

Hannah snaps her napkin down on the table, causing me to jump at the abrupt sound. "Uncle Steve was the—"

"Hannah." Molly flashes an admonishing glare at her daughter.

"No, Mom." Her blazing eyes brim with tears. "You guys tell us we should talk about Uncle Steve, Clayton, and Chloe whenever we want to. So I'm going to now."

Harlan gently sets his roll and knife down and gives my niece his complete focus.

Hannah balls her hand into a fist. "Uncle Steve was the car. Chloe was too little. But Clayton played with the shoe because he liked to say the word. Only he said it wrong and it came out 'soo.'

We all thought it was cute, but you were worried he was going to swallow the piece. Remember, Aunt Meredith?"

"I remember, sweetie." I offer a watery smile with my whispered words.

Harlan folds his hands in front of him and massages the inside of one with a thumb. "I, uh . . ." His eyes down, he nods. "I really messed this up, didn't I?"

I reach over and cover his fidgeting hands with mine.

"I'm sorry, you guys. Sometimes I dive in too fast without thinking." He shrugs, shaking his head, still looking down. "Maybe I should leave."

I close my eyes, and a tear escapes.

But a clap from the opposite end of the table jolts all our attention.

"All right," my mother says in a commanding tone. "Harlan, we're learning how to navigate this part of life right alongside you. There's no need to apologize. Sometimes it gets a little messy. But if you can handle a few tears in your mashed potatoes, we'd love for you to stay."

He fixes his eyes on my niece. "Hannah, would it be better for you if I left and came back another time?"

I suck in a breath.

Something works behind her eyes. After a beat, she sits up straight. "Instead of the race car, I think you should be the top hat. Because you're in show business."

Harlan takes a moment to swallow. "I think," he says, his voice low, "that's a really great idea."

The deflating tension is almost tangible, and I release my hold on Harlan. When he shifts his focus to me, I offer him a smile of forced confidence.

We defused that bomb.

But whether it be during this meal or on another day, there will be more explosions of grief. And I wonder if Harlan will want to stick around in the craters left behind.

# 18

FOR SOME INEXPLICABLE REASON, my mom, sister, and niece tackle the Black Friday sales every year. I've never done the calculations, but I don't think the savings balance out the post-shopping-massage costs.

Still, they insist on going.

Leaning against the doorjamb to the kitchen, I observe the planning process. The Pentagon's got nothing on these women.

A few hours ago, our Thanksgiving feast covered the table. Now the surface is littered with innumerable print ads, prioritized shopping lists, and one color-coded master map of the DFW area. I think all they're missing are live feeds of the storefronts, and it wouldn't shock me if those appear as midnight approaches.

"You going to join them?" Harlan's deep voice surprises me almost as much as his hand grazing the small of my back.

I lurch forward, and he grabs my elbow to steady me as he walks past. When he reaches the table, he scans the situation room.

"Aunt Meredith isn't allowed to go." Hannah outs me while crouching over a flyer from Abercrombie & Fitch.

I roll my eyes. "It's not that I'm not allowed to go. I just don't want to go."

"Also, you aren't allowed." Molly yanks the flyer away from Hannah and examines the model on the page.

Mom leans over to look at the picture. "That girl forgot to wear pants for this photo shoot."

Harlan grunts. "Why isn't Meredith allowed to go?"

"She hates shopping. It's her one flaw." Hannah smiles at me. "I still love her."

Molly harrumphs. "Hates? She sucks the life out of any momentary shopping joy. Small or big."

I throw my arms out. "Can we not do this right now?"

My family made it through the Thanksgiving meal without any embarrassing stories. I made it through the feast without hyperventilating. So far, I'm counting today as a win. But now we're on shaky ground.

"Sure." Molly tucks the half-naked A&F ad under a HomeGoods flyer.

"There's no need to tell Harlan she got kicked out of Dillard's. They lifted the ban after her appeal to the manager." My mother pulls another sales announcement from Hannah's pile and points to the scantily clad woman. "This one is wearing her little sister's shorts. Does she not know it's wintertime?"

Harlan glances at me, taking a sip of his coffee with a smile partially hidden behind the rim of his cup.

Molly grabs the latest half-naked-model picture and shoves it in the pile to join its cohort. "You should be glad they didn't make you pay for the mannequin."

"I was hangry." I shake my head. "And I had to go to the bathroom. No one should shop under those harsh conditions."

Molly taps her finger on her upper lip. "True. Which is why we implemented mandatory snack times the following year."

"Was that the time she fell asleep in the Gap dressing room?" Now my mom is throwing me under the proverbial shopping bus.

"Yeah, that was the last trip she was allowed to go with us." Hannah sneaks a Target flyer over the Victoria's Secret ad on the top of her pile.

Bless her heart. No way is her mom letting her buy underwear from VS.

Harlan scratches the stubble on his cheek. "What do you have against shopping?"

"Nothing. I like shopping sprints. But these absurd people like shopping marathons." I decide to change the topic before they point out more of my questionable shopping history. "What I want to know is who's going to help me sort the change this year?"

Between my dad and Taylor in the living room and the women in the dining room, a collective moan rolls through the house.

"That's what I thought." I point my accusing finger at each person. "Did you at least bring your change jars?"

"They're in the guest room," Taylor calls from the couch. "I put them in there when I showed Harlan where to put his luggage."

All the oxygen leaves my body, and a tense vibe fills the room. Heat creeps up my face. Of course he's staying here. I told him he could stay here. But I didn't tell my family about his impending visit.

Harlan's blank-faced stare locks on me.

I swallow and shift my gaze to my mom.

"I hope you changed the bedding for Hercules. Greek gods shouldn't sleep on floral Laura Ashley sheets." My mother winks at me while everyone releases the tension with laughter.

But when I glance at Molly, she stares at me with enigmatic eyes. This doesn't bode well.

"Come on, Harlan. Let's go sort the change." I nod in the direction of the guest room.

"Save yourself," Michael says, while at the same time, without taking his eyes off the Cowboys game, my dad says, "Send up a flare when you get bored."

Harlan enters the guest room behind me. "What have I gotten myself into?"

Funny. I was just thinking the same thing myself. There's a low-level pressure system between Harlan and me that I don't want to address. It feels like it's either going to turn into a storm or simmer out, unaddressed. I don't like either forecast. I want to know what he's thinking and why he's here.

Instead, I decide to keep to the topic at hand. "Every year, my family collects all their spare change. We pool it together, split the total, and that's our shopping budget for Black Friday."

Harlan's eyes widen at the jars on the bed. They vary in size, but each family member has their own glass container with their name painted on the top. "Where did you get this idea?"

I sigh. "With all of this stupid money from Steve's insurance policies, suddenly there were no spending boundaries. I know it sounds weird, but there has to be a limit. It's not reality that someone gets to buy whatever they want, whenever they want. Spare change sets my limit for post–Thanksgiving Day shopping." I shrug. "My family decided to join me."

Expressionless, Harlan blinks.

"However, they are total slackers when it comes to the actual coin conversion." Returning Harlan's stare, I gnaw on my lip. "What?"

"That is oddly refreshing." He steps toward me and takes on a serious tone. "So, when I got here, I just dove into Thanksgiving with your family. But it feels like maybe we need to talk."

Apparently he feels the tension too. Of course he does. I think the fact that he wants to talk about it should be a good thing, but the pit in my stomach doesn't want to go anywhere near that conversation.

I glance to the door of the bedroom and nod in the direction of my family. "Maybe not here?"

He nods slowly, assessing. "Okay. Then what's next for these coins? This sounds like it might be fun."

I glance down at the bed, my stomach relieved we aren't talking about us, but still holding a knot of tension knowing that discussion is coming. Maybe our errand will smooth things over.

"Yeah, well, you might not think so after loading and unloading these jars." I pick up the smallest container of coins. "Let's go, Hercules. Show me what you can do. We're loading up and headed to Walmart."

With a wry smile, Harlan leans over to grab the two largest jars. His broad, muscular shoulders strain his shirt.

As I enjoy the scenery, I realize I'm brilliant. Ask the in-shape, beautiful man to lift heavy things. Suddenly I'm overwhelmed with the need to rearrange the furniture in my entire house.

Harlan breaks me out of my trance. "Lead the way, sweetheart."

The endearment causes my gut to clench and brings me back to reality. What is going on? Are we acting like this is normal? Is he going to bring up Olivia or am I?

As we drive, the leaky question faucet drips and drips, the pooling water threatening to break the dam holding back my anxiety.

---

Once we arrive at Walmart, Harlan pulls his frayed, faded ball cap low over his brow. He hops out of the car to grab a cart, then grins at me. "Let's load up the booty."

"What did you say about my booty?" My mouth had a mind of its own with that question, and I slap a hand over it before it says anything else without proper censoring.

Harlan stops the cart, throws his head back, and laughs.

The view is so mesmerizing, it erases my embarrassment. I giggle, shoulders shaking. "Sorry." I pick up one of the change jars and place it in the corner of the cart. "You don't have to go in the store if you don't want to. But, just saying, you'll miss the best part."

"What's the best part?" He does that attractive lifting-heavy-things act again, and I mentally applaud myself for bringing him.

"Watching the coins go down the chute, as the total gets higher and higher." I lift Mom's jar and place it in the opposite corner. "Total rush."

"I didn't come all this way to miss the fun part. Let's do this." After unloading the final container, he moves the cart aside and closes the back of my SUV. "But I am going to need some help maneuvering this thing." He shifts his hands to the right side of the cart's push bar and nods at the open spot he created for me.

"Wow, you really are a good actor. Your movies make you seem so strong and manly. I didn't realize you're such a wimp."

Harlan's gaping mouth turns into a knowing grin. "Yup." He shoves my shoulder with his. "Poor little ol' me needs some help."

Once we enter the store and approach the Coinstar machine, the anticipation takes over. I clap my hands and rub them together. "Are you ready?"

He chuckles. "I think so."

Our two-person system works well. He pours the coins on the metal shelf, and I put my hands on them to even the layers out as they slide into the machine. The raining coins clink melodiously down the shaft. As our treasure falls, the digital display tallies our bounty.

Turning to Harlan, I nod in the direction of the total. "What did I tell you? Isn't this fun to watch?"

His intense gaze doesn't leave mine. "Yes. It is."

I gulp and turn back to pluck at coins lodged in the crevice.

About three-fourths of the way through, I cannot believe what I'm seeing. I jump up and down on my toes. "Stop. Stop dumping coins."

Harlan pulls back the jar in his hands. "What is it? Are you okay?"

"This is amazing." I reach into the pile of change lined up for the chute to oblivion. "Look!" I shove a silver hoop earring in his face.

"An earring?" Harlan scratches a spot above his eyebrow.

"I've been looking for this earring for five months. Do you know what a find this is?" I draw the earring up and survey the damage. A little polish will go a long way.

Harlan squints. "Meredith, you're acting like you won the lottery."

I glance around, and sure enough, an older couple at the customer service desk is staring at us. The coin machine happens to be next to the lotto machine.

"I did win the lottery. It's my lost earring."

The woman at the service desk holds up her phone and takes a picture of Harlan and me.

"That woman just captured you trading in coins for cash," I say, "and I'm a little worried that picture is going to go viral with some post about a destitute actor collecting coins."

He glances at the woman and back to me. "Good. Keeps them guessing. Tell me more about this earring."

I hold it close to his face. "I thought I was losing my mind. I couldn't find this earring anywhere. I never replaced it because I refused to believe it was gone."

I rub it with my shirttail while Harlan finishes processing the coins. As I float on the clouds of my earring victory, we take our receipt from the machine to the customer service desk.

"I can't believe it. Can you believe it?" Gliding to the car, I cradle the treasured jewelry in my hand.

He opens my car door for me. "Sweetheart, how much did that earring cost you?"

"Well, the pair was $20." I hold it out for him to take another look at my precious commodity. "So not cheap."

He glances down at the earring. "Uh-huh."

"What?" I ask as he closes my door.

He rounds the car and gets into the passenger seat. "Refreshing."

I put the key in the ignition and start the car. "What's that supposed to mean?"

"We just traded in coins for $527.45 worth of cash. Mind you, not a shabby amount. But you are doing the happy dance because you found the lost half of earrings costing $20. A pair you refused to replace five months ago when you noticed it was gone."

I look back over my shoulder for pedestrians and catch his gaze. "And?"

"And that makes you . . . refreshing."

I am so zeroed in on getting ready to reverse the car, I don't notice him closing the gap between us. I turn my head and his face is an inch from mine. "Oh."

He pulls back and glances to my lips. "Olivia is financially conniving. It gets exhausting."

If he had punched me in the stomach, it would have felt better.

No. No, I counter myself. The hit to the gut is good. I needed a reality check.

"I'm sorry about that." My voice sounds flatter than I want it to be. I adjust the rearview mirror and put my hand on the gearshift.

Harlan covers my hand with his and stops the reverse motion. "Hey. Are you okay?"

"Fine." I force my brightest smile.

"Meredith." Concern etches his face, and he squeezes my hand. "What's going on?"

"Nothing. I need to get back to my family, and you need to get back to yours." Tears sting my nose.

"I need to—" He stares out the front of the car for a long moment, then back to me. "Why do I have the feeling no one in your family knew I might come today?"

My face fills with heat, and those stupid, stupid tears threaten to spill. I shrug and turn to look out the driver's side window.

He leans over and angles himself to me. "Did you not think I was coming?"

I curl a strand of hair around my ear. "How would I have

known you were coming?" My quivering voice does nothing to help my effort to appear casual.

"How would you have—" Harlan slams his body back into the seat. "Because I told you I was coming. That's how we left things. I was coming for Thanksgiving."

"That's how we left things? On Sunday, *this week*, you said you didn't know if you could make it." A tear escapes and I quickly wipe it away.

"Yes." His hand swoops through the air. "But on Sunday I also told you to assume I was coming unless you heard otherwise. That I thought I could work it out. *That's* how we left things."

My face is on fire for a different reason now. "Harlan, I barely heard from you for six weeks. How was I supposed to know what you were thinking?"

He shakes his head. "Sweetheart, I told you this shoot was going to be intense and you might not hear from me much. In the middle of it all, I had some unexpected travel . . . There was just a lot going on. But I'm confused." He turns to take my hands in his. "I thought we were on the same page."

"Harlan, I heard your words." I huff. "But I mean, what woman thinks a guy is still interested when all he gives her are a few voicemails, texts, and conversations that don't last more than ten minutes?"

"But I sent you a blanket," he says.

My indignation deflates some at the mention of his incredibly thoughtful gift on Chloe's birthday. "You did," I say quietly. "And I truly appreciated it. I just found the rest of your actions really confusing."

"But that's how we left things. At the hotel. I told you to trust me."

I pull my hands back. "It was, Harlan. It's how we left things. And for seven glorious minutes, I thought I could do it. Right up until I ran back into the hotel to go to the bathroom and I saw you holding Olivia." The last few words are pushed through a tremble, and two more tears escape.

Harlan closes his eyes. "Olivia." The guttural word is said like a curse. He rubs his hands over his face.

I swipe away tears and release a breath. My body mirrors his, and we both stare out the front of the car in silence.

"I was ecstatic, Meredith. You got on that shuttle, and I felt hope I haven't felt in a long time. And then my feet hit the lobby. Olivia was there, tears streaming down her face, holding our daughter." He shakes his head. "Her dad had just gotten a terminal pancreatic cancer diagnosis."

A pit forms in my stomach.

"I make it a point to interact with Olivia as little as possible," he says. "But Alex's PawPaw was sick. And in the moment you saw, I had to make a choice to support my daughter by supporting her mother."

I feel sick.

I know better than to jump to conclusions, but I hurled myself off the cliff without a parachute anyway.

"You're a good daddy," I whisper.

"Olivia's family is in Denver. I've spent the last six weeks traveling back and forth with Alex in tow. My director wasn't pleased with me. We moved her dad twice. Alex got sick. Olivia kept calling, and she was a complete mess every time I picked up the phone."

Leaning forward to rest my forehead on the steering wheel, I shake my head. I failed him. He needed support from me, and instead I distanced myself.

He runs a hand over his face. "He passed away, and the funeral was Tuesday. I didn't know if Olivia could still handle having Alex for Thanksgiving, but I didn't want to cancel on you."

I sit up and ask gently, "Why didn't you say something?"

"I thought about it, but you were a little skittish before leaving Colorado. And I didn't want Olivia seeping into our new relationship. I was trying to protect you." He presses against the headrest but turns his head to look at me. "And none of that matters because your last image of me was with her."

"She's going to be in your life long-term, Harlan. Whoever you decide to have a relationship with will need to understand this and learn to cope."

"Whoever I decide . . ." A dark expression covers his face before he masks it.

"This all sounds like a nightmare for you," I say. "I wish I had known, just so I could have listened. Been a friend."

"Whoever I decide to have a relationship with is *you*, Meredith." He shakes his head, then looks at me, sincere and imploring. "I messed up. I should have told you everything. Right from the beginning. I'm so sorry."

I nod, conflicted. He just told me he wanted to be in a relationship with me, and he apologized. But something is warring behind his eyes.

"But, Meredith," he says. It's not a tone I've heard from him. It's frustrated, almost impatient. "I'm having a hard time right now understanding why you ghosted me."

Almost offended at the thought, I say, "I didn't ghost you."

"You absolutely did." I open my mouth to deny it, but he continues. "You didn't respond to my texts. You didn't return my calls. You made assumptions and you stopped talking to me."

"It wasn't like I pulled something out of a hat. I had good reason to think what I did."

"Meredith." He rubs his forehead, and it's obvious he's trying to calm his tone. "Why didn't you just ask me?"

My chest rises and falls with heavy breaths. Guilt slinks into the memory of the day I saw him holding Olivia. I should have. I should have found the courage to ask him.

"I—" Tears hit the backs of my eyes. "I was afraid it was true. I was afraid that my feelings for you were one-sided and that the embrace with Olivia meant something else. So if I didn't talk to you, I didn't have to hear you say it first. I could just go on with my life."

His tone shifts to compassion with a slightly drawn-out "Sweetheart."

"I'm sorry I didn't trust you," I say with a watery smile. "And I'm sorry I ghosted you."

He cups my face and runs his thumb across my cheek. When he pulls back, he raises a finger as if to tell me to pause, takes his cell out of his back pocket, and presses a few commands on the screen.

The iconic sound of ABBA fills my car, and the background singers ask me to take a chance on them. Without breaking eye contact, I slide my phone out of my coat pocket and answer. "Hello?"

"I miss you. I just wanted to hear your voice. I've booked my ticket for Thanksgiving and can't wait to see you." Harlan gifts me with a full smile and shining eyes. He holds his finger up again. "Don't move."

Opening his car door, he shoves the phone back into his pocket. Through the rearview mirror, I watch him stalk around the back of the vehicle, and my belly does giddy flip-flops. He raps on my window three times.

I smile like an idiot as I open the door.

The smooth mover leans across me, presses my seat belt release button, and orders gently, "Hop on out, sweetheart."

The next thing I know, Harlan slides his arms around my waist and pulls me into a tight embrace. A low groan fills my ear, and something in me stirs.

I stand on my tiptoes and wrap my arms around his shoulders.

"I've been dying to do this all day," he says in a thick voice.

I am putty at those words, molding myself to his frame. His hand at my lower back pushes me closer, while the fingertips of his other hand graze up and down my spine as he kisses me, gentle at first, then with more intent. It's PDA at its best, and I'm here for it.

Before I figure out how we can remain like this forever, making out in the Walmart parking lot, he pulls back and rests his forehead on mine.

"Well." A smile tugs at my mouth. "I thought you were letting me go because of the eternal 'stop the snoring ladies' message I left on your voicemail."

"Are you kidding?" His thumb rubs across my waist. "I've listened to that message a thousand times. It's going in the permanent collection."

I chuckle and move in to brush my lips against his one more time.

When he pulls back, he pats me on the hip. "Come on, sweetheart. Let's get your booty home."

# 19

"COFFEE." **MOLLY DRAGS** herself into the kitchen, armed for Black Friday in deep purple leggings, a gray tunic, and running shoes.

Turning, I nod to the carafe. "Fully leaded with all the fixings. Where are the kids?"

"Passed out on the couch." She squints, studying my face. "It's six o'clock in the morning. Are you wearing makeup?"

Heat creeps up my neck as I wipe my hands on a dish towel. "You guys didn't have to get here this early. I told you I'd take care of the pre-shopping breakfast."

Molly turns her back to me to pour the caffeine into a blue stoneware mug. "Yes, but we have to talk. Where's pretty boy?"

*We have to talk.*

In the history of humankind, those four words have never meant anything good. Especially from Molly.

Instead, I focus my thoughts on Harlan. I attempt to sound casual about him but am thwarted by my giddy smile. "He went for a run and will be back in a little while."

Glancing at the cookbook on the counter, I make a mental note of the items needed.

She taps a packet of stevia. "Then start talking. Mom and Dad will also be here soon, and you have some ground to cover. Beginning with how you broke your Famous People Probation."

Knocking out two tasks at one time, I peruse the cabinets for various ingredients while diving into the story of how I met the handsome Hercules. After tales of the now legendary dance, the drama at the zoo, and our long conversations, I detail the last six weeks.

As I wait for Molly's reaction, I gnaw on my bottom lip.

"You rejected Stanley?" her incredulous voice booms.

Of course out of all those details, she homes in on Stanley.

"Hush." As I open the refrigerator door to grab homemade dough, I glance into the living room. Thank goodness Taylor and Hannah are still conked out on the couch.

My sister shakes her head. "No one is more committed to you than Stanley."

Her disapproval sears frustration through me. "But it's not real."

"You think Harlan is real?" She hitches her thumb. "This guy is Chad Tarkington. What does Claire have to say about this?"

My shoulders slump. I haven't told Claire because she's had a busy fall in the classroom, which made it easier to avoid, and for six weeks I didn't know if there was anything to tell. I was confused, embarrassed, and hurt, all of which are things I usually tell my best friend. I'm going to have to call her as soon as I can. No, not a call. This conversation requires us to be in person and eating chocolate.

I deal with the matter at hand. "Chad Tarkington is Chad Tarkington because I never saw him again after camp. Harlan is here. In my house. You watched him yesterday. He hung out with our family, fit in naturally, and enjoyed himself. Do you think this is real?"

She stares for a beat and exhales with a regretful smile. "Yeah. I do."

"But?" Throwing flour on the counter, I prepare to roll out the dough.

She places her cup down. "Meredith, you aren't normal."

The words knock the breath out of me.

"I'm not just being a big sister here." Her voice lowers. "If he breaks your heart, it might break you."

My gasp cannot mask the bruise of her blow. "But that's going to be the case with anyone. I either risk now or risk later. Do you want me to be alone the rest of my life?" I dump the dough, causing a halo of flour to poof into the air.

"It's not that simple, Meredith, and you know it. What if something happens and you come undone? Do you want me to remind you what the last four Christmases were like?"

I pummel the dough flat with a little more force than necessary. "Harlan and I haven't even talked about Christmas yet."

"You will. You will because yesterday was real. He likes you." She draws her coffee up to take a sip. "And don't pretend grief at Thanksgiving and grief at Christmas are the same. They aren't."

In terms of loss, Christmas is Thanksgiving on steroids. It's more everything. More flashbacks. More things to miss. Gifts. Children having fun. Santa Claus. Cards with family photos. Shiny, screaming, decorative reminders of what was taken from me.

Picking up a stick of butter, I unwrap it, then drop it in a bowl. I shove the dish in the microwave, slam the door shut, and pound the timer. "What is your endgame, Molly?"

She scoffs. "What's that supposed to mean?"

I stare at the butter going round and round, angry bubbles forming. "How long will you protect me from holidays? For the next five years? Ten years?"

"You are so ungrateful—"

"No." I turn on my heel to face her. "I'm eternally grateful. You cannot imagine. But, Molly, I'm worried that my life has engulfed yours." A growling exhale of frustration escapes. "Let me ask you something. When you aren't trying to take care of me, what do you think about?"

"What kind of a question is that? What's going on with you?" She paces two steps and whirls back my direction. "First you took this odd trip to tour properties in Colorado. Then Francine Clyde told me you never returned her call about helping with the church database system. You worked way less hours at the food pantry this season. Next thing I know, you've broken a good man's heart but invited a flaky actor slash YouTube star into your home."

She did *not* just say that. "Molly—"

"No. This is bizarre behavior, Meredith. But somehow you're turning this onto me and criticizing me for trying to help. I can't believe you." Tears spill down her flushed cheeks, and she covers her face with her hands.

Our family is like a musical nursery mobile. Hanging above the crib of life, small, perfectly balanced animals circle securely to the calming, repetitive lullaby. The homeostasis is alluring as long as no one shifts. It's a system that hides and protects me well. But if someone removes their piece, the system destabilizes.

"Molly." Seething, I wait for her gaze to find mine. "It's not about you. You have served me sacrificially. I'm saying maybe it's time for both of us to let go a little and see who we are now. Without my life being about the accident all the time. And without your life being about holding me together at every turn."

"It's that easy for you, is it?" She grabs a napkin and pats tears from her cheek.

"No." The microwave dings, and I open the door. "No, it's not that easy for me. I'm terrified sometimes." I walk the melted-butter bowl to the counter with the dough and stare at the ingredients. "But I also hold to a sliver of hope that if I lean in a bit . . . risk . . . maybe life has something else for me." My voice cracks through the last words, and I look back to my sister.

"Do you mean Harlan?" Her face blanches. "You think he's going to swoop in and save you?"

"This isn't about Harlan." I pound my fist on the granite, and my voice rises in anger. "Who is *not*, by the way, a flaky actor slash YouTube star. It's bigger than him. It's everything. How long will I hide in my home? What do I have to offer now? What role do I play in this world?" As the words spew out of my mouth, I point to the window. "There are answers for me somewhere out there. And whether or not Harlan is part of those answers doesn't matter." My voice carries through the house, and I don't care who it wakes. "I want to live. I want to participate in my own life. Do you hear what I am saying? I want to live. Again."

Molly gapes, and for a few seconds she doesn't respond. Before I know what she's doing, she scurries over and wraps me in a suffocating embrace.

"I thought I'd lost you." She whispers her teary confession into my ear. "Steve and the kids were gone, and then . . . I thought I lost you too."

A sob sticks in my throat. Maybe the mobile won't collapse if I leave. Maybe the figures will find a new equilibrium, but they won't fall apart.

While she clings to me, I hear the front door open.

"Hey, guys." Harlan's voice floats through the house, causing my insides to flutter.

Molly releases me, nods, and wipes her face. We both inch toward the door to peek into the living room. A post-run, sweaty Harlan leans over the back of the couch, rustling Taylor's hair and giving a groggy Hannah a high five.

My sister sighs. "He *is* pretty."

Harlan glances up and grins. "Morning, ladies."

I purse my lips as I watch him saunter toward us. Molly slips past him on her way out the door.

"Hey." He squeezes my hand as he passes me.

"Hey." I never want to wash my hand again. "How was your run?"

Harlan opens the cabinet and reaches for a glass. "Good." He fills the cup with tap water, turns, and gives a chin lift to the baking concoction. "What's going on here?"

"Homemade cinnamon rolls. The Pioneer Woman swears people will love me more after they eat these." I point to the batter-splattered picture of Ree Drummond in my cookbook.

Harlan's eyes flash with a hunger that makes my stomach jump. Oh my. The sweat causes his clothes to stick to his well-defined body. Oh my again. Not breaking eye contact with me, he gulps down his drink.

Fidgeting with the hem of my T-shirt, I find a loose thread to wrap around my finger. Unable to withstand the scrutiny, I break down laughing. "What? What are you thinking?"

"I kind of want to kiss you."

What I would like to say is something to the effect of "Don't ever walk into my kitchen looking like this again or you won't have any choice but to kiss me."

He places his cup by the sink. "Only I think I'll wait until I don't smell like this. I need a shower."

*Oh, please. Please kiss me when you smell like this.*

A smile breaks over his face as if he heard me.

Was that out loud?

My face is on fire, and I cover my mouth with my hand to stifle a laugh.

"Harlan, Meredith's out of orange juice." Molly's entrance causes me to almost jump out of my skin. "Do you want to come with me to the grocery store?"

Wait. What's she doing?

For all the progress I thought we made with our earlier talk, the stench of her old antics is strong. Over the years, she's scared away more than one male prospect with her grilling. I've seen this movie, and it doesn't end well.

I elbow my sister. "I'm not out of orange juice. What are you doing, Molly?"

She ignores me, eyebrows raised to Harlan.

"Sure." He strolls across the room and stops in front of me to lean in. "I'll shower when I get back." Then he winks and lowers his voice. "I got this."

Without looking at me, Molly follows him, and I'm left alone with so many swirling thoughts, I don't know which one to process first.

Someone upset the mobile, and who knows where the pieces might land.

# 20

"BUT I DON'T NEED orange juice." I mutter the words to no one as I stare out my kitchen window.

Harlan opens the car door for Molly, and she folds her body into the driver's seat.

Grasping the edge of the counter, I bow my head. "I don't need orange juice." I repeat my declaration to the sink with more force than before.

Varied thoughts claw through my mind, vying to crest the mountain peak of my anxiety. Which version of my past will Molly throw at Harlan? How much weight will he give her words? Should I pack his things so he can make a quick getaway upon their return?

Muffled sounds from the living room break into my climbing questions. I turn and amble to the door. "Did someone say something?"

"Orange juice?" Half asleep, my nephew poses the question, face down on the sofa, head in the crook of his elbow.

I plant my hands on my hips. "I don't need orange juice, thank you very much. Why does everyone think they need to get me orange juice? I can handle it on my own."

My niece, curled up in a ball at the opposite end of the couch, lifts her head off the giant cushion. "So, is there orange juice in the house or not?" She peers at me, one eye closed.

"Yes. There is no need for someone else to go for orange juice." My pulse quickens with my escalating frustration.

"Everyone needs a little orange juice, Aunt Meredith." Taylor sits up, puffing his chest out as he stretches. "Especially before a big undertaking . . ."

I lose the rest of Taylor's thought as his words echo in my head. The tips of my fingers touch my mouth, and I close my eyes. *Everyone needs a little orange juice. Especially before a big undertaking.*

Flashes of the last four years play a montage of information Harlan should know. An accident so horrendous in nature, it warranted a week of news coverage. Debilitating depression. Massive migraines. A secret suicide watch. Being carried out of the house. Treatment facility. Recovery. Unequipped friends abandoning our relationship. Not wanting to leave the house. A few years of baby steps. Some breaths of fresh air. Awkward, intentional functioning.

And one day, a search for more that led me to Colorado Springs.

A peace descends on my mountain of questions like pouring rain, washing away my anxious thoughts. I'm not scared of him knowing any of those details.

"Maybe I'm wrong," I murmur. "Maybe I do need some orange juice."

Tell him, Molly.

Tell him everything. Buy the Costco-sized jug of orange juice. Get the apple. The grape. The pomegranate. Purchase it all.

And bring him home to me.

"Okay, I'm really confused." Taylor wipes sleep from his eyes. "I would like some orange juice. Do you have any here at the house?"

"Sure, sweetie. I'll pour you some." Entering the kitchen, I remind myself what is true about Harlan. He can deal with obstinate grief, he communicates he likes me, and he's here. If he wanted an excuse not to pursue me, he could have taken it—he's had several.

After I deliver the drinks, complete the cinnamon rolls, and clean up, there's nothing left to do. Pacing, I pull on a hangnail until I hear the front door open, followed by greetings.

Harlan strides into the room and sets a grocery bag on the counter.

"You get the orange juice you wanted?" I wring my hands, shifting my weight from one foot to the other.

He stills and studies me. "I already had the orange juice I wanted."

A beat passes. "Do you know we're not talking about a breakfast drink?"

Harlan's deep chuckle fills the kitchen. "Yeah, sweetheart. Come here." His long, muscular arm reaches out, and he tugs me into a solid embrace. "Chad Tarkington really did a number on you guys."

"You have no idea." I snuggle in deeper, my face resting in the crook of his neck. How can someone who has not taken a post-workout shower smell so completely marvelous?

"You okay?" He gives me a squeeze.

My bravado from earlier has left the building, and I ask in a small voice, "Did she scare you away?"

"No. She filled in some gaps of your story." His voice catches.

"Did she scare you away?" I repeat my fear on a whisper.

He pulls back and cups my face. "She confirmed what I already knew. You've had enough anguish for a lifetime."

Not knowing where the conversation is headed but wanting to appear brave, I swallow back tears. I'm unable to form words, so I just nod.

"I don't want to add to your pain." He releases my face and

slides his hands to my shoulders. "Molly doesn't want me to hurt you. But I'm a step ahead of her. I'm terrified of hurting you."

I offer a fake smile. "You're in a tough position."

"I'm falling in love with a strong, brave, and funny woman. Have I mentioned beautiful?"

Falling in love. Falling in love? My heart pounds. It's like it knows it needs to tell me to pay attention, to hold the gravity of the conversation with the giddy feelings his words cause while coming to grips with my own feelings.

He folds a strand of hair behind my ear. "I just want to be around her. Why is any of that bad?"

My hands at his waist, I clutch the fabric of his shirt. "Because no one wants to be the one who breaks up with the wounded widow."

Harlan's body jolts at my statement. His intense gaze causes me to squirm under the scrutiny.

"I'm a lot to handle, Harlan."

"No. Molly is a lot to handle." His eyes narrow. "This is real for me. If you walked away, I would be a wreck."

I swallow. I blink.

He steps back but takes my hands in his. "I didn't know your story the first time I saw you."

I tip my head to the side. "Yes, you did. The maître d' told you about the memo. The one about being sensitive to the widow."

A sly grin kicks up one side of his mouth. "Yes, but that morning I was in the lobby when you checked in to the hotel." He gazes over my shoulder as if lost in his memory. "I thought you were so beautiful. And when you showed up at the Penrose Room, I knew it was my lucky day."

Wait. What? My belly whooshes.

Harlan moves forward and lifts our hands up between us. "So if you think for one second, Meredith Harper, that I'm going to allow you to kick me to the curb just because you're scared, you're wrong."

"I'm not scared." When I say that, I'm pretty sure we both know I'm lying.

"Sweetheart, you've been listing reasons why we won't work since we met." He rubs his thumbs over the tops of my hands. "I'm not intimidated by Molly. Not afraid of your grief. And your fears won't run me off."

Tears fill my eyes.

"I'm not worried about breaking up with the widow because I don't plan on breaking up with her." He makes his final rumbled statement while staring at my lips.

My heart squeezes, and there's just no way to run from the truth. I whisper, "I'm falling in love with you too."

His eyes flash.

The timer on the oven beeps, and for all intents and purposes, it is a loud gong invading our moment.

"Aunt Meredith, does that mean the cinnamon rolls are ready? I can smell them from here," Taylor calls from across the living room.

Harlan drops my hands, winks, and steps back. "Later." His tone implies a promise.

With my eyes locked on Harlan, I answer Taylor. "Yes."

As the family rushes through the door, our moment ends and a mad dash for the breakfast treats ensues.

"Who wants coffee and who wants OJ?" My mother shakes the new gallon.

"Orange juice, please." Harlan's commanding voice fills the room, his gaze searing into mine.

I purse my lips, trying to contain my grin.

He gives me a chin lift and turns to accept a cup from my mom.

Thirty minutes later, stomachs full, sugar highs intact, everyone leaves for their respective post–Thanksgiving Day festivities. The women drive away armed with a retail attack plan that would've made Patton proud. The men load up the car for high-caloric tailgating at the SMU football game.

After a quick shower, Harlan joins me in the living room. He rocks sweatpants day. His well-worn navy sweats hang low on his hips, and a tattered used-to-be-white Henley covers his broad shoulders.

With his hair still wet, I want to run my fingers through the dark tips curling at the ends.

Harlan joins me on the couch and removes a fluffy throw pillow from behind his back.

"I'm thinking through our options. Are you sure you want to stay in today? I'm sorry I didn't have anything planned." I pick at a thread on my hot-pink yoga pants. "Plus it's my fault the guys didn't grab you a ticket for the game."

He covers my hand, stopping its nervous movement. "I think we need a lazy day. Tomorrow I'll take you out on the town."

Are those butterflies in my stomach? Dragonflies? Or a giant pterodactyl?

"Okay." Did I just bat my eyes at him?

"Should we watch a movie?"

"Oh. Yes. Okay." I have no clue how to navigate movies with him. I should have sent him to the game.

He freezes for a second as if contemplating something and shifts his body to face me. His deep brown eyes bore into mine. "I should probably confess something to you." The gentle but teasing voice matches the glint in his eye. "As an actor, I have quirky rules about which movies I watch. You might even call me high-maintenance."

"Right." I scoff.

"Nothing with plotlines involving actors, directors, or screenwriters. No film scores composed by people whose names end in *L*, *E*, or *P*. And the deal-breaker. No Tom Cruise."

"What?" I shove Harlan in the shoulder. "What's wrong with Tom Cruise? You're eliminating some epic cinema classics."

"I suffer from an inferiority complex." Mockingly, he crosses his muscular arms over his chest. "Are you making fun of me?"

"You're just trying to make me feel better." I roll my eyes. "I bet you guys are best friends."

"Only Facebook friends." Harlan hauls me to him, fitting us into the corner of the sofa. "Is it working?"

Releasing a sigh, I close my eyes. "Yes."

"Your movie rules won't scare me," he says gently. "Let's have them."

"It's probably easier if I tell you what I don't watch." I tug at the stray thread. "No death. No car wrecks. Nothing where a child's life is threatened. And basically, understand I can veto a movie at any time for no reason at all."

My list is met with silence.

I cringe. "I'm sorry—"

"No, ma'am. No apologies." Harlan kisses the top of my head. "That's good information." He leans forward, taking me with him, to grab the remote. "I think I've got a solution."

Scrolling through our options, he settles on my worst nightmare. Only his film choice doesn't fit any of the taboo categories, and I don't know how to skirt the issue.

"*Divergent.*" He raises his hands in victory, Rocky style.

"Yeah." My exaggerated response isn't convincing, even to me. "*Divergent.*" Most-embarrassing-moment flashbacks attack my vision. I glance at Harlan.

His lips twitch, breaking his earnest stare.

Wait a minute.

As I sit up, I take a better look at him. Gasping, I shove a finger into his firm chest. "Molly put you up to this."

Harlan doubles over laughing. "Please, tell me the story. I have to hear it from you."

"I cannot believe this." I run my hands through my hair. "That little traitor."

He twists to me and props his knee on the cushion. "All she said was to ask you about *Divergent* and CPS."

*Divergent* and CPS, indeed.

Heat crawls up my neck, and I shake my head. "Fine." I reach over him and snatch a handful of candy corn from a decorative crystal dish.

"Emotional eating is required for this story," I say as I stuff a few candies in my mouth.

Big, masculine Harlan Holcombe sits crisscross applesauce, grabs a snack bowl off the same table, and focuses on me with the excited anticipation of a child. "Excellent." The word is muffled through the popcorn he shoves in his mouth.

"Pretty early on, I had the kids enrolled one day a week in a Mother's Day Out program. It was glorious." I devour a few more of the yellow and orange candies. "For five precious hours I could do anything I wanted. My friends understood how important they were to me if I scheduled a lunch with them during that time. It meant they were MDO worthy."

Harlan chuckles. "MDO worthy."

I place my hand over my heart. "I truly believe it would have been more than acceptable to sit in my pj's and eat bonbons for those five hours. But in social settings, I felt pressure to come up with justifiable reasons for taking time away from my children."

With popcorn halfway to his mouth, he grins. "Like what?"

One finger raises with each excuse. "I volunteer at the prison to teach a GED course. Or I'm on a board to cure cancer. Or I need to purchase raw goat milk from a local farm."

"That's not a thing." He throws a piece of popcorn at me.

"Yes, it is. My friend Charlotte couldn't breastfeed and made a carrot-juice-and-goat-milk concoction for her babies. Her kids temporarily turned orange because of all the beta-carotene."

Shaking his head, he grabs another handful. "You're making this up."

"I'm not." He launches another morsel of popcorn at me, but I smack this one down before it makes contact. "But one day I let myself do the unthinkable." I hold my hand out like a stop sign.

"For almost two years, not once—not *once*—had the school ever called me in the middle of the day."

Harlan's shoulders shake with silent laughter.

"So I did it." Adding to my dramatics, I lean in. "I went to a movie while my kids were in Mother's Day Out."

"*Divergent.*" He slaps his hand on his knee.

"Yeah. *Divergent.* And just as the big kissing scene finally happens, my phone vibrates." I pause for dramatic effect. "It was the nurse at Mother's Day Out."

Harlan laughs and holds his stomach. "Stop. I can't breathe."

"She informs me Chloe has a fever. And in my brilliant, flustered state, I confess I'm at the movies and . . . wait for it . . . ask if I could pick her up after the kissing scene ends." I bury my face in my hands. "I broke the sacred mom code, and I thought they were going to call CPS."

Harlan's cackles fill the room. "That is amazing. Did you ever finish the movie?"

"Read the books but didn't finish the movie." Popping the rest of the candy corn in my mouth, I glance at the TV.

"Well, then. Let's find you some cinematic closure." Uncrossing his legs, he exchanges popcorn for the remote and hits play.

As *Divergent* begins, Harlan stretches his arm behind me and rests it on the cushions.

I purse my lips in an effort to contain my smile.

Who knew Hercules had high school cuddling moves?

When I scoot toward him, he tucks me against his side and presses my head down on his chest. Wrapping my arms around him, I decide there's nothing wrong with high school moves.

The first few scenes roll, and I settle into his embrace. We fit together. The two of us. I place my hand over his heart. The beat is just like the man. Steady.

I pause the movie, twist, and gaze up at his handsome face.

He returns my stare with molten dark eyes pouring into mine. His strong hand cups my face, thumb grazing my cheek. He leans in, and his lips brush my mouth tenderly. He moves back just a touch, our breaths tangling.

With my eyes still closed, I smile. "Again," I whisper.

The word barely escapes before he kisses me a second time, this one deeper. He draws me closer with one arm as he runs his other hand through my hair.

Tris and Four's big kissing scene will have to wait again.

Only this time, I'm not that upset about it.

# 21

**"WHAT'S HARD** to understand?" Leaning a hip on my desk, I pretend to sort through mail. Who can concentrate after our earlier make-out session?

Harlan places his hand over mine and halts my nervous movements. "You make the last six weeks of your life sound like you're working off a prison sentence."

I grin. "Right? I told Molly that Al Capone wouldn't have had this many community service hours."

"It's worse." He throws out a hand. "It's like asking Jack the Ripper to work in a woman's shelter."

Covering my mouth, I giggle.

He tugs on my hands, drawing me to him. "Or Bernie Madoff offering free financial services to college graduates."

"Stop." With my shoulders shaking, I plant my forehead on his chest.

"I'm all for volunteering your time, but it seems forced." He pulls me close for no reason at all, and the affection feels good. More than good. "Do you like what you're doing?" he asks.

As my thumbs rub down his ribs, all I can think is I like what I'm doing right now. Probably not what he means.

Harlan leans toward my desk, shifting us. "Hey, what are these?"

Turning my head, I glance at the stack of colorful papers closest to us. "Something I made for Sally."

He releases his hold on me to grab the top sheet. "What are they?"

I stand a little taller. "Stickers." I graze my fingertips over a three-inch blue accolade that says "Fed BOTH my kids" next to a chubby baby holding up a victorious fist. "You know how children go to the doctor's office and receive a sticker after their appointment? There's some cat with the words 'Purrfect Patient.' Or a giant trophy with 'Number 1 Attitude.' I always wondered where the stickers are for parents."

He glances from the designs to me. His eyes light up. "This is a brilliant idea."

"I mean, I'm the one who held the kid down while he screamed through a shot. Didn't I earn the 'I Didn't Cry' sticker?" I point to a baby-blue circle on the page.

"Or this one." He draws attention to a different design with balloons and a wine glass that says "Still Sober."

"Yeah. Sally's had a rough time the last couple of weeks with the dregs of mommyhood. I sent her a box with a few pages of stickers along with chocolate and a CD mix of non-mommy songs."

Harlan narrows his eyes. "You're really good at this."

"Oh, gosh." I shoo his compliment away with my hand. "The care package was for fun. I wrote her a note and told her to let herself off the hook. Just for today. She can go back to beating herself up tomorrow for all the things she thinks she's doing wrong. But for today, I dared her to go easy on herself."

"Seriously." He leans in and puts a hand on my shoulder. "I don't think you get it. You're really good at this."

I can't comprehend what he's saying. "Good at what? All I

did was send Sally a message that she isn't alone during the Groundhog Days of early-childhood parenting. It's not that big of a deal."

"You're right." Harlan's tone drips with sarcasm. "Instead of encouraging people like Sally, you could do more Molly-mandated volunteer work. I hear Billy the Kid is burning some hours running the kiddie trains at the fair."

His joke falls flat, and I pull back, wrap my arms around myself, and turn and scour the pristine sunroom for a distraction. Shouldn't there be a stray glass I need to take to the kitchen? "There's nothing wrong with charity work."

"Meredith." Harlan runs his knuckles down my spine. A whisper of a touch. "You have a choice. You know that, right?"

"I have time and resources. Shouldn't serving others be fulfilling? Shouldn't that be enough for my life to mean something?" My voice breaks, and I'm surprised by the flood of sadness.

This. This is it. I feel lost inside my own life.

Harlan takes one small step toward me, his gaze searing into mine. "Can we be fulfilled if we aren't working and serving in ways that we're wired and love to do?"

"I don't know." I rub the spot above my heart.

We both breathe hard, staring. At this point, I'm not sure whose life we're discussing.

The back of Harlan's hand grazes my cheek. "You aren't irrelevant, Meredith."

Sighing, I say, "What else am I going to do?"

I peek through the kaleidoscope of choices and freeze at the infinite colors. My options are unlimited. Am I supposed to merely exist? Do I get to have more dreams? Am I designed for something specific in this life, or will I play out the rest of my days swimming in grief?

Maybe Harlan's right. Maybe my stickers are more than farfetched ideas. Or maybe this isn't about stickers at all.

"You'll figure it out." Harlan's deep voice resonates in my ear as he wraps his strong arms around my shoulders, engulfing me in comfort.

I push back enough so I can study him. Exhaustion lines his brown eyes. "What about you?"

He gives me a squeeze and releases his hold. "Got a call from Penelope yesterday."

I scrunch up my face. "She always work on Thanksgiving?"

"I don't think she grasps the meaning of the word 'rest.'" He scoffs. "There's a reason her most recent contract with me contains a required vacation clause."

Something in me warms at the thought of her required vacation clause and Harlan taking care of his people.

"There's talk of future movie promotions." He bends his head to look at his phone and scrolls through it. "Most of what I do is contracted, but a few things are negotiated along the way. I prefer to stay out of the spotlight more than a lot of actors. But Penelope mentioned that the way the Oscars are lining up, they're looking at using a couple of us to announce an award."

As he takes a breath, he turns the screen to me. Front and center on Harlan's phone is the official letterhead of the Academy of Motion Picture Arts and Sciences.

I start giggling. "I'm sorry." Clearing my throat, I place a fist over my mouth. "Please continue."

"What's so funny?" His lips quirk.

"Look, I know it's your job. And I understand"—my explanation is broken with snickers—"you're a practical and down-to-earth famous person. But it's a little bizarre to listen to you talk about maybe attending the Academy Awards. I have zero ability to act like this is normal."

He hits me with a smile that doesn't reach his eyes and nods slowly. While he's staring at me, his smile disappears and the mood in the room shifts.

"If I had a typical life, I would want to show you off." He shakes his head. "But my world isn't going to protect you."

Gazing at my feet, I consider the kind of woman Harlan needs. I hate being a woman someone has to shield.

"Meredith." The call of my name is a gentle demand. "I would be proud with you on my arm at the Oscars." He pauses, then adds with amusement in his voice, "Though we might need some famous people training. Pitching a script to Steven Spielberg about conflict in space may not be your best move."

My only response is to roll my eyes at the ceiling.

"I want to take you to an Oscar ceremony. But, Meredith, God forbid a reporter makes your personal story part of his byline. It's not worth it to me." He shrugs. "So I told Penelope to send Charlie and Spencer."

Shame is sticky and will not release me from its grasp. Isn't enduring my astronomical loss enough? How is it I'm a prisoner of it years later?

My breathing increases. I benched myself from my own life to deal with grief, but I can't ask anyone else to stand on the sidelines with me.

"We're not talking about some appearance at the local Elks Lodge, Harlan. This is the Oscars. You can't not go." I grab his cell and shake it at him. "Call Penelope. Fix it. You have to go. You have to go without me."

In one swift movement, he removes the phone and grasps my hand. "It's better this way. Besides, I don't want to be there without you."

Shaking my head, I step back. "This is a little hard to take in. I don't think I can let you skip this because of me."

He moves a hand over the second-day growth on his face, then slides it to grip the back of his neck. "What if that's not the only reason?"

His blank expression gives me nothing, so I wait in silence.

"Charlie Boyd will take my place. The guy you met at the Broadmoor? He's hungry. He's keeping his head down and doing the work. And I want to see what this kind of experience will do for him." He drops his hand. "I think being at the awards show could be a significant catalyst for him."

Charlie. Young actor. Someone Harlan met with regularly while on set.

I study the man in front of me. "You help people figure out how to work their dreams."

He slides his gaze to me with a sheepish glint. "I don't know about that."

"Then what? What is it you want to do for those guys? Because I know it's important to you."

"I want them to have groundwork. Personal, professional, financial. I just see so many idiots, talented idiots, with nothing underneath them while this industry opens up and consumes them." He taps himself on the chest twice. "I had excellent support, and this industry still ate me alive."

"Olivia shook your foundation." I whisper the words, trying not to scare him.

Harlan's pained eyes take my breath away. "I did everything wrong with Olivia. Her disillusionment caused a fog in my intuition that I rarely have to face."

"And you think you can protect your guys from the pain of growing up?"

"No." His answer chokes through a laugh. "But maybe I can help them. Maybe my life can be more meaningful than a movie no one will remember in ten years."

His broken expression almost undoes me, and for the first time, I see the wounded man before me, grasping for purpose to make sense of his life. I'm not the only one who's searching for more.

Wiping his hands over his face, he growls. "I don't know how we got off on this. You're changing the subject."

"And you're making a mistake by not going to the Oscars." I shoot back my response, mirroring his intensity.

"My decision's already been put into action." He exhales and throws his arms wide. "And it didn't feel like a sacrifice when I hit the send button."

Glaring at him, I have no idea what to say. I so desperately want to allow him to extend this care for me, yet I so desperately don't want to need it.

"The Oscars are Sunday, February twenty-fourth. If you're not helping Bonnie and Clyde clean bathrooms at the bank, I want you either in a fancy dress or your best sweatpants. You choose." He prowls one step toward me. "I will be dressed in either a tux or a tuxedo T-shirt, according to your lead." Another slow, predator movement in my direction. "We will order an obscene amount of takeout. Consume all the chocolate you can handle. And we will text Spencer and Sally obnoxious messages during the entire show." His last stalking stride lands him in front of me, and I can't help but smile at his perfect plan. Then he takes my breath when he wraps me in his arms and gifts me with a quick brush of his lips on mine.

At his kiss, my entire body tingles. But I can't ignore a tiny kindling of doubt. Sighing, I rest my hands on his chest. "Promise me if you're ever nominated, you'll go."

"I don't think superhero movies are what the Academy is looking for." He presses his lips to my forehead with his words.

I poke him in the side. "Promise."

He pulls me in closer and speaks into my hair, "Only if you go with me."

"Hmm." I nod. "We'll have to find some kind of cotillion for socializing with celebrities."

He kisses the top of my head. "I'm impressed with you, Meredith Harper. We talked about my career, the possibility of meeting famous people, and our future without any freaking out." His tone is light, but he takes a loaded breath. "I want our relationship to be ours. To the extent we can control it, I want to stay out of public scrutiny."

I agree, not because of his words but because he is stroking my hair, coaxing me into oblivion. Then I shoot my head up and smack my hands on his shoulders. "I just realized the best part."

The impact shifts his weight backward, causing him to release an "oomph."

Full of glee, I grin. "Sally is going to rock the red carpet."

Harlan leans to the desk, grabs the top sticker sheet, and wrestles one off the page. "She can wear this to the show." He pulls off a bright pink sticker and presses it to my shirt, studying it with amusement.

*Showered today.*

# 22

## I BROKE HERCULES.

The quiet moan emanating from the guest bedroom for the last few minutes makes me nervous. I lift my hand to knock on the closed door but hesitate, second-guessing myself.

What should I do?

A loud thud calls me to action. I clutch the doorknob and press my forehead to the door. "Harlan?"

A grunt is the only reply.

"I'm coming in." I crack the door open and peek in. The pitiful picture of Harlan in the fetal position, shaking, is more than I can bear. "Oh, honey."

His arm is extended toward the side table, and I glance down and notice his phone on the floor.

Kneeling by the edge of the bed, I place the back of my hand on his forehead. My opposite palm finds his sheets drenched in sweat. He is sweating out a fierce fever.

Harlan shudders. "I may not be up for taking you out tonight, sweetheart."

At least I think that's what he said. The intermittent shakes break up his words.

I scratch my head. "I think you caught the flu. This year's strand is supposed to include super high fevers." Vomiting is also on the list, but I can't bring myself to mention this. "I'll find you a MinuteClinic. But at some point, I need tomorrow's flight information. No way are you going to be able to travel."

"Trying to get me to stay longer, are you?" This might sound cute if he wasn't coughing up a lung.

"You're the one who got sick. If you wanted to stay longer, you could have just asked." I bend over, pick up his phone, and place it on the side table. "Okay, let's nail down the logistics. Where is your itinerary?"

Harlan's teeth chatter. "Call Penelope. She'll know what to do. Do you still have her number?"

Penelope is handy. I need a Penelope.

I pull my phone out of my back jeans pocket and shake it. "I've still got her number. I'll be back in a minute, honey." I run a hand through his damp hair before I step out of the room.

Rushing into the kitchen, I throw my phone down on the counter. After scrubbing and drying my hands, I pull antibacterial wipes out of their container and proceed to clean my cell with the meticulous detail of a surgeon. Satisfied with my decontamination process, I thumb through my contact list and hit Penelope's number.

Just as she answers the call, I catch the uneven pounding of feet through the hallway, followed by the most horrific sounds.

"Penelope." My breathing becomes labored as my frantic eyes dart around the room.

"Who am I speaking with?" The curt words cut through the line.

"Penelope." I grasp my chest and pull in a choppy breath through my nose. "It's Meredith."

"Is Harlan with you? He's supposed to be in Dallas until to-morrow."

I claw at a drawer, pry it open, and grab a paper bag. I shove the phone between my shoulder and bent neck and give words to my biggest nightmare. "He's throwing up."

"Harlan's throwing up? Well, that kind of thing happens, Mer-edith."

Her reply gives me a chance to shake the bag loose and fix the opening around my mouth. I inhale and exhale three breaths. "Not in my house," I say into the paper.

"I'm not surprised. The flu spread through the cast the last few weeks of shooting. High fever? Coughing? Vomiting?"

"Don't." The bag expands. "Say." The bag contracts. "The V-word."

"I'll contact the on-set doctor to call in prescriptions for him. Can you text me your local pharmacy number, or do you want me to look it up?"

More gagging noises fill the house, and before my knees give out, I sit at the breakfast nook. Phone still cradled to my shoulder, one hand on the lifeline bag and the other covering my head, I start rocking back and forth.

"Meredith? Should I figure out how to get a sedative ordered for you?" Her offer might sound comical, but her voice is no-nonsense.

"I prefer Xanax and Reese's Peanut Butter Cups." Obscene amounts of the latter.

The bag crinkles with my inhale. My phone alerts me to an incoming call, and I glance at the screen.

Prissy.

I ignore the call. She'll want to know about the property search, and I can't talk about real life right now.

My next exhale stretches the limits of the paper.

Penelope clucks her tongue. "Text me the pharmacy number

and I'll take care of the details. I'll also alert his boss and look into getting his flight changed."

As I pull the bag down, I lean over my thighs and rest my head on my knees. "Penelope? What about Alex?" I have no idea what the custody agreement entails for this kind of thing.

"I'll take care of it."

Her clipped words confuse me. Is she angry? "Do you want me to ask Harlan—"

"I deal with Olivia on a regular basis. I will handle this." Even her sigh is curt. "A warning, Meredith. Olivia's behavior is erratic on a good day. It seems the stress of losing her father has sent her into a tailspin. I don't know what it is, but she's up to something."

The hairs on my arms stand on end, and I sit up straight. "I appreciate the warning, but I can't imagine I'd have an occasion to interact with her."

"It's not about your interactions with Olivia. It's about your interactions with Harlan."

I drop the bag and use my free hand to put pressure on my chest. "What does that mean?"

"Olivia makes empty threats, and it's hard to tell if she'll follow through. This time she's spouting off about challenging the current custody agreement."

Terrified to know the answer, I whisper my question. "On what grounds?"

"She claims being around Alex during her father's illness and death reminded her of the mother she wants to be. But there's no mistaking the timing. She didn't speak of this until she found out Harlan was going to visit you."

My stomach churns, and I might be the next one to throw up.

Me. Olivia wants to challenge Harlan's custody of Alex because of me.

My thoughts spin faster than I can process them. If she has someone look into my past, they'll find a long-term treatment facility stay. Not the most stable girlfriend choice to be around a precious three-year-old.

Moisture pricks my eyes. I won't be part of causing Harlan to lose a child.

"Meredith, I want to be clear with you. I like you. Harlan has been different since he met you. Lighter. Happier."

The kind words are not a worthy opponent for my swirling anxiety.

"But if you're not serious about a future with him, would you consider letting him go sooner rather than later?"

The phone slips from my shaking hand, and I fumble to regain control. "Um. Okay." I swallow down the lump in my throat. This conversation has taken a turn I never saw coming. "Thank you so much for your help today, Penelope."

When she signs off, I gently bang the phone against my forehead. How am I supposed to know what a future with Harlan looks like?

My past is peppered with love. I've always fallen quick and deep. My present is filled with the solid possibility of Harlan. But my future? What if we don't want the same things?

Risking his custody of Alex isn't an option.

I stand, shake out my arms, and peer down the corridor. No sounds answer my stare. After I send out a few texts, I shove my phone in my back jeans pocket. "Okay, Meredith. Suck it up."

I woke up this morning with a pit in my stomach, understanding this would be our last day together. What a difference an hour makes. Squeezing my eyes closed, I beg God to save us from the vomit.

After tiptoeing down the hallway, I stop at the open door of the guest room. "You all right?"

The prone, pale-faced man in front of me squints. "Why do you look like I should be asking you the same thing?" His frail voice is choppy.

"I can't do vomit." My confession sounds like that of a scared little girl. Maybe a seven-year-old little girl named Meredith.

The noise he makes resembles a dying horse. "Is this like how you can't do famous people?" Lying on his side, he clasps his hands and tucks them under his head.

"I'm so sorry." I take one tentative step into the room. "I don't do vomit. Ever. It's not one of my more attractive qualities. Steve's and my marriage agreement stated if he puked, he was on his own. If the kids puked, they understood to go to their father."

"All your qualities"—he moans—"are . . . attractive."

Nope. Flirting doesn't work while the threat of vomit lingers.

I shift my right foot back, considering how to flee. "I can't help it. Kim Sterling threw up on my head in the second grade."

One side of Harlan's mouth twitches, and he clutches his stomach. "Don't make me laugh."

"We were driving back from a Blue Birds campout. We got lost, and my mom pulled off the highway to look at a map. I was lying down on the back seat floorboard, and out of nowhere Kim says, 'I think I have to . . .' And then she did. *All over my head.*" I grab my hair and pull with each of the last four words.

Harlan's laughter fights with his groans.

"Direct hit, Harlan. No exaggeration." I point to my crazy hair. "With both of us screaming, my mother drove to a gas station to clean us up. She put my head under the sink faucet to try to—" I cover my mouth and shake my head.

"Okay." Harlan clears his throat, causing me to jump back. He holds out a hand, palm forward. "Clearly this is tougher on you than it is on me. What did Penelope say?"

Bless his heart.

Balling my hands into fists, I step toward the bed. "We're taking care of you. I texted a friend to pick up your prescriptions so I don't have to leave you."

I might be curled up in a comatose ball in the corner if he

throws up again, but by God, I will not abandon him in his time of need.

Harlan's face softens, and he offers a jerky nod. "What happened to Kim Sterling?"

With my arms folded across my chest, I scowl. "The next day at school she spread a rumor that I didn't wash my hair."

"Stop." Harlan coughs and throws a hand out to me. "Stop making me laugh."

"Nothing funny about almost going to jail for murder. Which is what would have happened had she not moved away during the following Christmas break."

"Meredith. Please." His lips twitch in a miserable smile.

"Okay, honey." I clutch a hand over my mouth and speak in muffled words. "Call if you need anything."

While I walk to the kitchen, my phone buzzes with an incoming message from Claire. She'll grab the meds and bring them to the house. In the meantime, I field calls from Penelope with new travel details, set up a tray for Harlan, and practice my deep breathing.

In the forty-five minutes between the text and when Claire arrives, poor Harlan makes three more trips to the bathroom.

And I make three trips to the laundry room to cover my ears, hum, and wait it out.

The doorbell rings, and I glance in the direction of Harlan's room. "I got it, honey," I call to him. Because he's going to rise from the dead and welcome a guest? I shake my head. If he still wants to date me when this is all over, it'll be a miracle.

When I swing the front door open, the sight of Claire makes me want to cry.

Dressed in her typical running gear, long blond hair pulled back in a ponytail, she reaches out for a hug but stops midmotion. "Oh, Meredith." Claire's deep blue eyes grow big. "How bad is it?"

Claire. Childhood friend sitting in the front seat of my mom's car when the incident happened. She knows. And she's pulled me out of the Bad Place several times over the last few decades when vomit was in my vicinity.

Ridiculous tears fill my eyes. "It's really bad." I hope Harlan can't pick up on my whisper.

Coughing and hacking float from the guest room into the entryway, and my body seizes up.

She grabs my hand and drags me outside. "Let's ignore what's happening in there." She waves a hand toward the house.

I pull in a deep breath and nod.

"I don't know who this Penelope person is, but by the time I got to the pharmacy, the entire order was packaged up, paid for, and ready to go. The clerk let on he wasn't super happy to do a rush job on a holiday weekend, but it got done." She holds out one large brown paper bag, stapled at the top, and one white plastic bag. "But I added a few survival things for you. Everything full of gluten, dairy, sugar, and preservatives just like you like them."

Claire can't eat any of my favorite stress foods, but she supports my consuming enough for the both of us.

I take both bags from her, clamp the brown one in place under my armpit, and open the thin plastic bag. *People* magazine, a book of sudoku puzzles, a giant bottle of hand sanitizer, three cans of Lysol, and seven kinds of chocolate. My girl knows me well.

When I finish pawing through my stash, I glance up to thank her. But her intense stare stops the words from coming out of my mouth.

She turns her head and looks at Harlan's rental car for a beat, then directs her attention to the bags. "When you're ready, I would love to hear about your new friend who is holed up in your house. Because that's not Stanley's car."

I feel my face flush. Stupid caring, observant teacher friend.

She rummages through her purse. "I'm gonna take off if I can find my keys." Her head snaps up. "Oh, the weirdest thing happened at the pharmacy. They asked me if I knew Harlan Holcombe."

My heart races. "What did you say?"

"There were a lot of hushed tones behind the counter, then the guy told me to forget it." Claire laughs. "Can you imagine? If I knew Harlan Holcombe, you couldn't be my friend anymore because you're still on Famous People Probation." She shakes her head. "He sure was hot as Hercules, though."

He still is hot.

I force a smile and some laughter. "I'm so grateful for your help."

She shoos the words away with her hand. "No problem. I'm sorry we didn't catch up this week, but maybe over Christmas break we can swing a lunch."

"I'll pull you away from your grading, Miss Stark, to make sure we connect." Holding up the bags, I cringe. "I hope you don't think I'm a wimp."

"Sweetie, I was there." She takes a step closer. "*I was there.* Anyone would experience panic attacks if their mom pulled cheese-filled hot dogs from their hair while under the running water of a dirty gas station sink."

My body shudders as I giggle. "Love you."

She turns on her heel and, without looking at me, holds up her keys and shakes them. "Love you too."

Upon entering the house, I freeze and listen for the sounds of illness.

Nothing. Thank God.

I return to the kitchen, unpack the various meds, and dole out the appropriate doses. After placing them on a tray with crackers and Sprite, I carry the load down the hallway.

When I arrive at Harlan's room, I gulp. Shifting the tray to balance precariously on one arm, I knock on the door.

"Come in," he calls, his voice sounding like sandpaper.

I plaster on a bright smile and shove the door open with my elbow. My face falls when he comes into view.

Pasty-white Harlan sits on the end of the bed, elbows shaking, while gripping his knees.

"I come bearing gifts."

Harlan's eyes slowly move to find mine. They are glazed with signs of a fever.

"I'm not sure what you can keep down, but here's the Tamiflu and Advil. We're supposed to alternate with Tylenol. And I set out some crackers and Sprite."

His silence unnerves me. Setting the tray on the side table, I step back and wait.

He clears his throat, and the pained expression on his face is disturbing. "I've got something for you."

Harlan outstretches his arm, and for the first time I spot something stuck to the end of his finger. The round sticker quivers with his movements. I reach out my forefinger at a careful, painstaking angle to tag it, avoiding contact with Harlan's skin in the transference.

I rotate my wrist to see the sticker. Once the picture and words are in my vision, I grip my stomach with my free hand and burst out laughing when I recognize one of my sticker creations. Staring back at me is a fat-cheeked, cheerful bunny.

*No bunny helps with vomit like you!*

# 23

**FLU FEST DAY THREE.**

Harlan has been vomit- and fever-free for twenty-four hours. So far, my body has not betrayed me. We just might survive this with minimal damage.

I glance at Harlan stretched out on an oversized, cushioned patio chair, feet resting next to mine on the matching ottoman, hands clasped over his chest, eyes closed. The pallor of death is gone, and his gorgeous tan coloring has returned. Covered by the awning of my deck, enjoying mild Texas November weather, he looks peaceful as the wind blows through his dark hair.

"Is your success as a caretaker proportionate to the amount of Lysol you use?" he asks. Without opening his eyes, he smiles. "I thought the flu would kill me, but it turns out I should've been worried about chemical poisoning."

Sitting in an identical chair next to him, I elbow his forearm. "I buy in bulk so I can disinfect for a solid month after anyone pukes. You can never be too careful."

His shoulders shake with his chuckle. "I thought germs could only live on a surface for twelve hours."

"Yes, but their shelf life in my head is much longer."

He opens an eye and peeks at me. "We'll take as much Lysol as you want when we go camping."

"Ugh." I roll my eyes with dramatics that should impress this actor. "Are we back to this again?"

While hanging out with a sick person is not ideal for someone who suffers from emetophobia, the official name for my vomit phobia, the last few days gave us time together. In between naps and an *MST3K* marathon, we discussed everything from terrible auditions to first kisses. When he gained more energy, we covered deeper topics like life's disappointments and surprise joys.

Each conversation drew me into the beauty that is Harlan Holcombe.

Sometimes our relationship feels like an unpredictable vortex that could lead to pain and heartbreak. What does Harlan Holcombe dream for his future? What if we don't want the same things? But in quiet moments, I picture Harlan guiding me down the same spiral into the clutches of something real. Something safe.

"I don't camp. Lysol can't help any of my problems while being one with nature." I hold up my hand, ready to raise a finger for each point. "Sleeping on a hard floor, eating food that may or may not be cooked all the way through, and going to the bathroom without the use of a toilet are not my ideas of fun. Not to mention impending bug or animal attacks."

"I still think you've camped with the wrong people." He sits up and turns toward me. "I'm offended you won't consider going with me just once."

I don't care how blinding his smile is right now, I'm not budging. "Camping is for high school youth group make-out sessions, or single people who need to prove to their friends that they're low-maintenance. I have nothing to prove."

"So you won't hang out in a tent with me." He reaches across the arms of the chairs and grabs my hand. "But will you celebrate

Christmas with my family in Colorado Springs?" He kisses my palm. "Top-of-the-line mattresses." Another kiss. "Fully cooked meals." Kiss. "Running water." A final kiss and a wink.

I blink. The kisses were lovely, but fear is seeping into this conversation.

He leans in. "The flu wasn't on purpose, but I'm constantly thinking about how we can make our schedules match up. Almost to stalker status."

I blink again. Penelope's warning about Olivia flashes through my head. How am I supposed to respond to him?

"Honest." He grins and shakes my hand. "I was going to lie about a favorite barber in Dallas just for an excuse to come in town every two weeks. But a visit at Christmas would be easier."

"You cut your hair every two weeks?"

"Meredith."

With no alternative escape route, I double down. "Every two weeks for the disheveled look?"

He growls, part frustration, part amusement.

I close my eyes, inhale, then open them and look at him. "I can't go, Harlan."

His tone gentles. "Why not?"

"Um." I pull my hand back and rearrange the afghan covering my legs. "Have you talked to Penelope?"

He straightens his spine. "What does Penelope have to do with this?"

Oh no. What do I do now?

"Meredith. If you won't tell me, I'll call her."

I stop tucking the blanket around my knees. "No. Don't. It's not her."

"If there's been a misunderstanding with Penelope, let me help." He swipes the screen on his phone.

"It's Olivia." My face cringes after her name bursts from my mouth.

His eyes slice to mine. "What about Olivia?"

"I don't know details, but Penelope said Olivia's going to challenge you for custody." I reach out to grab his arm. "If she brings me into that battle, it might be a disaster. My history over the last few years could make me appear unstable. And I won't do anything to jeopardize your relationship with Alex." The last words wobble as tears simmer in my eyes, blurring my Hercules.

My gut clenches. I'm falling in love with Harlan Holcombe. And saying goodbye to him will take more courage than I can fathom.

A lethal vibe emanates off Harlan. Standing, he shifts away from me and stomps a few feet. He runs a hand through his hair and grips his neck. When he turns back in my direction, his eyes are blazing. "Sweetheart, come here." His bossy command is somehow gentle.

"I think it's best if we—"

"Sweetheart. Come here. Please." He holds out a hand, but it's the expression on his face that draws me to him. Bridled fortitude with flashes of vulnerability.

I walk to him and grasp his hand.

Standing in front of me, he thumbs through his phone and dials a number. As he puts the phone to his ear, his eyes bore into mine.

I swallow, nervous and unable to figure out what's about to happen.

Harlan clenches his jaw. "Do not start with me, Olivia," he says into his cell.

The sharp words surprise me.

"I'm only calling to say one thing. There will be no discussion." His nostrils flare, and his eyes never leave mine. "Whatever it is you think you're doing, stop it. Now." He shakes his head. "Don't act like you don't know what I'm talking about. You're dropping threats to Penelope about taking me to court over the woman I'm dating."

The warm whoosh filling my belly is at battle with the original acidic reaction to the situation. I'm rooting for the warmth.

"Do not act like this is about your father's death. This is one hundred percent because I have a woman in my life." He grips my hand tighter and breaks eye contact to lower his head. "And do not force my hand. Your unstable emotional history will not serve you here. I'm not afraid to subpoena medical records or witnesses. Is that what you want?"

Whoa.

He grumbles at her response and looks up to the sky. As he opens his mouth, the doorbell rings. We both turn our heads to peer through the open sliding glass door.

I glance up to Harlan, and he gives a chin lift in the direction of the house.

Rubbing my thumb against his, I offer a feeble smile. As I shift to traipse through the house, I shake my head. What a mess.

Claire is supposed to drop off some chicken noodle soup from Panera. So when I swing the door open, I'm surprised to find Molly. "Hey. Everything okay?"

She plants a hand on her hip. "You tell me. You're the one who hasn't shown up to decorate for Christmas at the retirement community."

I slap my palm to my forehead. "I completely forgot."

She bulldozes her way past me into the house. "If you don't want to help, please call the director. It makes me look bad when you stand her up."

After I close the door, I turn to face my overinvolved sister. "Molly, I made a mistake." As I take a breath to describe the last few days, Harlan's raised voice floats through the house.

"What's going on? He was supposed to leave yesterday. I thought I saw his rental outside, and now I hear his voice and *know* that's his rental." Molly's narrowed eyes peer through the living room. "Is he why you've been such a flake?"

I breathe through the shock of her audacity and wring out my now shaking hands. This tension has been building for a while, but her sharp reaction still cuts me. "I knew this might be hard for you, Molly, but I didn't realize that when I started living my own life, you would take it personally."

"Take it personally?" She spits her words at me with an incredulous tone.

"I love you." My face burns and tears sting my nose. "But I need you to let go of me. You have sacrificially cared for me, but you are now overstepping your bounds. I need you to let me find my own way."

Her head rears back at my verbal slap.

"And you need to find your own way too," I add. When she starts to respond, I shake my head. Holding up a hand, I walk past her. "Claire's coming by soon to drop something off. Can you please answer the door?"

Not waiting for her reply, I step onto the back porch.

Harlan stands with legs slightly apart, one hand splayed on his hip, his head lowered as he stares at the phone in his other hand.

I gulp. "Everything all right?"

Face unreadable, he nods. "So." He shifts his gaze to me and waits a beat. "Let's start with the basics. Are you still falling in love with me?"

My head jerks back in surprise, and I blink. "Well. Yes."

His eyes darken. "I'm definitely still falling in love with you. Will you please spend Christmas with my family and me?"

"What about Olivia? I can't be something that causes you custody issues."

He gives me a curt shake of his head. "She doesn't get to be in this relationship, Meredith. I'm not worried about her. Penelope will contact my lawyer, and he'll be ready for any of her moves."

My shoulders slump. That's still not ideal.

"Which is why you're going to have to trust me on this one." He steps closer. "So what about spending the holidays with me in Colorado?"

I know I can trust Harlan. It's Olivia who gives me pause.

My cheeks fill with air as I blow out a long exhale. The transition from discussing Olivia to visiting him in Colorado is not an easy one. But it's time to talk about the realities of December grief.

"Christmas can get a little tough. I love the idea of spending the holidays with your family, but I can't risk a full-blown meltdown as their first impression of me."

He reaches out, pulls me to him, and wraps his arms around my waist. "I will respect whatever you want to do, but let me explain a few things first?"

Am I supposed to be able to concentrate with his hold around me like this? Still, I nod.

"The ranch has four separate houses spread out across the acreage. You'll stay in an entire house to yourself, fully stocked with Meredith-esque items of comfort, but also with total privacy."

I pull at a lock of hair and wrap it around my finger.

"I've thought about this, Meredith. I know it won't be all reindeer and mistletoe. If you want to share the hard part with me, I'll be there." He shrugs. "If you want to lock the door, I'll wait for you to come out. In the in-between times, you can see my life." He rests his cheek on mine and says close to my ear, "And if you need to go home in the middle of your stay, there's freedom to make that choice."

For the past four years, my family has set up a way for me to hibernate during the holidays. They'd stock me up with food and leave me alone while they protected me from the outside world. I sat frozen in the shelter of my cave, waiting for some of the roughest days of the year to pass. In the beginning, I needed those tough days to pass *over* me. But staring at Harlan, I understand that if I say no, this holiday will pass *by* me.

The subtle difference is powerful.

He doesn't shield me from the pain. But he continues to assure me he's available to see me through some of it.

I don't blame my family for the way they've loved me. However, I'm growing through something I can't define.

Sometimes I wonder if it's time to let go of them a bit and see what happens. Maybe that's why I went to Colorado in the first place.

I study each line on Harlan's face, and I hope visiting his home will reveal their stories. I take a breath. "Will the house be stocked with Oreos? The ones covered in white chocolate only come at Christmastime."

A blinding smile spreads across his face. "I think I can handle that."

"No, ask Penelope to handle the cookies. These only come around once a year, and if you buy the wrong kind, it could get ugly."

His eyes narrow with mock earnestness. "Yeah, that does sound more like a Penelope thing." He cups a hand to my cheek. "So, does this mean you'll come?"

"Yeah." I grin. "I'll come celebrate Christmas with you, Harlan Holcombe."

He draws me in to kiss me on the forehead. Leaving his lips there, he says, "Thank you."

The thought of Christmas with Harlan settles into the squishy sensation in my belly, but voices sound from the living room and interrupt the moment.

"What now?" I ask.

As I twist in Harlan's arms, Claire charges onto the porch, her eyes full of panic. "Meredith, I was at Panera grabbing your order for you, and look who I found who wanted to come check on you because he thought you might be sick." Her words sputter in such quick succession, they don't register.

Which is unfortunate because the next person to join us outside is Stanley. Only instead of panic, his eyes are loaded with confusion. Then anguish.

"Oh. My. Gosh." Claire's awe-filled tone whispers through the tension. "Hercules totally puked in your house the other day."

"Meredith?" Stanley's glare flashes from Harlan, to me, to Harlan's arms around me, and back to me. His face clouds in thunder.

Molly ambles out to the patio, arms crossed over her chest, completing the trifecta of disaster. She stands behind the others and narrows her angry eyes.

Where is Harlan's camping gear? I need to send up a flare.

I turn to try to pull away from Harlan, but he clamps his grip to my waist and plasters me to his side. Heat infuses my cheeks.

"Stanley"—I throw out a limp arm in his direction—"this is Harlan, my . . . uh . . . Harlan. And Harlan"—I dart my eyes to him, not making eye contact—"this is Stanley, my . . . friend."

Harlan's body is stilted when he pulls me forward with him and offers a hand to Stanley.

Stanley stares at the greeting a touch too long. Finally, he moves forward to shake Harlan's hand once, then retreats to his position. "How do you know Meredith?"

I glance at Claire, and it looks like her eyes are going to bug out of her head.

"Harlan, that's my friend Claire." I point to her. "Claire, this is Harlan."

Claire cracks a giant smile. "So nice to meet you."

Harlan nods. "Same to you." Then he nods to my sister. "Good to see you again, Molly."

Waves of distaste roll off her haughty stance. She shifts her gaze to me. "Christmas without your family, Meredith? Really?"

Now my face flushes for a different reason.

Enough is enough. This little scenario is full of fish to fry, and Molly is swimming to the top of my list. I lean toward her. "Were you eavesdropping?"

"I'm sorry, I didn't catch your answer," Stanley says to Harlan. "How did you meet Meredith?"

"Met her in Colorado Springs," Harlan says with a clipped tone, the first hint of his waning patience.

"And now she's going back for Christmas." Molly holds her hand out like she's in a courtroom offering exhibits.

"Why would you do that?" Stanley scratches his chin. "Christmas is a really tough time for you."

"Because we're dating." With Harlan's firm tone, it's clear he's done with niceties.

But Stanley doesn't deserve that tone. He's just been blindsided, evidenced by how destroyed he looks. Then again, I'm about done with Stanley inserting himself into my life.

One more glimpse at Claire and I see her gawking between each of us, enthralled with this nightmare of mine. All she needs is a bucket of popcorn and a comfy chair and she'd be set. At least she's not causing problems.

"Okay, I wasn't going to butt in, but clearly I need to say something." Molly steps toward me. "Harlan, you have no idea what you're getting into. It's fine if you want to spend time with Meredith, but just don't do it over Christmas."

Claire slides her eyes to my sister. "Molly, that is not cool."

Molly shoots a death glare at my friend. "With all due respect, Claire, you aren't around her as much as I am."

"With all due respect, Molly, you have no idea what my relationship with Meredith is like."

"You're hardly around," Stanley says to Claire.

I want to scream, but I'm not sure which of them I should start with. "Stop talking about my life like I'm not here."

Stanley leans toward me. "How long have you been dating?"

"Since her trip to Colorado," Harlan answers for me.

Stanley frowns at Harlan, then focuses on me. "When we talked, you said there wasn't anyone else."

Harlan turns to me, blocking Stanley from my sight. "You said there wasn't anyone else? When exactly did you talk to him?"

"See," Molly interjects, "you haven't been together long enough for you to dive into the Christmas holidays."

Peeking around Harlan, I throw a pleading look to Claire. Her eyes fill with alarm and she shakes her head.

"Meredith." Harlan's grunt pulls me back to my conversation with him.

"Harlan." I lower my voice. "I wasn't sure about us for a while."

He looks to the sky, then back to me. "I told you to trust me."

"Meredith," Stanley calls to me. "Doesn't sound like you're sure now."

Harlan cranes his neck to look back at Stanley. "Back off."

"Back off?" Stanley asks, his voice raised.

"Stanley," I growl so loud that everyone freezes. Pushing Harlan out of the way so I can see each person, I swallow and say with finality, "You are way out of line."

"He doesn't even know you."

"*You* don't even know me!" I yell, surprising no one more than myself. "I get that I treated you terribly after Steve died, but I will not tiptoe around you any longer. You've overstepped your bounds, offered your unsolicited opinion, and made massively incorrect assumptions about what I've needed. And I know—" I squeeze my eyes shut, shake my head, then look at Stanley and say with a softer but firm voice, "I know you do these things in the name of your friendship with Steve, but that suffocates me in manipulation."

Stanley gapes. "What's that supposed to mean?"

Harlan, his face granite, gives a chin lift to the door. "I think it means it's time for you to leave."

Stanley looks from me to Harlan. "This has nothing to do with you."

"If you've been paying attention, man, this has nothing to do with you either, and everything to do with Meredith."

Stanley shoves his hands in his jacket pockets and points his eyes to the ground. "I guess I know when I'm not needed."

I feel Harlan's hand on the small of my back, but his face is unreadable.

Claire nods as if she's having a conversation with herself. "Meredith, I left the soup inside for you. But I have to get going." She asks Stanley, "Will you please walk me to my car?"

Without looking at me, he turns and walks back into the house.

Following Stanley, Claire looks over her shoulder at me and mouths, *I love you.*

Once they leave, Harlan turns to me. "Why haven't you mentioned Stanley before?"

Is he . . . is he upset with me?

"See?" Molly says. "You're not ready to spend Christmas with him. He didn't even know about Stanley."

"Molly!" At this point, I don't care if my neighbors hear. I want to completely unleash on my sister.

She stands straighter and returns my stare.

Taking in a deep breath, I close my eyes. "I need you to leave."

"What did you say?" Her shocked whisper hits me in the gut.

When I open my eyes, I catch a fraction of pain in her face, then it disappears. "I'm asking you to leave," I say in a tone that she cannot mistake.

With slow movements, she looks at Harlan, then back at me. "I'm just trying to—"

"I know." I shake my head. "Don't I know it. You're just trying to help. But, Molly, I'm just not sure I can take any more of your help. You parade around my life like you're the grand master, but maybe I don't want to be in the parade anymore!"

Her face turns crimson and her lip quivers. She pats her hair down, dazed, as if she doesn't know exactly where she is right now. "Right," she says to herself. "Right. Somehow, while you went through hell, I kept you alive, and now you're ungrateful. That makes sense."

"Watch it," Harlan says in a low voice.

Molly's face screws up in an unattractive scowl. "You can't just insert yourself into Meredith's life and know what's best for her."

"And I'm going to say the same thing to you." Harlan's eyes flare, and his voice sounds sinister even though the words are beautiful to me. "If you've been paying attention, this has nothing to do with you and everything to do with Meredith."

"Who do you think you are?" she whispers.

"I'm the man asking you to honor your sister's wish and leave her house."

Molly looks at me as if she's going to say something, then at Harlan as if she knows she shouldn't. She storms out her exit while Harlan and I stand frozen. She crosses the threshold of the house, and a few seconds later the front door slams.

"Sweetheart," he says as he steps toward me.

I shoot my hand out. "Just give me a second." My snapped words stop him short, and I collapse into the deck chair. Leaning my elbows into my knees, face in my hands, I try to use deep breaths to avoid the impending tears. My MO lately has been huge buckets of grief tears. But Harlan won't recognize these tears. They are stronger-than-dirt, unfiltered anger tears.

He plops in the chair next to me. "Are you okay?"

I raise my head and turn it his direction. "Am I okay?" He can't miss my infuriated tone. "What was that all about? I don't mind talking to you about Stanley, but could you do the courtesy of waiting until he leaves to have that discussion?"

Harlan clamps his mouth shut.

"He was Steve's best man. He's been trying to push into my life for a while now, and it never felt right to me. And when he told me he had feelings for me a few weeks ago, I made that more than clear to him." I rest my elbows on my knees and let my hands hang down, feeling my blood pressure returning to normal. "I didn't tell you, Harlan, because I'm so busy trying to figure out how to walk you through my dead husband and kids that Stanley wasn't even on my radar. Also, he's not on my radar because, honey, he's just not *on my radar*." I shift my focus to the yard.

He scores a hand through his hair. "Okay," he says on a big sigh.

I take a minute to think through everything that just played out in front of Harlan. Lovely.

"Well, that was some good yearslong drama you just got a front-row seat to." Still staring at the yard, I whisper, "Wanna bail on me?"

"Not on your life." His answer is immediate, sure. "Still wanna go to Colorado for Christmas with me?"

"Yup."

In unison, we lean back into our chairs. He holds his hand out for me, and I take it. He squeezes.

"I changed my mind," I say, my eyes directed to the trees but unfocused. "I think we should go camping. But only under one condition."

"What's that?"

"For entertainment, we throw Molly and Olivia in a tent together."

# 24

**ALMOST A WEEK LATER,** over dinner with Claire, I tick off the points on my fingers. "Let's see, I hurt my only sister to the point that we're not speaking."

"Necessary," she interjects.

"I completely lost it to Steve's best friend."

"Also necessary."

"I quit all of my volunteer jobs only to consider buying a ranch I'm sure I don't need."

"Love it so much."

"And to top it all off, I'm in a serious relationship with a movie star."

"There it is." She points her fork at me, Caesar salad and all. "That's what I want to talk about. I've forgiven you, by the way, for not telling me about Hercules earlier. While I would have liked to have been on ground zero when you broke Famous People Probation, I always knew when you dated again you'd keep it to yourself for as long as possible."

Claire always knows how to keep it light and give me space.

"Well, that's good." I nod, knowing we'd come back to that now that we've finally found time to catch up. "Because I haven't talked to Stanley or Molly. Maybe they're in a support group, plotting an intervention for me. So I need you to still be my friend."

"Done." She shakes her head. "Watching Stanley meet Harlan was so dang awkward. He was the perfect storm of anger, judgment, and betrayal, all wrapped up in a nice-guy package."

"Worse than watching my sister become the worst version of herself?"

"Meredith, this blowup with Molly was bound to happen. You recognize that, right? She's always been on the codependent side of protective big sister."

"She held pieces of my life together for a long time. Her smothering *did* provide comfort."

"Doesn't make it okay," she says before she shovels salad in her mouth.

"No. It doesn't. Everything I'm frustrated with, I allowed, so I'll take ownership of that. But change is here, and I think she's filled with fear because she can't predict or control it." I shake my head, disgusted and still a little bit in disbelief. "I believe her parting words were something about my ungratefulness and that I'm only alive because of her."

Claire gapes, but she says nothing.

"The thing is, it's true. She orchestrated getting me professional help when I couldn't advocate for myself. But I'm hoping while I taste the freedom of change, she gets her own morsel of it too. She needs to go back to her life, and I'm figuring out what mine looks like now."

"She's a piece of work. Let's talk about the good part." My childhood friend grins at me. "How are things going with Mr. Change?"

I chuckle. "We're going to talk about him like he's normal?"

"I teach high school kids. Nothing fazes me." She looks at me with a pleased smile. "Plus, you now talk about him like he's normal. And I love that for you."

"I think we're settling in." I take a drink of my water and know that I'm glowing when I smile at her. "And that feels really good."

---

It turns out Harlan has strong long-distance-relationship game.

"Did you get them?" he asks over FaceTime the next evening. "Show me."

"I did," I say, grinning. I point the camera on my phone down at the pink cowboy-hat-covered flannel pajamas he sent me.

"We match," he says, showing me his blue-with-cowboy-hats pajamas.

I get settled into the cushions of my couch and pull a throw over my legs. "What are we watching?"

"In honor of the showdown last week with Stanley and Molly at your O.K. Corral, we're going to watch *Tombstone*."

Giggling, I lie down, hugging a throw pillow and keeping Harlan's face in my sights while I pull up the movie.

"Ready?" he asks. When I nod, he says, "Hit play."

A few minutes into the movie, I glance down at Harlan. He's propped on his elbow, staring at me.

I smile. "Are you watching the movie?"

"Nope. I found something better to watch."

And then I melt.

---

A week later, he orders me dinner to be delivered to my house. We were to receive our food at the same time and eat it over FaceTime together. Virtual date night.

I thought it would just be casual takeout. But Claire shows up dressed in all black with a long white apron, will not say a word to me, and sets up beautiful white linens, fine china, and exquisite crystal.

"You're seriously not going to talk to me?" I ask, arms folded, watching her in my dining room.

"I'm following my instructions," she says, unable to contain the grin on her face.

"He told you not to talk to me?"

"He told me not to steal the show," she says while lining up the silverware like a professional.

I laugh out loud. "He's a quick learner."

"He is. And I respect that about him." She pulls out a silver crumber to smooth over the table and ensure the presentation is pristine. "I also respect Penelope, by the way. She set this entire operation up, and I'm pretty sure she could run the country if asked."

"And it would probably be easy for her," I murmur. Harlan's assistant has proven herself to be a gem—not that she needed to. She just does it naturally. And she has become someone I hope I get to spend more time with.

ABBA announces to me that Harlan is calling, and I hit the screen to accept the FaceTime call. When I see his beautiful face, I say, "You told me to wear sweatpants and then brought in formal tableware."

"Let me see those sweats." I show him, and he whistles. "You look comfortable."

I laughed. "What have you done?"

"I'm providing you with a fine-dining experience while you get to be in comfy pants."

"You're my dream man."

His voice lowers. "Working on it."

---

Two days later, little Alex is live on my phone screen. Face scrunched up in concentration, she stares down at the playing pieces to Candy Land.

We don't want to overwhelm her with my presence in her life, so this is a first step to easing me naturally into the conversation.

So far, our Candy Land playdate is not going as planned.

"I want pink," she says.

I heave a dramatic sigh. "Me too," I say sympathetically.

Harlan moves his phone so I can see his face. "Are we going to be able to get over this?"

"I don't think so," I say. "The color of your playing piece is just too important. I'm with Alex on this one. We want pink."

He raises his eyebrows and says in an amused tone, "I don't think I saw this coming."

I shrug, loving the dramatics. "Do you have something else in the house that we could try to use for playing pieces? Preferably pink?"

He leaves the phone face up so I'm looking at the ceiling, but I can hear Alex's sweet voice singing "Row, row, row your boat" in the background.

When Harlan returns, he grabs the phone and holds up a can of pink Play-Doh.

"Pay-Doh!" Alex grabs the can.

Harlan laughs. "Let me get it open for you, sweetie."

At once, Alex begins to mash and push the Play-Doh.

"Do you have any of this stuff at your house?" Harlan stage-whispers.

"No, but I'll get some for the future."

The future. A future with Alex in my life. A future with Harlan and his daughter in my life. That feels good just thinking about it.

"That would be great, Meredith. Thank you," he says with a thick tone. He's thinking about it too.

"Guess!" Alex thrusts her creation at the phone's camera in a way that allows me to see only a dark pink curtain.

"Oh," says Harlan in his best game-show-host voice. "Ladies and gentlemen, we're playing Guess the Animal. Today, our guest, Meredith Harper, is playing for a trip to Colorado."

I giggle.

Harlan draws back Alex's arm so I can see her creation. An unrecognizable, four-legged pink thing.

"That's *beautiful*," I say, dragging out the word.

Alex smiles proudly at me.

I tap my temple as if I'm thinking really hard. I go for the big guns, knowing that my guess might be a complete disaster. "There's really only one appropriate guess. It looks like Rocky, the Rocky Mountain bighorn sheep."

"Wocky!" Alex throws her arms up and runs around in circles, holding her creation in the air. "Wocky wocky wocky!"

"You're unbelievable," Harlan says to me while we laugh.

Alex stops, wobbles, and looks at her dad. "I want to see Wocky."

I watch as it occurs to Harlan what I've done.

"Sorry," I say through giggling, knowing full well she will hound him until they go.

"You're unbelievable," he says, this time in a humorous but incredulous tone.

---

The next day, I receive a special delivery. A box of gorgeous pears with the message, "It apPEARS I really like you."

I pick up the phone and call immediately. When he answers, I say, "I'm going to post this card on Facebook just to out you in the cheesy department."

"I was going to send cheese"—I can hear the smile in his voice—"but I could only come up with things about strong smells to put on the card. It didn't seem as romantic."

"But pears did?"

"They made you call me, didn't they?"

---

"And that's how the last few weeks have gone," I say to Claire.

Her belly laugh fills the store as she clutches her stomach in mock pain. "Hercules is a dork."

"He is," I say with full affection, thinking of the most handsome man I get to call mine. "He is a total dork."

I stare at the full-length mirror propped on the brown-carpet floor at Western Warehouse, assessing the latest cowboy boots I've tried on.

Claire stands next to me, arms crossed, head cocked. "I like these the best. The black goes with anything, but the stitching gives them some personality." She steps behind us to a bench where ten boxes of rejected footwear tower dangerously.

Turning my body, I study the boots from the opposite side. "Yeah. I agree. This pair is a solid option." As I observe the crowded store, I shake my head. "I cannot believe I'm boot shopping on the way to the airport. On December twenty-second, no less."

When I shift to face Claire, she cradles an oversized shoebox to her chest. "Your boyfriend's taking you square-dancing on New Year's Eve, which means you need to shed your city-girl shoes." Her eyes glitter with mischief. "And I think you should go with this pair."

"Where did these come from?" I snag the box and sit down on the bench. After a failed attempt to pry off the left boot, I straighten my leg toward Claire. "A little help, please."

Pulling, she grunts out her answer. "I picked them up as an afterthought. But they might be the exact thing to complete your travel wardrobe." When the shoe releases, she falls backward, landing on her tail end. Her surprised eyes find mine, and we both laugh.

I open the shoebox and grin. "What are these?"

"Perfect, right?" Claire sits next to me and gazes at the Texas flag–embroidered boots in my lap.

While pulling the left boot out of the box, I remove the tissue paper from the toe.

Claire claps her hands together and rubs them back and forth. "I have a good feeling about these boots."

"This pair will make everyone in Colorado hate me. We Texans are so obnoxious." As I push in, my heel gets stuck. Folding my body over to wrangle the boot on, I shake my head.

"Wear them with pride."

"Well, he's also a terrible dancer." I step to the mirror, studying the different boot on each foot. "But either of these should protect my toes on the dance floor."

My eyes dart from one boot to the other. One is a neutral color, safely matching the other items in my existing wardrobe. The other is an uncertain purchase, destined for one use, then for years in the back of my closet.

"Finding where you belong isn't easy." She flashes a smile and taps her toe to my foot wearing the Texas boot. "But it kind of feels like you should do it dressed in this pair. Take a piece of your history with you, but walk boldly into the next phase."

"What am I doing?" I murmur to myself in the mirror. Christmas in Colorado with Harlan. This feels like a big step. One that I'm excited about. But nervous about all the same.

Claire rises, wraps her arms around me from behind, and rests her chin on my shoulder. Holding my gaze in the mirror, she says, "You're living."

Living. That word settles somewhere deep. Somewhere important.

I am living.

# 25

**"I'M NOT GOING."** Clutching the kitchen counter behind me, facing the room, I stare Harlan down.

The guesthouse on the Holcombe ranch outside of Colorado Springs provides a secluded hideaway. Which is perfect since I plan on doing just that. Hiding in this immaculate but homey, everything-looks-like-Pottery-Barn farmhouse.

A smile tugs at his lips. "Is it meeting my family, or skiing?"

"All of the above. Plus, I think I'm coming down with something." I fake cough. "Some kind of weird throat bug going around on late-night flights. The pilot mentioned it right before we landed. The first twenty-four hours are critical. I shouldn't be around anyone."

Harlan swaggers to me and places his hands on my hips. "Do you know why my family's going to love you?"

"Because I protected them from this terrible disease?" Turning my head, I release the most obnoxious hacking sound I can create.

His lips twitch. "No. They're going to love you because you're mine."

My belly whooshes, but I snap back into my fears. "Stop being all handsome and charming."

His fine physique contained in those black form-fitting ski pants and hunter-green thermal shirt is almost more than I can handle.

Leaning in, he gifts me with the most delicate of kisses. "I admit I'm pulling out the big guns to distract you."

I shake my head. "And this is how you show your devotion? By hurling me off of a mountaintop?"

"It's my family tradition. When I was eleven, my dad took my brother and me skiing on December twenty-third to keep the peace. The twenty-fourth is our official Christmas celebration, and Mom asked Dad to take her two rowdy boys away to save her sanity." He shrugs. "We've been doing it ever since."

I scrunch up my nose.

"But I brought you something that I think will help." Out of his pocket, he removes two safety pins and an unlined, square piece of yellow paper covered in black block letters.

As he holds up the note for me, I read it out loud. "My name is Meredith Harper. If I get lost, please return me to Harlan Holcombe or anyone in the Holcombe family. Their phone number is 555-4367. If you cannot track them down, please take me to the Ski Hill Grill at the base of Peak 8 and buy me a cup of hot chocolate. I will wait for the Holcombes, who will come to claim me at the end of the day."

A warmth starts in my core and spreads to my limbs. The message reads as if I'm a member of Harlan's family.

Could I find my purpose here?

Harlan holds one safety pin between his lips while poking the other through the paper. "One of your concerns is getting lost alone on the trails. If we get separated, you have a reminder about where you belong." He opens my puffy pink ski jacket and starts to attach the note to the inside lining.

"What if an axe murderer is hanging out on the slopes waiting for people like me who don't know what they're doing?" I blink in earnest.

His gaze darts to mine, and he grins through the metal fastener. "Sweetheart, if that's the case, then I will miss you."

As he leans in to kiss me, I quickly draw back. "Watch the sharp object, mister. Maybe instead of an axe murderer, you're the one I should worry about."

Harlan pulls the safety pin out of his mouth and grabs my shoulders. "If an axe murderer gets you on the mountain, I will do everything in my power to turn your story into an above-average made-for-TV movie."

I squint. "Will you play yourself?"

He offers a mocking solemn nod. "If that would make you happy."

"Who will be cast as me?" I jut my chin out and use a weighty tone. "Because it has to be someone good."

He fastens the remaining pin to the bottom of the paper to secure it to my coat. "Are you playing the game where you get pretend mad so you don't have to go skiing?"

I feign shock while I jerk my head back. "Can't you grant a woman her dying wish?"

A low chuckle rumbles in his chest. "Okay, I will work on getting Emily Blunt. TV movies aren't her normal gig, but when she learns the circumstances behind your unfortunate death, I think she'll be on board." His gaze turns to my zipper, and he runs the slider through the teeth, up over my sweater.

Dear Lord. I'm dating someone who knows Emily Blunt.

I stretch my neck to give him access to the two snaps at the top of my ski coat. "Thank you for honoring my memory. It means a lot to me."

"Uh-huh." While placing his hands over mine, he leans in and brushes his lips to my cheek. "Now, let's load up the Jeep." He pries my left hand off the counter edge, draws it up, and kisses the palm. "We're going to meet my family." He peels my right hand off the ledge and repeats his sweet affection. "And we're taking the first step to jump-start your professional ski career." The final peck is to my forehead, where he leaves his lips when he says, "Sans serial killers."

———

Sleeping the ninety-minute drive to Breckenridge did nothing for my hair. As Harlan and I maneuver through the village at the bottom of the mountain, I wrangle in the strays, tucking them under my knit hat. Because of my glove-clad hands, I'm not sure this hairdo is much better. Just as I yank my hat off, my hair defying gravity in the power of static electricity, Harlan homes in on a group of people standing under the awning of a ski rental store.

Harlan, his mom, and his brother William own equal parts of the vast and successful Holcombe ranch. William and his wife run the family business. When the man in the group turns around and grins, it's clear he's a Holcombe.

Oh my word. The genes in this family.

For a split second, I debate whether Harlan's sibling should have been the one to go into show business. Instead of dark hair, his is a fabulous mix of blond, brown, and a few distinguishing strands of gray. His deep-hued brown eyes match the set that I enjoy getting lost in. William's frame is as tall as Harlan's but leaner.

"Hey, big brother," he says.

"William." Harlan's grin lights up, and he clutches his brother in one of those manly pat-on-the-back-that-could-knock-over-an-ox hugs. He turns to me. "Meredith, this is William."

"Ma'am." William shakes my hand. "Mama's upset she won't make your acquaintance today, Meredith. But when you taste her chocolate cream pie, you'll understand why she never comes to the mountain." He shifts to the woman behind him, tucks her under his arm, and shoots a proud grin to me. "This is my elementary school sweetheart, Gracie."

Gracie is a little shorter than I am, and her stout frame speaks of country living. The sparse makeup and brown bob haircut outline her heart-shaped face in a flattering manner. But as I study Harlan's sister-in-law, I wonder why her smile doesn't quite reach her eyes.

After patting down my flyaway hair, I offer a handshake. "Nice to meet you."

Gracie's blank eyes glance to me when she takes my hand, then she turns. "Boys, come say hello to Meredith."

Two young guys looking through a storefront glass at a snowboard display turn at the sound of their mama's voice. The sight of them takes my breath away. The taller one shares his mother's blue eyes and his dad's lighter hair. But the younger one . . . The younger one is the spitting image of Harlan. Dark eyes, dark hair, and a very familiar gleam in his smile.

"Clark here is thirteen." Gracie loops her arm through her son's.

"Ma'am." He makes eye contact while he shakes my hand, thus defying the reputation of aloof teenagers.

William grips the other boy's neck and gives a gentle shake. "This is Scott. He's ten."

Harlan's clone offers a more bashful "Ma'am," then he turns. "Hey, Uncle Harlan."

"Hey, man." Harlan completes a complicated high-five-turned-handshake-turned-pull-in-for-a-hug thing with Scott.

Clark repeats the same ceremony with his uncle and says, "I was hoping Alex could join us on the mountain this year."

I slide my gaze over the group. What are they thinking? She's three. I'm thirty-six, and I think I'm too young to ski.

"Yeah, I know. It's not my year for Christmas with her." Harlan claps his hands together. "I know you all want to hit the slopes, so here's an overview of the day. You guys go do a warm-up run while I get Meredith situated with her rentals and find her ski school. After that, I'll join you. Later, we'll meet up for lunch with Meredith and then enjoy the rest of the day together on the mountain."

"Uncle Har, when we race Cimmaron this year, I'm gonna kick your—"

"Language, son." William clamps a hand on Clark's shoulder.

Harlan winks at his nephew. "You wish."

William opens his map of the resort, and Harlan, Gracie, and Clark circle around to plan slope runs and meeting spots.

Scott hangs back with me, glances up, and catches my eye. "I heard it's your first time to ski."

"Yeah." I offer a shaky smile.

He steps toward me. "Are you scared? I was really scared my first time."

I bug out my eyes at him and nod.

"I brought something for you." My new best friend pulls a Sharpie out of his blue Columbia jacket pocket. Before I understand what's happening, he grasps my right hand, yanks down the glove, and writes a big *R* in the flesh between my thumb and forefinger. When he's finished, he repeats his actions with my left hand, labeling it with a ten-year-old, wobbly *L*.

"Uncle Harlan said you might be nervous. He did this for me when I learned to ski. I had a hard time remembering which way was which." Scott offers me a somber nod. "That should help."

I am completely in love with Scott.

I am also completely in love with Harlan.

Which is why when I study this precious boy, almost the exact replica of the man I am dating, something deep inside me aches. Placing my hand just under my collarbone, I rub the spot over my heart.

Harlan doesn't have any sons. No one to pass down his family name. Is that something he wants?

From me?

"Ready to tackle the mountain?"

Harlan's enthusiastic words jostle me out of my thoughts, and I shift my gaze to his.

Am I ready for the mountain? I answer with the word that is repeating on high volume in my head.

"No."

*Dream big.* Harlan's last words before he abandoned me at ski school a while ago. It's not an exaggeration to say that small children are skiing circles around me. Dream big?

"Do you know what I'm dreaming right now, Harlan Holcombe?" Talking to no one, I stick my hands through the ski pole straps and, with fumbling gloved hands, try to unzip my coat pocket. During this failed attempt, the pole-tip things hit my shins repeatedly. "I'm dreaming of staying alive today."

Why am I doing this? It's freezing. I keep falling on my tail. My pants are going to split any second now. God help me if I have to go to the bathroom anytime soon.

"Meredith, you're doing great." Walking toward me is my real-life Hercules, dressed in his own tight ski pants.

Oh yeah. That's why I'm doing this.

"Liar," I call to him. I would make an attempt to meet him halfway, but my mobility is unstable. Who invented this god-forsaken sport?

Harlan struts toward me with ridiculous ease as if he isn't wearing Frankenstein boots. "How's it going?" He leans down and touches his lips to mine.

Glancing around to make sure my instructor isn't within earshot, I grab his forearm. "Listen. You gotta break me out of ski school."

Harlan squats and knocks on the shell of my boot. "I think these might be a little loose."

"All throughout my childhood, I was a rule follower. Never

skipped class. Never cheated. Always followed directions." I lower my voice. "But right now, my inner rebellious teenager wants out."

Harlan grunts when he pops one of the buckles open.

"Let's play hooky." I throw a hitchhiker thumb over my shoulder. "Bust me out of here, man."

He glances up and grins while pressing down on the adjusted buckle. "You would be disappointed in yourself if you quit now."

Narrowing my eyes, I frown. "Did you read that somewhere on inspirational toilet paper?"

Harlan chuckles, leaning over to work on my other boot.

"Never mind." I shoo away the thought with my hands. "Listen, I'm a self-aware woman, at an age where I'm comfortable with my strengths and weaknesses. And believe me that I'm okay when I say that I am not a skier. You're just going to have to love me through it."

He stands and brushes snow off his gloved hands. "I think I can love you through a lot of things."

I snap and point at him. "Do not do that charming thing."

He chuckles, but I sigh and press into his side, give him my weight, and confess, "Do you want to know the worst part about this?"

"Always."

"I am trying really, *really* hard."

He wraps his arms around me, and his shoulders shake in silent laughter. "You're better than you think. I watched you go down the bunny hill."

Burrowing into his jacket, I sigh again. "My kitchen floor has a steeper grade than the bunny hill."

"Exactly." He kisses the top of my head. "And I've never seen you fall down that either."

Out of the corner of my eye, I catch my ski instructor approaching.

"Everything all right?" the drill sergeant asks. "Break's almost over."

"She's doing really well," Harlan says, tightening his hold on me, "but I think I'm going to steal her away for the rest of the morning."

I crane my neck. "But, Harlan, I *do* want you to be with your family and ski the mountain."

He peers down at me. "I get the feeling that if I leave, you'll call a taxi and head back to the airport."

No truer words have ever been spoken.

After waving off my instructor, we head out to grab Harlan's gear. Him dragging me by my poles makes this task much easier. Once we get situated, dread washes over me.

The death chair awaits us.

I stare at the ski lift for the longest time before Harlan places his hand on the small of my back and offers an encouraging shove in its direction. While we wait in line, my silence speaks for my fear.

Harlan brushes my temple with his lips and murmurs, "You got this."

When it's our turn, we awkwardly shuffle-sidestep-move over to the loading spot.

The altitude mocks my Texas lungs, and in spite of only moving a few feet, I strain for oxygen. "No matter what happens, I apologize in advance for injuring you." I twist my torso to the outside, looking for the chair and bracing for the impact.

Once we swing out above the ground, I let go of the breath I was holding.

Harlan shifts in his seat. "You're a pro. No harm during the takeoff."

My eyes slide to his. "You aren't out of danger. We still have to jump off this thing."

I'm surprised when the gentle sway of the lift, the beauty of the mountains, and the solid mass of the man sitting next me coax my spirit into settling. Several minutes of silence pass, and my breathing slows.

"My family enjoyed meeting you." Harlan holds out his hand. "Let me take your poles."

"I'm excited about spending more time with them." With laser focus, I release each pole to his possession. It would be my luck to drop one into the snowy abyss below. "I know I just met her, but Gracie seemed distant this morning."

Resting the poles across his lap, he nods. "William said she wasn't feeling well. She stayed at the bottom of the mountain."

Not wanting to rock the chair, I keep my body facing forward but turn my head to glare at him. "If I had known that, I would've called Sally to go shopping. I'm sure she has enough sense to stay off this mountain. Skipping was an option?"

"Not for you." He winks. "Besides, Spence and Sally are spending Christmas with his brother in Denver. We won't see them until the twenty-ninth. And I should probably mention that Sally was a ski instructor in college."

"Of course she was." Sighing, I shake my head. "Why are you being so patient with me?"

Still holding the poles, he places his free hand over mine. "Because I'm proud of you."

I roll my eyes.

"I'm serious." He chuckles. "It's hard to try something new."

"Thank you." As I hold on to the side bar, I throw a gloved hand out in the direction of the austere scenery. "I admit, it's good to get out. The sunshine makes the temperature warmer than I expected. Plus, it's gorgeous up here."

"Dad and I had some of our best talks on ski lifts." Harlan turns his head away from me and stares out over the mountains. "Ski lifts, the pasture, and the chapel on our ranch. I always knew I'd get something honest from him in those places."

Still clutching the bar at my side, I reach with my opposite hand and squeeze his knee. "I wish I could have met him."

His stare shifts to my hand, and he takes my palm in his. "Me too."

Lifting our hands, I scratch the skin near my wool cap. "What was the best and what was the toughest part about him being your dad?"

Harlan's gaze returns to the open air. "He was a man of few words. More like William."

I shift my weight as far back in the chair as I can. When I'm sure I won't fall to my demise, I release him and unzip my ski jacket. "Which part was that? The best or the toughest?"

He nudges me with his elbow. "Both."

Grabbing a protein bar out of the inside pocket of my coat, I nod.

"When he was disappointed in me, he could level me with a fierce, convicting stare." Harlan exhales a weighty breath. "If he actually spoke words, that meant whatever you had done was especially bad."

My gloved hands do nothing to help me open the snack. I place the wrapper between my teeth and tug.

He slides a glance my way. "If you fall off this thing trying to open that, what do I tell the coroner? Death by protein bar?"

"That isn't funny." I giggle anyway. "What about when your dad was proud of you?"

"It was almost the same look of disapproval, but you knew the difference because his eyes would gleam." Harlan shakes his head. "I'd give anything to see that gleam again."

With extreme care, I remove one of my gloves and tuck it under my arm. "What would he say to you now?" I use my freed hand's dexterity to pry open the wrapper.

Just as I smile with victory, the ski lift stops abruptly, and my hold on the protein bar releases when I grab Harlan's hand. "Oh no." My only shot at nourishment falls toward its powdery white ruin.

As our chair swings, Harlan leans forward. "Well, at least we aren't over a trail. Then someone really would have experienced death by protein bar."

His remark might be funny if I wasn't in a panic. My stomach drops with each lurch of the bench. "This is like the baby swing from hell. Make it stop."

He grips my hand tight. "We're okay. It'll calm down in a minute."

Every muscle in my body tenses. "This chair is going to hurl me off onto another mountain to be eaten by wolves."

"Unless the axe murderer gets you first."

I bite the inside of my cheek to hold off a smile. "Don't think I won't push you off this thing."

His barked laughter fills the thin air. As the swing finally slows, he leans over and kisses my temple. "I love you, Meredith Harper."

I gape and blink. I don't move so as not to scare the moment away.

Lips remaining in place, Harlan chuckles. "See? You forgot all about the swinging."

Forgot about the swinging? No. I know all about the swinging. For a long time, I swayed through the murky depths of grief, only recently finding the ascension to living my life. Considering a future. Searching for purpose. And now, out of nowhere, the pendulum has thrown me right into the arms of an unexpected gift.

As my eyes fill with tears, I turn my head. My response to him is immediate. Easy. Peaceful. "I love you too, Harlan Holcombe."

Our faces are so close, all I can see are his eyes crinkling with a smile, right before he leans in to kiss me.

This is not a simple peck. This is a seal. A slow, deliberate, sweet seal of our commitment to each other.

"Get a room," jokers yell from the chair behind us.

He pulls back, and I don't try to hide my has-to-be-blinding smile.

Harlan Holcombe loves me. Not the actor. But Harlan Holcombe the man. Loves me.

I grab my glove and wrangle it back onto my cold hand. After zipping up my jacket, I loop my arm through his and rest my head against his strong shoulder.

"Dad was all about loyalty." Harlan's gravelly voice cuts through the silence. "He wanted us to be loyal to the family but also to ourselves. Regardless of my success, I think he understood my career wasn't about being true to my ultimate purpose in life. And I think I disappointed him."

Squeezing his arm, I snuggle in a little deeper. "What do you want to be when you grow up, Harlan?"

"I want to hand down a legacy." Harlan taps his skis together, loosening the settled snow. "Dad taught us to leave something here on earth that makes an impact."

I lick my chapped lips. "What does that look like for you? The guys you mentor?"

"I don't know, Meredith." He knocks his skis with more force, causing a giant clump of snow to fall to the ground. "But I was thinking it might have something to do with you."

My pulse quickens, and I'm stilled in scared anticipation of what he might say next.

He kisses me on top of my head. "It would be an honor to leave a legacy with you."

My stomach drops. At the same time, the chair lift restarts and jerks us back to our path up the mountain.

Ominous tingles skitter across my body.

What does he mean, leave a legacy with me? I close my eyes. *Please, no.* Legacy could imply a number of things, right?

Harlan moves, and I feel his face close to mine. "You okay?"

Swallowing, I nod. "Yeah. We got moving again, and it threw me off." I grit my teeth, fighting back the tears that will out my lie.

He nudges me off his shoulder and brushes his lips against my cheek. "Well, I need you to look alive, because we're about to ditch this ride."

My eyes pop open, and now I'm terrified for a different reason.

Impending doom is approaching.

Maybe it's not a different reason.

Drawing in a deep breath, I focus on the immediate problem. Getting off the death chair.

Harlan shifts his weight. "Tips up."

While exiting the ski lift, I veer toward him, grasping his wrist for balance, and almost take us both to the ground. Once our comedy routine of a dismount is completed, I stare at the bottom of the hill with dread.

"Here's the plan." He offers me one of my poles. "We'll stay on the easiest green runs down to the base. Then we'll meet up with my family."

When I struggle to loop the handle of the pole around my four fingers, I grunt my frustration. "It's almost lunchtime?"

"Someone needed extra time studying the chair lift before we got on." He adjusts his bright red knitted hat.

I shoot him a fake glare. "It wasn't that long."

"You're right." He leans over and fixes my second pole to my hand. "Only half an hour."

"You can't rush these things." I point to a skier who struggles to stand after getting off the lift. "Which is why I think I need more time up here to observe my fellow Alpine friends before I throw myself down the mountain armed with metal sticks in my hands."

"You're going to do great." Lacing his fingers together, he adjusts his gloves. "All you have to do is get behind me and line your skis up with mine. We'll take it wide and slow while we snowplow. Just follow my tracks."

I try to will the zombie apocalypse into coming. That can't be as terrifying as what he's asking me to do.

Harlan pushes off, and as I observe his form, I expend every ounce of energy to stay in his tracks. True to his word, we snowplow. And we are slower than Christmas. Which is saying a lot because Christmas is only two days away.

But a small miracle starts to gather momentum. With each turn of our journey, I gain a little more confidence. About three zigzags into our descent, a smile crosses my face. It dawns on me that I am having fun.

This is playful. This is freedom. This. Is. Living.

Five-year-olds skiing without poles fly by me. But somehow in my mind, I am an Olympic downhill skier. There is no stopping me.

However, somewhere during my personal Eddie the Eagle moment, it registers that I should slow down.

Only, I can't remember how to stop.

We near the end of the run, and my speed only increases.

Even though I'm completely out of breath, I try to call out, "Harlan." I dig my poles into the ground, trying to gain purchase. They drop to the snow. And now I'm toast.

"Snowplow." Harlan's bellow breaks through my panic.

I glance up.

He cups his mouth and yells again, this time indecipherable.

At that exact unfortunate moment, I lose my balance and my skis bump over something, causing me to veer to the left. My arms flail in an effort to steer my out-of-control body.

Ten feet away is a huge red plastic banner with giant white capital letters saying, "STOP." Unable to break my forward propulsion, I make a direct hit. And take the sign down with me.

"Meredith? Meredith? Are you okay?"

Writhing, I fight the crimson monster. I can't see anything but red. But I hear the crunching of boots on snow, and Harlan's stressed voice is getting closer.

"Harlan." I'm lying on part of the sign, with half of it wrapped across my body. Pushing, stretching, punching, I battle the banner. "Get me out of here."

Hands grip my shoulders. "Quit moving, sweetheart." I halt my struggle, and Harlan pulls the sign off and throws it down on the ground. He hauls me to my feet. As he frames my face in his hands, his worried eyes draw me in from head to toe. "You all right?"

Nodding, I gasp for breath. "I kind of forgot how to stop."

Because I'm not embarrassed enough, the ski patrol approaches. "Everybody okay here?"

"She's fine." Harlan waves him off. "But the banner might need some medical attention."

A blue-coated blur skies by us and comes to an abrupt, impressive stand, spraying snow ten feet in front of him. "Woo-hoo! Nice one, Stop Sign Girl!"

Great.

I wave at my fan. "I'm sorry to dethrone you, Harlan, but I'm the famous one today."

---

On the drive home, with the setting sun turning the snow into shadows, I reflect on the day as a beautiful picture of our relationship. Harlan moves ahead of me and asks me to follow him in his tracks. Each progression is slow and methodical. At first, all of it is terrifying, but he continues to reveal that moving forward is safe with him.

I open my jacket and reach for a package of Kleenex stored in my front pocket. Instead, my hand finds the note Harlan gave me this morning, reminding me that if I get lost, I now have a place to belong.

But what if our purposes don't line up?

What if he wants something I can't give him?

Staring out the window, I worry Harlan is unknowingly leading us straight into a giant stop sign.

# 26

AS I ENTER THE MAIN HOUSE on the Holcombe ranch, I glance around at the Christmas Eve preparations. From the back door, the open plan allows a full view of the kitchen, dining room, and den. Harlan told me the property was updated recently with dark wood floors that match the planks in the vaulted ceilings. The swirling dark granite complements the stainless-steel accents.

After I hang my coat on one of the hooks, I nudge my boots off and make a mental note to sink into the den's oversized couches for a nap later today.

Clark and Scott shove each other in an elbow war while they put place settings on the distressed-wood dining table. William stands next to the grand Christmas tree and stokes the fire. I don't spot Gracie anywhere, but a sprite of a woman with shoulder-length gray hair and sparkling blue eyes walks toward me.

"Meredith. Merry Christmas Eve." The lines in her face hint at a life of hard work, but her smile is breathtaking. "I'm Mama Lee."

When she hugs me, I take in her soulful warmth. I lower my head to speak into her ear. "I'm so glad to meet you." How did a person so tiny produce two brawny men?

"Word on the street is you turned down a serious triple-dog dare yesterday." She pulls back to end the hug but keeps a grasp on my arms.

"She refused to go down an easy blue with us," Clark calls across the room while pointing a handful of forks at me.

"I didn't want to cramp your style." Shrugging, I lean in for a conspiring whisper with Harlan's mom. "I chose survival."

With one final pat, she releases me. "I'm glad you did, otherwise I wouldn't have gotten to meet you."

She has no idea the truth of her statement.

Clark shakes his head as he haphazardly places a fork at the end of the table. "I think she fell down a lot on purpose so she wouldn't have to go down a harder run."

I think I fell down a lot on purpose so my hulk-of-a-man boyfriend would have to help me up again.

"Meredith, this is our ranch hand, Hank Browning. He's been with us since the boys were little." Mama Lee turns to a figure holding up the wall near William.

He doesn't acknowledge her words. Instead, he stares into the blazing fire.

Harlan's mother cups her hands and yells across the room, "Hank." She turns to me. "Hank's a little hard of hearing."

Head to toe, he looks like he walked out of an old Western, complete with hat and pearl-snap chambray shirt. Peering around Mama Lee, I search for his holster. He may be older in years, but I wouldn't want to cross him in a dark corral.

"This is Meredith." Mrs. Holcombe's declaration is loud enough for the neighboring ranch to hear. "She's from Texas."

Hank's mouth hitches in a half smile. "What about the sexes?"

A short burst of laughter comes from Scott and Clark.

"I forgot to mention," Harlan's mom says out of the side of her mouth, "his misinterpretations aren't always socially appropriate."

Trying to mask my shocked face, I wave at Hank.

He nods in return.

"Morning, sweetheart." Harlan's husky voice comes from behind me, and he pulls me back to lean against his chest. "How are you?"

I squeeze his forearms, thankful for the distraction from my introduction to Hank. "You didn't mention that I wouldn't be able to function today. I have taken soreness to a new level."

"I bet that stop sign feels the same way." He kisses my cheek.

"I don't think you're allowed to say mean things to me on Christmas Eve." I crank my head back and flash a fake glare at him.

"Just call him the Harlan Shake, Meredith." Scott snickers. "He hates it."

I spin in Harlan's embrace to face him, pursing my lips to contain a giggle.

Harlan rolls his eyes. "Some people think my dancing is out of control like the Harlem Shake."

Turning to his mom, I bug out my eyes. "Exactly. I mean, how he can be so good at something like skiing but is a lethal weapon during a waltz?"

Her lips twitch. "I don't know what you're talking about. I refer to him as Twinkle Toes."

I offer an understanding nod. "You enable him to boost his low self-esteem. I get it."

"Hello?" Harlan throws his hands in the air. "I'm standing right here."

Mama Lee pats her son on the shoulder. "Go grab some Advil for your girl. She'll need her muscles to recover before the New Year's Eve square dance."

"Thrown under the bus by my own mother." He leads me down a short hallway to a half bath. As he pulls me into the tight room, he shuts the door behind us and scans my face. "How are you this morning? Really."

My eyes mist, belying my happy facade. "I'm okay."

"We can go back to the guesthouse and hang out if that's what you need. Everyone knows what today means for you, and they want you to feel comfortable." After grasping my hands, he rubs my wrists with his thumbs. "How can I help?"

I release a shaky breath. "Will you just stay by my side?"

"Done," he says with an affirmative dip of his chin.

I snake my hands around his waist and burrow my head into his chest. "You okay without Alex here?"

"No. But she'll be here in time for the square dance, and that'll be fun." Harlan releases a frustrated sigh. "The daily parenting grind isn't Olivia's specialty. She's a better parent at big celebrations because it gives her tasks and she likes showing off. I trade holidays because it's best for my daughter. But I do miss Alex."

I sidestep, giving him room to crouch down and open the cabinet under the sink. "How did Alex sound this morning when you called?"

"Good. The whole family FaceTimed. William even played her favorite song on his guitar." He grabs a plastic shoebox, stands, and sets it on the vanity. While rummaging through the container, he inspects each label. "I'm disappointed you didn't get to talk to Alex, but I think it was best not to provoke an episode from Olivia. I hate it, but until my lawyer figures out her game plan, I need to be careful."

"I agree," I say through a stifled yawn.

Harlan pulls my hand up and glances at the top of it. "Nice cheat sheet."

Smiling at the leftover permanent-marker *R* on my right hand, I nod. "My new best friend, Scott, helped me out yesterday."

"The boys have really taken to you." He opens the bottle of Advil and taps two pills into my palm.

I grin.

"Brunch is ready." Mama Lee's voice carries through the house.

Harlan nods at my hand. "Those will loosen up your muscles before I swing you around the dance floor next week."

"Lord, help me." With Harlan's hand on the small of my back,

I walk down the hall, muttering to myself, "Do I need to take out more insurance before the thirty-first?"

Entering the food line, I'm sandwiched between Gracie and Scott. As I pick up my plate, I scan the choices. Shoney's buffet is for amateurs compared to this feast. No wonder Mama Lee stayed home yesterday. Bacon, two kinds of sausage, eggs, three kinds of bread, pancakes, waffles, and an enormous platter of fruit cover every inch of the surface. Syrup, whipped cream, four kinds of jelly, two kinds of buttery spread, orange juice, and coffee with all the fixings fill the end of the counter.

After the feast and the opening of the gifts, there will be an assortment of desserts to consume. I'm now thankful I burned off so many calories skiing down Mount Scary yesterday.

While making selections, I glance at Gracie's plate. "I'm told I have to pace myself. Are you saving room for the dessert?" I offer her a friendly smile and nod at her lone piece of toast and slices of banana.

Her lips press together in a straight line. "I'm fine. Thank you."

My eyes follow her as she rounds the smorgasbord to find her seat at the table.

Scott leans into my shoulder. "Don't mind her. She hasn't been feeling well." His preteen voice cracks in the lowered tone.

"Oh, sure." My eyes grow wide when I see what he's holding. "Good news is you're consuming enough to cover her."

His plate is adorned with an obscene amount of meat covered in a pile of bread products. I gape as he adds a whipped cream smiley face. "The trick is, you put the fruit on top so Mom thinks you're eating healthy." He dumps strawberry pieces over the precarious dome of food.

"Son, did you just say something about a kiss that's stealthy?" Hank reaches over Scott's shoulder to grab a roll while the rest of us stifle guffaws and giggles.

"No, sir." Scott's recovery to answer the question is impressive.

But more shocking than Hank's words, Scott eventually sits

down and devours his entire plate. Then he goes back for seconds.

After brunch, we congregate around the tree and begin the festivities. Inside our stockings are small gifts. Mine holds a beautiful nail kit and some stationery made by a local artist.

With each passing tradition and gift, I manage deep breaths. Memories of precious Christmases past pop up, and I shove them down along with the tears threatening to spill. Staying emotionally and mentally present in this room requires focused energy.

Harlan sits next to me on the couch and offers constant affection and support, reaching to push my hair behind my ear or rubbing his hand on my knee.

Various gifts of sweaters, purses, books, and boots for the adults. Video games, hunting gear, and clothes for the kids.

Before I left Dallas, I shipped Texas-themed care packages for each family. The gift baskets are a hit with their bluebonnet napkins, giant pecans, hot sauce, chocolate oil rigs, and Texas-shaped chunks of soap.

"So much Texas." Clark's words are muffled around an armadillo praline.

I wink. "Wait until you see my boots at the square dance."

Hank leans toward Harlan. "What did she say about her pants?"

My face flushes, and I bug out my eyes at Harlan. Thank goodness the group is too occupied with the Lone Star State paraphernalia to hear Hank's latest listening faux pas.

After all the gifts are opened, Harlan catches my eye with a mischievous grin.

"What?" I ask.

Each member of the family wears a varying degree of the same expression.

Scott pulls a package from behind his couch cushion and hands it to me. "This is to you from all of us."

As I tear the paper, neon orange peeks through. I cover my

mouth and giggle. In front of me is a workman's vest with the word HAZARD written across the back in block letters.

Everyone erupts in laughter.

William points to my present. "We wanted to make sure you were safe the next time you went skiing."

With a giant smile on my face, I take a moment to study each person in the room.

The possibility that I might belong here whispers to me.

After losing Steve, Clayton, and Chloe, I didn't think I would ever view the future as anything other than necessary. But now I'm intrigued. What if there is a place for me here? A purpose? A family?

When the gift opening comes to a close, William stands up, clasps his hands, and clears his throat. "I just want everyone to know—"

His wife, sitting next to him on the oversized chair, reaches up to grab his arm. "William?"

"It's okay, honey." He beams at her. "This is the fun part."

Eyes darting around the room, she shakes her head. "Now is not—"

"Gracie here has given us the best Christmas news." William opens his arms wide. "We are going to have another baby."

An ecstatic energy fills the room. The boys jump up and down with shocked faces. Mama Lee and Harlan walk over and offer exuberant hugs.

But I am frozen.

With tears streaming down my face.

Scott lets out a whoop, jolting me out of my stupor.

*Move. Move out of this room and let them celebrate.*

The closest door opens to the porch, and I make strides in that direction. Grabbing a random coat off a hook and slipping my feet into a pair of house shoes, I open the door, rush through, and close it. I cannot afford to look back.

After I slip my arms through the sleeves of the barn jacket, I clutch the railing of the wraparound deck. Snow-covered fields sprawl out for miles, but deep anguish hinders my view of the beauty in front of me. Angry, judgmental tears cloud my vision.

What was I thinking? That Colorado would swipe away my reality? That somehow my gaping wounds would ignore Christmas? I know better. I know better than to burden anyone around me with pain they can't help. As I close my eyes, hot tears streak down my face. Christmas. Family. Babies. How stupid of me. My thoughts spiral down to lies I shouldn't believe, and I lose the mental battle.

I am a giant stain on this picturesque Holcombe family holiday.

After several minutes of sinking into dark thoughts, I hear the door open. Once again, Harlan's strong arms wrap around my shoulders. A sob escapes as I lean back into his solid chest. He rubs his cheek against mine, soaking up my tears. Tightening his hold on me, Harlan whispers soothing sentiments as my body shakes.

"I'm sorry." My voice cracks with the inadequate apology.

"You're okay." When he kisses my temple, he holds his mouth in place. "You're okay."

My heartbeat slows as I try to match my breaths to his. One breath. Two breaths. Three.

"Hot chocolate, anyone?"

At the gentle voice, we turn toward his mother. With a quilt hanging over her arm and a mug in each hand, she offers a small smile. "Why don't you go make yourself useful, Harlan. Those dishes aren't going to wash themselves."

Holding my face in his hands, he wipes away the remaining tears with his thumbs. He peers down at me, lines creasing his face with concern.

I nod to tell him to go.

Mama Lee points to the hanging porch swing, and we both settle into it, draping the quilt over our legs. She transfers a cup to me, and it warms my chilled fingers. Glancing down, I spot the package of Kleenex she placed between us on the blanket.

When I draw my knees up to my chest, the bench sways. "I'm so sorry, Mrs. Holcombe. I ruined a special moment for your family, and—"

"Meredith, we're all so glad you're here." As she gazes out over the fields, she pats my knee.

Shaking my head, I stare at my mug.

"There isn't one person in the room back there that hasn't experienced pain." She pauses, then swallows. "I'm not going to tell you I think our loss is equal with yours, but losing Harlan's dad so unexpectedly was pretty big in our little world."

Dropping my feet to the porch, I sit up straighter and turn my face to her. We are now talking as one grieving widow to another.

"We all have our ways of dealing with it. William clears his throat when emotion hits him, and he excuses himself to check on the kids. Gracie sometimes hides in the bathroom. The boys get angry." She sips from her mug. "Harlan, well, I'm sure he told you his story. He made poor decisions to deal with his grief. The sadness seeps out sideways, but it all represents the same thing that happened back there to you."

I adjust my grip on the cup. "What about you?"

"I cry in private so as not to worry the others. But I'm not ashamed of my tears. Forty-six years of marriage gives me the right to miss Harold like crazy." Mama Lee sighs. "I have a dark place I go to every now and then, but I always come out." She turns her head and her gaze falls on me. "You're welcome in this house, Meredith Harper. And everything that comes with you."

My hands shake, and I tighten my grip on the hot chocolate. "What if I'm too much?" With the last word, a tear escapes.

She picks at a spot on the blanket. "You're going to be faced with that question for the rest of your life. It'll be yours to carry. But I'm asking you not to use it as an excuse. Part of your journey is about how others receive your story. But the other part of it is about how you decide to define yourself. Unfortunately, there'll be people who you are too much for, yes." Her thumb traces the stitching in the quilt. "But there are others who will be able to come alongside and do life with you." She nods to the fields. "Harlan can do it."

Mama Lee nudges the ground with her foot, giving the swing a gentle push, and I watch steam rise from my cup, swirl through the air, and dissipate.

Harlan thinks he wants to do it because he only has part of the story.

And I'm going to have to tell him the rest.

# 27

**"PLEASE TELL THEM** Merry Christmas for me." My raspy voice carries through the small chapel on the Holcombe property. The quilt pulled over my shoulders soaks up my tears. Maybe another day, I will take time to admire the simplicity of this one-room, eight-pew building. But this Christmas morning is burdened with grief, and I stare at the stained-glass window behind the small stage.

Loss comes in countless forms. The initial deaths were a shotgun blast to my heart. But the pellets from the shell blast out, causing holes in every area of life. Christmas is just one of a thousand casualties from a terminal collision with an eighteen-wheeler.

The door to the chapel opens, and heavy footsteps draw closer to me.

Harlan.

He sits, puts an arm around my shoulders, and gathers me against his side. I cannot control the sobbing, and he kisses the top of my head as he wraps his other arm around me. "I'm so sorry, Meredith."

Nodding, I grip his shirt and burrow deeper into his strong chest.

While he strokes my back, I concentrate on slowing my shuddering breaths. After a few moments, I pull back and focus on Harlan's sympathetic eyes.

He cups my cheek and wipes moisture away with his thumb. He grasps my hand, his face full of concern. "You're freezing. Where are your gloves?"

"I forgot them." I ball my fist and shove it in my coat pocket. "How'd you know I was out here?"

He stands. "Hank came and got me."

As I rise, I gather the quilt over one arm, and he takes my hand in his. Walking down the aisle, I glance around. "This is a lovely chapel."

"My grandparents got married here." He swipes at settled dust on the arm of the last pew as we pass. "It didn't see a lot of use for a while, but Mom comes out here more now that Dad is gone."

As Harlan opens the door and we step out into the cold, I catch sight of Hank standing against the building.

Arms crossed, toothpick in the corner of his mouth, he's bundled in total ranch getup. Wranglers, shearling coat, leather gloves, jeans, and boots. He tips his hat.

Guardian angels come in many forms.

I curl a stray strand of hair around my ear. "Did you shovel the sidewalk for me this morning?" I ask him.

Hank shifts the toothpick to the other side of his mouth.

Half of me expects him to misunderstand and ask me an inappropriate question. But the other half cannot ignore his keen, staring eyes. I release Harlan and take two steps to stand in front of Hank. "You did. You got up early and shoveled the sidewalk for me."

Hank grinds his teeth on the small piece of wood. "I may not hear very well, but I still listen."

Tears take over, and words get caught in my throat.

His strong hand squeezes my arm, and then he disappears around the corner of the building.

As I return to Harlan, I gaze out over the rest of the Holcombe property. On the other side of the fence is an oddly familiar house. Goose bumps run down my arms.

I yank on Harlan, pulling us to a stop. My fuzzy brain is missing a piece of a puzzle. "Who lives next door?"

Harlan looks across the field. "The Carsons."

"The Carsons?" Studying the property, I notice a building behind the main house. I shove the quilt into Harlan's arms and veer off the path toward the wooden fence, my heart racing. "The Carsons."

"Meredith." Harlan catches up to me. "What's going on?"

Once we reach the fence, I grab the top rail. "I can't believe it." I point down the gravel road. "Twelve Bluebells Ranch. The property Prissy showed me."

The frigid temperature awakens my senses, filling my mind with cool winds of hope and possibility.

He turns his gaze to the house and rubs his chin. "Old Man Carson is known for yanking everyone's chain about selling this place. I didn't realize this was the ranch you were considering. Prissy said he officially listed it for sale?"

"Yes." My breath materializes in the cold.

He shifts behind me, cages me in with his hands on either side of mine, while we both stare at the neighboring land. He says into my ear, "Your loss is unfathomable. It will always be part of your story. But it's not your whole story. So dream big, sweetheart." He kisses my cheek. "Dream big."

Stuck in the safe cocoon of all that is Harlan Holcombe, I breathe in his words. This is my hope. This is why I wade through the horrendous pain of grief. Because I have to believe that it won't always be my whole story. "I think that's why I came to Colorado."

Harlan's day-old stubble scratches my cheek when he nods.

I angle my face to his. "What about you? Do you dream big?"

He grunts. "I'm thinking about a job change." Shaking his head, he pulls back. "Making movies used to be fun, but it just doesn't mean anything to me anymore."

I turn and wrap my arms around his waist. "What will you do?"

His eyes flash with intensity. "My stab at consulting went better than I expected. I've got a few more opportunities lined up. It feels good to help people."

I study the man in front of me. "You're going to help people figure out how to work their dreams into reality."

He slides his gaze to me with a sheepish glint. "I don't know about that."

"But what do you need out of life, Harlan?" I suck in my bottom lip, holding it between my teeth, and wait for his answer.

Harlan's gaze darts from my eyes to my mouth. He leans in and gives me a kiss so soft and sweet I think I'm going to melt. After a few seconds of bliss, he pulls back. "You know what I really need?"

I shake my head, trying to reenter our conversation through the fog of his kiss. "What's that?"

His lips quirk. "I just need someone who can sit by me and hold my hand when I'm throwing up."

Giggling, I push him away. "Then you need to find yourself another woman."

"Come on." He pulls me back into his arms.

"This is nonnegotiable for me." I fail to wipe the smile off my face. "And if this thing between us goes any further, this issue will be in the prenup."

His body stiffens. "You would get a prenup?"

As I wrap my arms around his neck, I push up to my tiptoes and kiss him on the cheek. "Not for money. Just for the vomit clause."

He growls. "Fine. No vomit hand-holding required."

"Mmm. I love it when you whisper sweet nothings to me."

Holding hands, we return to the guesthouse.

I enter the living room, and the heaviness of the day returns. "Are you sure it's okay if we stay here?" I ask. "I'm fine if you want to spend time with your family."

As I slide my coat off, Harlan takes over and hangs it on a hook. "Our big celebration was yesterday, so no one's expecting us today. But if you need time alone, I can make myself scarce."

"I just want to veg out on the couch, maybe take a nap." My eyes are heavy, and I yawn. "Not sure if I have it in me to talk anymore. But if you keep me watered and fed, you can stay."

"I can do that," he says. After a quick kiss on the forehead, he bends down and begins to untie and wrangle the hiking boots off my feet.

"I think there's a John Grisham movie marathon on TBS." Almost losing my balance at his strong foot tug, I grab his shoulders.

I stand in a mumbling stupor while Harlan sheds his jacket and work boots, then guides me to the couch. He grabs the remote and flips through the satellite channels. Without speaking, he situates me cuddled up against him. My eyes droop as Tom Cruise frantically runs from someone.

The next time I glimpse at the television, the picture glows because the house is dark. But this time, Samuel L. Jackson is in jail. Did I really sleep all day? Shifting to a seated position, I blink and rub my hands over my face. In the glow of the TV, I see a note from Harlan.

*Sleeping Beauty, you were out like a light. I left to take care of a few things. Call me when you wake up. H.*

Stretching my arms above my head, I stand. The monster nap cleared through the fog of this morning's grief, and I'm ready to function. I glance around. The open floor plan makes the small kitchen seem more prominent than it is. A refrigerator, dishwasher, stove, and oven line one wall. An island offering extra counter space separates the kitchen from the rest of the house.

My phone charges on a plug next to the stove, and the screen lights up with a text message.

MOLLY
Thinking of you today. Hope you're tucked away somewhere safe at Harlan's ranch.

Holding the phone in my hands, I sigh and stare at the screen. An olive branch.

A few days ago, I would have broken the twig over my knee and thrown it in the trash. But today is Christmas. And I love my flawed sister.

I'm okay. Love you.

The kitchen is stocked with enough leftovers to feed an army, but I don't want dinner yet. Just a snack. As I rummage, my thoughts float back to the earlier conversation with Harlan. *Dream big.*

I open the refrigerator and stare. A quiet alarm beeps, and it doesn't stop until I close the door. The fridge doesn't appreciate how long my musings take.

"You know what I need to dream big?" I walk over to the small pantry and peruse the shelves.

Bingo.

Five boxes of white chocolate–covered Oreos. Harlan remembered.

As I tear open a package, my gaze falls on a pad of Post-it notes located on the counter by a small canister of various writing utensils. I sink my teeth into the first cookie and moan my delight.

But as I chew, I can't take my eyes off the office supplies.

---

"Meredith?"

No, that's not the right category. I move a Post-it note over a few feet on the wall and step back.

"Meredith?"

Wrong again. I unstick the paper and place it back in its original position. There must be fifty Post-its on the wall. It has to fit somewhere.

Three loud knocks sound on the door, but I can't pull my attention away from the plans in front of me.

"Meredith? Are you in there?"

Harlan's stressed voice breaks through my deliberations. "Oh. Yes. Come on in." Chewing on the end of a pencil, I continue staring at my creation.

"I thought you'd call when you got up." The door creaks when he enters the room. "I didn't realize you were awake— Whoa." He approaches the wall.

"Don't touch anything." I grab the back of his long-sleeve T-shirt and pull.

Turning to me, he smirks. "You have no idea how much I want to move just one piece of paper."

I jab him in the gut with my elbow. "Don't you dare. But if you make yourself useful, you can stay."

"I won't dare," he says on a grunt. He chuckles as he walks behind me, places his hands on my shoulders, and works his thumbs into my knotted muscles.

"I think I'll keep you," I say while his hands work magic.

"Did Office Depot throw up in here?" He squeezes both shoulders and gives them a gentle shake.

I giggle. "Just for that, you're not getting any cookies."

He leans over my shoulder and nods to the more-than-half-empty package of Oreos on the desk. "Looks like I came just in time to eat one."

Oh my word. Did I eat that many cookies? I write on the notepad in my hands, "Go work out," and smack the message against my chest. Harlan's chuckles rumble in my ear.

"Okay." He squints at the scene in front of him. "Are you redecorating, or what?"

A rainbow of blue Post-it notes frames the window. Words about buildings, design, finances, staff, and networking cover the little pieces. Very little of the peaceful gray paint of the bedroom walls peeks through my project.

He steps around me, grabs a cookie, and shoves the whole thing in his mouth.

I gape and put a hand on my hip. "Have you no respect? That cookie is a work of art that should be savored in bites."

"I'm more of a dive-in-and-experience-the-whole-thing-at-once kind of guy." He swallows. "What is all this? It looks like you're planning to build a city."

"A small city," I whisper as I return my attention to the rudimentary ideas. To the untrained eye, the papers probably look like the future contents of a trash can. To me, this could be my purpose.

"I blame this on you. And Sally." Skimming my hand over the pieces, I speak to the wall. "Sally and her kids showed me I might be able to do this kind of thing. Then you told me to dream big." I turn to face him and gather courage through a deep breath.

His eyes grow big, then shift to an intense gaze.

"I want to open a home for troubled young women who have nowhere to go." My opening statement is loud and rushed, and my face flushes.

Harlan's expression is unreadable.

"I couldn't find any other colors of Post-it notes, but let me explain the method to my madness." I swallow, step to one group of the notes, and plaster my hand flat against a clean spot. "Maybe they're pregnant. Maybe they've been kicked out of their homes. Maybe they're too old for foster care but need help getting their feet on the ground. They've given up on their education. Their lives. Maybe they have no one. I want to love on them, believe in them, build into them, help them find their gifts."

Taking a step around the desk, I point to my scribbles above the window. A new grouping of notes. "Place teachers and counselors on staff to guide them. Tie the house into community programs that can be safe places for them to find belonging and grace. Maybe they learn to help out on the ranch. Or maybe we create a work program with local businesses."

I glance back at Harlan, his eyes locked on my written work.

Shifting to the far side of the window, I knock on the wall with my knuckles. "Over here are my fundraising and networking ideas. My contacts in Colorado Springs are few, but Sally and Spencer will have some ideas. Maybe I could also brainstorm with Prissy about her connections."

He takes a wide stance and crosses his arms over his chest. Two creases appear on his brow as he concentrates on the information.

I run my pointer finger down the edge of a separate grouping of notes. "This is a projected timeline with what I think needs to be put into place, but what do I know? I'm super limited in my knowledge on this kind of thing. And last, these are basic funding thoughts. Again, I'm taking guesses."

Pursing my lips, I turn from the safety of the wall and face him.

"Prissy will for sure have connections." His gaze shifts to the window, Twelve Bluebells Ranch off in the darkened distance. "You're thinking of the Carson property."

"Yes. But I guess I could do this anywhere." Even as the words leave my mouth, that sentiment doesn't sit well in my gut. I didn't realize until this moment that I'm attached to the Carson property.

"So Prissy's your first call." He nods, still not making eye contact. "I've got a finance guy who's been with the family for decades. He's trustworthy. If he's in over his head, he'll know where to direct you."

I reach up and pat a blue note that says HANK. "I'm going to need to steal your ranch hand. There's no way I can run that place on my own."

"You can't have Hank." His eyes slide to mine. "He'll scare the girls away with his inappropriate hearing. Also, I'm not sure you've thought of this, but with pregnant women around, it'll be hard to enforce the no-vomit rule."

A nervous giggle escapes. I draw the pencil to my mouth and chew on the end again.

Harlan squares his shoulders to me but says nothing. Then in one beautiful moment, his eyes soften into a look filled with awe. "This is incredible, Meredith."

"Yeah?" I ask, vulnerable. Exposed. But also relieved. It's out there, and he gets it.

"You did it. You dreamed big, and it's incredible."

My smile is so huge, the muscles in my cheeks protest.

Without breaking his gaze, he reaches for my hands and removes the pad and pencil from my grip.

"Don't mess up my creation." I hitch my thumb in the direction of the wall.

"I will try not to mess up your creation." Looking down, he writes something on the top page, pulls it off, and posts it smack in the center of the window. "I just need to know where this one fits."

His stark, lone Post-it note sits in the middle of my blueprints with a simple message written in all capital letters.

HARLAN?

# 28

I TEAR DOWN Harlan's Post-it note, grab the pencil, and draw a dollar sign on it. "You're going to be my eye candy for fundraisers. A hundred dollars for a hug with Hercules." Turning to him, I hold out the amended paper and plaster on a smile that I hope covers my unease.

He takes a deep breath, the mood in the room shifting to something more serious. "Your wall of ideas is amazing. But I've been doing some planning too. I have choices to make about my career."

I remain quiet, not sure what's coming next.

"When I consider my future, you're standing right in the middle of everything." He offers a small smile, but it's not one I've seen before. This one is a little unsure, or maybe cautious. "I'm wondering if we should talk through some of these options. Think about what life together would be like."

A terrible combination of exhilaration and fear courses through my nerves. My heart beats wildly in my chest. I knew this moment was inevitable. I just wish I had more time with him before we needed to have this discussion.

He reaches for my hand, concern etched on his face. "If it's too soon, we don't have to discuss this now."

"No, it's time." I clear my emotion-clogged throat. "But first, I need to show you something."

His eyes never leave mine and he nods.

As I pass by, I squeeze his hand for him to follow me into the kitchen. I snag my purse and rummage through it, crinkling Harlan's Post-it note in the process. When I find what I'm looking for, I draw in a long breath.

Harlan stands on the opposite side of the island, his hands splayed on the marble counter.

"I want a thousand tomorrows with you," I say, my voice wobbly. I can't look at him.

In reverence, I run my fingers over the top of the small, fabric-covered accordion folder that's lived in my purse for years. The pink floral pattern has long since faded, but not the pain represented inside.

My words get stuck in my throat, and it takes unbelievable fortitude to push them out. "But I don't think I can give you the future you want. The one you deserve."

His posture stiffens.

With shaking hands, I set down the blue Post-it note. After I release the black tie on the folder, I pull out two items. I turn them to face Harlan's side of the counter.

"Clayton and Chloe." His gravelly voice is gentle as his fingers graze the sides.

"I can't have more babies, Harlan." A tear falls to the marble as I place my hand over his. "I can't give you children."

He draws his eyes from the pictures to my face.

Our stares lock. I want to turn my head and cower at the strain, but I force myself to remain unmoved.

"Are you—" He shifts his weight. "Can we talk about what that means? I mean, are you okay? Are you sick? Or is this because—" He pauses. "I mean, I understand if you're scared, Meredith. Anyone who's been through what you've been through would be scared."

His intense energy starts to unravel, and I wait to respond.

Pacing two steps away from me, he shakes his head, then turns and slices a hand through the air. "First. Are you physically okay?"

"I'm healthy, Harlan." I offer him a watery smile.

"Good." He releases a relieved breath and nods. "Good."

I take a shaky inhale and whisper the next strike. "But my doctor advised me not to carry any more babies."

His head snaps up, and a heart-wrenching understanding dawns on his face.

His pained expression is more than I can endure, and I shift my focus to the folder, praying I don't have to deliver the final blow. I pick up the abandoned blue Post-it and fold it over, creasing the middle. Out of the corner of my eye, I see Harlan rub his hands over his reddened face.

In four strides, he rounds the island and locks me in a frantic embrace.

When I clutch his T-shirt, it's more out of fear than comfort for him. "I'm sorry I can't have children with you," I whisper.

"It's okay," he murmurs into my hair. "We can adopt, Meredith. We'll figure this out, and we'll adopt."

At his words, I become wooden.

Pulling back, he cups my face, his eyes filled with concern. "Meredith?"

I exhale and close my eyes. "It's not as simple as my body not being able to carry a baby."

He puts gentle pressure on his hold. "Sweetheart, look at me."

When I comply, his beautiful, confused face comes into focus.

"Because of Clayton and Chloe?" He scans my features as if the answers can be found in my face.

I anchor a hand to the island. "Because of all of them."

His body jerks back. "All of them? What does that mean, 'all of them'?"

I turn to the marble, pick up the folder, and pull out the remaining photos. My hands tremble while I lay out each grainy, black-and-white picture one by one. Two rows of three. Each one is separate. A little bit different from the one next to it. Siblings.

Harlan braces a hand on the counter.

"The top row is sonograms." I point. "The bottom row is embryos in petri dishes."

He touches the edge of one of them, and his eyes draw up to mine. "What happened, sweetheart?"

This is it. Will he understand?

"The only thing I ever wanted to be was a mom. I thought that's what I was supposed to do. My purpose." I swallow a lump of sorrow.

"Your purpose." Harlan directs his words to the pictures of my lost ones.

"Steve and I married and waited a year before trying to get pregnant. After a while, we consulted with a reproductive endocrinologist. He told us our only shot at having a baby was through in vitro fertilization. We saved every penny we had for two years and then returned to the clinic for IVF." Clearing my throat, I tap the first sonogram on the top row. "I lost this one at eight weeks." My finger moves to the second picture. "Six months later, this one left us at nine weeks."

Harlan settles a shaky hand on the small of my back and closes the gap between us while we stare at the counter.

My lip quivers. "The twins stayed with us for a trimester," I can barely say on a scratchy whisper.

He places his fingers on the third sonogram.

I nod. "Then came these two." While shaking my head, I slide Clayton's and Chloe's pictures in between the rows of sonograms and petri dishes. "I couldn't believe it."

"Miracles." Harlan squeezes my waist.

"They were all miracles." I study the family in front of me. My heart pounds faster with each passing second.

"Tell me about the bottom row." His quiet question cuts through the tension.

"I couldn't get them all here." My eyes fill with tears as I try to control my quivering voice.

He nuzzles my ear. "What does that mean, sweetheart?"

"I had terrible pregnancies. Chloe's almost did me in. Six weeks of bed rest at the end to give her more time to grow. After she was born, the doctor told me carrying another baby would put my life at risk." I pick up Harlan's folded blue Post-it note. "But we still had embryos." When I tear off the corner, it floats to the counter. "After all the money we drained into the IVF process, we couldn't afford a gestational carrier." I rip off another scrap and drop it with the first one. I repeat the monotonous movements to ward off my angst as I wait for Harlan's response.

He covers my hands, which halts my nervous movement. "Where are they now, Meredith? The bottom three?"

"Six." I shred a longer piece when I correct him. "Each petri dish contains two embryos. There were six more." My hands tremble. "We had to let them go." My shed tears land on the remaining paper. Shedding. Shredding. Releasing. "Steve and I went to the cryopreservation facility. And we stood by as a staff member removed the containers from their frozen state and laid them in a bin in front of us." I hiccup and whisper the last words about one of the most difficult days of my life. "Eight seconds. It only takes eight seconds for them to lose viability."

Harlan wraps one arm around me and presses his strong hand over the three rows of pictures.

I hold my body stiff. "I couldn't get them here. I couldn't fulfill my purpose and get all of them here." Something in the depth of my gut aches, and I clutch my stomach as I say the next excruciating words. "And I couldn't even keep the two who made it to us alive."

Harlan's grip on me spasms. "Meredith."

Shaking my head, I step back and pull out of his hold, tears streaming down my face. "If I choose to raise more babies now but let go of my precious six? My brain can't wrap itself around that option, and my heart wouldn't be able to endure it."

He lifts his hand off the pictures and faces me, his glassy eyes troubled. "I understand why you'd be scared. But—"

"I made this decision before I lost Steve and the kids. He wanted to adopt, and I just couldn't fathom it. It was all wrapped up in the same category for me." My fingers knead the mutilated Post-it. "Before life was filled with total loss, I came to the realization that I couldn't do it again. I have limits."

He runs a hand over his face, ridding his cheeks of tears.

Unable to handle the wounded face in front of me, I squeeze my eyes shut. "I'm so sorry, Harlan. But I have *limits*."

I release a choppy sigh and focus on the remnants of blue paper as they fall to the marble. "I would be a wonderful stepmother to your Alex and love her until the day I die." I brush my pictures and the fragments of the Post-it into a pile. "I can be the greatest aunt to your nephews." Cupping my hand, I scoop the heap into my weathered folder. "But either through a gestational carrier or adoption, I cannot bring any more babies into my family. I cannot have more children with you. Which means I can't give you your legacy."

Harlan paces away, runs his hands through his hair, and turns back to me. "Through it all, how many did you lose?"

Squaring my shoulders, I take a breath. Each IVF attempt used two embryos. Though we lost them in different ways, the original number of embryos is seared on my heart. A picture of all of us as a whole family. "Fourteen. I may not have carried some of them for very long. And not all of the final six would have made it to term—maybe none of them would have. But each of them was mine." My voice hitches. "Fourteen."

His anguished expression threatens to destroy me. "After

298

everything you've been through, Meredith. All of your loss. How do you keep going?"

"Because even after this, even after all of the loss . . ." I circle the black tie around the portfolio, stare down, and caress the frayed edges. "What's left over is still my love for them."

# 29

**DAWN SHOULD BE HOPEFUL.** A sign of possibility in an uncharted day. But this morning, the clouded sun brings hazy prospects.

Last night, sleep was plagued with spiraling questions. *What's wrong with me? Why can't I just give him children? Am I that selfish? Why can't I be happy with what's in front of me?*

I have limits. My heart simply cannot get there.

Which is why I must leave.

Harlan knocks before he lets himself into the house. While he wipes his feet on the doormat, he catches sight of my luggage. He shoves his hands in the pockets of his jeans, slumps his shoulders, and closes his red-rimmed eyes. After a sigh, his pained gaze finds mine. Without a word, he approaches me and pulls me into his arms.

Neither of us says anything. The embrace feels loaded. Heavy with sadness.

"I need you to know something." His whisper breaks with anguish. "I am so in love with you, and I want a life with you."

"Me too." Tears flow as I burrow into him. "I'm so sorry, Harlan."

Pulling me back, he cradles my face, wiping away moisture. "Why in the world would you apologize?"

"Because I want to give you everything. And I can't." I force the last words out with a sob and return my head to his strong chest.

He moves his hand along my back in soothing strokes. "This is my fault."

My scoff is muffled. "Because you want more children? I would call that normal." I pull out of his hold and walk behind the kitchen island.

As he surveys the room, he throws a hand out to my luggage. "When do you leave?"

"Soon." I rummage through my purse. "Here. Will you please deliver these to your mom and your brother?" Holding out sealed envelopes, I avoid eye contact. "I canceled my appointment with Prissy and am on the next flight out of Colorado Springs."

His fingers graze mine as I pass the cards for his family to him. "You can't let go of Twelve Bluebells Ranch, Meredith. You lit up yesterday explaining your vision."

I imagine my effort to smile is as grim as I feel.

"I wish you'd reconsider talking to Prissy." He shakes his head. "But I'll take you to the airport."

I trudge to the pantry and stop to look at him. "Don't make me say goodbye to you in public. This is hard enough as it is."

Thumbs hooked through his belt loops, he blows out a loud exhale. "I'll ask William if he can drive you."

After I grab the leftover boxes of white chocolate–covered Oreos, I turn. "I'm covered. I caught Hank working the grounds this morning and asked him for a ride." I put the packages on the counter next to him.

The wrapper crinkles when he traces a finger down the side. "How'd that go?"

Walking to the bedroom, I call back, "He said, 'You want me to tan your hide?'"

Harlan chuckles half-heartedly.

When I return to the kitchen, I place the blue Post-it pad and pencil beside the other items.

He rubs his day-old whiskers. "I'm not even sure not having kids is a deal-breaker. It just blindsided me." Distress covers his face, and his words are a plea. "I thought we were going in one direction, and I assumed we were on the same page. I need some time. Can you give that to me?"

My knotted stomach clenches, but I don't have words to respond.

His eyes mist as he stares at the items on the island. "I need more time," he whispers.

"Your heart's desires won't change with more time," I say gently and place my hand over his. "And that's okay."

"That's not fair. It's not about changing my heart's desires." He paces two steps and clasps his hands to the back of his neck. "I just—" He turns, and his expression rages with confusion, devastation, and frustration. "You're making a decision for both of us. You've had time to think about this, and you're making this decision for both of us."

"At what point in a relationship is it time to let the person you're dating know this kind of thing?" I don't want to sound defensive, but I know the strength and slight rise in my volume are matching his. "There's no manual for this, Harlan. It's all just hard. It's all just impossible."

"Don't do that." He steps to me, takes my hand, and places it over his heart. "This is not impossible. Do not give up on us."

"I'm not giving up on us."

"Yes, you are. You've made a decision for both of us."

"If I don't make this decision, you'll give up what you want out of life. That can't be the foundation of our relationship. You'll resent me for it. I'll always feel guilty about it. I'm making this decision so we don't implode later."

His face is set. Determined. "Yes, it's a lot to let go of and adjust to overnight. I can't tell you I'm okay with it right now. But"—his voice cracks and heartbreaking emotion crosses his face—"I also can't tell you I'm ready to walk away from you. Don't do this, Meredith."

His heart pounds underneath my hand, and I stare into his pained eyes, barely able to speak. "I don't want to walk away from you either. But I can't do this. We can't do this."

He studies my face, exhales a long breath, and pulls me in to press a kiss to my forehead. "I love you."

"I know. I love you too." Tears rush down my cheeks as he tightens his arms around me in an embrace that could consume me whole.

In a blur of hushed words, final squeezes, and soul-wrenching pain, Harlan leaves the guesthouse.

I press my palms to the closed door. My choppy breath calms in time for Hank to arrive and load my luggage. I'm comatose watching him enter, pick up a bag, and exit the house.

When he returns, he inspects the room. "What about those?" He nods to my pair of Texas-flag cowboy boots lined up next to the door.

The memory of square dance shopping and the hope that filled those boots seeps bittersweet sadness through me. I may not belong here anymore, but somehow those boots do. They can't go with me.

I lock eyes with Hank. "Leave them here."

# 30

**"I'M GOING TO SCARE** everyone away." Talking to the reflection in my bathroom mirror, I cringe. Five days of minimal showering has been unkind. I'm just grateful to live in a city with a wide range of food delivery services. It makes staying in bed so much easier.

My current lifestyle isn't sustainable. Today is New Year's Eve, and if I don't leave my house and do something, this new sorrow could swallow me whole. Plus, I don't think it's a good sign when you're on a first-name basis with the restaurant delivery guy.

After taking two hours to trudge around my house and get ready, I leave for the food pantry. Even turning the key in my ignition requires an abnormal amount of energy.

Monotonous volunteer work.

I'm back to square one.

Second to losing Harlan, I've lost the possibility of new dreams. A new purpose. It's hard to tell which one drags me back to my bed of depression with a stronger hold.

The good news is, the annual black-eyed-pea-pancake breakfast should be a distraction. That concept is gross enough to challenge the worst melancholy day.

Today, volunteers do early prep work on the food and facility to prepare for tomorrow's New Year's Day breakfast. I chose this shift because interacting with people isn't required.

But Cordelia, the administrator in charge, didn't receive the memo about my no-talking rule.

Ten minutes after she gives me the rundown in the kitchen, she's still chattering. She modified akara, a Nigerian recipe, with Bisquick to create the holiday-appropriate-but-probably-disgusting dish. "My nephew went on a mission trip to Africa. He studies medicine at UT Southwestern and wants to work for Doctors Without Borders when he graduates." After a pause, she raises her eyebrows.

Right. We're having a conversation. I should probably interact with her.

"That's wonderful." I stand in front of the ingredients spread across the top of the large, square, stainless-steel island.

She leans in. "He's also dating the former Miss Grand Prairie."

Grabbing the provided apron off the counter, I restrain my eye roll. Always a joy to hear about someone else's perfect life. "Oh. Great." I wrap the long ties around my waist and then back to the front.

"Cordelia?" A familiar masculine voice comes from outside the entrance to the kitchen.

I freeze. *Please, no.*

As Cordelia turns to the door, her face lights up. "Stanley? So nice to meet you." She reaches out her hand.

When Stanley returns her greeting, he glances at me. Then does a double take.

"What are you doing here?" My words blurt out in an unfortunate accusing tone as I tie the apron strings a little too tight against my belly.

Stanley pales. "Molly called. She said you weren't in town to do your usual duties. I thought I was filling in for you."

Retying the bow, I exhale. That's what I get for ignoring Molly's calls. "I had a change of plans." I'm not sure if that tone is an improvement.

Cordelia claps her hands once. "You two already know each other. Excellent." She winks at me, oblivious to the tension in the air. "Did I mention this Nigerian dish is wonderful on dates?"

Squeezing my eyes shut, I make plans to hurt her. I'm going to take this can opener and hurl it at her. And during my sentencing, I will ironically be refused the opportunity to work off my conviction through community service. But it will be worth it.

I cannot do this today.

I couldn't book an appointment with my counselor until next week, and I'm hanging on by a thread.

Stanley points to the counter. "I think we've got this, Cordelia. I'll let Meredith explain what I need to do."

"Very well, then. I'll leave you to it." She nods with an annoying gleam in her eye and exits.

Once I'm sure she's out of earshot, I address Stanley. "You don't need to stay."

"I'll help." His tone is light, but he seems jittery as he steps to the giant silver bowl next to the Costco-sized carton of eggs. "What was your change of plans?"

"Crack twenty eggs in that bowl." I slide the 117-ounce can of black-eyed peas in front of me. After I attach the opener to the metal top, I lean my weight in to break the seal. "I just needed to come home." *And I need you to go home.*

He holds up the laminated recipe. "I thought she was kidding on the phone when she mentioned black-eyed-pea pancakes." Shaking his head, he picks up an egg. "What was your change of plans, Meredith?"

I don't care for his direct tone. Where is Mumbling Stanley? "Nope. She's not kidding. At least this year, half the batches will be normal pancakes. Maybe they had complaints last year." I turn the handle and crank the device to free the peas.

"Because you look terrible." He almost fumbles the egg, and his voice falters. "I know you were in Colorado with that guy."

Using a spatula, I pry open the top of the can, heft the container up, and pour the contents into an industrial-sized blender. "All due respect, I'm not doing this with you."

He cracks an egg on the side of the bowl and it splatters everywhere. A breath of a curse escapes his mouth while he grabs a nearby towel. Once he cleans his hands, he lets out a frustrated sigh. "Did he hurt you?"

With one hand covering the top of the blender and the other gripped around the sides, I flip the power switch on and glare at Stanley. The appliance rocks to life, and the deafening grind fills every last corner of the room. I thought this would give me time to calm myself. Instead, my emotions spiral down, churn, and whirl into unrelenting animosity.

To his credit, Stanley holds my gaze of fire, but he shifts his weight.

He wants to know?

Fine.

I stop the machine. "No, Stanley. He didn't hurt me. I'm a joke. I'm like the bad TV movie of the week. We've all seen it. Melissa Gilbert plays a woman who is so broken she doesn't think she'll recover. But then a man gives her hope and shows her a new way, only *he isn't the one.*"

After I pull off the top, I run the rubber spatula down the inside of the blender. "There's some takeaway from the movie about how Melissa Gilbert flourishes after the man leaves her. And then we all turn off the TV and come to the healthy conclusion that we don't need a relationship to thrive." My gestures cause black-eyed-pea remnants to fly off the spatula and splatter on the counter. "We're supposed to feel empowered to go find some dream and live it out. Don't tell me you don't remember that one."

Even as I point my accusatory finger in his direction, the ugly truth pierces my gut. My own cowardice is sabotaging any hope of empowerment and dreams.

Stanley's eyes darken in an expression I've never seen him wear. He leans his weight into his hands on the counter. "Did that idiot break up with you?"

My lip curls. "Only, just for fun, I was dating a movie star in real life. And I followed the clichéd movie plot to a tee, right down to finding myself a new purpose in life." I'm laughing through my seething words. "And I am that much more the fool."

I grit my teeth to stop the tears from flowing. *No way. Today doesn't get my tears.*

Stanley brushes his straight hair back, and it falls limp. "Why did he break up with you?"

Seriously? Angry spots flash in my eyes. I slam the spatula on the counter. He wants to go there, I'll go there. "I broke up with *him*, Stanley! I can't give him any children, so I broke up with him."

Stanley's face flushes, but he seems to know my diatribe isn't over and remains silent.

"There's not a brochure for being barren and broken. At what point in a relationship is it okay to tell someone you aren't going to have kids so they can decide if they want to stay?" I take two steps toward him, my voice quivering. "To say to someone, 'I can't give you this . . . but I want you to pick me anyway.'"

He fidgets with the dish towel.

My anger continues to spew. "I was in love with him before I understood what he wanted. I let our relationship go too far. So it's all my fault. And the second I understood he'd have to sacrifice his happiness for me, I broke up with him." I step around the island and dump the black-eyed-pea puree in the giant bowl.

Stanley edges back, his face blank. "What else you got?"

With incredulity simmering, I slowly draw my eyes up to his. "What else is there?" I force out.

"I understand you're hurt. Embarrassed even." He wipes a spot of egg on the counter. "But that's not what you're upset about."

You have *got* to be kidding me.

I hold out my arms. "My husband and children died, and I just lost another man who I loved, not to mention my new dreams. All of which are being used as some trite lesson in my life." My voice rises. "What in the world else is there to be upset about, Stanley?"

He squares his shoulders and clears his throat. "You're irate because you did some terrible math about yourself, and you decided to believe it."

I open my mouth to respond but blink instead.

"You added your grief, your loss, and your inability to have more babies and came up with something incalculable. Your brokenness is bigger than you originally knew." His compassionate voice is incongruous with the harsh truth he spews. "Now you're terrified that you're so unlovable and needy that no one will choose you."

It feels like the breath has been knocked out of me. "Get out." My raspy whisper is barely audible.

He holds my eyes in his and shakes his head once.

Humiliation crawls over me like spiders running down my skin. "I mean it, Stanley. Get. Out." The last word releases on a sob.

"You wear your grief like a badge of honor, Meredith. A badge you earned by experiencing more loss than most people do in a lifetime." He shakes his head. "But you would have felt this way about yourself even if you hadn't lost your family or had been able to have more babies."

A spark of pain lights in my chest. I take a step back, put a shaky hand in the air, and point to him. "You are so full of it. Why would you possibly think that?"

He gulps. "I've accepted you aren't going to love me the same way I love you. But it doesn't mean I don't know you, Meredith." Regret fills his eyes. "You lost your husband, but I lost my best friend. We met every Tuesday morning for twelve years." He jabs the counter with his pointer finger. "I hoped and pulled for you guys through every step of your infertility journey. And I can't tell you how many times Steve would confide in me about his concern for you."

Each piece of information stokes the small flame, and I rub the heat building in my chest.

"For years I've watched you. You put on a pretty face. But you're worried you aren't good enough, that you don't belong on this earth or have a purpose. And Steve knew it too." Moisture brims his eyes.

My breathing becomes labored, and I move back, bumping the counter behind me. "Please leave."

Where the timid, awkward Stanley has gone, I have no idea. But the man in front of me gains strength with each hit. "You told me once you didn't need to be rescued. But I think you do. Do not turn away from this. Figure out the answers to the questions that terrify you."

The fiery truth sears through me. Still facing him, I grab the counter behind me and inch away.

"You can do this." He holds out a placating palm. "You've faced bigger mountains. But this one is an old friend of yours that you don't want to let go of. Lean in. Find your peace."

I clutch my chest and wheeze. "I have to go."

"I'm here for you, Meredith." He slumps his shoulders, looking defeated somehow. "Just like always."

My hip catches on the corner of the counter when I turn to grab my purse off a hook on the wall. Without looking back, I scurry out the front door of the building. Tears stream down my face, but they can't put out the blaze.

As if on autopilot, I trudge down the street to a gated garden maintained by the community center next door. I visited this haven often when I first started volunteering for the food pantry. After hours, the gate always remained unlocked. With my soul scorching, I need that to be the case today.

My legs wobble as I head for my spot in the farthest corner. A sturdy bench carved of wood and smoothed for comfort rests under the solace of a tree. The bench looks a little worse for wear, and I wonder if it thinks the same of me. I sit, elbows on knees, head in hands.

Choppy breaths escape as gut-honest questions run through my head.

What's wrong with me?

Am I good enough?

Am I worthy of being loved?

Why am I here?

Am I a disappointment?

My questions sit in raw pain.

I fumble through my purse looking for Kleenex and try to soak up all the tears. But it's to no avail because the floodgates have opened.

"I want answers." My guttural words are soft but forceful. "Everything I have loved is gone. I can't make the love I have work. I have no idea what to do with my life." I cough through sobs. I curl my hands over the top of my head and clutch my neck. "This is all that I have and all that I am." My lips tremble. "Is it enough?"

There it is. I've said the ugliest things I can think of about myself. I've asked the scariest questions I can ask. I've voiced the things that I thought could break me.

But instead of breaking me, the returning silence coats me in an odd peace. I don't move.

The fire in my belly extinguishes, and soft tendrils of smoke release the last of my anguish into the air. I don't have an exact answer, but somehow my shattered soul knew it had to voice my cries out loud.

I slide my hands across the top of my head, rest them over my closed eyes, and draw in a long breath. Here in the dead of winter, the garden smells of tranquility.

In the distance, the gate creaks open and footsteps approach.

"Meredith?"

First Stanley. Now my sister.

"Are you okay?" Her worried tone lacks the judgment I've been dreading.

Holding up a hand, I shake my head.

"I thought I'd find you here." She plops down next to me, hands intertwined, resting on her purse. "Stanley called. He told me about your breakup with Harlan. And the fun discussion you just had with him." She sighs. "Who knew he could be such a jerk?"

I sit up and look at her. "He's right about everything he said."

We let the conversation rest for a few minutes while we stare in front of us.

At the crinkle of a wrapper and a faint spicy smell, I glance down at Molly's hands. Peppermint discs.

She pops the candy in her mouth and digs in her purse to pull one out for me. "A peace offering." Her thick words accompany what looks to be a reluctant smile.

"For what?" I untwist one side and slide the treat out of the wrapper with my teeth. My mouth salivates with a taste from our childhood.

"I'm told I'm highly codependent and if I don't work on myself, I'll 'ruin our relationship.'" She uses air quotes for the last portion of her shocking statement.

I freeze, not wanting to scare away this new version of my sister. "What do you mean?" I ask quietly.

"You stopped talking to me, Meredith, and I fell apart." Irony fills her short laugh. "And then"—she touches a hand to my knee—"I don't mean this in a bad way, but I felt relief. I wasn't in charge of you anymore."

I just stare at her.

"Finally." She shrugs. "I wasn't in charge of you anymore."

I close my eyes, take a breath, then return my attention to her.

"Michael gave me some Stanley truth." She flicks off a piece of lint from her wool pants.

"Is that what we're calling it now?"

"I think it deserves a name, since who knew Stanley had it in him? Anyway, Michael dragged me to a counselor's office. She scheduled weekly appointments for the next three months, then ordered me to CoDA meetings. Co-Dependents Anonymous." Molly exhales a heavy breath. "I haven't been doing life very well for a long time."

"Molly," I whisper, compassion drawing through me and wanting to reach out to her.

Her voice cracks and her eyes mist. "You got the help you needed after Steve and the kids died. But I didn't. I thought I had to hold everyone together."

Guilt slices through my heart. I take her hands in mine. "Molly, you did a great job in our time of crisis. But at some point, we should all live our own lives."

She leans in and places her head on my shoulder, and I wrap my arms around her and squeeze.

After a while, she asks, "Do you want to talk about Harlan?"

I let out a long sigh. "No."

Maybe it's the peace in the garden, but by some miracle, she allows the topic to lie.

She nods. "Do you want to talk about how gross and bizarre the concept of the black-eyed-pea pancakes is?"

My shoulders shake with laughter.

Molly sits up. "Seriously. The least I could have done is gotten you volunteer work that didn't betray a classic American breakfast food."

An ache hits my soul, but I smile.

There she is.

My sister.

It's been a long time.

But while Molly is probably willing and ready to nurse me

through a breakup, I'm aware of the inherent backward slide in that plan.

This newfound space in our relationship is going to take work.

My job is to dream again. Hers is going to be to let me.

# 31

**"YOU DIDN'T NEED** to pick me up from the airport, Prissy. I could have taken the shuttle." I heave my bag into her trunk, thinking that any other form of transportation is probably safer than riding with my realtor.

Ironically, my broken heart has brought me back to Colorado Springs. Two weeks after my painful and productive epiphanies with Stanley and Molly, I'm ready to move forward with life, whatever it might hold.

Prissy pushes a button to shut the back of her SUV. "The Feldmans insisted. They're so grateful you're subletting their brownstone, they want me at your beck and call."

"I don't think you can be at someone's beck and call if you're dressed like that." I throw a hand at her sleek ensemble while I climb into the vehicle.

Peeking through the opening of her coat is a black jumpsuit paired with half-stacked, heeled ankle boots. The faux fur surrounding her collar is oh-so-Prissy.

"Don't be silly. I delegate when I'm dressed like this." With admirable grace, she maneuvers into her car, buckles in, and presses a finger to the start button.

"Hello, Priscilla." The voice of Prissy's car sounds different than my last visit. "While you're driving today, please remember your husband loves you. But if you are arrested for speeding, he will make sure you're locked up in a facility where the uniforms consist of baggy shirts and mom jeans."

With so much breakup grieving, my laughter feels foreign to me, and I clutch my stomach. "That's amazing."

She rolls her eyes. "My husband got a new gadget for Christmas. I haven't figured out how to disable this one."

Taking deep breaths to calm my giggles, I flash a smile at her.

She pulls out and drives toward the exit. "Do you want to talk about how Harlan's in LA while you're here in Colorado?"

Ignoring the punch to my gut, I run my finger over the window and gaze outside. "No."

"Very well. Let's go over our plan." With a graceful wave to the parking attendant, she exits the lot. "Three new properties hit the market last week. Peter Grundle, an architect highly regarded in his field, is available to go with us on our viewings and discuss how to turn those houses into your halfway house vision. I sent him your notes, so he's up to speed. But he's also developing plans to convert Twelve Bluebells into a more user-friendly ranch concept."

At the mention of the property that sides up to Harlan's, I sit at attention and face her. "Prissy—"

"This search may take some time, so it's nice that you have the freedom to stay in town a while." As we stop for a red light, she clicks her pristine nails against the steering wheel. "Because you have more clarification on what you want this time around, it might be a good idea to make your funds available. We don't want to miss an opportunity for a quick sale."

Grateful she moved on from discussing the ranch, I decide to play along. "Okay. I'll move some money around from my Swiss bank accounts."

She slides her eyes to me. "Are you engaged in a criminal enterprise?"

"I'm just kidding." I chuckle. "I'm more of a Swiss chocolate kind of girl."

"I understand why you're nervous about the possibility of residing next door to Harlan's family—"

Snapping my mouth shut, I cross my arms over my chest.

"—but living in the country is different than the city. Borrowing a cup of sugar requires a car ride, which means you rarely interact with your neighbors."

I nod and ignore the things she said. "I'm also an I-would-like-Swiss-cheese-with-my-ham-sandwich kind of girl."

"You love that property and need to keep an open mind." When the light turns green, she punches the accelerator. "Wait until you see what Peter's got in store for the boardinghouse."

This woman is relentless. "I'm also a Swatch girl." I rub my wrist. "I had one growing up. Do they even make those anymore?"

She takes a right turn as if she's Danica Patrick. "Peter's an expert. His work is impeccable."

"Can I call him Peter the Great?" I grip the handle on my door. "Don't forget Swiss cuckoo clocks."

"You're a little cuckoo right now." She straightens out the car and guns the gas. "Maybe we should be looking at properties in Switzerland. I have a superb contact in Bern."

"You're the one that keeps bringing up a property that's less than a football field away from the Holcombes." Remembering the seats in this car warm themselves, I adjust the appropriate control. Whoever came up with this concept should get an award. "I would be open to a place in Switzerland. Their train tunnels are cool. But I heard there are a lot of thyroid disorders. Something about lack of iodine." As I snuggle deep into the heat at my back, I forgive the car for allowing Prissy to drive so fast and settle in to enjoy the ride. "So maybe let's just stick with Colorado."

Living in a Broadmoor brownstone has some perks. I can access all the amenities as if I were staying at the hotel proper. I'm within the resort's reach, and it wraps me in a protective cocoon with its spa, delectable eating, and personal care.

In the meantime, Prissy hooks me up with the Center for Nonprofit Excellence, located in the heart of Colorado Springs. Using her contacts, we conduct several meetings to formulate an effective business plan and brainstorm fundraiser ideas.

Sally joins us on occasion to throw her encouraging two cents into the mix. She's gracious and supportive. It's been a good distraction from discussing our mutual friend, Hercules.

My therapist back in Dallas networks her connections to aid in the search for long-term facility staff. People who can counsel, oversee support groups, provide self-care education, and help the women thrive. I want these girls to understand their needs and strengths, and how to operate in this world in light of that information.

Without knowing what is logistically possible, I'm hoping to create a haven for community and healing.

My solitude during this time is purposeful. Instead of feeling sorry for myself, I spend an hour every day in complete silence, waiting for answers.

An intensity builds in my quiet spirit.

I don't know exactly what I'm waiting for. But at the beginning of each day, I release what I want to hear, how I want to hear it, and when I want to hear it, creating space for something different. New. Undefined. I don't know. Just something that isn't how I've felt about myself for a lifetime.

I give all that I know of myself to the process.

I journal, I listen to all kinds of music, I draw, I make lists, I reflect, I cry. I take walks through the Broadmoor property, make visits to the zoo, and spend days at the spa being pampered.

Sometimes I stare into a fireplace, other times I study the ducks swimming in the lake. And I eat decadent food at the fabulous restaurants.

Always at a table for one.

But every day, without fail, I make space for silence. And wait for something.

―――

"Open up, it's cold out here."

As I hurry to grab the door, I glance at my watch. "Prissy?" I take the giant gift basket from her while she removes her coat.

She pats her perfectly molded hair. "Did I miss the beginning? The dresses are the only part that matters about tonight's show."

"No, the red carpet coverage hasn't started yet. The local news is wrapping up." I blink. "Where are your pj's?"

She glances down to her clothing. "These are my pj's." Decked out in a pale pink silk long-sleeve shirt and pants, she defines Academy Awards Pajama Party. Her feather-tipped, opaque, high-heel slip-ons remind me of a pair of plastic dress-up shoes I stomped around in as a child. Though her feathers are probably bound by diamonds instead of plastic crystals.

I peek through the transparent cellophane wrap of the basket. "You brought reinforcements."

Various sizes, flavors, and brands of Toblerone, Lindt, and Nestlé chocolates are displayed. The multiple Swiss goodies cause me to smile. Even her chocolate is fancy.

We walk into the den, and at the sight of Spencer and Sally on the red carpet, I rush to put the sweet confections down and grab the remote. "I can't hear them."

Glittering from head to toe in a black Versace gown, Sally looks radiant. Spencer isn't so bad himself, but he is definitely upstaged by his wife tonight.

"Good evening to the beautiful Mr. and Mrs. Dean." A *Good Morning America* host greets my friends by amicably shoving a microphone in their faces. A cheer erupts from the crowd behind them. "I haven't seen you guys since the Valentine's Day Make-A-Wish Fundraiser. Sally, you look amazing this evening, but I can't help but notice a new accessory." She points to something small and round at the top of Sally's dress.

I squint.

*No way.*

Sally smiles wide and proud. "It's a reward a friend of mine gave me."

The host leans in and laughs. "This is a sticker." She looks beyond the camera. "Can we get a close-up? It literally says, 'I showered today.'"

The camera zooms in to show one of my infamous-now-famous mommy stickers. A cat wearing a shower cap, holding a bar of soap.

"Yes. Being a mom is tough some days. We need stickers too. Shout-out to all the mothers out there." My friend waves at the fans.

I wave back and giggle. Without taking my eyes off the screen, I sense Prissy standing with me. "I gave those to her."

"I love it," the host says, her eye catching something off camera. "And what about this guy? Harlan Holcombe, everyone."

While the crowd's roar soars, my heart drops to the floor. Breathing is difficult, and I clutch my chest as he comes into view. Classic black tuxedo. He's simply beautiful. But I ache for the man who wears jeans and boots.

I feel a strong need to put my hand on the television and touch his face.

"This evening you and Spencer will be presenting the Best Foreign Film award. How does it feel for you guys to be back together?"

"I'm presenting with Holcombe?" Spencer fake glares at Harlan, then looks at his wife. "Babe, let's go home." He takes Sally's hand as if he's going to lead her off the stage.

The host throws her head back and cackles. "You can't go now. Your wife showered for tonight."

"I think I'd rather present the award with Sally." Harlan runs a hand through his hair. "There's no telling the last time Spencer bathed."

The host laughs again. "Harlan, word on the street is that you've got plans to headline a unique theater arts concept."

Harlan leans toward the microphone and nods. "I've been brainstorming with several colleagues in the industry about a mentoring program for younger acting professionals. It's been exciting to talk through the possibilities."

I grab Prissy's hand and close my eyes. "Good for you, Harlan." Prissy acknowledges my whisper with a squeeze.

"That sounds wonderful. Best of luck to you. Spencer, Sally, always a pleasure. Have a great time tonight, you guys." The host points to the camera. "Laura, I hear you have a report on some new arrivals. Back to you."

The shot cuts away from the interview stage.

Prissy tsks. "I should have brought something stronger than chocolate."

We make the best of watching the Oscars. Trying to put on a good front, I laugh at all the jokes and clap for my favorites. The camera catches Harlan in the audience once, and I want to squeeze my eyes shut. When it's time for him to present, I grip the arm of the couch and hope the Feldmans don't charge me for the permanent nail marks.

After the show ends, Prissy leaves, reminding me of our appointment with the architect tomorrow.

Once I close the door and turn the lock, I return to the den and plop onto a comfy oversize chair.

It's time to face the gaping hole I've tried to ignore since Harlan's face filled my TV. As I curl up under an afghan, tears spill down my cheeks.

I repeat the scary question I've been asking for weeks. Only it's not scary anymore. For a while it's like I was searching. Then more like pondering. But tonight, my soul asks it differently. "Am I lovable?"

In a whisper so soft I barely hear my words, I answer myself for the first time. "Yes."

Then I understand. Only in the midst of brokenness. This had to happen in the midst of brokenness. Because if I believe I am beautiful, precious, beloved when I am in the pit, then it will always be true. Never again will I have to wonder about my worth. I am enough. And I am lovable.

Instead of familiar grief tears, these are ones of relief. A celebration. A declaration.

A new beginning.

There's still room for love.

---

The day after the Academy Awards, Prissy and I meet at the Grundle Architectural Firm to discuss remodeling concepts attached to three different properties we've viewed. But, of course, Peter the Great begins with Harlan's next-door neighbors. This move has Prissy's well-manicured claws all over it.

"Ms. Harper, I took some liberties with these blueprints, but we can change or shift most anything you desire." Peter points to the gridded plans of the boardinghouse at Twelve Bluebells Ranch displayed on a drawing table. "We'll keep the kitchen, dining, and living area in the same places. But we'll get rid of this wall here to open up the space."

After studying a picture I barely understand, I nod.

"Breathe." Prissy nudges me. "We're just brainstorming, Meredith."

Peter pulls the top page off, revealing a new drawing underneath. "The upstairs is where the real restructuring will be."

At present, the lodge holds numerous small rooms lined up in a row on either side of a long hallway. Not much creativity, but it's functional. I don't know a lot about architecture, but the plan in front of me is nothing like the simple, symmetrical building that currently stands. Peter describes knocking down walls, adding bathrooms, and varying room sizes to accommodate different needs.

My eyes glaze over as his hand floats across each item he discusses on the page.

He knocks on the table twice when he finishes. "All in all, you'll have fourteen rooms to work with in the boardinghouse."

His words draw me out of my overwhelmed daze. "What did you say?"

Peter pulls his bifocals off his weathered face. "We can make space for fourteen resident rooms."

Tingles start at the top of my head and travel down my body. "Fourteen." I whisper the number of my lost ones.

All my children are represented here on this table.

The precious abandoned women who walk through the doors of Twelve Bluebells Ranch will fill spaces left by my little ones.

I grab the edge of the table, squeeze my eyes shut, and smile. "Prissy, I need to move some money from my fake Swiss bank accounts."

Looks like I'm going to be Harlan Holcombe's neighbor.

# 32

**"I'M NOT MOVING** to Colorado this morning, Molly. The property sale has to go through before we can even start on the renovations." I stand in my Dallas living room, arms crossed, eyes glued to the TV.

Speaking of Twelve Bluebells, I check my phone for Prissy's call. Nothing. Here at the end of the option period for the ranch, unexpected structural issues threaten the deal. I need to hear from my realtor.

"Do you really want to move somewhere that gets these mega storms?" Molly motions to the news coverage.

A massive cold front is shutting down airports across the central states. Pictures of downed electricity poles, roads blanketed with snow, and brightly colored maps noting torrential weather fill the screen. The groundhog wasn't kidding about an extended winter.

She rubs her forehead. "It's just hard to swallow that you're leaving."

Hopefully. Hopefully I'm leaving.

After I stayed in Colorado for six weeks, returning to Dallas feels a little odd. This will always be *a* home for me, though it may not always be *my* home. Between my newfound peace, new friendships, and Twelve Bluebells Ranch, my world has shifted. It feels purposeful. Solid.

Uncertainty exists, pain is inevitable. But an unexplainable equanimity underscores my days.

When my phone rings, I do a double take at the screen. "Hello?"

"Meredith."

"Penelope?" I glance up to Molly and shrug.

"I'm calling about Alex. There's been an accident. Can you get on a plane?" As efficient and professional as I remember Harlan's assistant to be, her tone is uneasy.

At the blunt explanation, I lose my breath. An accident. An accident.

Deep inhale. I command my brain to separate reality from assumption. Truth from fear. Deep exhale.

"We're in LA. Can you get on a plane? Due to the weather, the Holcombes are grounded in Colorado. Olivia too. The earliest anyone can travel is twenty-four hours. But I don't know what's going to happen to Alex." Penelope's voice breaks, and she pauses. "Can you come be with Harlan?"

The words drag through thick syrup before they make sense to me. "Yes. What do you need?" I cover the speaker on my phone and say to Molly, "Grab my luggage out of my closet, please. The small blue rolling carry-on bag."

Her eyes grow huge, but she follows my instruction.

"A car will be at your house in thirty minutes to take you to the airport. I'm emailing you your itinerary."

"What else can I do?"

"Just get here. Harlan needs you." She ends the call.

Dread fills my chest, and it's hard to breathe. Harlan may need more than I can offer.

After landing at LAX, I find Penelope's driver. We travel through the city in silence. Scrolling the news on my phone, I catch several stories about the storm. On a separate feed, a paparazzi picture of Harlan walking into the hospital is paired with a blurb that the famous actor's daughter has been in an accident. I only feel small guilt pangs when I pray that a newsworthy scandal breaks elsewhere to distract the photographers.

Now able to focus, I read through my emails and listen to voice messages. All from Prissy. With each piece of information shared, impending doom draws near. The owners withheld details about needed foundation repairs that greatly affect the structure. Prissy needs me in Colorado to sign off on the new discoveries before we can close. The sellers won't extend the option period, which means other buyers are waiting in the wings. And Prissy's latest text sinks my heart.

> You are going to lose the house if you don't call me.

But I don't reply to her pleas because I can't deal with this right now. Everything is happening too fast.

Only Alex matters. I know this. I've lived this.

Only Alex.

I'm sad about the possibility of losing the house, but I will not regret traveling to California for Alex. For Harlan.

Penelope waits for me just inside the doors of Saperstein Critical Care Tower at Cedars-Sinai Medical Center. Her pencil skirt, silk shirt, and heels can't mask the stress evident in the dark circles under her eyes.

Alex has a special place in Penelope's heart. And holding it together for everyone else can't be easy. When is the fabulous Penelope Reid allowed to break down?

Rolling my luggage, I follow her. "What happened?"

"She fell off a climbing tower on a playground." The elevator doors slide open, and after we enter, Penelope hits the second-floor button. "Harlan and I were in a meeting when I got the call. The babysitter says Alex was unconscious for three or four minutes. A CT scan shows swelling on the brain." Her voice wavers. "She's in the ICU. They have her medically sedated and on a ventilator." Penelope's focused gaze shifts to me. "We were all supposed to go to Disneyland tomorrow. That's the only reason Harlan brought her on this trip."

I'm stuck on the word "ventilator," and I rub my chest.

Once we arrive on Alex's floor, Penelope guides me to the left.

At the end of the hallway, Harlan sits on a bench. His elbows rest on his knees, head in his hands.

I tell myself I'm not allowed to fall apart until this is over.

When I sit next to him, I touch his back. "Harlan?"

Without looking at me, he slumps over and rests his head in my lap. His hands still cover his face, and he begins to shake. I stroke his hair and trace his arm with my fingers as his body racks with sobs.

Nurses, orderlies, and strangers pass. Penelope stands in the corner, arms crossed.

And I hold a broken man in my arms.

Once he sits up, he wipes his face. "I was with her in her room, but I started to lose it." His eyes well. "I don't want her to be alone, but I can't . . ."

"I can go with you. Would that help? Or do you want me to sit with her until you're ready?"

He stares at me.

I gave him too many options. He needs direction. "How about this. Grab a snack. Go to the restroom. Take your time. I'll stay with Alex until you come back."

When I rise, he squeezes and releases my arm.

Grateful for an actual task that can help Harlan, I head toward Alex's room.

But when I stand next to her bed, I have to steady myself. My knuckles turn white as I cling to the rail. Her face is oddly peaceful while machines help her little body function. As I study her, I'm blindsided by how I feel for this precious, beautiful girl. We haven't had much time together, but I care for her. Deeply.

After taking a seat, I scoot the chair in, cringing when it grates against the floor. But when I glance at Alex's listless body, I wish the noise had woken her.

"Alex, it's Meredith. Your zoo buddy. Your Play-Doh buddy." Gingerly, I take her hand in mine. "You're doing really well. So many people are here taking care of you." I comb my fingers through her hair. "I'm going to sit with you for a few minutes until your dad gets back."

When I pull Kleenex out of my purse, my fingers graze the accordion folder full of my children's pictures.

I didn't get the chance to fight for my own children. Clayton and Chloe were gone in an instant. But here I sit, my simple, newfound love for this child boundless.

And I feel like I am somehow in a battle for her.

My thoughts shift from waging war to blueprints. I picture a newly renovated boardinghouse. But instead of fourteen rooms, the space is undefined. *Don't limit the love you think you can give.*

I'm a warrior for a little girl who isn't mine. But in this moment, I know there could be room for others.

Tears stream down my face.

With my eyes closed, I whisper prayers. Moments later, I feel a warm hand on my shoulder. Harlan's fingers skim my cheek.

We switch places. He leans into the side of the hospital bed and cradles Alex's hand.

Keeping an eye on the monitor, I place my palm on his back.

"Hey, doodlebug." He sips from a water bottle he brought in and places it on the side table. "It's Daddy. I'm here." Gone is the unsure, panicked father from earlier. He's found his footing. His voice steadies and sounds gentle as he offers updates on the day and reassures her of his love.

While Harlan murmurs to his daughter, Penelope signals me from the door. I step out into the hallway.

"I've got to take care of some logistics. I'm going to run by the hotel, get a few hours of sleep, and pick up a change of clothes for Harlan. If Alex's status changes, you have my number. The driver is on call through the night, so if you need anything, text him." She offers me a business card for the chauffeur company. "Per Harlan's orders, I informed the producers he was meeting with not to come by tonight or tomorrow. But I'll update them. They sent the giant cookie bouquet in the snack room."

I take her elbow and guide her out of earshot. "Penelope, you're not my assistant, so please feel free to say—"

"What do you need?" She pulls her phone out of her coat pocket.

"Prissy Prestidge is a realtor I'm working with in Colorado Springs. She's connected to the Broadmoor—"

"I'm acquainted with Prissy." While pressing commands onto her screen, she raises her eyebrows.

"We're in the middle of negotiations on a house, and she's called me all day. Will you please contact her and tell her I can't do this now?" I fold a piece of hair behind my ear. "Assure her that I realize the deal may fall through."

She shifts her focus from her phone to me and searches my face. "What if I can work with her on it for you?"

"No, thank you. The deal's too big for me not to be completely involved at this point. I need to be here. It's okay." I wrap my arms around my pained stomach. "If I lose the property, I lose the property."

"What can I do, Meredith?"

In spite of the intense energy coming from her, I silently hold her stare. There's nothing she can do.

Resignation registers on her face, and she sighs her defeat. "How long are you planning to be in LA?"

"Just until Harlan's family gets here. I mean, if he needs me longer, I can stay. But I don't want to be in the way." I pause. "I don't want to make Olivia uncomfortable. And I don't want to confuse Alex."

She takes in a deep breath and nods. After she steps on the elevator, she turns. "Thank you for coming, Meredith."

Penelope and I stand on the front lines, side by side. I don't know when it happened, but we are now allies. Under different circumstances, we might have even become friends.

With one bed and one chair in Alex's hospital room, Harlan and I switch off staying awake with Alex through the night. We don't say much to each other. A pat on the back here, a squeeze of support there.

The night nurse comes and goes, checking vitals, drawing blood, and offering somber smiles.

With no change in her condition, Alex sleeps peacefully in sedation while we wait.

Not entirely sure how much later, I wake to the sounds of an orderly shuffling a cart. Sitting up, I stretch my arms over my head.

Harlan's bloodshot eyes remain fixed on his daughter's face. "I keep trying to figure out how to fix this. I should have been there." His gravelly voice fills with regret as he locks his eyes on mine. "Do you ever think that? That you could have stopped it?"

I bite the inside of my cheek to stop the tears. "Every day," I force out.

His stare returns to Alex.

The clack of high heels against tile announces Penelope's arrival before she crosses into our room. "I've been working with the airlines this morning. It looks like everyone should be here by noon."

My chest tightens, and I swallow the lump of disappointment. Somehow I wanted more time.

I sense Harlan's attention on me, but I keep my eyes on Penelope. If I even glance at him, I'll fall apart.

"I'll go look at flights and figure out when I can leave," I say. Penelope's probably already done this, but the comment is my getaway car. "My trip home to Texas won't be affected by the storms."

I force myself to move my feet and make a beeline down the hallway to the women's restroom.

The small area only holds two stalls. I step into the larger one, slide down the wall, and sit on the cold tile floor. Tears flow down my cheeks. Some are for the whirlwind of the last twenty-four hours. Others fall for a little girl who fights for her life. Then others for my own broken heart. My separation from Harlan. Flashes of different hospitals. Three cherished ones lost.

"Meredith?" Penelope's plush black heels peek from under the door.

"I'm sorry, Penelope." I pull toilet paper off the holder. "I'll be out in a minute."

She pushes the unlocked door open, sits, and folds her legs under her as if she gets on the floor of a public bathroom wearing a pencil skirt every day. Without saying a word, she takes my hand.

"The good news is we're in a restroom, so there are plenty of supplies for cries like this," I say, pointing to the toilet paper. My attempt at humor is lame.

She offers a small smile. "I couldn't have planned it better myself."

"How long until I need to go to the airport?" I wipe the tissue under my eyes.

"Two hours." She releases her hold and smooths her skirt. "I wanted to reroute you to Colorado Springs to salvage the real estate deal, but I called Prissy first." Her movements stop. "You lost the house, Meredith. I'm sorry."

The pain is acute, and I swallow it down. "When does Olivia get here?"

"After you leave."

I try to toss my toilet paper into the trash can, and it bounces off the side. "That's for the best, I think." Leaning over, I pick up my missed shot and drop it in the metal container. "Thank you."

The next two hours pass with encouraging developments. While making morning rounds, Alex's doctor evaluates her progress. They test her without the ventilator, and she attempts to breathe on her own. Now her medical team will lower the medication dose in increments to see how she reacts. With a decrease in brain swelling and a fully functioning little body, all indicators point to a calming storm. Everyone sits easier after learning the positive prognosis.

The second breath of fresh air comes with the arrival of Harlan's brother and mother. William doesn't plan to stay in town long but didn't want Mama Lee to travel by herself. Gracie, still sick from pregnancy and home alone with the boys, is eager for her husband's return.

Much to everyone's surprise, William brought his guitar. Sitting on the end of the bed, he strums a few of Alex's favorites. Harlan leans against the wall, arms crossed, eyes on his child. Mama Lee holds her granddaughter's pudgy hand in her weathered one. As I consider each person in the room, I'm reminded of the warmth of belonging.

But I no longer belong to the Holcombes, and the ache is almost unbearable.

When it's time to get to the airport, Penelope glances at me.

I move to the door, and William asks, "Taking a breather?"

"No, actually." After readying my purse and luggage, I turn back to him. "I'm heading back to Texas."

He slides a glance to Harlan, then back to me.

"I was just the backup." My gentle words are meant only for him. "You're the ones Alex needs now."

His piercing gaze is unnerving. "I'm not sure that's right."

Mustering up a gracious exit, I square my shoulders. "Good to see you again, William. Keep playing your guitar." I point to the monitor next to Alex's bed. "Her heart rate slows down with the music. And please give Gracie my best." As I step past him, I squeeze his arm.

Mama Lee reaches across the bed for me. With our arms linked over Alex, I dip down to kiss the sweet girl on the forehead.

In heavy silence, Harlan and I trudge to the elevator.

"I don't feel right about this." He speaks his quiet words to the floor.

"Penelope will update me. I'll keep praying for each of you." Looking away, I try to gather my resolve. I finally lean in to push the down button. "My presence will cause unnecessary stress."

He stops my arm. "Not for me."

"Mostly for you. And for your daughter." I shrug. "Alex needs her parents here. She needs Olivia to be the best version of herself. And she needs consistency."

"I just . . . This is wrong." With a sigh, he shifts his weight. "I needed you. I didn't know how much," he says almost to himself. He takes my hand, caressing it with his thumb. "I know it's not fair to ask. But everything in me wants to beg you to stay."

Tears sting my eyes. "I'd do it, Harlan. You know I would. Because I love you, and because I love that little girl in there." My voice wobbles as I stare into his deep brown eyes. "It will cost me. But I will stay if you ask me to."

With a tortured expression, he pulls me in, wraps his arms around me, and presses his forehead against mine.

A tidal wave of regret crashes over me.

I should have given him time. The thought steals the breath right out of me. *Please, make this excruciating pain go away.* I should have given him more time.

I'm such a hypocrite. I walk around asking everyone else to give me time and space to grieve, but I couldn't give him more than one night to figure out the rest of our lives.

"I'm sorry." I hiccup through a sob. "I'm so sorry." I'm only beginning to understand all the things I'm sorry for, and it's more than I can take in, standing in his arms in the hallway of a hospital. It takes great effort to suck in my next intake of oxygen.

"You were right, Meredith." He whispers his words against my lips.

I close my eyes, terrified of what he thinks I was right about.

He lifts his head to press a kiss to my forehead. "Even after all of this. There's still love."

My body melts into his as we share oxygen between us. But when the elevator dings, I peel myself away.

His comment is so final, I know he won't ask me to stay.

Which is why I turn around and step onto the elevator. And when the doors close, I stumble to the back wall so it can hold my weight while I sob. My tears again are for my loss. Only this time, the fault lies on my shoulders alone.

# 33

"ARE YOU STILL MAD at me, Prissy?" Leaning against her SUV, I stare at Twelve Bluebells Ranch. Two weeks since I lost the property, and my realtor has been curt with me at best. "Don't be mad at me. You know I couldn't come."

"I understand you needed to be with Harlan. Lee reports Alex is back to her lovely self. Thank goodness." Prissy sighs, her gaze not leaving the house. "Besides, I don't get upset with clients. They're the ones who have to live with their choices."

"You love me." I bump my elbow to hers and flash my most endearing smile. "I know you love me. Who else would bring me out to the country for one last look around on casual Tuesday?"

I can't be sure, but I think she's wearing a three-thousand-dollar Dolce & Gabbana pantsuit as she strolls through the cow-patty-filled countryside.

"I can't decide if you're sentimental or some kind of masochist for wanting to come back one more time after you lost the sale on this property. I've not had a client make this request before."

I feel a smile curve at my lips. I wondered last fall if I was some kind of masochist widow for going back to the Broadmoor. But sometimes closure means different things to different people. Sometimes closure means you're grasping the hope that came from the past and letting it tether you to the possibilities in the future.

The faint smell of manure reminds me of the welcome cow I almost purchased with the house. "Where's Isabel?"

Prissy passes me and climbs the porch steps. She turns, staring at me with an ambiguous expression. "She probably couldn't bear to say goodbye."

I love my realtor for many reasons. She obtained permission from the new owner for me to take pictures. This house and land gave me space to dream. I want to pin these photos to a board and figure out how to emulate the warmth and hope in this property, especially the boarding lodge. Meandering through the upstairs, I fight back tears. I pause and run my hand over the smooth front of a bedroom door.

When I arrive back downstairs, Prissy strides across the room, drawing my focus to her. She stops in front of me, presses a hand to my arm, and says softly, "Did you get what you need?"

I stare at her for two beats. "I'll still open a halfway house for women who have aged out of the foster care system. It just won't be here." I open my arms and circle 360 degrees. "Maybe Twelve Bluebells was never supposed to be mine. It was just supposed to put me on a path."

Prissy says nothing.

On our way out, the weathered wooden sign above the door catches my eye. "Alba." Dawn. This property will be someone else's new beginning.

Once outside, I glance at the neighboring Holcombe farm. "Just give me a minute, Prissy."

I traipse over to the fence, prop my foot on the lower rung, and rest my forearms on the top one. The view of the chapel is beautiful, even on this cloudy day.

Before I can talk myself out of it, I climb over the fence and start walking. My legs work as if I'm on autopilot. Harlan told me the building is rarely used. He'll be at work. And it's so far from the ranch proper, I can't imagine anyone would see me.

When I step inside, the musty smell hits my nose and I sneeze. Touching each pew as I advance down the aisle, I head toward a seat at the front. The tears that I thought had dried out start to fall, and I bury my face in my hands.

One last release. Then I'll walk away.

As I wipe my face with my sleeve, a noise in the back of the room startles me. I turn around.

Harlan.

I shoot to my feet. "I'm so sorry, Harlan. I—you—you aren't supposed to be home." My words blurt out in stuttered beats.

*Breathe, Meredith.*

"It's okay." He uses a gentle tone and takes a slow step toward me.

Concern washes over me. "Is Alex all right?"

"She's doing great." Another step.

My chest tightens at his third movement forward. I'm blindsided by the pain of his nearness. "I-I'm so sorry. I should go." I make a move to squeeze by him.

But he takes my arm. He leans in and says in my ear in a low plea, "Meredith."

I turn into him, half-heartedly pushing him away with the fingertips of one hand while grabbing his shirt and pulling him to me with the other. He places his hands on my waist to steady me while I war with myself, but also so he can gently pull me closer to him. I rest my forehead on his strong chest, and we stand in thick silence. With a final exhale, I raise my head.

His eyes fill with tenderness and concern. "Can we sit down for a minute? Would that be okay?"

My forehead hits his chest again, and I shake my head no. He slides his hands from my waist up my back and runs his fingers through my hair.

"You aren't supposed to be here. I can't see you. I can't say goodbye to anything else today." My body melts into his, and I place my hands on his chest.

He wraps his arms around my back, presses me closer to him, and kisses the top of my head.

"You aren't supposed to be here," I say in a broken whisper.

I want to leave and never come back.

I want to sit and stay forever.

"I know." He softens his voice. "But I found out you were going to be at the ranch."

I pull back, searching his face for an answer. "Why? Why would you come?"

With one hand still holding me to him, he cups my face and uses his thumb to wipe a tear from my cheek. "I'm sorry, Meredith. I shouldn't have surprised you."

"Why are you here?"

"Well . . ." Eyes glittering, he looks around the room, then back to me, and shrugs. "I'm supposed to be here. You're the one trespassing on my property."

Blowing out a sigh, I nod. Sure. There is the breaking-the-law thing. I glance down at the dusty floor. "I have to go," I say more to myself than to him.

"Before you do, would it be all right for me to show you something?" He swings his hand toward the door. "It won't take long."

Stupid handsome actor with a masked face. I can't work out in my head how he knew I'd be here. I'll figure it out after the long and expensive therapy session I'm about to schedule.

I bite my lower lip and nod. "But then I have to go."

"Fair enough." He offers me his hand.

*One last time*, I tell myself as I take hold. One last time I will hold his hand.

Harlan leads me across the small field in the direction of Prissy's car. We stop at the fence I jumped earlier and gaze out over Twelve Bluebells Ranch.

Gripping the top rail, he takes a breath. "Prissy called me the other day."

Confused, I shift my attention to him. Why wouldn't she mention she talked to him?

Because she's Prissy. She probably sells houses to the president and doesn't tell anyone.

"She told me about this real estate deal." His eyes remain focused on Twelve Bluebells. "Properties don't typically interest me. But this particular one was different."

A nervous energy fills me.

He scratches his chin. "It had a buyer, but the transaction got messy."

My stomach roils. What is he saying?

"Needs a little work." He turns to me. "But I think it would make a great home for people who need help."

I wrap my arms around myself. What's happening?

"Harlan?" I whisper, part scared and part frenzied with hope.

After retrieving something out of his jeans pocket, he takes my hand, opens it, and places a key in my palm. "It was always supposed to be yours, Meredith." His eyes travel from my face to the ranch.

"Harlan." I trace the edge of the key. "What have you done?"

"Well, I almost ruined everything. That's what I've done." His focus shifts back to me, and he grazes the back of his hand over my cheek. "I hope it's not too late to make it right."

"Stop."

He pulls back an inch and studies my face.

"Please don't apologize. I'm the one who's sorry. I'm the one who ruined everything. I was so scared of what you wanted for our future that I beat you to it and broke it off. I didn't give you the space you needed." My shaky voice breaks. "And I should have. I should have given you space and time. I should have given us both space and time to figure it out together."

He wraps his arms around me and lowers his head to rest his

cheek against mine. From somewhere deep in his gut, he groans his acceptance of my apology. "Meredith, I love you. And I want to spend the rest of my life running Twelve Bluebells with you."

Tears stream down my face. "But what about—"

He draws back to look at me. "This is what I want." He shakes his head, his voice firm. "You left the hospital, and I thought William was going to tan my hide. Even without his talk, everything became clear to me." His beautiful eyes bore into mine. "Let's love Alex until she can't stand it. Let's open this ranch to people who need a home. Then we can love them until *they* can't stand it. I want to raise *that*"—he nods toward the house—"family with you. It doesn't matter who we get to love along the way, I just want to do it with you." He presses his forehead to mine. "I want that legacy with you, Meredith."

Before I can respond, he steps back and pulls something else out of his pocket.

Harlan Christopher Holcombe gets down on one knee, opens a small velvet box, holds my left hand, and smiles, his eyes gleaming. "Meredith, will you marry me?"

I clutch my chest with my free hand, trying to remember how to breathe. "Yes," I whisper through a watery smile.

He slips the ring on my finger and brushes a kiss on the top of my hand.

Pulling him up to me, I throw myself at him.

His arms wrap around my waist, and he whispers soft, sweet words in my ear. When he draws back, he cups my face in his hands and kisses me. It's slow, tender, and thorough, filled with promises of more to come.

Breaking the kiss, he guides my newly adorned left hand into view between us. "Twelve diamonds around the band for the tiny ones, and two baguettes flanking the main stone for Clayton and Chloe." He rubs his thumb over my finger. "So they'll each be a part of our family."

I whimper. My throat closes up.

His love. His heart. His beauty. All shining through the sentiment of this ring.

I bury my face in his chest, and he runs one hand around my waist and the other up the center of my back to press me close. I slide my hands up his back, his heartbeat strong in my ear.

When I gaze up, I see beautiful, deep brown eyes. Eyes that I will blissfully get to swim in for the rest of my life.

He takes my face in his hands and places sweet kisses over every inch of my face.

During a pause in our celebration, I turn around in his arms. He locks one around my waist and one around my shoulders. We both look at the house. Something on the porch catches my eye, and I squint. "Are those my Texas cowgirl boots?"

"Yup." Harlan rests his chin on my shoulder.

I rub my cheek against his. "Someday you're going to have to tell me how you pulled this off."

"Penelope and Prissy."

"Traitors."

His shoulders shake. "Are you complaining?"

"Never."

"I talked to your family yesterday." His gorgeous rumbling voice fills my ear. "Molly almost didn't grant me permission to marry you."

"My sister knows?" Craning my neck, I glare at him. "Of all the times not to be codependent and share inappropriate information. I'm going to kill her."

Harlan loosens his hold so I can turn in his arms to face him. "She wants me to pass along a message to you."

I brace myself. "What's that?"

"She took you off Famous People Probation."

Giggling, I say, "I don't think that matters anymore."

"It doesn't?"

"No."

"If I'm not famous, then what am I?"

I lean up and whisper in his ear, "You're just mine."

He draws back and throws me a heated look before he captures my lips with his. When we stop kissing, he says at my temple, "She also thinks we should go camping for our honeymoon."

"Liar."

"I'll table the camping thing for now," he says. "But I insist on dancing at the reception."

"Can surgeon general warnings be put on wedding invitations?"

I study his face, then shift my gaze to the precious ring and finally to Twelve Bluebells Ranch. Wrapping my arms around him, I rest my cheek on his chest.

My Hercules. My family. My love.

Even after this.

# EPILOGUE

**"HOW MANY DIFFERENT** shades of pink paint does one person need?" In the Home Depot parking lot, Harlan stares into the back of his Jeep, his daughter on his hip.

Alex holds out her silver wand with silver and pink streamers coming out the top of a plastic star. She pops each of the paint cans with her wand as she counts. "One. Two. Free. Four!"

He looks at me. "I thought we were getting paint for the set of our backyard play. Apparently I shouldn't have left you in the paint section unsupervised for"—he uses air quotes—"'one more thing.'"

"We did get paint for the play. Those are the fifth and sixth cans. The pink cans accumulate to be the"—I use my own air quotes—"'one more thing.'"

"Uh-huh. And why do we need all the pink?"

"We're painting my room!" Alex booms before she pushes up and gives her daddy a loud, demonstrative kiss on his cheek.

He leans in and stage-whispers to me, "I thought we painted her room pink last week—"

"We did—"

"Pepto-Bismol pink."

I grin. "Yes."

He scratches his chin. "Then why do we need four more cans of pink paint?" He looks at Alex, horrified. "Are we painting the entire house pink?"

She lets out a beautiful giggle. "No, Daddy. We need an ash-ent wall."

He looks to me, confused.

I close the back of the Jeep. "While I love the thought of a house full of pink rooms on a ranch, what I think Alex is refer-ring to is an *accent* wall."

"Hold that thought and stay there," he says to me. He helps Alex clip into her car seat and closes the back door. Then he stalks my direction, a mischievous look on his face. When he gets to me, he pulls me in and kisses me. Not too much for pub-lic, but something almost too much for public. With his hands around my back, he asks, "What in the world, Meredith? An accent wall?"

I rest my hands on his shoulders and get mock serious with him. "Harlan, I tried."

"Clearly"—he nods to the trunk and says in an amused voice—"you did not try."

"You weren't there," I say, shaking my head. "You didn't see how she was looking at me."

"Oh, I can imagine."

"I *did* try. She got ahold of the paint samples and found the pink family and started naming off which color everyone's room was going to be. She had your nephews in hot pink and bubble-gum rooms. I thought my idea to take the paint chips and create a piece of art to hang in her room was a brilliant idea."

"That is brilliant."

"Right? But then she took it and ran with it, wanting each of her walls and ceiling to be different shades of pink. You should be glad I got her talked down to an accent wall."

His lips twitch. "But there are four shades of pink in my car."

I let my forehead fall to his chest and finally admit the one area of defeat. "Stripes."

His chest moves with his chuckles. "Did you say 'stripes'?"

I nod against his chest. It's not a bad place to be. "Pinkalicious, Bashful, Pink Pizzazz, and Pretty-in-Pink will join Bubblicious on the wall in different widths of stripes."

"You're kidding."

"Nope."

He lifts my chin so I have to look him in the eyes. "You're amazing."

"She's amazing," I whisper.

The last three weeks have included more and more time with Alex. On special days, we have tea parties and movies. On normal days, we have rides from preschool with singalongs and, at night, discussions about dinosaur-shaped chicken nuggets. I like the normal days the best. They're a picture of our lives to come, and they settled in Alex the same way they settled in me once I said yes to Harlan. Peacefully.

Harlan squeezes me. "I've gotta get my girls home. We have one week before we need the set finished for the one and only showing of our backyard play. And apparently we now have an accent wall to paint."

*My girls.* I hope I never get used to that.

"One more thing," I add, pulling away strategically before I land the punch line.

"Yeah?" he asks in a skeptical tone, squinting one eye. I deserve this reaction. I've been the queen of "one more thing" over the past several weeks.

"There's been a costume change for you in our play."

"I already have a prince outfit."

We had discussed his Hollywood ties and his options for the perfect Alex-requested prince costume. Instead, Harlan bought a T-shirt that said, "Isn't it obvious? I'm the prince."

Alex was not pleased. Which is why, my guess is, she came

up with this idea. Give a girl some room to be creative and she comes up with a genius idea.

"You are still the handsome prince. You just have a different costume," I say, walking around the edge of the car. I peek back and add, "It's more organic to the original roots of the play."

"Meredith," Harlan says, stone-faced with a playful warning tone.

"It was her idea to do the play to announce to everyone that we're engaged." I shrug as if to say what can we do? "I think we have to go with it."

Grinning, I get into the car and buckle my seat belt. Harlan does the same, then looks to me, then to Alex, then back to me.

Shaking his head, he puts the car in reverse and backs out of the space. "I don't think you two should shop alone anymore. You seem to get into a lot of trouble. And I don't even know what you guys have planned yet."

I glance back to Alex, we lock eyes, and we both laugh.

Harlan once told me he loved the sound of my laughter. But I like Alex's better.

---

With my stomach in knots and our audience in place, it seems we're ready for our Twelve Bluebells Ranch production of "The Three Billy Goats Gruff."

Prissy and Harlan's family sit on the front row of folding chairs that face the back porch of the ranch house. The second row holds my parents, Molly, and her family. Sally insisted she and her kids sit in the back row because Toby and Layla like to work the crowd.

The good news is that our stage debut coincided with Easter weekend, so my family can be in the audience. The bad news is that I'm missing Claire, who stayed home to be with her parents, but she has known I'm engaged since the day Harlan put a ring on my finger because that's what happens with best friends.

I smile at Claire over FaceTime. "He's going to kill me," I say through a giggle.

"Please tell me that whatever he's wearing, you're going to post this on social media so the world can see," she says from her parents' backyard swing.

"Not on your life. He wants no part of publicity."

Her face softens. "I kind of love that for you. You don't have the pressure of the spotlight."

No one wants my story plastered for the public. But it's more. He told me he wants to focus on our life here and let his mentoring take root. He'll still be connected to the industry, so I still need to work on being around famous people. But for the most part, for us, we'll just be a normal family here at the foothills of the Rocky Mountains.

"Are you wearing your cowboy boots?" she asks.

I move the camera down to show the Texas flags on my boots. "Only because a small pink fairy named Alex told me I could."

"Maybe she'll be a costume designer someday."

"Just wait until you see Harlan. Okay, I'm handing you off to Penelope, who is going to keep FaceTime going during the show. Love you."

The chiffon layers of my long, pink princess gown flow against my legs as I step to Penelope and hand her my phone.

She nods, gives Claire a quick hello, and says to me, "Showtime. Everyone is in their place."

"Even Harlan?"

Penelope can't keep a straight face. It's subtle, but her lips twitch with a small smile. "He refused to go on stage and told me to call his agent."

I cover my hand with my mouth and laugh. "What did you do?"

"I sicced Alex on him. It worked. He's in place."

Penelope. Beautiful, kind, and the most brilliant, efficient, and productive person I know.

I step to take my place at the side of the porch, knowing Harlan is behind the door to the house so he can make a grand entrance at the end of the play.

Harlan cracks the door open. I can't see much, but he is for sure glaring at me. "I cannot believe you did this to me."

I purse my lips, trying not to laugh. "It was Alex's idea. She's the writer and director of this production."

"I feel sure you could have told her that this particular getup wasn't available."

"You want me to lie to your daughter?" I ask as if I'm offended.

"You should've had to wear the counterpart to this."

"She told me I had to be a princess." I shrug and look as innocent as I can. "What could I do? Plus, I'm sure you've had movies where you didn't care for the costumes."

"Is this what life is going to be like from here on out? My daughter and almost-wife laughing at me?"

I lean into the door and whisper, "I don't know, honey, but I sure hope the future holds as much laughter as the three of us have had in the last few weeks."

Our makeshift bridge sits in the middle of the porch, the green and brown paint we purchased at Home Depot giving our set some definition.

Spence trudges up to the stage and sits in front of the bridge with his legs cocked up and his hands around his knees. As our resident troll, he wears a pair of brown jeans and a ripped-up green T-shirt. For kicks, he added a wig full of short auburn crazy hair and a big gray nose. He's the only one in the play who has the wrong script and doesn't know how the production really ends.

He sighs loudly and dramatically.

"Daddy!" Toby yells as Layla squeals. The crowd chuckles.

Alex walks onto the stage, fairy wings, crown, and wand in place, and announces, "'The Thwee Billy Goats Gwuff.'"

Everyone claps.

Spence crosses his arms and says in a loud, low voice, "I wonder who will try to cross my bridge today."

Alex walks behind the set to give the picture that she's on the bridge.

Spence rubs his belly. "Who dares to cross my bridge? I sure would like to gobble someone up for a snack today."

"It's me," Alex says. "Don't eat me. Merweradith is coming."

I know someday she'll say my name correctly. But I hope it's not anytime soon.

The audience chuckles again.

"She might be more tasty than you are," Spence says. "You can cross."

Alex flutters her wand and tiptoes adorably to the other side. Once she stops, she looks at me, smiling, and I begin my trek across the bridge.

Spence bellows, "Who dares to cross my bridge? I sure would like to gobble someone up for a snack today."

"It's me, Princess Meredith," I say. "But please don't eat me. There is something, someone"—I look back to the door that hasn't opened yet and can't contain the giggle that bubbles up— "much, much bigger and better coming along for you to feast upon."

"Who is this you speak of?" Spence the Troll asks as I step to the other side of the bridge.

The door swings open, and Harlan steps out in all his glory with his arms stretched wide. "It is I, Harlan, cousin to Rocky the Bighorn Sheep," he says through the giant head of his mascot costume, an exact replica of the atrocious Rocky from Alex's favorite pizza parlor.

The crowd goes wild. I can even hear Claire cackling from the FaceTime call. Alex jumps up and down, causing her crown to fall off.

"Dude." Spence breaks character, laughing.

"Get on with it," Harlan growls.

Spence stands to full height, trying to scowl but failing miserably. "And why do you want to cross my bridge?"

Harlan places his fists on his waist and stands taller when he says, "Because the woman I love is on the other side, and"—he steps across the bridge to hold my hand up with his—"we are getting married."

Alex raises her arms in the air and yells to the audience, "We're getting mawwied!"

Chaos ensues, but it's the best kind.

Spence looks at both of us. "What?!"

Sally hugs her kids and yells from the back, "That's amazing!"

Harlan pulls off his giant costume head just in time to pick up an excited Alex and put her on his hip. He places his other hand around my waist and looks down to grin at me, then back to the audience.

Mama Lee remains sitting but hugs Prissy, then looks at her son, emotion behind her eyes. The rest of the Holcombes rush to Harlan, and the boys and William give manly, back-slapping hugs while Gracie tells me how happy she is for us.

Molly stands, watching the joy, then her eyes find mine and something good passes between us. *I love you*, she mouths.

*I love you*, I mouth back to her.

Hannah runs up to me and almost tackles me in an overexuberant teenager hug while squealing something about marrying Hercules. Taylor rolls his eyes at his sister and says a quiet "That's cool, Aunt Meredith."

My mother snaps a picture of all of us and says, "Can I post this on Facebook? My book club ladies are going to love this."

"No, Mom!" both Molly and I say while laughing.

Almost everyone knew the big news already. Prissy, Penelope, and Alex were a given. Prissy probably keeps state secrets but would never keep something from her best friend about her kids. Which means Mama Lee knew. But Mama Lee already knew because she's a mom and moms just know things about what's best for their kids, even if their kid is a famous movie star. William knew because he kept badgering Harlan until Harlan told him in a huff that he should back off because he was going to propose. William said once Harlan's good mood returned, he knew I had said yes, so he told his wife and kids.

Molly knew, which I figured meant my parents knew because there hasn't been a secret about me that my sister has ever kept. But Harlan had also asked my parents for permission to marry me, so they knew.

The four people who were truly surprised were my niece and nephew and Spence and Sally.

The one secret we were able to keep from everyone was Harlan's Rocky the Bighorn Sheep costume. And, honestly, seeing him in that thing is almost better than announcing our engagement.

When Alex grows up and gets married, at her rehearsal dinner I will thank her for not asking me to wear Rockina's horrendous matching costume.

Once the congratulations die down, everyone heads into the house for some light snacking, leaving Harlan and me on the porch alone.

Harlan stalks to me, a smoldering look on his face and the bighorn sheep mask dangling off one hand, its horns sticking out from his side.

"You are simultaneously the sexiest and funniest man alive right now," I say, grinning at him. "I told you that you could have a future in mascot wear."

With his eyes not leaving mine, he drops the mask on the floor and swoops—yes, swoops—me into his arms. Without saying a word, he kisses me something thorough, long, and lovely.

Once finished, he pulls back and whispers against my lips, "Happy?"

I lean further into him, giving him all my weight. "Yes."

He draws back more and studies me. "So how long do you

think we have until Molly has her dream wedding planned for us?"

"She's already planned it."

"What? I mean, she knew I proposed, but what?"

"She's known for three weeks," I say as if this explains it. Because it does where Molly is concerned.

Realization crosses his face, and he nods. "A tactical error on my part."

I run my hands up and down his back. "You wanted to ask her permission. You made a trade. It's understandable."

"She's made some big changes in her life. Maybe she's going to let you do this on your own."

"She just told me she had some ideas and wants to have some girl time while she's in town, which means she's planned it."

He looks over my shoulder. "She totally has it planned."

"Yup."

He cringes. "What do you think she has planned?"

"She'll assume we're getting married in Dallas and have three venue options. One church, one arboretum, and one fancy hotel. There will be a binder."

"A binder?"

"With tabs." I pat his arms in conjunction with the two words. "She'll have it planned, but she won't have the deposits down, so we might have more time."

"How long?"

"Forty-eight hours. Tops."

He looks worried, so I say, "We have a secret weapon."

He raises his eyebrows in question. I give him a minute to think it through, and we say at the same time, "Penelope."

"We totally have a secret weapon," he says with a confident grin. "How long do you think until Penelope has the real wedding planned?"

"I'm sure it's already planned in her head. But she's playing the long game. She's probably waiting for us to take a few days, become miserable, then walk right into the realization that she could help."

He draws me closer, and I wrap my arms around his neck. "Do you want to get married in Dallas?"

Nothing feels right about that. It's not just that Steve and I got married in Dallas. It's that my life isn't there anymore. "No." I stand on tiptoe and kiss him. Just because I can. "I want to get married here."

He flashes me a smile and lowers his head to kiss me again, but Penelope opens the back door and walks out of the house. "I'm sorry to interrupt, but your presence is being requested in the dining room for the cutting of the engagement cake."

Harlan releases me, bends to scoop up his Rocky head, and looks to Penelope. "If I find out you had anything to do with this costume, there will be words."

Without batting an eye, Penelope says, "You won't find a receipt for that costume anywhere in your accounts. Sometimes I do work for your fiancée's nonprofit, but the work I do there is confidential."

"I knew it," he said, shaking his head.

A smile tugs at her lips, but she turns her attention to me. "Meredith, there are some lovely wildflowers at the edge of your property. I wondered if you wanted something like that for your wedding."

Wildflowers from my property that butts up against Harlan's family property. For our wedding. That sounds perfect.

Harlan shoots his eyes to me. She is totally about to be our secret-weapon wedding planner.

Penelope ducks back into the house. Harlan and I follow, but before he walks over the threshold, he turns to me, snakes his arm around my waist, draws me to him, and kisses me one last time. Then he says, "If you want me to wear Rocky's costume to our wedding, I'm drawing the line."

# DISCUSSION QUESTIONS

1. Harlan debates the perfect ringtone to represent him. What song represents your personality, and why?

2. Which character in *Even After This* do you relate to most? Why?

3. Meredith and Harlan have both been married before. What strengths do they bring to their relationship because of this? What are some possible pitfalls?

4. The clerk at the Apple store accidentally calls Harlan from Meredith's phone, resulting in a humorously long and awkward voicemail message from Meredith. Describe the worst I-didn't-mean-to-call-you moment you've ever experienced.

5. Harlan enjoys mentoring people. Have you ever been mentored? What was valuable about that relationship?

6. Grief applies not just to the death of a loved one but also to categories such as relationships, jobs, fertility, expectations, and purpose. Share a time when you grieved a loss, big or small, and had to reframe your life.

7. Meredith enjoys shopping sprints as opposed to shopping marathons. What kind of a shopper are you? Why?

8. Meredith knows that Stanley is a good and safe option for her to date, but he might not be best for her. Is there a time in your life when you chose to reject a "good" option to wait for the "best" option? How did that feel? How did the situation turn out?

9. The author suffers from a vomit phobia and gave it a humorous voice through Meredith's story. Is there a funny or quirky phobia you suffer from that challenges you?

10. What did you dream of being when you were little? What do you dream of now? Is there a baby step you can take to capture a piece of those dreams?

Read on for a sneak peek
at the next book in

# THE
# SHELTER AND SKY
## SERIES

AVAILABLE OCTOBER 2026

# 1

**HOW HARD WOULD** it be to locate a bulletproof stained-glass window?

Standing at the foothills of the Rocky Mountains on the far edge of the Holcombe property, I scan the outside of the quaint chapel. I could find one, but not before the Thanksgiving Day wedding that starts in—I flip the sleek band of my gold-link watch—sixty-eight minutes.

Besides, such a precaution would be overkill.

The on-call security consultant arriving soon will cover my bases for the last-minute situation I discovered. Another item completed on the list attached to my black acrylic clipboard.

Efficiency is my love language.

The wind catches the corner of the message that arrived sometime during the night. At least I think it's a message. I found it this morning amid a shattered floral arrangement at the front of the chapel. The gust grabs the fluttering edge from my hand, whisks the glossy paper through the air, and plasters it around a fence post that delineates the property lines. Before it can take flight again, I snatch the paper, smooth the edges into submission, and secure it under the clipboard's clamp.

Once I manage this detail, everything will be in place for my boss's nuptials. Bosses'. Both of them. My professional multi-tasking duties straddle the property line on which I currently stand. West of the fence rolls out the vast acreage of Harlan Holcombe's childhood, where he now runs a consulting company. East of the fence sits Twelve Bluebells Ranch, his fiancée's boardinghouse for young women aging out of the foster care system.

A master's degree in business administration prepared me for work with Harlan's company. A master's degree in misery from a group home during my teenage years prepared me for work with Meredith's halfway house.

West of the fence holds my expertise. East of the fence holds my heart.

And it's almost time to ask the soon-to-be newlyweds for my dream job.

I stride toward the white wooden chapel, crunching the brittle grass with each step of my four-inch heels. As if a personal wedding gift to the Holcombes, the sun breaks through the smoky clouds, streaking well-wishes across the grounds for the noonday ceremony.

Upon entering the one-room building, I proceed down the aisle and study the floral decor. Bound by brown ribbon, modest wildflowers adorn the ends of each of the eight pews. Light fragrance dusts the room with a romantic autumn perfume. Bold colors complement the fall palette of the golden aspens and Rocky Mountains outside the church windows.

An out-of-place daisy catches my attention.

I hike up my knee-length trench coat, and flares of boysenberry chiffon fabric peek from underneath, hinting at the hidden cocktail dress. Before I can crouch down to fix the flower, someone at the chapel entrance clears his throat.

Shoulder leaning against the doorjamb, arms crossed, eyes glittering, he chews on a toothpick. "Luke Granger."

Two words. It only takes two words to appreciate this man's electricity. Something's vaguely familiar about him, but I need to focus on the task at hand. Cargo pants accentuate his tall, muscled body but aren't enough to throw me off my game. Even if the black fleece he wears causes those green eyes to pop. But I don't recognize his name.

"I'm from the LG Security Team," he says. "I know Logan usually handles your account's on-property needs, but he has the day off to celebrate Thanksgiving with his family."

"Of course." With a calming exhale, I approach the back of the room and extend my hand to him the way my education taught me. Palm neither up nor down. Straight across and equal. "Penelope Reid, Harlan Holcombe's assistant. Thank you for coming on such short notice, Mr. Granger. I'm sorry you're here on a holiday but grateful your company offers on-call services."

"Not a problem. Call me Luke." He matches my firm grip. "The after-hours operator briefed me with the basics. She mentioned we don't have long before the ceremony begins. Show me what we're dealing with in here."

"Today's wedding is a small family affair. Several of us worked yesterday to set up the chapel. We finished by 7:30, and I'm positive I shut the door before we left the premises. But when I arrived this morning, it was cracked open."

Luke crouches down, inspecting the latch. "Entry doesn't look forced."

"No need," I say. "The family keeps the chapel unlocked."

He stands, runs a hand up the dark stained wood, then closes and reopens the sturdy door. "The wind wouldn't be able to budge this thing open."

"I don't think so either. Everything appeared to be in place with the exception of a shattered floral arrangement on the stage. While cleaning the debris, I found small pieces of ripped paper. I gathered them and taped them back together." Earlier, I'd pains-takingly pulled each scrap from the pile of flowers, glass, and water. I hadn't needed to tape the pieces of the puzzle together before I recognized it as a shiny brochure for Twelve Bluebells Ranch.

I slip the mangled leaflet from the top of the clipboard and pass it into Luke's hands.

He shifts the toothpick to the opposite side of his mouth while studying the paper.

"I'd like for this to be handled without burdening anyone else," I say. "Harlan and Meredith deserve a day to celebrate without this added stress."

With a curt nod, he takes booted steps across the hardwood planks and inspects the front of the chapel.

Outside the open doorway, a flash of color catches my eye, and I see the three tenants of Twelve Bluebells Ranch skittering across the field. Meredith purchased each of the women burnt-orange taffeta dresses for today's occasion. Three beloved gig-gling pumpkins scurry across the plain toward the barn for the upcoming group pictures.

One yells in my direction, her hand flailing in the air with excitement. "Hey, Penny Lady."

I hold up my clipboard in a responsive wave.

Once today's celebration is complete, I'll be in charge of the boardinghouse tenants for nine days while the Holcombes are on their honeymoon. Ample time to prove I'm more than capable of being the new program director at Twelve Bluebells Ranch.

This morning's mess in the chapel reeks of prank more than threat. Still, my uncertainty nudged me to call the ranch's se-curity company. We need to shut down the matter at hand so I can proceed with the schedule for today and the goals for the coming week.

"This is interesting." Luke's comment recalls my attention, and I turn toward him, hugging the clipboard to my chest. "If it was just a broken vase, it could be an accident. But this brochure you found ripped up is for the ranch next door? Is that right?"

"Yes. The groom lives on this property, and the bride owns the neighboring halfway house." I keep my tone neutral. "Do you think we have an issue?"

"What issue?" asks a voice from behind me.

At the sound of my boss's question, I close my eyes.

Harlan Holcombe. The groom.

After pasting a fake smile on my face, I turn. "We were discussing a matter with the grounds." I cringe inwardly at my terrible attempt to lie.

Harlan raises his hands in surrender and offers me an easy smile. "I recognize that look, Penelope. But I come in peace. Scout's honor." He shifts his attention to Luke, and his face lights up in surprised recognition. "Hey, man. Good to see you." Reaching past me, he grabs Luke and pulls him into a hug, each man pounding the other on the back. "Shouldn't you be globe-trotting? I didn't think I'd catch you until the New Year's Eve shindig."

Today's ceremony is limited to immediate family, the pastor, the girls, and me. The official wedding celebration with friends and extended relatives will be at the Broadmoor in six weeks. Luke Granger is on the guest list?

Trying to gain ground on the scene in front of me, I rack my brain for Luke's connection to the Holcombes. Dread claws at me as the reason for his familiarity stays out of my mind's reach.

Luke pulls the toothpick out of his mouth. "Penelope called the company about your last-minute wedding problem here. I came to check it out."

Harlan's body stiffens. His gaze moves to me. "Do I have a last-minute wedding problem?"

"Not you. I'm taking care of it." Pressing a hand to his shoulder, I attempt to usher him out of the chapel. "Family photos are in a few minutes. Please don't be late."

But he doesn't budge. Rather, he draws his tuxedo jacket back and splays his hands on his jean-clad hips. "I know what Luke does for a living. What's going on, Penelope?"

As I open my mouth to make another attempt at sending Harlan away, Luke leans in and hands my boss the patched brochure.

Anger spots dot my vision. Who does he think he is? I know I called him, but this is not what I expected. We were supposed to shield the bride and groom while we privately handled the situation.

I squeeze Harlan's forearm, trying to redirect his attention. "I'm handling everything."

Frowning, he examines the vandalized leaflet.

Luke's stoic focus doesn't waver from Harlan, and he misses the death glare I aim in his direction.

Harlan snaps his head up. "I don't understand. What is this?"

"Last night someone came into the chapel and destroyed a flower arrangement and its vase," I say. "They left this brochure torn to pieces on top of the debris."

"Meredith came over here last night." He cringes. "She loves this place. Wanted a few minutes to herself. What if something had happened to her? Did you call the police?"

"No. I can if you want me to, but I was trying to avoid squad cars at the wedding."

His focus darts around the chapel. "Where is the broken vase?"

I swallow. "I cleaned it up."

"You cleaned up all the evidence?"

*No, I ensured the ceremony would happen on time.* I hold out my hand. "I took pictures on my phone, caught the broken vase from all angles. The pieces are in a trash bag in the dumpster if someone wants to take a look, but there really wasn't much to see."

Harlan gapes at me, but Luke takes a step forward and says, "With the door unlocked and very little touched, I'm not sure the police would've found much anyway. Probably nothing to fingerprint either." He nods to me. "Still, it's a good idea to notify them after the ceremony."

"This is a private family gathering. Only eighteen people are attending, and we didn't send invitations. Who else would know about today?" Harlan shoves the brochure in my direction. "And why would they do something like this?"

My boss's rare display of frustration isn't the only factor causing a nervous lump to fill my throat. But I straighten my shoulders and push past the feeling of foreboding that this might have something to do with one of the girls at the ranch.

"My best guess? An uber fan from one of the superhero movies you starred in. Or an obsessed person who caught wind of your viral YouTube video." I shift to address Luke. "A little over a year ago, Harlan saved a teenage girl from drowning. The footage went viral."

Luke nods. "Yes. I believe two and a half million people deemed him Hercules." To his credit, his face remains blank when he mentions the embarrassing moniker.

Harlan's glower shoots from Luke back to me.

"In the beginning, he had a few obsessed teenagers contact him," I say to Luke. "It was all very benign. Other than that, nothing. The bulk of the social media attention subsided after a month. Other than normal fan mail, we've never dealt with anything like this before." I study Harlan and take a breath. My boss has never been anything but honest with me. "I hope it's a teenage prank. But I called the security company to come evaluate the chapel just in case."

In spite of the crisp Colorado Springs autumn morning, the air in the room hangs heavy.

Harlan runs a hand through his hair, a combination of frustration and worry etched in the lines around his eyes. "Luke, what do you think?"

Luke plants his feet wide and crosses his arms. "I'll point out that this incident wasn't aimed at a specific person. It could be meant for anyone on either property associated with the halfway house."

"It has to be for Harlan," I say, the pitch in my voice higher than I prefer. "He's a fairly well-known celebrity. This is just a local wayward adolescent acting on the dare of a classmate. Something for attention. I think you might be blowing this out of proportion."

"You're the one who called me," Luke says.

"Because I wanted discreet monitoring of the chapel. Not because I wanted to escalate the situation an hour before the wedding starts."

"Listen, I don't know what happened in here. But this feels a little personal. Why didn't the perpetrator unleash a can of spray paint? Why only destroy one flower arrangement, leaving everything else in place? It seems controlled. Intentional."

I curl my hand into a fist, fingernails digging into my flesh.

"It's too vague to assess if there's a true threat," Luke says. "I don't know what this person's endgame is. It could be nothing."

Pressing a palm to his forehead, Harlan turns and takes two steps. "What needs to happen next?"

Luke sticks the ridiculous toothpick back into his big mouth. "Your existing security on the ranch is all solid. No sensors or alarms were set off, so that's good. I'll walk the property and look for signs of stakeouts, additional damage, or unwanted visitors. I'll also stick around today and keep watch. It'll all be fine." His eyes glitter when he adds, "And if you're interested, I can send two undercover bodyguards on your honeymoon with you."

Harlan angles back in our direction, shaking his head. "I'm not double-dating on my honeymoon."

Luke laughs, the sound grating on my nerves. Why is he having this reaction? Not one thing about this is funny.

Rubbing the stubble on his cheek, he downgrades his outburst to a chuckle.

Wait a minute.

The stubble. The green eyes. That dumb toothpick attached to a cocky grin. And Harlan's thirty-third birthday party. The one where I met a man named Luke who asked me to dance. Whose intoxicating energy and sincere interest pierced right through my typical negative response to such a request and tempted me to say yes. As I recall, I took a breath to accept, but his phone rang before I could utter a word. He barely apologized as he hurried out of the restaurant, leaving me with the taste of watered-down lemonade and bitter embarrassment.

"All right. No roommates on your honeymoon," Luke says. "But I think while you're traveling, someone needs to keep an eye on the ranch in case this joker shows up again."

"I know you're usually on the road," Harlan says, rubbing the back of his neck. "But can you stay on the property? Beef up our existing security system? Watch the place?"

My entire body jerks back. What? Stay on the property? I know I called for help, but this is not what I meant. My control of the situation seems to be unraveling, and the snag is a man named Luke Granger.

"Not a problem," Luke says, chewing his toothpick like it's cud.

How hard would it be to yank that thing out of his mouth and stab him with it? Death by toothpick.

"I want you next door at Twelve Bluebells with the girls." Harlan hitches a thumb toward the adjacent property across the wooden fence line. "My fiancée's halfway house serves young women who've aged out of foster care assistance but need help getting their feet on the ground. It doesn't officially open until next spring, and we have yet to hire a program director to run the place. But Meredith can't turn anyone away, so we already have three boarders."

The girls. *Nothing can touch those girls.*

"Sounds like Meredith's doing good work," Luke says.

Harlan nods. "The women work hard. They just need a little direction. We're grateful Penelope agreed to look after them while we're on our honeymoon. She can smell when rules aren't being followed."

I peer at Harlan out of the corner of my eye. "We're trying to have a civilization here."

"I know. It's your life's motto. It's also why you're in charge while we're gone." He wraps one arm around my shoulders and squeezes.

In charge while they're gone. Hopefully in charge long-term after they come home.

Harlan returns his focus to his friend. "Thanks for handling this, man. I'll let you work out the rest of the details with Penelope. But, you guys"—his intense stare bounces between Luke and me—"Meredith knows nothing about this. She's been through enough in her lifetime. I'll tell her later, but I want today to be perfect for her."

I square my stance to him, and for the first time in five years of employment with my boss, I make a promise I'm not sure I can keep. "This won't go anywhere near her."

As soon as Harlan leaves the chapel, I spin on my heel to face the man who stole my breath away four years ago at a birthday party.

I point at his chest. "I knew there was something familiar about you."

A blinding smile breaks over his face, and he winks.

Whoever said lightning doesn't strike twice was dead wrong. His sway is as powerful now as the first time I met him. Maybe more so.

"So, you do remember me," he says.

"Yes." With my arms outstretched, clipboard still attached to one hand, my voice rises. "How could I forget your opening line? 'Excuse me, ma'am, I don't think you've had the pleasure of meeting me. I'm Luke.'"

"The one and only." He grins. "At your service."

My face flushes. Will he bring up his disappearing act? I don't have time to be embarrassed. I have a job to do.

I lower my voice. "This situation isn't a joke to me, Luke."

All hints of humor leave his face, and he aims his fierce green eyes at me. "It's not a joke to me either."

"I can't let anything happen to them." My whisper carries the weight of my world. This job is my home. The only place I've felt like I belonged since I was twelve. "The Holcombes. Meredith. The halfway house girls. Any of them."

Luke moves one heavy cargo boot a step toward me. "I'm a professional, Penelope. I specialize in the security of large acreage property. You took great care of them when you called the company for reinforcements."

I proceed to a pew. Aware of his scrutiny of me, I study the floral arrangement hanging on the end of the bench with the out-of-place daisy. After setting my clipboard aside, I bend down to rearrange the flowers. Maneuvering the blooms with a gentle touch, I shape the arrangement into perfect symmetry with the bow. My boss trusts this man. I need to trust him too.

I rise and turn to him, dusting my hands off. "All right. What's your plan?"

He scowls while staring at the brown ribbon I adjusted. "Like I told Harlan, I'll walk the property. I've got some temporary cameras I'll strategically place for additional short-term monitoring. I've also got one drone ready to go. Everything is linked to my colleague's computer at the office. He'll be in constant contact with me."

I sidestep to the next pew and repeat the reorganization process with the next floral decoration. "Where will you be?"

"Not far. Watching. No one will get anywhere near the door to the chapel unless they're supposed to be here." He picks up the newly pristine sprays and messes with my rearrangement.

"What are you doing? That bouquet was perfect." I grab at the bundle in his possession, but his quick reflexes evade my reach. "I need to introduce you to Hank, the main ranch hand on duty for the holiday. He'll need to know you're on property."

"Thanks, but not necessary. I met Hank through the Holcombes

369

a few years back. I saw him earlier on my way to the chapel and briefed him. He'll have eyes on this building too." He rehangs the flowers and moves to the second bouquet. I dart an arm out to snag the decoration, but he uses his body to deflect my effort.

Shifting my foot one step, I attempt to reach around him. To no avail. His bulky mass is a wall. A giant, regrettably attractive wall.

"Well, good. Then you probably already know he's hard of hearing and often has difficulty understanding others. Half the time, he refuses to wear his hearing aids." I grunt with a repeated effort at stealing the bouquet, this time grazing his solid bicep.

"I told him to send up a flare if he found trouble. He thought I said something about his underwear." Luke chuckles and pushes a cream-colored rose in front of a deep-orange daisy. While this is a definite improvement to the arrangement, his finger catches on the brown grosgrain ribbon and pulls one of the loops free.

He pauses, examining his bouquet handiwork. After an approving nod, he flashes a confident grin my way.

I roll my eyes. "Hold still and let me at least fix the ribbon." Leaving the flowers in his hands, I lean in and, with practiced precision, retie the bow. The fresh floral scent combined with something manly teases my senses. "Hank's an honorable man. But I swear he misinterprets things on purpose to get a good laugh."

"He's hilarious." Luke crunches the ribbon I just tied, relieving it of its perfection and somehow creating depth to the display.

I pick up the clipboard and tap my finger on the shiny, smooth surface. We need to be aligned for the next nine days to run well, but everything seems to be a joke to this man. "I can't handle you here with us every day if you don't take the welfare of those girls to heart."

He turns and locks his gaze to mine. "The only reason I'm staying is because I'm concerned about the welfare of those girls."

"Right." I nod. "I appreciate your help today. But you must know that we follow a purposeful regimen around here. I don't want your presence over the next week and a half to disrupt the girls' lives." *Or mine*, I want to assert, tracing my index finger along the tattered edge of the ranch brochure.

"All I'm going to do is secure and monitor the grounds. The rest of my time here, I'll ask around, see if anyone has any leads on today's incident. I'll get my job done, then I'll be out of your hair. And"—he leans an inch toward me and nods at my clipboard—"I won't disrupt your purposeful regimen."

Before I can respond, his eyes dance, and a heavy dose of confidence zaps around the room. "But you can't fire me if someone happens to smile while I'm here. Even if *you're* the one who's doing the smiling." Bending over, he hangs the flower arrangement on the end of the pew.

The swirling, giddy sensation in my stomach is an unfortunate reaction to this man. Studying the two pews seems like a favorable distraction. But when my gaze takes in the stunning result of Luke's floral creations, I shake my head in utter disbelief.

"I must admit," I say through clenched teeth, "the arrangements look better your way."

He crosses his arms over his chest, eyes never leaving the flowers. "The beauty's in the wild."

Something in my soul aches to reach out and grasp at the fragments of his words. Words I don't understand, but words that somehow hang on wisps of hope.

*The beauty's in the wild.*

I tighten the belt of my coat. "I need to check on the wedding preparations. I trust I won't see you until this evening. But if you need anything, you have my number."

As I stride through the doorway and onto the path, he calls after me, "Penelope."

I turn to face him.

Luke raises his forearm over his head and leans his weight into the doorjamb. His gaze, full of intensity, bears down on me. "If there's a threat, I'll know. And I'll take care of it."

A flash of something unfamiliar streaks through my chest. What is that? Fear? Comfort? Tuning out the uncomfortable feeling, I offer a slow nod.

"I'll catch you later." He knocks the doorframe twice with his fist before he heads down the edge of the property line.

My stare lingers on his exiting form just a tad longer than I intend.

## DEAR READER,

Thank you so much for being with me through Meredith and Harlan's story. It's very difficult as an author to tell you what it means to me that you took time to read something I wrote. Picture me holding your hand, staring you in the eyes, and saying a heartfelt thank-you.

By the time this book makes it to print, it will be thirteen years in the making. Whatever it is that's been written on your heart and you have no idea how to do it or how long it will take, keep going. Take the next step. The journey might be heartbreaking. The path may change. But honor that voice in you that wants to try something new. I am jumping up and down, cheering you on.

This book is my heart bled onto a page. It began with a funny, offhanded comment from my husband about how if he died, I would just go live at the Broadmoor Hotel because it's my happy place. But the guts of the story came through losing my mother to a quick journey with cancer, and the subsequent accident that took the lives of a childhood friend and her two beautiful girls while they traveled to my mother's funeral. It took me years to unpack those losses—and it all came pouring out on the pages of this story.

Grief is such a loaded topic, but grief is also universal. We've all experienced it. Something changed in our life, big or small, and now we're left with feelings. All the feelings. It hits each of us at different times and in different ways. We have individual needs inside of it, and then those needs change. Understanding grief can feel like a moving target. Some of us may be in the throes of it right now, and for that I am truly sorry. You are not alone.

I'd love to stay in touch. I have placeholder accounts on social media that the fabulous Team DC runs, but I'm not there. Maybe someday I'll write about why. But for now, I would love to connect with you through my monthly newsletter. We get into some shenanigans. Head over to DeborahClack.com to sign up. I've got a free novella for you with an opening scene that may or may not be based on one of my most embarrassing moments.

And if you enjoyed meeting Penelope and want to see who was able to wrangle her type-A heart, look in bookstores October 2026. I cannot tell you how much fun it was to write cavalier, flirty Luke into this opposites-attract story. It's not what you think it is, and it's everything you want it to be.

And finally, my thank-yous.

Kelsey Bowen, I can't even type words about you that don't make me cry with gratefulness. Your belief, enthusiasm, and passion for this manuscript . . . well, now I'm crying again and can't finish that sentence. This manuscript spent over a decade in rejection and heartbreak. But I think God knew. He knew it had to be you. And I'm so glad He knew how to get me to you.

Jessica English, I'm not saying galleys are my favorite. I'm saying that doing them with you was a gift to me. Truly. Thank you for your polish, insight, and encouragement.

To Rachael Betz and the marketing team, the title of this book still makes me tear up. You guys knocked that and everything else you did out of the park.

Laura Klynstra, I just want to walk into the cover you and your team created and get lost in the beauty. Thank you.

Karen Steele, I did not quite understand what "publicity" meant before this all began, but let me just say that now that I'm on this side of it, I'm so glad you were in charge of mine.

To my fellow Haven authors Chelsea Bobulski, Jennie Goutet,

Andra Loy, and Roxanne LoMarc. I'm so glad to be buckled in next to you on this ride. I can't wait to read your books!

Tamela Hancock Murray, thank you for taking this manuscript on so many years ago with hopes of getting it to today.

Joy Tiffany, you know what you did. I am grateful.

Sarah Hepola, thank you for not laughing at me when I whispered to you, the first, that I wanted to be a writer. Also for not laughing at me when I wore super big bangs in the ninth grade. I think that's why I knew you'd be safe to tell about the writing thing.

Thank you to Julie Marx and her fabulous crit group with Brittany Ali, Bill, Loved Carmack, Jennie Gorman, Tonya Hamilton, Jim Head, Marie Sontag, Byna Whitlock Terndrup, Alicia Van Huizen, and Jen Weaver. You guys believed in Meredith first, and you made me get rid of all my adverbs. (Is now when I apologize for adding some back?)

Becky Wade and Lynne Gentry, thank you for such special leadership over myself, Sherrinda Ketchersid, Kay Learned, Shelli Littleton, Kelly Scott, and Stacy Simmons. To each of you: I love you. And I'm sorry I didn't have better snacks when we met.

Bethany Kazmarek, you get me. You get Meredith. And your encouraging edits in the early days of this book only spurred me to be a better writer. I want to be like you when I grow up.

Kelly Jo Fernandez, I don't mind one bit that we're twins separated at birth. I'm just so glad we found each other.

Lynn Blackburn and Debb Hackett, I hope our eight-year-long text strand never ends. You keep me sane and laughing in the trenches.

Anne Alexander, you pray so boldly and so big it inspires me to do the same. Leigh Klotz, thank you for loving me even after you cleaned out my junk drawer. To you both: Real friends tell their author friend that young people use their phones and not paper and pen. Thank you.

T and M, if I thought there was a way to put into words how

much I love you, I would do it here. I'm so proud to call you mine. You have no idea.

Lance, if you had told me that my first manuscript was any good, we wouldn't be here today. I'm not saying I want to repeat that conversation. I'm saying you were kind enough to tell me the truth and then give me your full-on support to attend conferences and critique groups and learn the craft of writing so I could put the stories I believed in on the page in a stronger way. Thank you for being by my side. I love you. I'm sorry there aren't more monkeys in this book.

Thank You, Lord. Every word is Yours. The path to here was paved in so many ways that could only be You. I pray I never forget to trust You with whatever comes next. In anything.

I love you guys,
Deborah

Award-winning author **Deborah Clack** is a native Texan who believes in the power of fiction, in the lost art of lip-synching, and that chocolate should be eaten without nuts. A high school AP history teacher for ten years, Deborah earned a master's degree in education and was awarded Teacher of the Year for arts in education. Now she creates stories of her own filled with endearing characters and a hard-fought romance. Learn more at DeborahClack.com.

# Sign Up for Deborah's Newsletter

Keep up to date with Deborah's latest news
on book releases and events by signing up
for her email list at the website below.

DeborahClack.com